THE WALLS OF SPARTA

FORGOTTEN HEROES OF ROME, BOOK 6

JERRY AUTIERI

1

Varro squinted at the ancient stone walls of Argos, lingering over the black streaks that stretched from the parapets to the ground. They marked the long years these walls harbored the Argives from enemies. Sun and rain had been equally relentless on the old stone. To Varro, the black stains looked as if the walls were bleeding.

No stretch of my imagination there, he thought. For the blocky stone gates had swung open and the shadowed outlines of armed men surged into the bright gap in the tired gray wall.

To his right, Varro glanced across a stretch of pleasant green plains that fled away to the sea on the horizon. He could smell the salty air even at this distance. Though he had no love of the open water, he was seized with a desire to steal a ship and sail toward that distant horizon. He had no idea where, just anywhere but the rigid formation of a heavy infantry line.

Yet the bucina sounding behind him broke into his idle daydream.

"Tenth hastati, form up!"

He shouted the command from the front of his century. To his left and set back from him on the line were Falco and the Ninth hastati. As his century stepped into position, he nodded to Falco.

"We'll make this fast," Falco shouted back. "These bastards don't know who they're running at."

This was their first action together as centurions of the Tenth Maniple of hastati. Varro was the senior centurion to Falco, who had only been appointed to his rank a month ago. They were both young, but so were the men they led. In any case, neither of them had command of this operation, and so listened for the orders of the task force tribune assembling their defensive line. Varro and Falco simply had to keep the right flank anchored against the enemy.

Consul Flamininus had sent them to protect the camp surveying task force. The Argives had not welcomed the Romans' arrival from the start. Varro had been the first to notice the pantomimed curses hurled at them from the Argives on their city wall. Within the hour, the gates were now opened and spilling out an army.

"Light pila, ready!"

Varro prepared the thinner of his two pila, hefting it in his right hand. He easily tossed it into the air, reversed his grip, and caught it again for the cast. The pilum had become an extension of his own arm by now. The pila storm, as Falco liked to call it, never failed to stagger an enemy charge. Many times the devastation of the pila attack broke up the enemy completely. So he had drilled himself and his century relentlessly, slaying the same straw soldiers for hours at a time so that when real battle came the men would be prepared.

He was premature to call for the pila. No one would question this but himself. Still, he demanded precision both in himself and others. So now they stood with pila readied as the Argives filed out of the blockhouse gates into serried ranks before the hoary walls of their city. Their officers formed infantry blocks, and their thin-voiced commands drifted over the distance to the Roman line.

Fortunately, the Argives did not waste time marching forward. Otherwise, Varro's ill-timed order might leave everyone with stiff elbows, himself included.

The Argives were lightly armored, if at all, and depended on their round shields and bronze helmets for protection. They had long spears at their shoulders. The sun glinted off these as they marched in shallow blocks. Varro licked his lips, tasting the salty sweat that beaded there. He felt the comforting press of his chain shirt on his shoulders and the heavy weight of his scutum. It imparted an invincible feeling to him, one he knew was spurious. Yet as a senior centurion, he would be leading from the front and only injury or death would take him off the line. He needed every bit of encouragement.

The Argives now increased pace, gleams from their helmets bobbing as they jogged forward. It seemed they would not negotiate a withdrawal but jump right into the fighting. Varro appreciated reaching the ultimate conclusion and skipping pointless threats. Rome would not back down, and the Argives were right to contest an army encamped at their gates.

"Get ready," Varro shouted over his shoulder, watching the approaching line for a sudden charge. He would wait until he could see the eyes of the front rank. By the time the pila landed among them they would have walked deeper into the rain of iron-tipped shafts, ensuring their charge would falter.

The Argive line now swept forward and their officers shouted commands that produced war cries and jeers. In contrast, the Romans stood in stony silence. Varro smiled. This was going to be an easy battle. From the enemy's ragged formation he decided they were conscripts with little training. They were probably all that had been left to Argos after the war with Macedonia, where they had chosen the wrong side in that conflict. These poor bastards likely had been drafted to keep the peace in Argos while their best fighters died miles from here.

The Argives roared and charged. Varro felt the ground vibrate with the thud of their sandaled feet.

"Cast!"

He picked out what seemed an officer at the head of the Argive line and sent the light pilum sailing at him. The long, thin shaft arced across the gap then plummeted down to plant its iron point into the target's chest. He crashed back, his scream lost among the shouts of the men running aside him. Varro had indulged himself to watch the result of his cast. But he had already shifted the heavy pilum into his hand, repeating the same carefree toss-up to catch it for a proper throw.

All along his line, the hastati repeated the same motion.

"Cast!"

The heavy pila had less range but were more devastating to the enemy. The Argive charge stuttered as the soldiers attempted to evade the incoming pila. The light pila had taught them fear, and now the heavy pila twisted that fear into chaos.

Their brave war cries turned to painful screams. Men crashed into each other as they leaped aside, stalling the charge and damming the momentum of their companions following behind. Rather than presenting an even line, they tripped forward in disarray. The Argives had done better than some trained soldiers Varro had faced. But despite his admiration for their bravery, he had orders to fulfill.

With ease learned from long hours of practice over the years, Varro's right hand reached down to his harness where his gladius suspended from the same hip. He drew the blade with a sharp rasp of metal and held it forward.

"Let them hear you roar. Charge!"

The throaty war cries of a century of heavy infantry were nearly as withering to the Argives as the pila had been. Every man had drilled his war cry just as well as his swordplay. Fear was just as much a weapon as pilum and gladius, and the riotous cries for death and blood swept ahead of their charge and set the Argives back in hesitation.

Varro ran at the left end of the front rank where his signifier held the century standard over the heads of the men. Even in their surge forward they maintained an even line with massive shields raised and swords pointed to stab into the gap.

The Argives had lost the advantage of their spears when their charge collapsed. Varro led the century into close quarters protected behind a wall of reinforced wood that was his scutum. The front ranks were already scrambling to draw swords.

Even against such lightly armored opponents, the collision of two battle lines created an astounding crash that never failed to ring Varro's ears. He slammed forward with his shield, as much a weapon as a defensive tool. The Argive he had targeted vanished behind it. Varro only recognized his defeat from the Argive's muffled scream and the bone-snapping crack against his scutum.

Without losing momentum, he stepped into his sword thrust at the following enemy. The blade rebounded off a shield and the defender let out a cry of joy at having blocked it. But Varro slammed his own shield against the enemy and knocked him into the thrust of the Roman beside him in line. Unbalanced, the gladius stabbed into his exposed neck and his surprised shout died as he did.

So the battle began, and Varro knew a patient churning of shield and sword would grind down these thin blocks and teach the Argives to respect what might have seemed a token force to them. One Roman was generally worth five of any other enemy, at least in his estimation. City guards, no matter how numerous, were doomed to obliteration on an open battlefield against veteran Roman infantry. As far as Varro knew, the tribune had not even sent out the cavalry yet.

Battle was like a tide, and as such had an undertow that had to be respected. Varro found himself flowing deeper into the enemy ranks as his hastati tramped the Argives down like grain in a field. His men followed where he led and he realized that he had probed too far ahead and that now the recovering Argives were threatening to lap his flanks.

"Hold the advance here," he shouted across the length of his line.

The men seemed to have endured the battle with minimal if any injury. Thus far, Varro's worst complaint was the numbness in his shield arm from battering down so many enemies.

But the Argives were finding their courage, whipped on by an officer who walked among them and bellowed orders in a brash, striking voice that cut through the clank and thud of swords on shields. He was a tall man and unafraid of the threats before him. All down the line, other maniples of hastati pressed the enemy, but this one man kept his section fighting.

A spear clipped against the greave on Varro's left leg as an enemy sought to bring him down. He had let his shield rise up, which was a mistake he would've whipped out of any recruit under his command. Fortunately, he had been protected where so many other hastati would not. He could afford a mail shirt and bronze greaves to protect against his own lapse of discipline.

He put his shoulder into the curve of his shield and shoved forward to slide down the length of the spear. Without its reach advantage, Varro's gladius ruled the combat. This Argive had the wisdom to melt away rather than let Varro stab him. This told on the loose ranks behind the enemy, for otherwise front rankers had nowhere to go but forward.

Realizing his own front line must be as tired as he felt, he ordered the tubicen to sound three short notes on his bucina to signal the line change. He would remain at the front to keep enemies off his side of the century. The sharp, metallic blasts echoed in Varro's ear as the tubicen completed the signal.

The front rank of hastati shoved forward with their shields until they created a gap for the next rank to step into place. The Argives were too happy to retreat, which seemed to indicate their imminent collapse. But until they were relieved Varro was obliged to keep the pressure on them. The second rank slotted into position and the front rank melted back through the fighting men to the rear of the century.

The Argive officer had worked his way up the ranks and ensured men remained in place and plugged gaps in their blocks. His efforts seemed successful, for in the moments Varro had turned aside from him, the Argives were renewing their attack in this section of the line. He could not see beyond the helmets of the combatants to the center, but guessed they had held up as well.

A swift fury rose in Varro. This officer was delaying the inevitable outcome of the battle, and thereby leading to more bloodshed on both sides.

Before he even understood what he was doing, he had stepped ahead, pointing with his bloodied gladius at the officer.

"You! Here's your challenge!"

The Argive might not have understood the words, but grasped the challenge. He saw Varro at the end of his century, his armaments proclaiming him an officer. The Argive shouted one final command then rushed to meet Varro.

Whatever had possessed him to make this challenge, he regretted it as soon as the Argive answered. For as he closed, Varro realized the man stood half a head taller. While he was not as well armored as Varro, his bronze shield was engraved with ornate patterns and splattered with blood. A black crest flowed from his conical helmet, beneath which a stern, scarred face glared at him.

The Argive bore a startling resemblance to Varro's own father.

In fact, it was such a similarity that Varro gasped, and the Argive, likely believing he faced a coward, gave a mocking laugh.

Both Roman and Argive forces yielded space for their leaders' duel. At least Varro had the comfort of knowing his optio would assume command while he rode out his own impetuousness. If he could kill this officer, the Argives in this section would likely crumble.

The Argive rammed Varro with his heavy bronze shield, and it was a match to his scutum. He found himself skidding backward as the older and visibly stronger man followed up with his heavy sword, the kopis. Designed to hack an enemy apart, it was more of an ax than a sword. As it slammed down, Varro had only enough time to knock it upward with the edge of his own shield.

The Argive roared and laughed, then battered Varro once more with his shield. But he had braced for it and now stood within its protective enclosure. Only, he could not strike while so turtled, and the Argive seemed to have boundless strength to hack away at Varro as if he intended to fell him like a tree.

Being driven back after having issued the challenge flared Varro's shame and anger. No matter if the man did resemble his father, he had selected this man to die. His father had been a shameless criminal, after all. So Varro would slay his twin on the battlefield as often as he had to to slay the ghost of his father haunting his dreams.

He let the Argive break over his shield like a storm-driven wave. In a flurry of attacks with a weapon as heavy as the kopis, any man would have been winded. But this Argive seemed immune and raged on, laughing as he battered away at Varro.

"Back to Hades with you!"

At last he employed sense over the brute force he had been content to rely on. He slipped aside and extended his foot to trip the Argive. But he was as nimble as he was tireless. The gods preserved him and he stepped over Varro's foot. It seemed he chided him as he strode past.

But Varro tracked with him, sweat pouring from beneath his helmet. He dared a glance to his own century and saw they remained in contact with the enemy. But he could spare no more or else again cede ground to this insane Argive.

The kopis hammered away at Varro, and wood splinters spun over the top of his shield. Shudders with every blow ran the length of his arm and it seemed he was once more in the same defensive situation. With a muttered curse he vowed to end this foolishness now.

With a fluid motion, he dropped to his right knee as he raised his scutum in his left arm. He tilted it forward, creating something of a roof over himself which he rammed into the Argive's chest. Within the same motion, he drove his gladius into the exposed groin of the Argive.

The soft flesh tore easily and hot blood splashed to the grass. Varro tore out the gladius with a twist, ensuring a gaping wound that would flush blood out of his enemy so that he might die before he fell.

He shoved the Argive away with the edge of his shield, and he careened back toward his men. He thumped to the earth and his black-plumed helmet rolled off his head. Despite the grievous wound, his dead face bore a strange smile. Nor did he seem like Varro's father any longer. He was just a dead enemy lying before his own men.

Varro spit at the Argives. "Will there be another?"

They looked fearfully at him and Varro felt a swell of pride. For a score of men with shields and spears clustered only two dozen strides away could have easily overcome him. He had taught them to fear the Roman soldier, and they would not advance easily on him.

But that pride came at a cost. For all of his victory, the Argive line was now closing about his century. They had come too far forward, and without support they could be lapped and cut off from the Roman line.

Worse yet, the Argives seemed to understand this. They had retreated to reform while Varro had dallied with their officer. And now they seemed in good position to attempt just what he feared. They had not hesitated out of fear of approaching him. They hesitated for orders to take advantage of their new opportunity, which Varro had handed to them.

Out of that mass of spearmen huddled fearfully behind bronze shields a shout came. The spears lowered and the mass surged forward at the Tenth hastati's left flank while they struggled to break the infantry block to their front.

Only Varro stood in their way, and he gritted his teeth and set his feet apart as if he would drive them back on his own.

2

"Get out of the way, you fool!"

Falco's curse broke through the clang and smash of metal on wood and the screams of the wounded. Varro felt the ground shudder with the thud of the Ninth hastati's charge.

"Cast!"

Varro's heart seized when he heard Falco shout the order. He was standing in the line of attack, and if one of those pila fell short—

One landed by his left foot, and he jumped aside both in shock and delight. For far more of the light pila stitched death among the charging Argives. Their sudden bravery turned to bloody fear as men toppled to the ground and tripped those behind them. Even as Varro sought to back up to his own century, he saw the Argives scrambling to reverse.

He laughed as Falco led his century past him. His tall friend glared from under his heavy brow as he carried forward.

The Argives crumbled under the next wave of pila, and to his right his own century shouted in victory as the enemy sought to disengage.

"Hold pursuit!" Varro shouted. "Don't be led to their walls or you'll be picking arrows out of your asses! Stay in line!"

His orders vanished under the shuddering thud of hooves and screaming riders. The tribune had sent the cavalry around Varro's end of the line to roll up the Argives. As he stood with his front ranks, chest heaving and throat burning, he watched the enemies flow back toward their city walls. This section of the line had fought the hardest and longest, and so the cavalry had come to instruct the Argives in their true predicament. They ran down the stragglers, but none of them followed to within bowshot of the walls.

The Romans let out jeers and shouts of victory. Varro encouraged his own men, all of them raising their bloodied swords and shouting themselves raw. It was a necessary act after battle. It told the men they had won and their shouts confirmed they had survived. So often Varro had seen men carrying on unaware of missing limbs or spears impaled in their bodies, only to drop dead when they realized their wounds. Many times at the end of the fight, he had no memory of what he had just endured. Only the blood and sweat pouring off his flesh served to remind him of the horror.

But today he was clear on the victory. The battle could not have lasted more than an hour, and most of it was the lead-up to the actual clash. They had probably clashed no more than a quarter of that time.

He spit the coppery taste of blood from his mouth and wicked it from his gladius. He stopped cheering even as the others continued. He would let them congratulate themselves as long as it seemed no other threat was at hand. He looked toward the black-stained walls again, noting the men atop them staring helplessly at their retreating brethren.

The Ninth hastati had halted once the Argives broke and let the cavalry sweep the enemy away. Falco stood at the fore shouting curses along with his men. He was an imposing sight, being taller and stronger than any other in his command. Looking at him from behind, Varro realized his childhood friend had filled out in size and strength. He was no longer a strong farm boy, but a solid war veteran with the scars and brawn to prove it. Both of them had left their farms unbloodied and innocent. Now both of them stood victorious and uncaring among dead and dying men bleeding under their feet.

With victory decided, the tribune in charge of the camp surveying force sounded the call to reorder the ranks. The battle was over and the cavalry could return and the infantry step down from their battle formations. Varro turned to his men and recaptured their attention from the last of the fleeing enemy.

They spent the next hours after the battle tending wounded, rounding up captives, and carting away the dead. With this site intended as an encampment, it would not do to have piles of dead Argives rotting around the perimeter, so the hastati were set to digging a mass grave in the fields Varro had admired before the start of the battle.

Overall, the Argives had sent more than three hundred men to their deaths and the Romans had lost almost no one. The Tenth hastati had not suffered a single casualty. The worst had been a cut to one man's shoulder, which had split it open and would take him off of active duty while it healed. In tougher times, he would have been ordered to remain in the battle line. But this was hardly the war against Macedonia. Varro was not even sure this was a war.

With the mass grave completed, the hastati were allowed a short rest. Council Flamininus was due to move up the main army and begin constructing the marching camp. While the exhausted men sat in the grass beside the mound of fresh-turned earth and chatted while looking toward the distant sea, Varro and Falco met up behind them.

"Thanks for not killing all the Argives by yourself and leaving something for the rest us to do," Falco said with a twisted smile as he walked the short distance. He stopped beside Varro and clapped his shoulder. "Were you out of your mind?"

"My blood was up," Varro said, returning the clap to Falco's other shoulder. "I'm glad you arrived when you did."

"It's how we drill." Falco and Varro both nodded then turned to look across the line of men resting in the grass. "This is hard to believe, isn't it?"

"It's not so hard," Varro said. "All the centurions before us are dead. We're all they had left to promote."

"I hadn't thought of it that way." Falco folded his arms and shivered. "For a moment, it looked like you wanted to add your name to that roster of dead centurions."

Varro did not answer. He thought of the Argive officer and how he had resembled his father. What had made his ghost rise up in an enemy's armor? After the battle, he studied the corpse and found only the shallowest of resemblance.

"Do you think we'll ever go home?" His eyes lifted beyond the men to the sea that sparkled with the late day sun.

"Why not? We've come this far." Falco spit in the grass then made the fig at Varro, tucking his thumb into his clenched fist but wrapping his index finger over it. "So don't curse us with evil talk."

"Why are we still fighting?" Varro pushed Falco's hand aside with a grin. "I thought the war was over."

"It's the fucking Greeks, Varro. They love fighting. You're the one who paid attention to the tutors when we were boys. I thought you'd know these bastards have been fighting each other since the start of the world and probably will continue on forever. Now we're here. So they fight us."

Varro shrugged. "I suppose so. But I keep thinking of those

soldiers who fought against Hannibal. We were just babies then, and they're still fighting today."

Falco waved dismissively. "Well, no one is alive from the beginning of that war except Hannibal. That's for sure. Those veterans came in at the end."

"It's still a long time to fight, and I'm afraid it will be the same for us." Varro blinked from staring overlong at the brilliant reflections of the ocean. "Maybe the ship that took us here will never return to take us home."

Falco sighed. "Well, suits me. What's at home anymore?"

"A family farm. Maybe a family of our own. Don't you want to start a family, Falco?"

"I know I don't want to be a farmer like my father was. I'm too rich for that anymore."

They both shared a smile. He, Falco, and Curio had been awarded a talent of silver each for rescuing the Macedonian war indemnity from theft by traitors. Council Flamininus held it safe for them, but they had easy access to their wealth. It would change their lives once back in Rome.

"Well, whatever we will do," Varro said. "We have to survive this and the next few years before we get to decide anything."

"It's just Argos," Falco said. "A single city won't keep us out for long. Besides, aren't the Argives going to revolt now that we're here? That's the whole point of this business, isn't it?"

Falco extended his hand to the mound over the mass grave.

"That's what the consul says. He should know better than anyone. When they see us encamped outside the wall, the revolutionaries will gather the people and topple their Spartan masters. They'll throw the gates open to us."

"Right, then. So Argos goes free and Sparta can go get fucked. I mean, I guess they were tough bastards a thousand years ago. But I bet we'd stomp them into the dirt now."

"Wait. So you want to fight Spartans?" Varro asked, raising his brow. "You were looking pretty pale at the thought of having to fight them just a few days ago."

Falco snorted. "No, I just ate some bad puls the night before. I'm not afraid of Sparta. Just another legend blown up way beyond what they're really about. Just like Philip's phalanx. Unbeatable, they said. But we were both there when they got cut to bits. The Spartans are the same. This whole land is full of puffed-up legends. Rome is the power and the future. You'll see."

"Well, I'll remind you of this speech if we get stuck in with Spartans."

"You won't need to remind me. It'll be obvious when we're standing on a mountain of Spartan dead."

A signal from the tribune broke into their rest with the sharp notes sounded on a bucina. Both Varro and Falco had to return to their optiones and coordinate their march back to the main camp.

"All right, Centurion Falco, our rest is over. Thank you for saving me back there. I really didn't know what I was doing."

The rest of their night was spent in building the camp ditch and stakes then constructing their row of tents. Varro had to review the men and ensure they had cleaned and repaired their kit after battle. Despite everyone's expectations that the Argives were going to revolt and throw wide their gates, Varro had to keep the men ready to fight if this did not happen. It seemed a bit too pat for Varro's tastes, but if the consul believed it would happen then he would not speak against the idea.

The next morning they awakened at dawn and Varro expected to find the smoke of chaos rising above the walls of Argos. Instead, he saw seabirds and clouds. So the tribune ordered them to conduct drills in full view of the city walls, where black shapes of guards observed. They marched and shouted and clapped swords to shields. But the shadowed figures watched and the seabirds circled and the clouds drifted away to the ocean. Nothing changed. No revolution came.

The next morning, Varro awakened at dawn to the same scene only with fewer clouds.

"So much for revolution," Falco quipped under his breath as they again walked the men to the fields for exercises.

"The Spartans keep better control than expected," Varro said. But Falco rolled his eyes before they split up to their centuries.

They had planned to drill formations together, since it had been a highlight from their last battle. But as they drilled their maniple, a runner from camp arrived, trotting up to Falco who then called over Varro. They both allowed their centuries a rest while they received the message. The young hastati did not hesitate to drop in place and groan, letting shields and pila clatter beside them.

"The consul has requested you attend him at his command tent immediately. You are to bring Hastatus Curio with you as well."

Varro blinked at Falco, who stared back with equal surprise. The addition of Curio could only mean the consul had a special plan for them. He stole a glance at quiet Argos and dreaded what Flamininus would require.

"Give us a moment to settle our men," Varro said. "We'll follow you."

Each met with their optio, decent soldiers who had both served at Cynoscephalae, and gave them the strange order to continue the drills without them.

"What if Centurion Falco and I are both dead?" Varro explained. "You'll need to understand how to work together. Make the boys sweat while we're gone. And I'll be taking Curio with me as well."

When called, Curio stepped out of the front rank. Varro had appointed him to his command group as tessarius, which handled their century's watch schedule in coordination with camp headquarters. While he was boyishly short with a young face, Curio was one of the toughest fighters in the century. He often surprised replacements and recruits with his ferocity. He jogged the short distance to salute Varro, who told him of the summons.

They followed their messenger back across the camp to the consul's grandiose command tent. Two men flanked the entrance on guard duty and one opened the flap at their approach while the other entered to announce their arrival. The messenger left them at the entrance, and Varro filed into the tent with the others following.

Flamininus sat in full war gear at his plain desk. His soulful, heavy-lidded eyes stared into the reflection of the polished dark wood before him. The impact from the grand size of the tent had not diminished over the years, but the screens and panels that sectioned off his tent had dimmed. They now showed the cracks, smudges, and chips from being transported all around Greece in his term as consul and now proconsul. The rug under Varro's feet was once full of vibrant color but now was worn to dull gray threads.

They saluted and stood at attention, Varro and Falco now standing in line with Curio slightly behind them. Flamininus sighed as if acknowledging their presence, but did not immediately put them at ease.

"It seems the Argives are not as willing to rise up in their own defense as I was told. In fact, sources tell me that the rebels have been identified and put to the sword. That has quelled any desire for rebellion by the people."

Varro stared beyond Flamininus's head into the blackness of the paneled-off sections of this audience area. He would not offer his opinion, but it was not surprising to him. The Spartans were ruled by a tyrant of some fame for cruelty.

"Sorry, men, you needn't stand so rigid. At ease, though I will have orders for you presently."

"Sir, if I may speak," Varro asked. The consul tilted his head to grant him permission. "Sir, the men we fought two days ago were of inconsistent quality. Some were brave but most were unwilling to risk their lives. Whatever power the Spartan garrison commands, it must be limited to their own warriors and not to those levied to defend their city. We can beat them, especially now that you have arrived with the alliance."

Varro knew that the main powers of the area had joined in an alliance against Sparta and their continued control over Argos. Varro was chagrined to find Macedonia now part of this alliance and even contributing forces to fight alongside Rome.

"Ah, yes, the alliance," Flamininus said with a mirthless grin. "Well, one thing you may count upon is no alliance ever agrees on anything. I appreciate your sentiment, Centurion Varro. But there are fifteen thousand men garrisoned under King Nabis's own brother-in-law. Even weak-willed men can stand up with a wall before them."

"I'm still certain we can beat them, sir."

Flamininus rested back in his chair and now a genuine smile crept up to his sad eyes.

"Well, I have decided along with the Achaean League strategos that Argos is not our main concern. The rest of the allies don't agree with this. They say that since Sparta's refusal to release Argos back to the Achaean League is the reason for this alliance, that we should pry it out of their hands."

"It seems a logical response, sir," Varro said. "But then Sparta will not be happy, I expect."

Flamininus slapped his hand on the desk. It made Falco wince in surprise beside Varro, but he remained still along with Curio.

"Just so, Centurion Varro. Sparta is the problem. Why should I smash my good men into the walls of Argos when the real culprit is King Nabis in Sparta? If we take Argos we will find that we have only exchanged position from laying siege to being besieged ourselves. Yes, the alliance would break any siege by Sparta. But we shall still be obliged to deal with Nabis after we've exhausted ourselves with Argos. By all the gods, the men are tired of fighting."

Varro raised his brows in surprise, and at last Falco murmured.

"That's the truth, sir. We've been fighting more since the peace with Philip."

While Flamininus shook his head in vigorous agreement, Varro did not believe the act as readily as both Falco and Curio seemed to. Flamininus had a lust for glory and power, and that was purchased through military victory. Victory over Sparta, with its legacy and ferocious reputation, should be something the consul craved. Moreover, Varro was beginning to see a pattern where the consul salted "querulous states" with Roman garrisons, further projecting Roman power through Greece. Sparta would be a prime location for a Roman garrison. Varro was learning to watch what his leaders did and rely less on what they said.

"So the strategos and I will divert our forces to Sparta." The consul spoke and gave a reptilian smile to Varro as if he had just read the doubts in his heart. "The rest of the alliance will keep Argos contained and possibly break through the walls. Though I doubt their success without our aid."

Flamininus paused and smiled as if they had accomplished all he had just described.

Varro craned his neck and glanced once more at Curio and Falco before speaking.

"Sir, I assume you've plans in mind for us?"

The reptilian smile widened.

"Of course I do, Centurion Varro. You are a useful man, after all. And I would not waste your talents strictly in the line of battle. Though you are excellent there as well." He extended the smile to Falco and Curio and swept his hand across his desk as if whisking away all his troubles.

"All three of you are going to help me hasten Sparta's fall.

You'll make yourselves ready to travel this afternoon. You're going ahead of the army to Sparta."

"Sir," Falco chuckled. "We're good, but the three of us can't topple Sparta alone."

"I think you'd be surprised at what you can do," Flamininus said. "But you needn't topple Sparta. Just its king."

3

Varro set his pack down in the copse of trees. The crunch of branches and leaves sounded so loud that he expected the gates of Sparta to open and expel thousands of battle-ready pikemen. But it was a moonless night of still air and every sound was like thunder to him. Sparta's gates remained closed. The shuffling of Falco and Curio behind him made the hair on the back of his neck rise for fear of being discovered. Yet Sparta was nearly a mile distant.

"Stop jumping at every noise," Falco whispered in the dark. "Gods, if you're this nervous now you'll piss yourself once we're over the walls."

"How are we getting over those walls?" Varro regretted the whining note in his voice. But Sparta seemed like an impregnable fortress nestled between two mountain ranges. The entire city was draped in blackness and only showed points of yellow light from where inhabitants lit lamps or hearths. These blinked like the stars splattered across the indigo sky above.

"We'll get over," Curio said. "That's no question. We've done this before."

"Right," Falco agreed, nudging Varro's shoulder. "Didn't you once say something like walls are for keeping out armies and not mosquitoes?"

"I doubt I'd make such a hideous analogy. We're not insects. We're Roman officers."

Curio cleared his throat. "Yes, sir. I do believe the centurion said something like this once before."

"Sorry," Varro said. "You should've been made an optio. Have you been studying your letters like I've shown you?"

"Have you been learning to swim like you promised?"

Curio was a small, blank shape in the dark, but Varro somehow still saw the crooked smirk on his face.

"No, I guess we've not had time for anything besides soldiering. Anyway, we're all equal here."

"No we're not," Falco said. He shoved beside Varro into the underbrush, creating another crunch of broken twigs underfoot that made Varro tuck his head down. "Centurion Varro, you are the senior officer. There is no possibility of me taking command of this totally mad operation."

"This is madness," Varro said, his voice low. No one replied for he knew each one was aware of their dire situation.

The consul had every confidence in them. He had supplied them well and sent them on the fastest horses through the mountain passes to catch the swiftest ferry down the Eurotas River to Sparta. He filled their packs with enough drachmae to buy anything or anyone they needed to buy. Further, he promised to add to their already substantial wealth for services beyond normal duty.

In return, he simply asked that they incite an uprising in Sparta and cut off Nabis's head if they saw an opportunity.

"Why do we keep getting missions like this?" Falco asked wearily as he settled in to stare at the night-shrouded walls of Sparta.

"Because we keep succeeding at them," Varro said. "Maybe we should fail this one."

Falco and Curio both chuckled. Falco snapped a twig in his fingers with a bright pop.

"Because failing this one means we'll be broken as easily as that."

Varro glimpsed the two halves of the twig flip away into the dark. Falco was correct, of course. This mission was a direct order and as such to disobey meant a flogging at the least and the worst might be more than he wanted to consider. Of course, they could desert the army. But they had all left that option in the past.

Despite the danger of it, Varro admitted to himself such missions stimulated his pride. The danger was not less than leading a century in battle. What did it matter if he died here or on the end of a Spartan pike? Even dying on the battlefield did not guarantee his corpse would receive a proper funeral. So while he dreaded what lay ahead, he was proud to be entrusted with it.

"So Curio thinks the walls will be as good as passing through air," Falco said.

"Wait, I only said we'd get over them."

"Sure," Falco said, putting his arm across Curio to silence him. "Curio has the wall handled. Now, who has these contacts we're supposed to meet? Varro, you spent the most time with the consul on this. So I'm counting on you to have a plan."

"I memorized contact names the consul gave me," Varro said. "But that's as far as my planning went."

Crickets chirped in the night and twigs cracked with the shift of their weight on the ground debris.

"Well, what the fuck were you thinking this whole journey here?" Falco slapped his hands to his thighs. "I left you alone because I thought you were planning something. Were you fucking sight-seeing?"

"I was not sightseeing." Varro shifted away from Falco's shadow to face Sparta. "There are certain Spartans with sympathies to Rome, or at least they want to be rid of Nabis which makes them our allies."

"Well, Nabis is a terror if there ever was one," Falco said. "I expect if anyone could speak freely they'd be glad to see him dead. But how are we finding these people? What are they going to do for us?"

"Flamininus said a spy is already working within Sparta. He'll likely find us once we contact one of the citizens. They're all merchants or other rich people." Varro forced a smile that seemed to ease Falco's nerves as his shadowed form sat back and relaxed.

"So we're looking for rich people unhappy with the king," Falco said. "That's something at least."

"We've got names," Varro said. "And I'm certain they won't be hard to find. We've got drachmae to pay for the information. From there, we let them know Flamininus is coming and coordinate an uprising. It won't be hard if we just keep our heads down."

Falco grunted. "Well, I hope these rich bastards speak Latin, or we're all going to be fucked."

"The merchants will," Varro said. "Or they'll have someone to interpret for them. Anyway, once we meet our contact that won't be a problem."

"What's his name, at least?"

"The consul wouldn't say. In case we're captured the name cannot be tortured out of us. He'll come to us when ready."

Falco and Curio both stiffened, and even in the darkness Varro could sense Falco's eyes widen beneath his heavy brows.

Varro folded his arms. "Come on, you know we'll be tortured for information if caught. Nabis will want to know where the consul is and what his plans are. He won't believe us even if we tell him the truth. He'll confirm it with torture. So, let's not get caught."

He heard Falco swallow. Curio remained frozen in place, but soon returned to his pack and began fishing around inside.

"We should climb the walls now before Centurion Varro gives us any more encouragement. I've got the hook and rope. It should get us atop the wall. But I'll need to get closer to find the best spot to place it."

They watched the walls of Sparta longer, studying the patterns of torchlight moving slowly across the walls as guards patrolled. Nabis was certain to have heard of the allied attack on Argos by now. In any case, he knew war was coming soon, and so his men were alert to danger. The torches carried from one tower and then back to another as the sentries patrolled.

"What good will the torches be from so high up?" Falco asked. "It just gives them away."

"They're not the ones hiding," Varro said. "And they can drop a torch from the wall to light up anything they suspect is a danger."

"Well, when did you become such an expert?" Falco sniffed.

"It's common sense. You never had much of it. Now, I think I see a spot less patrolled than the others. Let's make for it."

Before Falco could protest the insult, Varro emerged from the copse of trees and started forward. The fields before the city walls had been cleared to deny concealment for enemies. But the night was as dark as any Varro ever remembered. Still he bent at his waist to keep his profile hidden as he ran toward the walls of Sparta. He heard Falco and Curio jogging behind him.

To his left the walls converged on a stone bridge that crossed the Eurotas River. He could see the bright yellow watch fires reflected in the water below. He could never approach from that angle. However, to the right, he saw the walls climbed up into a rocky ledge. He noted the light from patrols there was sparse and it also seemed only a single patrol paced the wall. It made sense that the area already enjoying natural defenses would be less patrolled. But he was still a half mile away and would need to confirm up close.

When they arrived within a few hundred feet, they flattened to the grass to observe their final approach. The blades of grass were cold and sharp against Varro's face as he watched the torch travel down the wall toward the tower set into where the rocks pushed up from the ground. All three Romans lay in the grass, and Varro enjoyed the weight of his chain shirt over his tunic.

All of them wore chain, even Curio who had been provided one at his own expense just before setting out. When worn over a tunic, the chain was merely heavy but not particularly noisy. They carried their unfeathered helmets in their packs, but did not bring shields. Varro's pugio and gladius pushed into his hips as he lay atop them in the grass.

"Cover your mail with dirt," Curio whispered.

"It's not that shiny," Falco said.

"Do it anyway." Varro grabbed up clods of damp earth. It might have rained recently and it clung to his palms even as he scrubbed it onto his mail. "Just put it where the armor shows. We've got cloaks for the rest."

The three of them worked in silence, daubing mud on their exposed body and armor. Varro thought his legs seemed especially bright in the darkness and he scrubbed them down with dirt. He had left his greaves at camp, knowing they would only be a hindrance for his upcoming work. When he finished, he pulled his gray hooded cloak from the pack and unfurled it. The consul had gifted them to them, with plain wood pins to keep it cinched at their necks. He slung it over his shoulders then pulled the hood over his head.

When they were finished, Varro sat back in the grass across from Curio.

"You look like a beggar," he said.

Curio laughed. "Liar. You can't even see my face."

"Listen." Varro shifted closer to the others and they all drew their heads together. "Once we get closer, we can't speak aloud until out of enemy hearing. If we become separated, meet at the southern wall of the acropolis. That will be the easiest landmark to find. If any of us are captured, then we don't speak a word to the enemy about each other, our plans, or the spy we're looking for."

"Until the Spartans pull out all my teeth," Falco said. "And cut off my balls. I'll talk before that happens."

"Or burn my eyes out," Curio said.

"Don't be so imaginative. Hold out as long as you can so that the rest of us can get the revolt underway." Varro put his arms around both their shoulders. "If either of you are captured, I will find you. I swear it."

"Well, I might not want to be found with all my teeth shattered and my balls cut off," Falco said. "Maybe just let me die in that case."

"We won't be caught," Varro said, grabbing them tighter. "We're just three men among thousands. We're those mosquitoes you mentioned earlier. They're damn hard to swat."

"I'm not a bug," Falco said, and the three stifled their laughter before Varro gestured them forward.

They approached the final distance with deliberation. They paused whenever the torch bobbing along the top of the wall paused. Now that he had drawn closer, the angle prevented Varro from seeing how many sentries patrolled. But he guessed at least two if for no other reason than it seemed a military standard. When the torch moved on, traveling up the sloping wall toward the next higher tower, they carried forward as fast as they dared. Soon, they were pressed against the rough rock at the base.

Their first challenge was in climbing into the rocks to even reach the base of the wall. A wall here seemed a superfluous measure to Varro, as after just moments of climbing in his armor he already felt its weight yanking him down. No commander would try to send his army up this way.

Varro's feet had slipped often enough to rain sand and scree on Falco and Curio. But neither complained, and whenever this happened all of them hugged the wall lest they be spotted. Varro hoped under his gray cape in the darkness he seemed no more than the rock he clung against. No guards caught them, and so with silent persistence they scrabbled up to the wall base.

They had a meager ledge to stand upon. These walls were of tightly fitted stone that allowed no gaps for climbing other than the pitting that time and weather had inflicted. Once Curio was prepared, he had his hook and rope spinning for a throw.

But Curio's spinning slowed as he looked up. Falco stood behind him in the line against the wall, and he gestured that Curio should throw. But he shook his head.

Looking up, Varro understood. They were now so close against the wall that it was nearly vertical to them. It seemed to climb forever into the sky to vanish into the stars overhead. Without any angle, Curio would not be able to launch the hook, and they couldn't back up to improve it.

They looked to each other, and then to Varro.

Too much time had been wasted and this remained the best section available to them. Varro snatched the rope and hook from Curio and began to spin it. Looking directly up, balanced on the ledge, he felt about to fall. But propelled by frustration with himself, he hurled the iron hook directly up.

And it plummeted directly down.

The iron clanked against the stone then bounced down, pulling the rope taut in Varro's hand. Falco gave a low hiss and pressed against the wall.

Varro did as well, silently cursing himself. He hid his face, feeling like a child who closes his eyes believing the bad men would disappear for it. They hung in silence and heard nothing.

Varro at last looked to the wall and did not see any lights or activity from the lower and nearer of the two towers.

So he cast again with the same result. At last, Falco grabbed it from him with a curse and broke their rule against speech by delivering a harsh whisper.

"You're making too much noise. Let me do it, Lily."

In a single cast, Falco landed the hook. Varro wanted to throw him off the ledge, knowing Falco smirked at him even if it was hidden in blackness.

Falco yanked the line taut, then leaned out to test the hook's bite on the wall above. Satisfied, he then handed the rope to Curio with a haughty bobble of his head.

The rope had been knotted in sections to make it easier to scale the wall, another gift from the consul. Curio was the lightest and fastest of them, so he would be the first up the wall and signal them when he determined safety. Varro would go up second and Falco last.

Curio did not hesitate, testing the hook's hold for himself then scrabbling up the side of the wall. Even with the weight of his pack and his mail, he made it seem effortless. Varro watched him grow smaller until he reached the top. He then dropped his pack over the wall and followed it to vanish from sight. The rope slapped against the stone. Varro held his breath, waiting for a sign from Curio.

His head reappeared, looking right toward the higher section of wall. But he still waved up Varro, who tested the hook again then nodded to Falco before scaling the wall.

While Curio had made it seem easy, Varro felt as if he were about to plummet backward, drawn by the weight of his mail shirt and the pack on his back. Even his gray cloak felt like lead over his shoulders. The rope bit into his hands and the knots made it easy for him to pull higher. He paused halfway and looked up to Curio, who still watched the next higher tower. That was the direction of the patrol, and thus far they had not returned along their path.

Wasting no more time, he clambered up to the edge, where like Curio he unslung his pack and hauled it over the parapet. His hands found the cold stone of the ledge and he hauled himself over to land artlessly in the corner of the wall with his face pressed against the stone.

Curio was already gesturing at Falco, who Varro could hear scraping against the wall. They had gone separately to avoid stressing the anchor and causing the rope to break. Varro wished they had doubled up to save time, for he glimpsed the fringes of an orange glow brushing against the stone parapets where the wall turned a gentle curve.

He did not have to hold his breath long, for Falco rolled over the side with his pack still on his back. Curio dragged him over, and he slid to the stone floor like a fish being landed into a boat. His tunic rose up to flash his naked backside, and Curio stifled laughter.

While Falco pantomimed curses, Varro was already gathering the rope dangling off the wall. They would need it to scale down the opposite side into the city. He stuffed it under arm, working hand over hand as fast as he could, for that orange fringe of light brightened and bobbed closer. The patrol was returning for another pass.

Curio groaned as he wrestled with the iron hook. It had three prongs and one had sunk into a gap between the stones of the parapet while the other two had anchored against the wall. Varro spooled the rope under his arm to Falco, who made a neat coil out of it. But by the time the rope had all been retrieved, Curio was still grunting against the hook.

Varro looked up the wall. The light was brighter now and would soon round the corner.

Falco forced himself between Varro and Curio to help with the hook. But now both men grunted and leaned into it. Yet their exertions availed nothing. Varro shuffled nervously behind them as they struggled. The torchlight was growing brighter and Varro thought he heard voices.

Faulting Curio for his smaller size, Varro pulled him back and stepped into his place. The iron prongs were warm under his hands. He and Falco both pulled and pushed, twisted and yanked, but it had sunk too deep to remove without a bar or another tool to extract it.

A ball of orange light appeared around the corner up the wall. The patrol was now returning and they were in full sight.

Both Falco and Varro looked to the iron hook lodged in the stone. Even if they escaped, the Spartans would know someone had slipped into the city and begin a search for them. Who else but Romans or their allies would attempt to enter the city unseen? The Spartans would figure it out and their entire mission would be that much harder.

All because this hook would not release.

The orange ball of the lit torch stopped suddenly.

They were spotted and trapped on the walls of Sparta.

4

The globe of torchlight paused but no one called out or shouted an alarm. They had not been spotted, but there was no way off the wall Varro could see besides the guard towers. Both Curio and Falco stood in fighting crouches with their hands on their sword hilts. The starlight created the barest outlines over their curved backs.

They were not going to escape, Varro realized. Whatever had paused the patrol was likely idleness in the guards. But they would have to check in with the tower lower down the wall and therefore encounter him. Any hope of not alerting the Spartans was gone now. The iron hook would not budge and the guards would expose them. They had to be killed, at least so they could not report details of what they had seen and also give Varro time to extract the hook.

There was no place to hide but for the corners of the walls. It was not a wide parapet either; being built atop a rocky hill, it did not need to be as deep to be defensible.

A plan flashed into Varro's mind. He hauled Curio and Falco closer.

"You two hide in the shadows down the wall. I'm going to hang off the rope with pugio ready. When they look over I'll strike, and you two take them from behind."

"That's mad," Falco said. But Varro shoved him away and threw the coiled rope over the side. As he slipped over, not even looking back for the others, he heard the guards call out.

At least he appeared to be someone escaping the city, he thought. He clung to the rope, just beneath the edge. His feet sat comfortably on the knot to keep him steady and flat with the wall. With practiced ease he drew his pugio as he heard the guards rushing toward him. A gift from his mother and blessed at the temple of Mars, this pugio was Varro's prized possession and lucky charm. He lavished care on the razor-sharp blade and tonight it would again prove its worth.

The Spartan guards reached the hook and leaned over.

Unfortunately, they leaned over to see much farther away than he had hoped. They were out of range of his strike.

He immediately clenched his pugio between his teeth then hid his head from them. He tried to act as if he had lost his nerve and now clung to the rope in terror.

The guards shouted at him, obvious commands that he did not understand by words, yet by their tone he knew they were ordering him to climb back atop the wall. He shook his head, drawing frustrated growls from the guards.

They spoke to each other, and one gave a derisive laugh. One shouted at him again, this time in a mocking tone. Varro again shook his head and both guards laughed.

The rope gently twisted as he hung from it. He wanted to see what the Spartans were doing, but from the pause in their cursing he assumed they were closing on him.

Instead, he looked down the wall. It vanished into shadow as if it were a vast chasm beneath him. If he fell, he realized, he would not survive. The rocks below would shatter his every bone. His gray cloak flowed around him, down to the middle of his calves. It seemed to drawn him down, and he had to close his eyes against the fear of falling.

Now he heard the voices overhead, speaking low and rough. They were out of patience and snapping commands at Varro. He offered a nod, as if agreeing to them. He kept one hand on the rope and with the other removed the pugio from between his teeth.

He at last looked up at two shadows staring down at him. Their bulbous helmets caught the errant starlight behind them. One shook his head and gestured Varro up. He braced his feet and held his dagger close.

As fast as he dared, he struck up. But he slashed into nothing. Both guards had fallen back. One gave a shrill but short cry. Varro heard the clatter of metal on stone and he smiled as he hung from the wall. Curio and Falco had cut them down. The distraction had succeeded, and Varro slipped the pugio back into his sheath.

His arms burned from the effort of hanging off the rope in a mail shirt.

Falco reappeared over the top of the ledge, a blank shape against the stars.

"They're dead," he whispered.

Varro laughed as loudly as he dared.

"I can't believe this plan worked."

"Neither can I," Falco said. Then he extended his hand over the edge to offer help up.

Varro reached for it, but for some reason Falco's hand was out of reach.

"If you're going to help," he said. "Make a better effort."

But before Falco could answer, he again shifted away from Varro.

Over the top of the ledge, he heard Curio shout. "Fuck! The hook!"

Varro heard the snap of it releasing and suddenly the rope slackened in his grip.

He clawed at the wall but the stone tore away under his hands.

The plummet passed in a blur. His body pressed against the wall, mail shirt firing sharp sparks under his chin.

When he crashed to the ground, he let his body crumple and roll back with the force. Bright pain engulfed his lower body and he slammed into a wedge between stones. The iron hook clanked in the distance.

He lay dazed and numb on his side, wedged between two stones. He was unsure how much time passed before he understood Curio and Falco called down to him.

"I'm alive," he shouted back, though it hurt his ribs to do so. "Be quiet!"

Both men fell silent. Varro lay still, unsure how he had survived this fall. He knew the wall was shorter here due to being built atop the rocky hill. But it was still twenty or more feet. Yet he had plunged down onto rock and survived. He flexed his fingers and toes, experiencing no pain. Eventually, he pulled himself from between the rocks that had caught him like two hands.

"I'm your man, Fortuna," he whispered. "I will make a great sacrifice in your name when this is done."

His side burned and he naturally bent to the left. His mail shirt had nearly melted from grating down the wall. Perhaps that had slowed his fall enough. Fortuna had held him against the wall and protected him from death yet again.

He heard Falco trying to communicate in a whisper to him. But he was too high up. Standing directly beneath the wall, it seemed an impossible height and he shook his head in disbelief.

The rope had drizzled all across the stones here, and he began to gather it up. Each movement of his arm hurt his side. But that he had not broken a limb or his head only proved the gods watched over him. Eventually he gathered the three-pronged iron hook. One of the prongs was bent nearly straight now.

Within minutes of his fall, he spun the rope and again launched the iron hook up at the wall. He heard Falco's shout of surprise and the hook came crashing down again. Varro groaned and hobbled like an old man to retrieve it for another attempt. Even if he landed the hook, he wondered at his ability to climb.

But he could not leave Curio and Falco stranded. They needed the rope and hook to scale the interior wall and enter the city. At worst, he could wait overnight and find a new opportunity in the morning.

"I'll catch it. Try again." It was Curio's voice, somehow softer but carrying better than Falco's.

Varro spun the hook, letting the knots pass loosely through his hand as the rope flowed upward. Both Curio and Falco extended themselves and one of them caught it. Varro was unsure of who as they were both mere shadows. A faint orange glow shined behind them and only deepened their shadows.

"Try to climb now." Curio's voice carried down to him. "We're holding it fast."

Varro jumped onto the rope and his side jolted with bright white pain. He bit back a scream, but forced himself up. Halfway along the length of the wall, he had to stop. Sweat poured off his head into his eyes, burning them, then leaked between his clenched teeth to salt his tongue.

"Just hang on," Falco said, now closer and clearer. "We'll haul you in."

Being heaved up the side of the wall was marginally less painful. The act of holding onto the rope alone spiked sharp pains into his joints, and every bump against the walls jolted him. Yet he gritted his teeth and eventually reached the top.

Now Falco's and Curio's hands seized him and rolled him onto the parapet. Their rough handling felt as if he were being battered with mallets over the length of his body. When he clapped to the ground, he landed in a warm puddle that splashed over his face. But the shocking pain of the final thump caused him to shout out.

He lay dazed, unsure of the passage of time. Every beat of his heart felt like agony, and lying flat on his stomach hurt his side and back. At last he realized neither Curio nor Falco had moved.

"All right," Falco said at last. "If the Spartans are awake, that shout should've brought them."

He felt Falco's light touch on his shoulder.

"I'm alive. Is this blood?"

"Sorry about that," Falco said.

"How bad are your wounds?" Curio asked. "Can you stand?"

"I was able to before you both hefted me to the ground like a sack of barley."

"Sorry, sir," Falco said. "Next time I'll have a pillow ready for your comfort. How in the name of all the gods are you still alive?"

"I don't know myself." He groaned as Curio helped him roll over. He winced at his side. "I think I broke a rib."

"You should've broken your head," Falco said. "Or maybe you landed on it and that's what saved you."

"It's the least used part of me," Varro said as Curio probed his side for the exact injury.

"Looks like your mail shirt melted," Curio said. "We'll have to get this off you later so I can wrap your side."

"Very well, Doctor Curio. But we've got to get off this wall and into the city. This patrol will miss their next check-in and we don't want to be standing here."

Only now orienting himself to the scene, he saw two Spartans laid out in the center of the narrow parapet. Their throats had been cut and blood like black ink formed wide pools beneath their prone forms. Their helmets remained strapped to their heads and their swords had dropped to their sides as if they were ready to grab them again.

"Take their helmets," he said. "It will help you two pass for Spartans at a distance."

He then noticed the torch guttering by his pack. The patrol had dropped it and now the dying flame singed the leather deep brown. Falco noticed him looking at it and made to kick it out.

"No, raise it up. We want others to think the patrol is still active here."

"Good idea," Falco said. "Looks like I cooked your helmet though."

"Don't worry for it. Now let's get into the city."

They helped Varro stand and put on his pack. He moved stiffly and gritted his teeth, but his nerves were already overriding the pain he felt. They had to get into the city and away from danger on the walls.

"You wear the helmet," Curio said. "Both of the guards were taller than me, and I can hide faster than you can."

Varro nodded and fit the awkward helmet to his head, thumbing the strap under his chin. Despite its strange fit, the weight of it felt comforting.

Then the lower tower door opened and a flash of yellow light beyond spilled into a rectangle before it. A figure appeared framed within and called out to them.

"Shit," Falco hissed. "What do we do?"

"Wave," Varro said.

Both waved at the Spartan shadow. But Varro's side caused him to jerk in pain.

The Spartan called up something that seemed a question.

Varro shook his head and waved the Spartan off. This seemed to take the man by surprise, as his head tilted and he put his hand to the back of his neck. He called out again, gesturing inside.

Once more Varro waved at him and pointed up the wall.

Eventually the Spartan shook his head and shouted something

that sounded offensive even in a foreign language before shutting the door.

"His sight must be terrible," Falco said, lowering the torch from holding it aloft.

"Good idea to hold the torch high," Curio said, emerging from the shadows. "It made your faces looks strange, so that he couldn't tell who you were."

"Of course," Falco said. "That was my plan all along. Worked brilliantly."

"We've got to move," Varro said. "He expected something from us. Maybe we just disobeyed an order. Hurry now."

At last Varro and the others looked inside the wall at Sparta beyond. The acropolis stood high above the flickering orange lights of the city. He immediately noticed how many of those points travelled in regular patterns, blinking in and out of sight.

"The city is patrolled," Varro said.

"That's the least of it," Curio said. "Look down."

The interior wall plunged down deeper than its exterior side. The Spartans had excavated the hill here to make more room for development, creating a wall that encompassed all the distance of the hill they had climbed outside.

"The rope is not going to reach the ground," Falco said. "This just gets better with every moment."

"There's nothing for it," Varro said. "We climb down the rope and drop the final distance. Curio, you're lightest. If you can drop down, then you can find something to break our falls."

"Thank you, sir," Curio said, staring over this side. "I'd be happy to if I don't shatter both of my legs."

"I'm waiting for another plan?" Varro said, not even looking for their answers as he snatched the iron-pronged hook from Falco. He set it against the parapet and then looked to the others. "Well? Short of flying, what else do you suggest?"

"We can throw you over the side," Falco said. "You have the most practice of anyone I know."

Despite their predicament, Varro winced as he smiled. He appreciated Falco keeping his humor up and it buoyed his own spirts.

"I've already tested the gods' love of me tonight. Curio, roll with your drop and don't fight it. You will be fine. It's not as bad as it seems from this angle."

Curio stared over the edge in silence like a boy searching for a lost toy. Without another word, he grabbed the coiled rope from Falco and flung it over the side. Varro heard it slap against the wall and he closed his eyes in hopes for Curio's success. For his part, he could not drop any distance without worsening his injured ribs. He needed a safer landing.

"Gods go with you," Falco said, slapping Curio's back as he climbed onto the ledge. His face was pale and bright in the weak torchlight. He looked between them and nodded, soundlessly lowering himself down the wall.

Both Varro and Falco watched him climb down, artfully walking the wall as if it were second nature to him. Falco leaned closer.

"Do you really think he'll be fine?"

"He has to be or we're truly fucked."

"I can hear you!" Curio's bright and exasperated whisper came up the wall.

Varro tucked his head into his shoulder and waved in apology.

When Curio reached the end of the rope, he dangled by the last knot. His body twisted against the wall as he looked down. Varro silently warned him to just close his eyes and hope for the best. The longer he waited, the worse his fear and the worse his fall would be.

Curio released and his fall was swift and short. He clomped to the hard ground in the shadows of the wall, then rolled onto his back where he lay without making any sound.

"Is he dead?" Falco asked, leaning over as if to get a better look.

"I'm sure it hurt, but he's not dead. Just stunned or nursing his pain." Varro watched for motion from Curio, but being hidden in shadow he seemed unmoving. He rested there long enough for Varro to worry. Then he sat up and staggered to his feet. He waved up at them, then looked around.

"Get over the side," Varro said, drawing Falco to the rope. "By the time he finds something to land on you'll be halfway down. We can't afford delays."

"You go," Falco said. "It's more important that you get inside with your list of contacts."

"I might agree with you, but I've no strength to hang from the rope. Now get on with it."

So Falco slung his pack over his shoulder, handed Varro the torch, then slipped over the ledge. Watching him descend, Varro wondered if even the simple act of getting on the rope would be too much for his injury. He would soon find out as Falco had swiftly descended and Curio was already returning with a small wagon filled with baled straw.

Heeding his own advice to be ready for fast action, he stepped across the short parapet to where the two Spartan corpses lay as if napping. He retrieved his pack then slipped it over his shoulder. Crossing back to the other side, he saw the iron hook grinding against the stone wall for Falco's weight. He hoped it wouldn't snap again, particularly while he was on the rope.

The lower tower door opened once more. It slammed to the stone wall with a loud clap.

The familiar shadow of the Spartan appeared and he once again repeated his angry shouting at Varro. Remembering that holding the torch higher cast strange shadow over his face, he raised it and waved back at the Spartan.

This elicited a stream of swearing and wild gestures. Clearly he had aggravated the man, for now he marched out of the door as he blasted foreign curses.

Varro glanced over the side. Falco had reached the end of the rope but had not dropped.

There was no time for Varro to make his descent and vanish. The Spartan would sound the alarm before they had made their escape into a city already alert for enemies.

One Spartan versus his injured self, Varro mused. At least he would have surprise on his side.

The angry Spartan charged up the sloping wall, sandals slapping against the stone. With each step he swore and seemed to be nearly whining in his tone.

Then he stopped when he saw the bodies.

Varro was still a distance away, but the Spartan had no weapon in hand nor any shield.

Taking every advantage of the confusion, Varro leaped forward as he gripped his gladius hilt. Forgetting all pain, in three long strides he was on the Spartan.

He yanked the gladius from its sheath.

And he held only a broken shard of bronze in his hand. The sword had been shattered during his fall.

Now he stood before the Spartan holding no weapon and robbed of surprise. In fact, the surprise rebounded finding himself disarmed.

The Spartan recovered his senses then grabbed for his longer, heavier blade.

5

The Spartan's sword hung from his left hip in a leather scabbard. It was a long blade that required precious seconds to draw. This guard, a faceless enemy shrouded in the night's darkness, had recovered from the shock and had the length of bronze at his hip halfway drawn even as Varro realized his own weapon was a wrecked scrap of metal. Yet that extra length and weight was all a trained veteran like Varro needed to exploit.

In his other hand, he held a torch aloft. He had not thought to drop it, anticipating a swift end to the Spartan's threat. Now, he thrust it at the enemy's face.

Fire caused men to lose their resolve and their senses. He had experienced this during a siege of a town early in his time with the Legion. This Spartan was no different, and the paltry flames must have appeared like a mighty ball of flames in his field of vision. For as Varro thrust, the Spartan flailed back with a terrified scream.

While he had surely alerted the tower now, Varro at least had created space again. He flung the hilt of his broken sword into the darkness, letting it spin off beyond the wall. Holding the torch forward like he would a shield, he drew his pugio.

The Spartan dodged out of the flame and finished drawing his weapon. He roared a battle cry then made an artless swing at Varro's extended arm.

The enemy blade caught a gleam of orange light as it swiped across Varro's front. He spun with the arc of the strike, so that his arm avoided the blade. At the same time, he plunged in with the pugio in his right hand. He darted at the Spartan's exposed side. But he had expected as much and backed away from the point of Varro's weapon.

Then he thudded against the wall behind him.

Varro wasted no time. He flung the torch into the man's face, which caused him to instinctively cross his arm over his eyes to avoid the fire. The torch smashed on his forearm, sending a cloud of orange sparks billowing over him. He howled with the pain of the burn and his sword arm flailed aimlessly.

Grabbing the enemy by his knees, Varro hauled him up and flung him headfirst and backward over the side of the wall. His scream was sharp and short, and a dull thud immediately followed.

"Only one of us is lucky enough to survive that fall," Varro said as he set his pugio back into its sheath. He looked to the tower, where shadows flickered across the door.

The remains of the torch burned in small yellow whorls in the corner of the wall. Voices echoed from within the lower tower.

Varro leaped back to the opposite parapet, only now feeling the stab of pain in his left side. He paused from the burning sensation, hoping it would pass. But it lingered and he cursed under his breath. New shadows filled the door and quizzical voices called out.

He did not even remember getting onto the rope, such was his panic. He was halfway down and staring at gray stone when he heard the horn sounded above him. Below, he heard Falco and Curio calling his name.

Looking up, guards searched over the sides of the walls. He noted at least three and one had a short bow that he hooked over the parapet.

"Just jump!" Falco shouted. "We've got to run!"

Yet he shimmied down, his feet finding the knot beneath him as he went. But rather than look down, he looked up.

Someone had found the iron hook and was pointing over the edge. One of the men got onto the rope and began to follow Varro.

"Jump!" both Falco and Curio shouted together.

He released both hands.

He plummeted straight down, the rope slapping his face as he sped down the final length.

The bale of hay beneath him was not as gentle a break as he expected. He let his legs collapse and tried to roll back rather than pound down into the straw. The bale aided his bounce and he flung back out of the cart.

Then he felt entangled in something soft.

Falco cursed and Curio grunted. But they had caught him as he fell back from the cart then set him on the ground.

Varro's side was in flames, or so it felt. They were in shadow here, but the Spartan archer still attempted to shoot. His first shaft broke on hard ground nowhere near them.

Curio dragged Varro away from the cart, while Falco fished around in his pack.

"They're following," Varro managed to stammer out as Curio hauled him over the rough ground toward a building.

"That's obvious," he said through his exertions. "But Falco's got a surprise for them."

Varro craned his neck as he saw Falco's shadow toss a flaming object onto the bale beneath the rope. Flames immediately spread out, and the hay bale easily took to the flame. Bright streaks of yellow now licked up the length of the rope.

The Spartan following down the rope screamed in horror as the heat must have scorched the bottom of his feet. He began to scrabble back up the rope while his companions hurled curses.

Falco now raced back, laughing.

"Get up, sir. We've got to run for our worthless lives."

Curio pulled him to his feet and Varro followed both of them in a stupefied run. He had no idea what had happened. The fire, the screaming Spartans, the sounding of horns. It all swirled around him in utter chaos.

But somehow, Curio threaded a path between dark and silent stone buildings away from the madness. It faded behind them with every step ahead until at last Curio planted them firmly in the pitch blackness of a narrow alley formed from two building walls without windows or doors.

They all slid down the wall to sit on the cold, hard earth. All three panted, but Varro's was harder and more painful. He leaned over the ache in his side. It had strangely transformed from a burning pain to a throbbing one. He was not certain if this was a good development or the sign of having worsened his injury. Cradling his ribs, he managed to speak.

"What sort of magic was that, Falco?"

"I stole a lamp from a nearby post."

"There were dozens of bales," Curio explained. "All stacked up. Some were still on carts and I grabbed the first one to hand, but didn't realize it was soaked in oil until Falco complained of it."

Only now did Varro realize a familiar bitter scent on his cloak.

"I smelled the oil and figured we could burn the bale as a distraction if we needed. So I went for one of the streetlamps while I was waiting for you. But then I had a better use in keeping those Spartan bastards from following down the rope. Anyway, are your ribs still together?"

"Together enough for now. I don't hear any new alarms yet. They must be focused on putting out that fire. So we have time, but not as much as I want."

Falco shifted closer to him in the darkness. Whatever light the stars provided did not reach the bottom of the alley. He was simply a deeper mass of darkness than their surroundings. Varro felt the heat of his body close to his.

"Hold on, Centurion Varro. Maybe we take some time to sort our shit out before running blind into Sparta. Let's not make this mission more confused than it already is. Besides, I still haven't figured out how you survived that fall. You might just be a ghost and we don't know it."

"Don't say that!" Curio shuffled closer, whispering into the darkness between them. "My uncle survived a fall like that once. He was hunting in the mountains when he slipped from a ledge and fell into a deep chasm. It was such a vast height that my father and other uncles didn't even climb down to find his body. No one could survive that fall, and the chasm was treacherous. They camped near the spot where my uncle fell, and sure enough he walked back into camp that very night."

"You saw this?" Falco asked.

"No, it happened before I was born. But my father and everyone else swears it's a true story."

"What did your uncle say?" Varro asked, wondering if the answer might suggest how he had been saved.

"My uncle was never right after that fall. They said it's why he was simple."

"The gods give and take," Falco said. "Easy enough to understand. Varro, the gods gave to you. So what did they take?"

"My sword," he said. "It was shattered when I drew it."

"Then it was a light price for your life."

"I think it was for their entertainment," Varro said, patting the empty sheath at his hip. "But enough stories. We've got to get moving. It may be quiet now. I know I would not alert the entire city for a few men sneaking over the wall. But I certainly would report it to my commander. With three dead, they are going to start scouring this city. It's big. So we can hide for a while. But the sooner we find our contacts the safer we'll be. Besides, we're going to need time to organize these citizens and get a rebellion started."

"I'm hoping our unnamed spy friend will have an idea how that bit of business works." Falco shifted in the dark, his cloak scratching against the wall where they leaned. "Because I don't."

"We don't have to know. We simply have to get the messages to the right people and assure them the consul is marching on Sparta soon. When he arrives, they rise up in time with the consul's attack. Then the gods sort out the living and dead."

"As simple as a backward march up Mount Olympus in blindfolds." He heard a puff of air as Falco likely clapped his hands together. "I'm glad you are confident in success."

"We'll succeed." Varro gathered his pack closer, taking the stiff leather in his grip. "Let's get into the light and I can read this list of contact names from the consul."

"Wait." Falco's hand gripped Varro's shoulder. "You have a list of names? If that list is captured, then all those people are going to be exposed and the entire plan burns up like that bale of hay."

"Yes, I have a list. How else am I going to remember a dozen Greek names? But don't be as simple as Curio's uncle."

"Don't make fun of my uncle. He was a nice man."

"I'm sure. But, Falco, the list is written in a code. The consul taught me how to decode it. It will appear as nonsense to anyone else."

"You learned a code in that short meeting you had with the consul?" Falco released his grip and chuckled. "That's quite a feat."

"I know just enough to read my list. Now, I'll need some light. Once we decode the list, then we'll need to find some of these people. They're all wealthy so it shouldn't be hard to contact one or more of them."

"Of course. We'll just ask at the local inn," Falco said. "In Latin. And in Roman war gear."

"Let's get to the light first," Varro said. "I need to see your mouth so I can punch it squarely."

They gathered their gear, scraping it together in the safe darkness of the alley. Varro's side throbbed and certain movements jolted him with pain. But otherwise, he could stand and move under his own power. He hoped to get his mail shirt off and wrap his ribs. Once they had found their conspirators, his part in the plan was mostly over. He would only have to do as much fighting as needed to rejoin the army when it arrived. Killing King Nabis was never going to be a reality for the three of them.

They crept to the end of the alley. Lamps burned at crossroads casting a faint orange light in a wide globe. Varro had lost his Spartan helmet somewhere between the wall and the alley. He regretted it, for now only Falco presented the outline of a native soldier against those lamplights.

Curio led the way, scouting for patrols or anyone else. Somewhere a dog barked. But for such a large city the quiet was unsettling. At last, they found a lamp close enough to an alley to make a swift escape if necessary.

"All right, it's on a wax tablet in my pack." Varro unslung the pack, looking about the crossroad that stretched into darkness only to be punctuated by another lamp farther on. The buildings lining the streets were all two levels and dark, as if no one lived here. Yet he occasionally heard voices, coughs, and other sounds of life. It reminded him they were in the center of enemies who were as famous for their callousness as their heroism. If caught, he would expect nothing less than a brutal death.

As he searched the pack's contents, he found the wooden slates that formed the covers of his wax tablet. The cord binding on one edge brushed against his fingers. He pulled it out into the light. Both Curio and Falco drew closer as if beholding a stolen jewel.

Varro flipped open the cover with his thumb.

And gasped.

The wax had melted, smearing out the names on the list.

"What happened?" He held the tablet away, no longer like a jewel but more like a cobra. Falco snatched it out of his hand.

"There's nothing on this," he said, turning it around in his grip. "How did this fucking thing melt?"

"The torch," Curio said as he plucked at Varro's pack. "Look at the scorch mark here. When those wall guards dropped their torch, it landed by the pack and sat there long enough to almost start a fire."

"And just long enough to melt the wax," Falco said, clapping the two wooden slates shut. "And so we see what the gods really took in exchange for your life, Varro."

"This cannot be." He snatched the wax tablet back and flipped it open. He held it to the light, trying to get shadows to fill the grooved writing. But the heat had done its work, turning the wax to an ugly blot devoid of any information.

"This mission is fucked," Falco said, folding his arms. "We better get back over the wall and report our failure. I'd rather be beaten to death by our own men than have some Spartan cut off my balls and break my teeth."

"Would you stop saying that?" Varro glared at him. "Get back into the alley."

He herded both of them into the darkness. They stood together, staring forlornly at the slate in Varro's trembling hand. The moment he noticed the tremor, he tried to hide it by shoving the slate back into the pack and turning aside. The twist pained his ribs, but he bit down on it.

"I remember one name," he said. "It's the one I used to learn how to decode the list. He's a merchant called Charax."

Falco repeated the name. "That's all you've got? What does he trade in?"

Varro stared at him as he thought. An intense anger coiled in his chest as Falco stood with arms folded and head tilted. That he wore an enemy helmet did not help ease Varro's irritation.

"Do you think I'm his clerk? We're looking for a merchant called Charax. How many can there be here?"

"I don't know. How many Charaxes can there be in Sparta?" The helmet on Falco's head bobbled. "Are we just going to walk around Sparta looking for him? Have you noticed how big this city is? And there's the small problem of three dead Spartans we left behind us."

"I know how big Sparta is." Varro's voice echoed through the narrow alley. "I know what is behind us. Can you do something helpful instead of poking holes in everything I say?"

"Setting that fire wasn't helpful enough? It was the best fucking idea of anyone so far."

"Then what is your next great idea? Quit before we even start?"

"Stop yelling, Lily. You're going to bring the guards around."

"Don't call me that name!" Varro stepped forward, butting his chest against Falco's. He realized his eyes only reached Falco's chin. But he pressed despite the pain in his ribs. "I'm sick of hearing that from you."

"I told you to shut up." Falco pushed back with his own chest. Then he stabbed his finger into Varro's shoulder. "We're in deep here, if you didn't notice. You're supposed to lead this mission, but you wouldn't share even a single name. Now, because you wanted the glory for yourself, we've only got one stupid name that could be anywhere in this stinking pit."

"Glory?" Varro stepped back and blinked, fists balling up. "I didn't share names because it's dangerous to the mission. It was the consul's order to me."

"Of course he had special orders for you. You're his darling."

"Well, Falco, maybe it's because he knows I can commit a code to memory. Unlike you."

Something jabbed Varro's injured ribs and the explosive pain made him bite down on a scream. His vision bloomed white. When the painful haze faded, he faced Curio, who stood between him and Falco.

"Sorry, I had to stop you two idiots from giving us away." Curio's face was covered in shadow, but his sneer was clear enough. He nodded back toward the crossroad. "Can either of you stop arguing long enough to read the sign on the building there?"

Falco shoved past Varro and squinted into the crossroads. "It's in Greek. I can't read that."

Varro muscled up to his side, pressing against his shoulder.

A wide building fronted a much larger building behind it. It seemed some sort of business, and as Falco noted, a large wooden sign carved in beautiful Greek lettering hung from a pole on the second floor.

The same sign was placed beside the door, but beneath it was Latin script.

It read, Charax, Finest Olive Oil and Cheeses.

Varro leaned back in shock.

"Finally, things are turning our way!"

6

The weight of a sleepless night pressed on Varro's eyes. He remained in the alley across from Charax's business along with Falco and Curio. All three of them slouched to the ground in the shadows now forming with the new day. He had stolen perhaps an hour of rest, as had the others. He knew from their fitful snoring they had dipped in and out of rest.

No alarm was raised during the night. Patrols had passed their position a few times during the night, yet never looked down the alleys. The pair continued past on their regular circuit. He was not so foolish as to believe it meant they had escaped the worst. With the coming of the dawn, reports would be made and searches conducted. Why the Spartans had delayed was not clear to Varro, but perhaps King Nabis had enemies even among his troops. Why else delay a search for infiltrators who had killed three men?

Having remained still throughout the final hours of the night had done wonders for Varro's ribs. The deformed chain of his shirt made it impossible to remove without cutting the opening around his neck. So he would have to beg assistance from Charax once they contacted him. Now that he climbed to his feet with the others, the dull pain resumed. He knew it would not take much more movement to bring it back to full strength.

Falco tapped his arm. He offered his flask of posca. "Have an extra drink. For your ribs."

He took the flask, realizing this was Falco's version of an apology. He was not ready to feel less aggravated with him, but he saw no need to make matters worse. He tipped the posca back. Being diluted with water from the river they had followed to Sparta, its sourness was properly diluted. The wine was refreshing, and besides hard bread from their packs, it was all they would likely eat for the day.

"Thanks," he said, handing it back. "Breakfast in an alley in Sparta. I never expected that when I joined the army."

"Nothing makes sense," Falco said.

Curio had crawled to the edge of the shadow and studied the streets ahead. Dawn traffic was light and only a few pedestrians had passed their alley.

"We need to get out of here and into Charax's place," Varro said. "When the city fully awakens, who knows what traffic might come down this alley."

"I was beginning to think of it as home. It's clean enough for an alley."

"Well, this is Sparta. I don't think they own enough to make trash." Varro nodded to Curio who scrabbled back.

"I think someone has opened the business," Curio said. "The door opened for a moment and someone stood there before going inside again."

"Then we need to get in there before Charax's other customers show up."

They finished a meager breakfast, providing enough to fill their stomachs and generate strength for the day ahead. Within moments, all of them crouched at the edge of the shadow.

A handful of people in the simple tunics of plain colors

crossed along the path. A mule and cart ambled up the road. The sun had only just risen, cutting deep shadows across the streets. The city was awakening and the sweet scents of cooking fires carried on the air. Dogs barked from distant points all around.

"Falco, you keep that helmet on. If anything, you look somewhat like you belong here. I'm torn about these gray cloaks. No one else is wearing them, but if we remove them our chain will be obvious."

Both Curio and Falco sat back in thought, but Curio answered first. "Chain shirts aren't just for Romans. I think most common people wouldn't want to bother with us. We'd look like trouble to them. As long as we don't run into real Spartan guards, it should be enough to get us across the street."

"Even crossing a street is a challenge," Falco said. "And you realize you just invited the gods to send a column of soldiers after us, Curio?"

Varro chuckled. "I think that column is coming for us sooner or later. We've done things like this before. The key is to act like you belong and others will ignore us as long as we're not doing anything implausible. We're just three men crossing a street to enter a merchant's store. Nothing strange there. But, let's time the crossing with that mule cart. It'll cut down one view of us."

They stowed their gray cloaks in their packs, then waited for the passing cart. The driver walked on the opposite side of the beast, mutually obscured from sight. So when he passed, Varro stepped out. He did not look around like a frightened man. His stride was long and confident, even if his ribs began to flare into pain. Curio and Falco walked alongside him with equal confidence.

Varro reached the door and pulled on it. It was locked.

"Soldiers," Falco mumbled under his voice. "To the left."

Carefully turning his head left, he spotted three men with long spears and round shields coming down the road. If Varro did not know better, they seemed to be marching for him.

"They haven't seen us," Curio said. "Open the door."

"It's locked," Varro said as he pulled the door hard enough to rattle it.

"Open up!" Falco shouted, banging on the door.

"That's not Greek," Varro said, eyes wide.

"Act normal and people will believe what they want, isn't that what you said? It's normal for soldiers to bang on doors like they own everything they see."

Falco banged on the door again, making angry shouts as if he had lost his patience.

Down the road, the guards drew closer.

"This is not working," Varro said through clenched teeth.

"Open this fucking door!" Falco shouted, then began kicking.

The few people on the street looked to them, but did not pause or question their action.

At last, an answering shout came from inside and Falco retreated.

The moment the door opened, Varro shoved inside with Falco and Curio both following.

The room was far smaller than Varro would have guessed. It was dark and cool, and smelled unsurprisingly of olive oil and cheese. The brief light from the opened door showed a room lined with shelves of containers and jars of all sorts. A desk piled with papyrus scrolls and sheets along with several small boxes holding everything down sat to his right.

The door slammed shut and the room fell to gloom, lit only by the lamp carried by the small man who answered the door.

He was old, perhaps in his sixties. From his poor and dirty clothing and emaciated looks, he seemed a slave. He stared in wide-eyed horror at the three Romans arrayed before him. His gap-toothed mouth hung open.

"Do you speak Latin?" Varro asked.

"I do, sir." The man blinked again. He ran his hand over this thin, white hair. "What is your business, sirs? The store has not opened yet."

"That suits me," Varro said. He nodded to Curio, who understood to set the bar behind them. Then he gestured Falco toward the slave. "What's your name?"

The slave did not answer as he quailed before Falco, who removed the lamp from his hand then took him by his thin arm. "You've been asked a question."

"Ajax," he said. "I belong to Master Charax."

"Ajax the slave," Varro said, smiling. "You speak good Latin."

"Thank you, sir. I learned it as a boy."

Varro scanned Ajax. He wore simple sandals, which spoke to better treatment than most slaves. Nor did he seem to have any obvious signs of abuse or physical labor.

"You're treated well, aren't you? You take care of business, record-keeping and such?"

"Yes, I help the master with inventory and certain parts of his business. I am old, sirs. But, why are you here? Do you have business with Master Charax?"

"We do."

Falco had placed the lamp on the cluttered desk. Curio stood with his back against the door, as if bracing it. Varro stood in the center, trying to ignore the biting pain in his ribs.

"Well, he will come down soon." Ajax smiled. "I could fetch him for you, if you'd give me your names and your business."

"I'd rather not. Who else is here? You can't be alone?"

"I am," Ajax said. Falco twisted his spindly arm and he winced. "You're hurting me, sir!"

"That's the point." Falco drew him closer. "I could fit a legion in the building behind here, and you mean to say there's only you?"

"There are other slaves in the warehouse. But they're not

allowed in the offices." Ajax groaned as Falco continued to twist, further convincing Varro the slave had not experienced much hardship. "Please, it hurts."

Falco did not relent. "And guards? Charax must have men watching his stuff."

"We're not allowed armed men," Ajax said, suddenly noticing the swords at their hips. "Who are you?"

"We're here to see Charax," Varro said.

A loud thump on the door and a challenge came from beyond. Curio nearly leaped into Varro's arms and Ajax shouted in surprise.

"Who is it?" Falco hissed, drawing him closer.

"A soldier."

"What does he want?"

The bang repeated along with the shout.

Ajax squeezed his eyes shut and shook his head. "I don't know. He wants me to open."

"Open up and deal with him,' Varro said. "Where can we hide? Don't say anything about us or your master will die even if we are captured. You don't want a new master who'll beat you?"

"No, sir! Hide in the offices. I will keep them out."

The shelves of the small front room funneled to a door directly opposite the entrance. It was old and gray wood, as if it had been salvaged from a shipwreck. But Ajax pointed them at it as the banging and shouting grew more intense.

"Wait behind the doors, sirs," Ajax whispered. "Hurry, now."

The three of them entered an unlit corridor with rooms on either side. The corridor traveled a short distance before ending in another, equally flimsy door.

"This must be the master's office," Falco said in a whisper, pointing into the only opened door.

Lacking any better choice, they piled into the room and closed the door. Varro readied his pugio as did the others. He drew their heads together to whisper.

"We may have a fight. If we do, get into the street and separate. Remain in hiding, then meet south of the acropolis like we discussed."

Both nodded and their small huddle broke up. They all faced the door of the room. A lit clay lamp rested on the massive desk opposite the door, proof that Ajax had been here before they had entered. Unlike the front room, this office was much neater, though equally packed. Sealed and empty amphorae lined one wall, but the other walls were fitted with shelves stuffed with all sorts of rolled papyri. It reminded him of the libraries of Rome, though he guessed these must all be business records.

As his eyes scanned over the shelves, he was shocked to find an armor rack with an old Corinthian-style helmet set atop it. A baldric and scabbard hung empty from the rack, but a care-worn bronze shield rested against the wall behind it. Both helmet and shield were gouged and pitted, signs of use in battle. It seemed a strange sight in this office. The helmet appeared to be returning his stare, as the faceplates left only black holes for the eyes and a linear gap beneath it.

Through the walls he heard the bass tones of the guard, though Ajax's answers were indistinct. While unable to understand the language, he heard the surly impatience of the guard. Soon it stopped and he wondered what Ajax was doing. Then a light rap sounded on the door.

"He's gone, sirs." Ajax's weak voice was muted.

Falco and Curio gave Varro a dubious look, but he nodded for them to open. If the guard accompanied him, he would be in for a surprise.

Yet as the door swung in with a creak, only Ajax stood in the frame. His wispy white hair was disheveled as if he had just been running his hands through it.

"What did he want?" Falco asked, pulling Ajax into the room.

The old slave gave a shout of surprise at the rough handling.

"He was looking for you three," he said, blinking. "Not by exact description, of course. But he said three men, probably Romans, had climbed the wall last night and are expected to be in this area."

Varro raised his brow at the Spartans expecting him in this area. But they had not gone far from where they had scaled the wall. So it made sense to search here first.

"That's all they said?" Falco pointed at Ajax with his dagger, drawing a vigorous nod from the slave. "And what did you tell him about us?"

"That I haven't seen you, and would alert Master Charax to report any sighting of the Romans."

"Ajax, you have done well," Varro said. He sheathed his pugio and the others followed. "I know you want to be done with all of this. So fetch Charax for us. Keep the store closed in the meantime."

The slave bobbed his old head and was about to turn away when Varro stopped him.

"There are many other offices here. Will other workers be arriving soon?"

Ajax paused then nodded. "There are clerks, accountants, and messengers. They will be arriving shortly."

"Then move us someplace where we won't encounter anyone else, at least until we can speak with your master."

The old slave's face lit up with a smile. "Of course, sirs, the warehouses are large and divided with stock. The slaves will be at the other end of it. That should do, I think."

They left the office and followed Ajax down the corridor to the door. This opened to another room and other short corridors until they reached the building exterior once more. They crossed a brief path to reach the large warehouse. In the moments outside, the sounds and smells of Sparta assailed him. In the time after sunrise, it had come to life and the familiar hum of the city made Varro think of trips into Rome with his family. It was a constant droning noise of thousands in motion. The air was already hazing with smoke from the activities of the new day.

It all vanished as he stepped into the cool, darkened quiet of the warehouses. Ajax led them a short distance from the door to an area where barrels and casks sat alongside empty amphorae and wooden crates. He gestured at some of the crates.

"Sit here," he said. "I will bring Master Charax soon."

Varro settled onto a crate which creaked and sagged under him. But he was happy to rest his back against the outside warehouse wall and relieve pressure on his ribs. Falco and Curio did the same, and he saw Curio staring at his side.

"It's not as painful as yesterday," he said in reply to the unspoken question.

"That doesn't mean it's not serious," Curio said. "You've seen men walking around telling everyone their injuries are nothing, and then they drop dead."

"My, you're the sunshine in the darkness, aren't you?" Falco, seated beside Curio, shoved his shoulder. "Varro's tough. He can take anything. I started training him from the day he could walk."

"We're not going to talk about our childhood again," Varro said, rolling his eyes. "But Falco's right about me. I'll be all right. Once I can stabilize my ribs, I'm sure I'll recover in no time."

Curio's boyish face clouded. "I suppose it might just be a bruise or a crack."

"A bruise," Varro said with a smile. "Now don't think on it. Instead, think about what comes next. We're going to meet a contact on the first day of our mission. That's already a success I didn't expect. But I'm not sure how Charax will react. The consul was certain all the names he provided would be sympathetic. But that doesn't mean they'll be welcoming or kind. So let me handle Charax."

Falco shrugged. "I'm here as the muscle. Curio is the sneak. As sad as it is to say, you must be the smart one."

"Well, Centurion Muscles and Optio Sneak, I would appreciate your ideas in addition to your other talents. We all need to be in our top form for this to succeed."

All three smiled and fell to silence awaiting their contact. Varro worried that everything relied on Charax now that the coded list had been destroyed. He had to be handled carefully. Being a wealthy owner of a merchant trading house, he had much to gain siding with the winner. In Varro's mind, this would doubtlessly be Rome and the allies. While Sparta had declared for Philip in the past, King Nabis had shrewdly changed his alliance when it was clear Philip would be destroyed. Had he only complied in releasing claim on Argos none of this would be happening.

But now Sparta was taking on all of Greece along with Rome. No matter how valiant the Spartans might be, eventually the allies would crush their city. Charax would want to ensure his business emerged in good shape from what would soon be the wreckage of Sparta. What better than to bring a swift end to the conflict by deposing a hated king and preventing a destructive siege where his oils and cheeses would spoil in the rubble of his warehouse?

As Varro clarified his arguments for aiding Rome, he heard the door open where he had entered and then two voices speaking low. Falco and Curio heard as well and reached for their swords and sat forward. Varro waved them down, wanting to strike a balance between preparation for treachery and openness. All three of them, however, stood up.

Ajax appeared around the corner, head lowered and bony arm sweeping forward to gesture to them.

"Here they are, master. The three Romans."

Charax rounded the wall of crates to join them in the

makeshift room. He was tall and walked with a strong and confident gait. Yet he was as bony as his slave. Shadows filled his gaunt face making his head look like a skull, for he was bald and clean-shaven, and his eyebrows so faint as to vanish into his olive-toned skin. Varro noted spreading ages spots on his temples and prominent cheekbones.

He folded his arms as if he were a disappointed tribune reviewing raw recruits.

"You three have put me and my business in great danger. You better explain why I should not have soldiers come take you away. And you better make it convincing, for I'm inclined to do just that."

7

Charax stood with his thin arms folded across his equally bony chest. He wore a plain brown tunic more suitable to a common man than the wealthy trader Varro believed him to be. His skull was so prominent beneath his spare flesh that it seemed only eye sockets stared at him in the low light of the warehouse. His thin lips turned down as he waited for Varro's answer.

He looked to Curio and Falco, then nodded to the slave.

"We are here to meet only with you. Is this the most privacy you can arrange?"

Charax lacked any visible eyebrows, but still the fleshy bumps there rose.

"What is this about? You dare to challenge me on my own property?"

Yet Charax turned to his slave, Ajax, and shooed him. "Go watch the front offices. Make sure no one disturbs us."

Ajax bobbed his head and for a moment Varro imagined he was in the land of the dead where the bones of the fallen walked as if in life. He could not tell master from slave. But then Spartans were famous for their austerity. They all watched the slave retreat around the wall of crates. Varro waited for the door to open and let in a gasp of light and sound from the city outside. When it tapped shut, both he and Charax squared up once more.

"Now, why are three armed Romans in mail armor in my warehouse?"

Varro swallowed and felt both Falco's and Curio's stares. He took a deep breath before speaking.

"We have been sent from Consul Flamininus. We were given your name as a contact."

The skull-like head of Charax did not move. His hairless brows did not move. He remained with arms folded and his mouth bent in an expression of impatient disgust. Varro wondered if he had been heard. The darkness of the vast warehouse seemed to close in on him, and he felt as if behind the wall of crates and trade goods a hundred ears pressed closer to hear him.

But it was all pointless speculation. He decided that his best course was to say no more and let Charax take the lead.

The awkward silence expanded and Charax seemed to have been turned to stone as good as if he had beheld Medusa's head of snakes. Perhaps this was a type of battle, Varro thought. If so, then he would do battle as he knew how and dig in against the weight of the enemy line and not budge. Eventually, Charax gave a frustrated chirp.

"I am a contact? For what, then?"

"You don't know?" Varro narrowed his eyes at the man. "Why would my consul send me to you under such dangerous circumstances?"

"Because he wishes you death."

Varro put his hand to his pugio, and from the corners of his sight Curio and Falco grabbed their swords hilts.

"Then we have made a mistake, and we'll not leave you or your slave alive to report on us."

The old man remained unperturbed, though his skull-like head tilted slightly as if trying to understand.

"Stay your swords, Roman. Of course I know why your consul has sent you. But how do I know you are who you say you are? What if you are spies sent by King Nabis?"

"You've not yet heard?" Varro nodded to where Ajax had left. "Your slave should have told you of his visit from a soldier searching for Roman infiltrators. We are those Romans. Would your king go through so much trouble to fool you? If he suspected you, from what I know, he would just arrest you and not bother with trickery."

At last Charax smiled, and it went a long way toward making him seem less a visage of death, for shadows filled laugh lines clustered at the corners of his deep-set eyes.

"King Nabis's reputation is known far and wide. So, your consul has sent you to me. But to what end? I am honest in saying I cannot guess why he would pick me. I am a merchant dealing in both olive oil and cheeses. Does the Roman army need supplies?"

"I come with a message," Varro said, ignoring the barb. "You are a wealthy and influential man in Sparta. You are in position to save the citizens of this city great suffering and to end the terror of the usurper Nabis."

Charax now unfolded his arms and set two thin hands to his chest.

"Me? I am a simple merchant. I will admit to the wealth your consul credits to me. But that is all. King Nabis holds the city about its throat. There is nothing a man like me can do to resist."

Varro again looked to Falco and Curio, who had not backed down from holding their hands to their weapons. He searched them for support, for affirmation that he was handling Charax correctly. But they had no more experience than he did, and they relied on him now as he would rely on Falco's strength or Curio's stealth. He turned back to Charax and looked him in his sunken eyes.

"There is much you can do," Varro said. "That is the message from my consul."

Charax's hands slipped from his chest and his head tilted to the opposite side and he shrugged.

"I cannot see what help I may offer. And I wonder at how he knows to seek me out, for I have never met him."

"But he does know to seek you out," Varro said, narrowing his eyes. "That was his order to me. Let me tell you plainly. You know the situation your king has created. Rome and a gathering of allies will shortly march on this city. It will be surrounded and destroyed. Before you brag about Sparta having stood so long and the protection of the mountains, let me stop you. If you are indeed the simple merchant you claim to be, then you have not seen Rome at war. I have. Sooner or later, Sparta will be dismantled stone by stone and every man alive at the end will be beheaded and all others sent to Rome as slaves. That is the fate of your noble city. We Romans do not retreat. We do not surrender. We do not negotiate. We win. That is what we do and will continue to do. All of Greece is behind us, and Pergamum and others as well. The Selucids are not coming to your aid. So don't fall back on that hope. Sparta is doomed. Unless we act today."

Charax once more remained still and silent, but now he had a pensive look in his shadowed eyes. His bald head lowered and he rubbed his chin with bony fingers.

"How do we act? I would not see my beloved Sparta destroyed."

Varro smiled and he noticed both Falco and Curio ease their hands from their swords. Charax suddenly seemed old and frail, less commanding than he had a moment ago. This worried Varro, since he needed Charax to be confident in resisting his king.

"That is why we are here," Varro said. "There must be others like you. Others who do not wish Sparta to be destroyed. Those who have businesses such as yours, that could only suffer from a protracted siege or be destroyed in the violence of Roman victory. If you and others like you cooperate with us, then you shall be shielded from the worst of what is to come."

Charax now dragged an empty crate closer and gestured the others to return to their makeshift seats. Varro, his ribs throbbing under heavy mail, did not waste time to sit. He winced and Charax noticed, but he swiftly looked aside. He seemed in deep thought.

"There might be others," he said. "I can think of some. But you have no other names of your own?"

Falco, who had thus far simply offered only scowls, now breathed in to answer. But Varro realized he might say more than was prudent. So he spoke louder, widening his eyes in warning at Falco.

"We only have your name, Charax. We were told you were the best to organize an uprising."

"Uprising?" Charax's eyes widened and he leaned back. "I told you King Nabis has this city under the sword. No one would dare. Nor would anyone succeed. Every street of this city is patrolled. There is no chance to move unseen, or to organize any rebellion large enough to threaten the king."

Varro waved away the concern. "Gather your friends and we will set our plans. When the Roman and allied armies arrive, you only need to capture the gates and allow Consul Flamininus inside."

"How will that ease the bloodshed?" Charax's voice echoed in the space of his vast warehouse. Varro again winced, but immediately felt foolish as any slave overhearing them would only hear Latin and not understand.

"I will work with you to understand the details," Varro said. "But we would have to secure both gates to the outer and inner city. The consul would bolt through the city and take control of both gates from us. After this, the fight would be over. Yes, soldiers will die. But the city and the people will be spared better than if we lob flaming shot into your city for months on end."

Again Charax nodded appreciatively. "Well, then there is much work. I have some names I could begin with, old friends I trust to feel as I do. There might even be those close to the king himself who could aid us. Did your consul mention this?"

Varro shook his head. "We were to seek you out and work with you alone. If there is a man close to the king, then you know better than the three of us."

"Of course," Charax again seemed to drift into thought and sat quietly for a moment before addressing Varro again. "Well, then in the meantime we should decide where to house the three of you. At least for now, this warehouse will be safe enough. You cannot be seen outside, of course. Even if you were to dress in my own clothes, the soldiers who patrol these areas know the people. You would be an unfamiliar face in a time when travelers are not allowed into the city."

"How long will it take you to begin organizing like-minded men?" Varro cradled his side and leaned forward. "We only have a few weeks, if that long, to prepare."

"The journey from Argos is hard, but not so long as that." Charax continued to rub his chin as he searched Varro's face. "Your consul delays so we have time to enact the plan?"

"As you can appreciate, we've been told almost nothing so if we are captured, even under torture we could reveal nothing." Varro smiled. "Though we hope our situation will not become so dire."

"It won't if you remain here," Charax said. "At least for now. Besides, you are wounded. I will have Ajax look at the wound. He has some training in medicine, and could at least help you brace those ribs."

"I can handle it, sir." Curio gently shook his head in disagreement with Charax, who shrugged in answer.

"Just as well," he said. "But rest now. You will at least want wine and something to eat. Can we trust each other enough for me to send refreshment to you?"

Varro smiled. "We trust each other enough for that."

Charax again gave a warm smile, further relaxing the impression of the skull so prominent under his spare flesh. "Good, and if we are to trust each other, then I shall know your names."

Seeing no harm in identifying themselves, Varro gave their names. Charax then repeated these back, pointing to each one in turn to ensure he had the identities correct.

"This place will be as good as any to rest," Charax said. "I will see that the slaves remain away. You might hear them at work, but pay them no mind. Over the coming days, we will reconsider the best place for you to hide."

"Do you have any family?" Varro asked on a sudden inspiration. Charax's hairless brows rose. "I have three sons, but only one still lives with me. My wife passed two years ago. Why do you ask?"

"I just fear we put them in danger by remaining here."

Charax gave a cool smile. "If we are to enact this plan of yours, they are in danger as long as they are my family. It does not matter where you are."

"Still, keep us secret from them," Varro said. "The fewer who know, the less chance of our being uncovered."

So Charax left them, and once Varro was certain he was gone, he dared to let his breath out.

"You don't trust him?" Falco asked Curio. "With that business about Varro's ribs?"

Curio nodded. "He looks like a vision of death."

"He is off-putting," Varro said. "But we cannot judge him by his appearance. We must see his actions. In any case, I want us to be careful about what we reveal to him. Until we've had some time to build trust, we should be wary and not keep our weapons too far."

"Do you think he's going to find those soldiers?" Falco asked, his hand drifting to his sword again.

"We'll know soon enough," Varro said. "Curio, I need you to get outside and learn the approaches to this place. I need to know who is here and all the entry points to this building. Find a place to watch the entrance, and a way to warn us to run if guards are approaching."

"I should wrap those ribs," he said.

Varro shook his head. "Once this armor is removed, I won't be able to get it back on again. I want the protection until we know what Charax might do. Even if he is on our side, maybe his slave is not, or maybe he is not discreet."

"If those ribs are broken, they'll set improperly," Curio said with a shake of his head. "But it's your body."

They waited for Ajax to return with wine, bread, olive oil, and cheese. It seemed a feast to Varro, who eagerly accepted the food along with the others. Old Ajax offered to examine Varro's side, but Curio chased him off. After the slave departed, Curio took up his mission while both Falco and Varro rested in the cool and dim warehouse. The sounds of workers in the far rear echoed through the building. About an hour passed and Curio returned with his report.

There was the front entrance they had used, a small side entrance, and then the rear where there was an open dock to load carts. Right now, empty amphorae were being returned and slaves were stacking these while a boss monitored their work. There were five slaves and one boss.

The day passed and soon the issue of relieving themselves arose. They would be perfectly fine to go in an empty pot, but feared the scents would give them away. Ajax, who had returned by nightfall, suggested they use the side door and relieve themselves in the alleyway. It was not ideal, but slaves could clean it up and the waste could be blamed on vagrants.

A full day and night passed before they saw Charax again. He brought them their evening meal with help from Ajax. Slaves in the far corners of the warehouse bumped around at the end of their working day. A small clay lamp was all that lit the semicircle of conspirators sitting on empty crates and eating.

They ate a repeat of yesterday's meal, with fish added as meat. To Varro, it was the most succulent food he could remember tasting and its quality set Varro's mind at ease about Charax. He would not feed them so well if he hated them.

Charax reported on his progress, saying he had met in secret with his closest friend to persuade him to join their cause. The friend, he said, was eager to prevent any conflict with Rome.

"And I have more news," Charax said, leaning closer. "It seems one of King Nabis's advisors might be less than loyal. I heard this from my friend, who has close ties to the court. There are rumors about him. Could he be the one who contacted your consul with my name?"

Varro coughed, a small fishbone catching in his throat at that moment. He could not answer, but Falco spoke up.

"Maybe. I suppose someone had to tell him." Falco patted Varro's back while he continued to cough. "Looks like your question made our centurion choke."

"You are a centurion?" Charax sat up straighter. "You seem quite young for that rank."

"All the older ones died," Falco said. "It has been a long war."

"Not as long as some," Varro managed to stammer. He guzzled the last of his wine, a sweet vintage unlike anything he had ever tasted. He regretted swilling it, but his throat called out for relief. When he set the cup on the upturned crate that served as a table, he looked once more to Charax.

"This advisor, what did your friend say about him? Can he help us?"

Charax shrugged. "It is just speculation now. It would be a

dangerous thing to approach him without knowing for sure where his loyalty is. But if you did know something that you were not telling me then we might know better how to proceed. A man in such a position could be of immense use."

"Why do you keep asking us about this?" Curio asked as he finished his meal, setting the wood plate down with a soft clack. "Someone knows enough about you to tell our consul you aren't loyal to your king. Why not just figure out who you've told this to, then you'll have your answer."

Charax sat back with a nod.

Varro's hands went cold.

The lamp flame flickered deep shadows across Charax's head, and Varro saw only a grinning skull looking back at him.

He shoved away from the crate and snatched at his pugio resting by his foot.

"It's a trap! Get your swords!"

8

Varro had no time to articulate his hunch. His fingers, slick with the juices from his meal, slipped across the handle of his pugio. Falco and Curio had not even reacted when Charax leaped off the empty crate he sat upon. He might be bone-thin with fat age spots clinging to his temples, but he moved with alarming speed. He drew a long dagger from beneath his tunic with fluid ease.

Yet even as Varro wrapped his hands on the handle of his pugio, men spilled around the wall of crates that had blocked the rest of the warehouse from them. They wore polished bronze Corinthian helmets and had lowered short spears with bronze points that gleamed with the lamplight.

Snapping to his feet, unsheathing his pugio, Varro leaped for Charax.

But the old man had anticipated this and sidestepped his clumsy charge. Varro crashed into the crate between them, sending all the plates flying atop Falco, who was still only reaching for his sword. The lamp crashed to the floor and gushed oil out that swiftly caught flame.

"You traitor!" Varro shouted, whirling on Charax.

But the old man was ready, and he rammed his blade into Varro's injured ribs.

The mail turned the blade easily, as it was not a straight-on blow. But the force of it carried through and the pain overwhelmed him. His vision turned white and his ears filled with the roar of his own blood pounding in his head.

He might have fainted for an instant. For he was now looking up into a thicket of razor-sharp spearpoints and had no recollection of how this had happened. A dull throbbing at the back of his head suggested he had fallen backward.

Beyond the spearpoints, the enigmatic Corinthian helmets looked down on him.

Both Curio and Falco called out, but they were lost from his sight.

"It's over," Charax said. "Your centurion is captured and you are surrounded. Put down your weapons."

"Don't do—"

A spear butted Varro's face, rebounding his head off the earthen floor with a heavy thud. He tasted coppery, hot blood flowing from his spilt lips into his mouth.

He heard the clank of Falco and Curio dropping their weapons. With a dozen spearpoints touching his throat, chest, and legs, he could not even lift his head to see them. So he closed his eyes in shame and sorrow.

They had been captured.

The inspiration had come too late. Had he not been so tired and so worried for his injured ribs, he might have realized Charax's charade earlier.

He had sought to lull them into trust and elicit more of their plan. His questioning about Nabis's advisor now seemed the obvious attempt to either frame or confirm suspicions about that man. Charax might be seeking to ingratiate himself with his king or else questioning them on the king's behalf.

In any case, when Curio pointed out that Charax should know in whom he had confided his true loyalties, Varro realized Charax had never done so. Therefore, this was not the same Charax from the consul's list of names. The gods had punished his conceit. They had set him before another merchant named Charax. Falco had been right. Perhaps Charax is a common name after all.

Men shouted as they stamped out the flames of the overturned lamp. Now only dim light reached them from the recesses of the warehouse. The bitter scent of the extinguished fire hung in the air and the cold spearpoints pressed into Varro's flesh. Charax's skull-like head appeared over the enigmatic helmets starting down at him.

"You'll be taken to King Nabis for judgement, which will surely be death. Let your foolish consul come with his armies. We are Spartans. Every man, woman, and child will take up arms against you. Rome has been defeated, Centurion Varro. Many times in my lifetime. And so Rome will learn defeat once more!"

Charax now sounded like a madman, his voice echoing into the darkness of the warehouse. The guards surrounding him pulled the pugio from his grip. They then hauled him up and came forward with greasy iron chains to bind his hands and legs. They then clamped an iron collar to his neck. The same was done to Curio and Falco.

Both men hung their heads in defeat. Varro could not stand to look at them, for he had led them to disaster. Once their chains were secured, the Spartans used their spears to march them out of the warehouse and into the streets.

Varro was surprised to find the lamplit streets filled with soldiers. He guessed a full company had come out to line the roads. Spartan citizens mocked them from behind the line of guards. Someone hurled a stone, and it thudded harmlessly into the dirt at Varro's feet. But the guards shouted down the crowd and threatened them with their spears.

It seemed they were to be spared physical harm until they were delivered to the king.

In a final humiliation, their collars were linked together with another length of chain that fit through a loop. Varro was placed in front and the lead soldier hauled the chain like a tether. With arms and feet bound, he could only walk at a shuffle. The Spartan yanked them forward with a shouted command then turned to set the pace.

Sparta seemed immense to him being led through it in chains. As darkness fell, the lamplights dropped globes of golden light into their paths. The lines of citizens eventually feathered out with the coming of night. Doubtless a curfew sent them back to their homes and spared Varro and the others humiliation.

They wended their way along streets toward King Nabis's palace. This was set on the acropolis, the highest point of the city. Along the journey, being bound at the feet, all of them stumbled at different points causing the others to stagger. Whenever this happened, the column of guards paused and kicked the fallen man. Whenever Varro fell, he protected his ribs from the Spartans' violence. For all their shouting, their beatings were halfhearted. Either they did not care for the duty or had been instructed to leave them whole for the king's torturers.

The palace seemed freshly built, though Varro had no time to admire its finer points. It was an imposing structure of stone columns and ornately peaked roofs. Statues of ancient heroes stood black against the new stars of the evening sky. Bronze braziers big enough to hold three oxen each roared with flames that lit the approaches.

Once inside, their chains clinked against the smooth stone of the palace floor.

The lead guard at last stopped and gave them instructions

which Varro did not understand. In their helmets each man seemed the same as another. It was an unsettling sight, and Varro thought it might bring them some minor advantages in battle. He shook his head at his own wandering mind, for surely he had come to the end of his life. He would never fight another battle again. What did the Spartans' helmets matter to him?

The lead guard paused to speak, but then seemed to understand the language barrier. Rather than burst into a rage as Varro expected, he simply picked up the chain and continued to march them into the palace.

Varro had never been able to turn around to see Curio's or Falco's conditions, nor who followed. The huge column of soldiers that had delivered them to the palace were no longer present. He could tell this from the sounds of feet clapping the stone floor behind him. At most a dozen guards remained.

But they were delivered into a side room where more guards awaited, men who were stationed within the palace. They seemed no different than the other Spartans, but their exchange indicated a definite superiority in the palace guards. They assumed custody of Varro and the others.

The lead Spartan handed the chain to his superior, gave Varro a short nod, then paused to speak to him before leaving with his unit. The man clapped his shoulder before leaving Varro confused.

"He said you are an enemy and a fool, but he admires your guts to come here alone."

The leader of the palace guards spoke heavily accented Latin. He was tall and strong. Varro imagined under his helmet he must be a handsome man. But at the moment he seemed like any of the others in this group of seven guards.

"What will happen to us?" Varro asked.

"What would happen to me if I was caught spying on your camp, Roman?"

Varro swallowed and looked down. The iron collar around his neck chaffed him and his side ached. The guard chuckled then turned to speak with his companions, leaving Varro and the others alone. Chained as they were, escape or attack was impossible. In any case, they had been disarmed. When Varro turned, he saw their weapons and his pugio set at the entrance to this guard station.

"I was too late to figure out Charax's game," Varro said, daring a whisper to the others. "I am sorry."

Curio and Falco both looked down, seemingly as afraid of meeting his eyes as he was of meeting theirs.

"He was just leading us on," Falco said. "Hoping we'd tell him all our plans. If I ever get to grips with that skinny bastard, I'm going to carve out his heart."

"Are we going to be tortured?" Curio's voice was small and weak.

"Probably," Varro said.

He looked to his feet and pressed his lips together. The Spartan had said it all with his question back to Varro. If a spy was found in the Roman camp, questioners would be set to work on him, applying torments to inflict maximum pain while leaving the spy alive to answer. Even if he told the truth, the torturing would continue until the tribunes and consul were satisfied. Then the spy would be executed, probably through crucifixion.

That's what lay ahead of them.

"Now would be a great time for that spy in the palace to show up with a rescue plan." Falco tried to laugh, but it died into silence.

"We'll be broken men within the hour," Varro said. "Too late for his aid."

Their brief conversation ended with the guard leader taking up their chains again.

"King Nabis is eager to see you," he said. Though his helmet hid his face, Varro heard the smile in his voice. "And I will interpret for you."

They shuffled through palace corridors lit only by bronze lamps in long intervals. It created a sense of wonder in Varro. With ceilings and walls lost to darkness, he felt as if he moved through an endless black space. By the time he reached the audience chamber, he had been through a half-dozen galleries and their connecting halls, all dim and forbidding.

A man in a stark white tunic with a gold border and scarlet cloak sat on a heavy, undecorated chair set atop a stone dais. Braziers were lit in the corners of the room, throwing dramatic shadows that flickered around him. His bare legs were muscular and his flesh browned from the sun. Most arresting was his expression of anger and intensity. He was an older man, but his pointed beard and curled hair remained mostly black. He grimaced as if he were wrestling with a lion and winning.

Their guard escorts went to their knees before him. Varro did not recognize kings, nor would any Roman. Nabis was proof enough of the evils of kingship. He murdered a path to his throne, and ruled through fear and violence. Varro would never kneel willingly before such a monster.

But he was helped to the ground with a strong butt from a spear to the backs of this knees. He and the others collapsed, and striking the stone floor lanced bright pain into his knees and jarred his ribs. Yet Varro kept his head high, even if forced to his knees.

With a lift of his palm, Nabis allowed his men to rise. Varro shifted to do the same, but found a spear blade pressing his shoulder from behind. He and the others were to remain on their knees.

Nabis's voice was rough and unsettling. Imagery of a snake shedding its skin came to Varro's mind as he listened to the king speak. He went on at length, apparently addressing his prisoners.

But without any translation, the king's words were so much bloviation to him.

Charax appeared from behind, escorted under guard by two men. He slid easily to his knees, and a long exchange passed between Nabis and his subject. Skeletal Charax only ever gestured to Varro, but never turned to face him. He also never spoke without Nabis's leave.

Left in the dark, Varro looked up to the Spartan who had promised to translate, but he remained standing at attention and in complete silence. It seemed unless Nabis designated a man to speak, he would not.

Nabis laughed at something Charax said, then rose ponderously from his plain but brightly polished seat. He gestured at Charax in dismissal, and the old merchant bowed then backed respectfully from the presence of his king. He averted his eyes from Varro and the others and vanished behind them.

Now Nabis stepped down from his dais, strong arms clasped behind his back. He paced before his prisoners, delivering a long speech that was not interpreted. Even without knowing the words, Varro understood the arrogance and smugness of Nabis's speech. No doubt he bragged how the Romans had been caught and their plans uncovered. Now they would face unending pain and ultimate death all at his discretion. What else could he be saying? Varro followed Nabis's pacing, hoping that his glare would pause the king's diatribe. But no one, not even Nabis, looked at him. It was as if he had died already and was merely a ghost watching a reenactment of his final hours.

But then Nabis did stop, standing over Varro with his arms tightly clasped. He gave the king an icy glare of hatred, which made him laugh. He asked a question and at last the guard translated.

"King Nabis wishes to know your names. Speak them now."

Varro paused as if he debated whether to answer, but knew

better than to actually defy the order. He named himself, as did Curio and Falco. This seemed to satisfy Nabis, who returned to his seat atop the dais.

He sat there a long moment, chin resting in his hand as if he had grown bored with them. Then he clicked his tongue and waved them away as he proclaimed something to his guards.

The leader took up the chain and yanked Varro and the others to their feet.

The audience was over and now they were dragged in chains from Nabis's presence. Varro looked back, over Curio's head, and around Falco's. Nabis watched them leaving as a group of servants and other men in plain tunics gathered to his side.

Rather than thread back through the palace, they were led in a different direction and eventually back into the warm night. No one spoke except as needed to pass some checkpoint or make an adjustment to their marching order. Not far from the palace they were delivered to a plain and squat building, and once inside they discovered it seemed like a guard barracks. Words were exchanged between their guard and the occupants of this building. At last, they handed the chains over and turned to leave.

With some room to move, Varro stepped in front of the leader.

"What is happening to us? Are we to be tortured for information?"

Spears lowered at Varro, as it seemed he might be threatening their leader. But the Spartan raised a hand to calm his men. He at last removed his helmet and as expected he was a handsome man with a white scar that ran from his left brow to his jaw. He gave a wicked smile.

"You have revealed your plans already, Centurion Varro. There will be no torture. Only death. Tomorrow you will be crucified on the board and hung from the city walls to warn your consul what fate awaits any Roman who dares enter our city. Enjoy your last night alive."

9

A vast crowd had gathered to watch the crucifixion. Their cheering and cursing along with the general bustle of thousands made it seem like a festival to Varro. He remained in chains, though he was no longer bound to the other two. They had been led from their prison to the agora, where they were surrounded by great works of architecture that were all a blur to him. Most of the crowd would be unable to see their crucifixion. But he could see them, a rolling throng shrouded in city smoke and checkered with shadow and sunlight from the noonday sky.

Spearmen surrounded the platform, three ranks deep. If anyone wished to get through, they would have to bring heavy infantry to the task.

No help was going to reach him here, he realized.

"This is really it?" Falco stood to his right and Curio on his left. All had been stripped naked, and Falco covered himself with his chained hands. "No one came to help?"

Falco had expressed confidence in a rescue the entire night

they had sat in iron cages. Curio had said nothing, except that he did not want to die like this.

"We were not promised any help," Varro said, his voice low and weak. The three men on the platform with them ignored their exchanges. They were bent over crucifixion boards in final preparations for the big performance culminating in their deaths.

"But that spy should know we're here now." Falco looked toward the throng that flooded into the streets of the agora. "Maybe he's out there planning something."

"Why? What does he gain except to expose himself? We're three soldiers, Falco. Rome will not mourn us, and certainly not miss us."

"He did it to take back the silver." Curio at last spoke, his voice trembling on the verge of tears. "Flamininus is a snake. We didn't even have time to write a will or anything. He'll just take it all for himself now that we're going to die."

Varro blinked at this and considered dissuading Curio as the consul could have just kept the silver in the first place. But then he shook his head. He had one more duty to the men he led, and that was to lead them on their journey to meet the Ferryman and their ultimate fate.

"Let us not leave the world full of hate," he said. "We have served well. We have been loyal and have fought for our city and our way of life. We have been friends to each other when there were only enemies surrounding us. Life was too short. There was much to do. But now it is over. Forget about wealth or rescue. Forget anger. I will see you both in the Elysian Fields, and let us meet there with smiles on our faces."

Curio began to weep and Falco lowered his head. To Varro's surprise, he felt no sadness. He thought of his great-grandfather and the vow of peace he had made. This was all that weighed on him now. For he had shed so much blood, and done it gladly, that he must be judged false after death. Falco and Curio might stride the Elysian Fields, but Varro wondered if he would spend eternity in a cold world of fog and sorrow.

The workers on the platform stood up from their labors. At the same time, a man in a white tunic with a blue cloak mounted the stage. He glanced at them, his face red with the effort and full of disgust. The new arrival to the platform called for attention. He was in Varro's reach, and he thought that with the weight of the iron manacles binding him he could split the man's skull like a melon. But what then?

He began calling out to the crowd, playing to their emotions and drawing shouts of approval and triumph. No doubt he derided Rome, spouted defiance, and carped about the torment of the three prisoners beside him.

Varro's mind drifted off. This was his last view of the world. He would not waste it trying to make sense of nonsense. Instead he looked to the blue sky and the white birds that wheeled freely through it. Curio's weeping grew stronger and even Falco began to crumble. He wished he could console them better. He had hoped his speech would've emboldened them. But instead they now seemed to fall apart.

"The two of you, get yourselves together. Don't give them what they want to see. By the gods, forget what I said if it will make you cry. Die like a Roman, with your head high until it cannot be held up any longer."

Falco sniffed. "You're right, Lily. I can't believe you're the one to hold it together and I've gone to shit. Come on, Curio. Stop it. This is the end. Be brave like you've been all your life."

Their exchange was barely audible to themselves, and the frenzied crowd drowned out even the blue-cloaked speaker. Varro could hear the strain in his voice, and at last he quit the stage with a snort of frustration and his face redder.

The three workers remaining on the platform did nothing yet. They sat on the edge, dangling their feet idly. One even brushed his bare feet against one the soldiers surrounding the platform. But his orders must have prevented him from turning around to stop the irritation.

The three boards set out beside them were like oversized doors. When Varro thought of crucifixion he thought of poles and crosses and not boards. In Rome, victims were normally beaten and had their legs broken. Oftentimes they were nailed to their fixtures to speed death. But it seemed today that they were to be clamped onto these boards then stood upright. Each board had iron rings for hands and legs and an iron collar for the neck. The wood was rough and old, and therefore probably used in previous crucifixions. He did not see any blood stains, which suggested he would either die from exposure or starvation if he did not choke to death first.

Now the throng of the agora parted as soldiers with bronze shields and shining helmets shoved them aside. Varro noticed that even where people were compliant the soldiers still swatted at them with shields. Even at this distance, the curses of the newly arrived soldiers carried over the hum of the crowd.

The workers on the platform with Varro now suddenly scrabbled up to stand. The guards surrounding them tightened their ranks.

For the procession entering the agora was King Nabis's.

He had arrived behind his men, seated on a great black horse. He kept his back straight and his red cloak flared in the sun to emphasize his greatness. Indeed, Varro judged he cut a fine figure. But while he acted with regal authority, the soldiers surrounding him did not contain their aggression against their own people. It seemed Nabis required a path three times wider than the width of his column, and his men were eager to stamp down anyone at its edge. Against Nabis's regality, they were all the more brutish.

"No wonder people want to rise up," Falco said.

"If he comes on stage," Varro said, "let's beat him to death with these chains. It will be our last service to Rome."

"I can agree to that," Falco said.

Curio remained silent, head lowered though his sobbing had ended.

Nabis did not approach closer, but stopped his horse in the opening created by his thugs. Some injured people either crawled or were hauled back into the crowd. Nabis rose his hand to accept the adulations of his citizens and turned to all corners. His mounted guards flanked him on all sides and close enough that even an archer hidden in the rooftops would be challenged to find a shot. His speech was thin and faint, and it went on too long. Yet when it ended, he pointed toward the stage and every head turned to face it.

Now six of the guards beneath the stage mounted. Three kept their spears ready and the other three each grabbed one of them. The man on Varro was short and thin, more a boy than man. He unlocked Varro's chains, which fell to chime against the wooden floor.

For a fleeting moment, Varro closed his eyes and savored the breath of freedom. It was no longer than a heartbeat, that space when the chains had fallen from him and his guard had not yet seized him once more. Yet it was the most precious thing Varro could imagine at this moment. He was free for a heartbeat.

Then the guard slapped a rough hand to his naked shoulder. The massive bruise on his ribs was a glaring sight and the guard gave it a playful punch. Still the pain of it made Varro groan. This entertained his guard, but the crowd made too much noise to hear it themselves.

Before he could stand up, the guard shoved him onto the board with the other spearman keeping his weapon ready. Varro thought about throwing himself on the spear and denying the

Spartans the spectacle of his suffering. But before he could act, the young guard effortlessly swept him off his feet.

He crashed hard on the wooden board. Beside him, Curio and Falco also thumped to the wood. Falco cursed his guards, who ignored him as they worked.

The two Spartans overshadowed everything, including Varro's view of the sky. Their helmets turned them into expressionless demons who hovered over him in his final agonies. They stretched out his arms and set his wrists into the iron rings. They hammered locking pins into place, one on each side. For now, he felt only cold and rough iron.

They repeated this process for both his ankles. He stared at the sky as they worked, the dull roar of the crowd drowned out by his own thundering heart. A hawk circled above, rising and falling with the wind. Was it a sign from the gods? he wondered. Had they sent their messengers in disguise to observe his death? Did the gods even care?

At last the iron collar was fitted to his neck, holding his head tightly to the board.

He heard Falco shouting to his left. He realized as he lay flat against the wood that he was trying to get his attention.

"I said I'm sorry for all the shit I did to you when we were kids."

"I'm sorry I wished for your death."

"Looks like you're getting your wish."

Falco laughed. It was delightful to hear and Varro smiled. Tears at last burned his eyes.

"You were a good friend, Falco."

He tried to answer, but their guards stepped in between, shouting at them. The workers then trotted behind the boards and as a group they set to the task of raising them.

Varro's was first. They counted down their lift, then levered Varro's board upright.

At first he simply bounced on the board as they got their leverage under him. Then in one swift motion the board rose vertically.

He slipped down against the iron collar. The panic was instant as it bit into his neck, cutting off his windpipe. He gagged and struggled, but realized he could still breathe. His body arched forward as if to fall, but the chains held him just enough that he could only bow forward so far. It took considerable strength to stay flat and relieve the pressure on his neck. He could fight to stay alive.

But it was a fight he was destined to lose. It was the point of crucifixion, to make a long, torturous death for the victim.

He heard both Curio and Falco being raised in turn. He had no idea what held him upright after the workers had finished with him. His mind was in no condition to consider the possibilities. He was vaguely aware of the crowd closing in on the stage, now wild with a lust for death and suffering. They were faceless and shapeless. Panic at being on the verge of suffocation made it impossible to see anything. His mind was blank with fear and his body immobilized.

It seemed he must hang there forever, but then more workers arrived with a wagon. Like moving furniture from a home, the new workers carried away each board to the wagon and set them on poles. The angle gave Varro some relief. His wrists and ankles throbbed and his side burned from having been stretched.

Being set at the front of the cart, Varro had only a view of the mob while Falco and Curio were loaded behind him. He heard the thumping and cursing of the Spartan workers. The crowd was kept at bay by a line of soldiers that had come forward.

He thought of Falco's hope, that the promised spy would somehow appear through the crowd and save him. He had once been under an executioner's blade and spared by a hidden ally. Where was he now? How would he be saved? Of course he would be saved. This was not how he should die. He had been a good soldier and an honest man. He had tried to do the right things. This was not the reward for such a life.

Yet the cart lurched ahead as a driver walked beside the two mules yoked to it. He steered them onto roads lined with guards to keep onlookers away. The Spartan citizens shouted curses and raised fists. Some tried to throw rotten vegetables, but these mostly landed wide of the cart. Being naked and chained to a board, Varro's humiliation could not be more complete.

Despite that shame, he was glad for the donkeys ambling pace on the trek to the main gate where Nabis had promised they would hang in warning to Consul Flamininus. The slight incline made his position more bearable. He knew there was no point in fighting the inevitable, but he considered he would have a better judgement in the afterlife if he tried to cling to life.

The cart bumped and creaked through the streets. The people arriving to watch him pass seemed endless. Even with the agreeable angle of his board, Varro felt the burn in his legs from trying to relieve the pressure on his neck. Once he was hung from the walls, he doubted he could last more than a few hours. Already weakened from his rib injury, he expected to be the first to die among the three of them.

When the cart rolled to a stop, even the sway of that force tugged against Varro's neck. The crowds had been kept back and he now faced a stone wall much like the one he had scaled to get himself into this mess. Raising his head, he saw a series of cranes were set atop the wall.

Rather than watch the process, he closed his eyes and tried to imagine all that he had loved and held dear. He would never see his mother again. He would never get to thank her for her gift of the pugio that had preserved him for so long. Its blessing had finally depleted, and his offering to Fortuna had been delayed too long. Still, he recalled his mother's tearful face on the day he left for the army. He had promised to return.

As he dreamed, he remembered Falco as a boy and the terror he had felt whenever he showed up, which had been too often. Strange now that he should be his best friend. He remembered his father working in his cubiculum. He had banished his father from his thoughts in light of what he had learned about him. But now as he endured the final hours of his life, he had less anger toward the man. As a person, he might have made mistakes, but he had done his best to be a father. Why go to the grave with anger at him?

Now his board rattled again and workers once more climbed into the cart. They were removed in reverse order, with Curio being first to go. Varro watched in horror as his board slid up the side of the wall, hauled by the cranes above. The teams involved called to each other as if raising a load of bricks. Such was the value of their lives. The dying moments of his life were just another workday to these men.

Falco went next. His board rattled up the length and he could see him writhing from the agony of it. But soon he too vanished beyond vision.

At last, Varro went. They hooked a heavy rope to the top of his board after carrying him out of the cart. The long draw up the wall was as torturous as Falco had made it seem. Each lurch and bump made him feel as if he must fall, but all he did was choke from the crushing weight of his neck on the iron collar.

He gracelessly bumped over the side, and his board turned and thumped as the workers set him in place beside Falco and Curio. They were not set over the side, but on a framework created above the parapet. When they were finished, they angled the board back to ease the tension on his neck. While it might have seemed a mercy, Varro realized they wanted a lingering death for their victims.

With no fanfare or ceremony, the workers cleaned up as if they had done no more than patch the wall. Eventually, they collected their tools and descended out of sight. The cranes remained in place to be taken down some other day.

Varro hung by arms, legs, and neck. He gagged and gasped, as did Falco and Curio to his right. He struggled to push himself upright and keep his torso from sagging forward. Whatever his success, it could not last forever.

The view from their position showed the sparkling waters of the river they had followed and the massive stone bridge that marked the entrance to Sparta beneath them. The bridge vanished off to Varro's right along with the river. Ahead were mountains and one impossibly high peak. It drew his eye, for it seemed as if he were set directly in front of it and made to study it.

So they hung, naked beneath the sun as the noonday temperatures rose.

Hours later, Varro was sagging and the collar pulling tight against this throat. His head roared with the rush of blood and his throat burned with thirst. His ribs throbbed. His legs ached. Blood ran from cuts in his wrists and ankles.

And as the sun went down, Varro realized he would never see it rise again.

10

The starless night wrapped Varro's naked and tormented body in cold. By now he could not think and could not see. His vision had become a blur and his head throbbed with sharp pain. He had passed hours in a state of near suffocation. His legs had lost their strength and his will to live had set with the sun. Now he sagged against his chains, wishing he could choke to death rather than die of thirst as it seemed must be his fate.

To his right, Falco and Curio had ceased their struggles around the same time. He no longer heard them fighting for breath. But he did hear gasping still, just as his internal reflexes sometimes forced him to gulp air. He could not turn his head to see them. The mountain he had stared at all day was now an angular blankness where no stars shined.

His mind had raced over every memory a hundred times since he had been abandoned to this board. By now, he had no will to review life again. Death was the only release and he would have it soon. In the meantime, the pressure behind his eyes and at the top of his head left him feeling as if his skull must explode. The torment would continue through the night. With luck, he would pass out from exhaustion and die unawares. Would that the gods be so merciful to him.

The breeze and cricket chirping were the only sounds to reach him. The crickets must be underfoot for they seemed too loud to be from the base of the wall. He wished for a comforting voice in his final hours, but it seemed only insects would accompany his passing. The loneliness was as strangulating as the collar about his neck.

A light bloomed to his left, the yellow glow of a torch. He did not expect wall guards to torment him. But of course they would. The Romans did it to their victims. Men were not so different in other countries.

The torch bobbed closer and he heard murmuring voices approach. At last, the light blazed and warmed his left side as the guards leaned over the parapet to look up at him. He could not face them, but from the corner of his hazy sight he saw two helmeted shapes. They stared at him without saying anything for a while before moving off. The light moved behind his board and eventually it reappeared at the other end, where it lingered. Again, no one said anything. No taunts or torments were heaped on them. The guards were simply curious, it seemed, and eventually they moved off again.

He endured this process twice more within the ensuing hours. Only now the patrolling guards no longer paused to look at the victims hung on their stretch of the wall. They continued past in quiet conversation.

Around what must be midnight, Varro felt a torchlight burning again to his left. He must have blacked out for there had been no sound or sign of the approaching light. The two guards seemed to be studying him.

"Are you alive?"

The Latin words were like a slap to his face. He pressed his body against the board to shimmy up and relieve pressure on his neck to reply.

"I live."

"I think the other two are dead."

"No!" Varro surged against his chains as if he could tear the iron like old sheets. But in reality he was too weak for even his mysterious visitors to notice.

One of the pair shifted behind him. He felt him bumping along behind his board, the thumps and knocks vibrating against his back.

"Ease yourself, Roman. Be silent and we'll have you down from here. Don't give us away."

The Latin was characteristically Greek accented. He wanted to face his rescuers, but could not yet shift his head. The man behind him tapped lightly with a hammer. It caused his friend to shush him.

"Be quiet, Charax."

"I can be fast or quiet," Charax said. "But not both in equal measure."

"Charax?" Varro's voice was a hoarse croak. "A merchant?"

"Of a sort," came the voice behind him. "Now be quiet."

Varro lay back and stared up at the stars in disbelief. The true Charax had come to his rescue. Then he realized that he was looking at the stars and the terrible weight on his neck had been relieved as his body flattened against the wood like loose dough.

"This is madness," said the other man. "He's half-dead. He'll never get back to his own, and we'll be put in his place."

"Don't be so negative," Charax said.

Both men now got beneath Varro's board. He heard them grunt with his weight as they lowered him to the narrow floor of the wall. They were both shadows lost in the glare of the torch that one of them now held again.

"The trick is these iron rings," said the man with the torch. "They're not supposed to give way once locked."

"They reuse the boards," Charax said. "So the pins can be tapped out. Just give me time and light."

The man holding the torch looked around. "We're fine for now."

"Please," Varro said. "Get the others. They are alive."

"They're dead," said the torchbearer. The finality of his voice brooked no argument. Varro closed his eyes and felt a piercing sadness. Then terrible rage gurgled up at these men who had arrived too late. Had they only come an hour earlier, all of them would have lived. Falco and Curio would have joined him in freedom.

Charax's shadow filled Varro's sight as he worked on the pin holding his neck clamped to the iron ring. He used a small hammer and what seemed a long nail. He tapped patiently at it while the torchbearer hummed his impatience. After a dozen taps Varro heard the pin plink against the wood board then felt it roll under his neck. Charax tore away the collar.

"I bet that feels good."

"Better than anything." Varro instinctively tried to reach for his neck, which burned at the touch of the fresh air. But the rings over his wrists held him firm.

The torchbearer spoked hurriedly in Greek to Charax, who had shifted to Varro's left hand. Whatever he said sounded urgent, but Charax shook his head.

"I thought he was a brave Spartan," he said to Varro. "But now he worries like my grandmother."

"How did you get up here?"

"We killed all the guards in the tower."

Charax tapped out another pin, then whisked it away with his hand.

As weak as he was, Varro lifted his head to regard Charax. The light of the torch held by his companion showed a strongly built man in a plain white tunic with a short gray cloak. But not a speck of blood dirtied him. He flashed a smile.

"Poisoned wine," he said. "Not all of them died from it, but enough were weakened. Killing them was simple. There were only six men in the tower."

"Nabis will put half the city to death for this." The torchbearer leaned closer to Varro. "So you better survive and you better get back to your consul. Tell him that Demas and Charax have the people ready. The citizens of Sparta will not stand for Nabis any longer. We side with Rome and will open the gates gladly if Rome will free us of this monster."

"But most importantly you don't forget the names Charax and Demas." Charax had released the final ring on his right ankle. "If you live, and we survive, then you owe us your life."

"I will not forget." Now freed, Varro remained flattened on the board.

"Can you stand?" Charax asked as he extended his hand. "The bread and wine, Demas, please."

Varro took the offered hand and hauled to his feet. He collapsed against his savior, who was firm and warm against him. The torchbearer called Demas pushed a hunk of bread into his hand and then offered the skin of wine. Varro chomped the bread down like a starved dog, then swilled the sour wine until Demas pulled it back.

"Here's a tunic," he said. "Now, we'll lower you down the wall. The rest is up to you. You're hurt, but you're tough. So run all night and all day. Bring the Roman army and we will do our part."

Charax helped him lift his arms as Demas fit the loose tunic over him.

"My friends," he said. "They can't hang here and rot."

"We've been fortunate so far," Demas said. "Whether they

hang here or not, you cannot return them to life. We all need to make our escape."

Charax dragged something from the darkness beyond the globe of torchlight. He grunted as he hefted it up. "This is an expensive gift, Roman."

It was a rope ladder that he threw over the side and secured to the parapet.

Demas took Varro's arm. "We'll help you onto the ladder. Then you go."

Varro pulled away. "I will say goodbye to my friends."

Neither Charax nor Demas hindered him, and Varro stepped up into the dismantled framework where he had been hung. He leaned forward to see Falco.

His eyes were closed and his head hung forward. In the flickering torchlight his flesh seemed blue. Of course he had choked to death. Tears pushed from Varro's eyes. He reached out to clap his friend's arm in a final salute.

But the flesh was warm, and Falco's eyes snapped open.

"He's alive!"

Both Charax and Demas hushed him, then drew to his side.

"So he is," Demas said. "He looked dead to me. In any case, we have no time for all of you."

Varro rounded on his rescuers.

"You'll save him or I'll go nowhere. We live or die together."

Demas inhaled to protest, but Charax already fetched his hammer.

"What are you doing?" Demas asked. "We'll be caught for sure."

"You waste more time arguing," Charax said. He gestured Varro to help him with the framework holding the boards upright. "Did you never have a brother-in-arms that you would do anything to save?"

Demas did not answer, but instead growled in frustration.

Charax winked at Varro and whispered, "We served together as young men."

Together, they set Falco's board to the wall floor. Charax immediately began tapping out the pins, while Varro and Demas both went to Curio. Now alert, Curio held his head up and smiled. His voice was thin and weak.

"Falco was right. We're saved."

"Not yet," Varro said. Then he and Demas both braced the board against their backs and lifted it off the framework.

Demas grumbled in Greek to his friend, who had just finished freeing Falco. The two had a curt exchange where both seemed irritated with the other. But Varro slipped past them to help Falco stand. Before he even spoke, Varro lifted the wineskin from Demas to his friend's lips. He gulped it eagerly.

"You're going down this ladder," he said while the dark wine spilled down Falco's neck. "Get back to the consul. Tell him Charax and Demas have the people ready to revolt on his arrival."

Varro grabbed the wineskin back from him before he drank all of it. His shadowed head tilted to the side.

"You've got a tunic?"

"Steal one on your way." Varro led him by the arm to the rope ladder. "Waste no time and get down."

"I don't understand what's happening," Falco said, even as Varro helped him to straddle the parapet. He felt his friend's arms tremble with weakness.

"You're escaping is all you need to know. I'll get Curio, and we'll follow. Remember what I just told you in case we are separated."

In the brief flash of torchlight, he got a good look at Falco's face. Though he had not hung from the board for even a full day yet, he looked as close to death as Varro had ever seen him. Even in the bright light, his eyes were sunken under his heavy brow. His flesh looked colorless and his cheeks hollow. He stared back, Varro guessing he was likely as shocked at what he saw as well. Then he swung over onto the rope and began to climb down.

When he turned back, Curio was chomping on a hunk of bread. He looked to the wineskin Varro had over his shoulder. He offered it to him while Charax and Demas collected their tools into leather bags.

"Finish eating later," Varro said as he guided Curio to the rope ladder. "You go down and follow Falco."

He repeated the same message for Charax and Demas as he had for Falco, then helped Curio onto the parapet.

"You're coming?" He paused as he stood on the rope, his head cocked to the side.

"Of course, but don't stop for anything. We're all getting free."

He gave Curio a light shove down on the shoulder, and his diminutive friend began to climb down.

"You're last to go," Charax said. "You are their leader, then?"

"I am," Varro said. "When I return, I will find you both and ensure you are richly rewarded. You have spared men tonight who have greater riches than you might guess."

Demas's frown lifted. "Well, then let's get you over the side."

The shrill blast of an alarm horn set all three of them leaping in shock. Varro felt cold ice trickle down his spine.

"We're caught!" Charax shouted. "Quickly, the tower is open. We can escape that way. You follow your friends."

But the horns sounded all around and on both ends of the wall, Varro saw yellow rectangles of light open like two eyes of a demon. Both ends were trapped.

All the weakness and pain he felt vanished with strength born of terror. He needed Curio and Falco to escape. Thus far it seemed the guards had only seen them on the walls. He had to give his friends time to reach the bottom of the wall.

"It's no use," Demas said. "We have to go over the side."

"No, we can still get through the tower." Varro pulled Demas back from the rope and pointed ahead.

In the same instant, an arrow shrieked between them. Varro felt the force of its trajectory. He and Demas blinked in astonishment at each other. Had either leaned a fraction closer he would have been skewered from the arrow.

The next shaft roused him from the shock. It shattered on the parapet, sending splinters showering across his face.

"They're on both sides," Charax shouted.

"Demas, with me." Varro flipped up the crucifixion board and set his shoulder to it. "I'm not strong enough. Charax, can you block the rear?"

Neither man needed further instructions. Demas threw his shoulder against the board beside Varro, and Charax groaned with the effort of hefting the other board to cover their back.

"Charge!"

Varro and Demas dashed forward as arrows thumped uselessly into the heavy board. Varro wrapped his hands into the iron rings that had bound him not long ago. With Demas to aid him, he hoped to smash back the archers from this tower entrance, then fight to the bottom while Charax covered them from behind.

Both he and Demas roared as they bashed into the doorway, driving back whoever had shot from within its frame. The board slammed like a door, but the archers had wisely backed away.

"Waste no time and escape into the city," Demas said. "We all go different ways."

They sloughed aside the board, as it could not fit through the door. But both of them ducked down, expecting the archers or spears prepared for them.

The arrows passed overhead and thudded into the board that Charax had covered their rear with. The merchant gave a yell of surprise, but Varro and Demas both leaped into the tower room.

Lamps from the prior occupants still burned. Dice lay on a

table between two men who looked as if they had passed out drunk. Their silver coins were still stacked by their elbows. Two men, both stowing their bows and drawing daggers in the tight confines, now faced them.

They were evenly matched but not even in strength. Demas revealed himself to be an older man in the brighter lamplight. Varro had been wounded and weakened enough that even his rage-fueled strength meant little.

Demas collapsed with a grunt as the first guard rammed his dagger into his gut. The older man had seemed to have had no plan of attack other than the throw himself on his enemy.

Varro instead shifted toward the open hatch where a ladder provided entrance to this floor. Setting it between himself and his attackers meant only one could face him at a time. The second guard skirted the opened hatch to reach him.

But Varro swept his foot out to unbalance the man, then punched his shoulder to cause him to stumble into the hatch. His scream cut off with a thud below. In the same instant, Charax entered, having set his board as a cover against the door. He turned to face the other attacker hovering over his friend.

Charax was as old as Demas but more powerfully built. He grabbed the guard's dagger arm, pulling him aside from Demas's prone body.

Varro snatched a dagger set on the table with the poisoned guardsmen. As Charax and the final guard wrestled, Varro drove that dagger into his kidney, causing him to slump forward onto Charax with a wet gasp. In turn, Charax shoved him aside to send him crashing into the two bunks against the opposite wall.

He immediately flipped Demas over, revealing a heavy stain of bright blood spread over his stomach. Demas gasped and smiled, then spoke in Greek. Charax roared in anger and tried to stanch the blood flow, but Varro knew a fatal wound when he saw it.

"Charax, quickly. Down the ladder."

"I won't leave my brother-in-arms," he said. "I will delay the guards coming this way. You must flee into the city. When you get out, find my home and you will have shelter. It is—"

But the makeshift door flew aside and the doorframe filled with angry guards with lowered spears.

Being so close and covering Demas on the floor, Charax presented an obvious target. The lead guard slammed his spear into Charax's back. The bronze head burst out of his ribcage. His eyes flicked wide and he screamed as blood gushed onto his fallen companion, who had gone slack in death already.

The guards turned to Varro as one. He could see at least two others behind the lead.

The guard's spear had penetrated too far into Charax's body and the guard cursed as he tried to wrestle it free. It was the delay Varro needed.

He snatched the clay lamp from the table and hurled it at the door.

It smashed on the lead guard's helmet, spraying oil that licked into flames that splashed into the recesses of his helmet and flecked the guard behind him. They all retreated, screaming in terror as the first guard clawed at his burning face.

Now he dropped into the hatch, his feet catching nicely in the rungs. He climbed down, feeling numb and cold with the prospect of being recaptured.

But he dropped off the ladder onto the body of the man he had knocked through the hatch previously. As his foot landed on the fallen guard, he slipped. He gripped the ladder to remain upright.

The drop had been too short to kill the Spartan. From underfoot clamped a strong hand onto Varro's calf and another slashed up with a dagger.

Varro jumped back up a rung to avoid the swipe, but now he was off balance and toppled to the floor to land on his back.

The heavy thud jarred his fragile ribs. Pain and weariness

exploded through the armor of his fear. He cried out as the man beneath him now flipped over and drove his dagger at Varro's neck.

Despite the bright pain and the weak tremor of his arms, Varro grabbed his enemy's wrist and stopped the dagger inches from his neck.

Now the Spartan, who had lost his helmet in the fall, climbed atop him, pressing down on the dagger so the point dropped to Varro's neck. He put both hands to the man's dagger arm. The Spartan did as well. The two struggled until Varro realized his enemy straddled him.

Then he kneed the enemy in his crotch. At first, he puffed out his cheeks and groaned. But even in his weakened state, Varro was a powerful man. He delivered two more strikes that forced the Spartan to shift as he moaned with pain.

It was enough to break the hold, and Varro wiggled free, just as two more men appeared over him.

One kicked his head, and he knew no more.

11

Arms in chains, Varro awakened in the same cage of black iron bars he had occupied before crucifixion. His vision swam as he tried to focus on the flickering points of light ahead of him. But instead he fell to the side and retched the wine and bread he had eaten. The sour stench of the half-digested food burned his nose and made his eyes water. He shimmied aside from the puddle on the cold stone floor.

A deep chuckle echoed before him. His arms were bound at his lap in iron manacles, so he had to raise both to wipe the spittle from his chin. As he did, the chains pulled taut against his ankles. He had been chained hand to foot, making it impossible for him to raise his iron-bound hands as weapons against his captors.

"You've had quite a night, Roman." The voice was warm and familiar. It was the accented speech of a Greek who lingered in the darkness beyond the edge of his double vision. "Yes, quite a near escape for you. Tell me, which one are you? Curio, Falco, or Varro?"

He did not answer but strained through his throbbing eyes to see who spoke. The dual points of light were actually one clay lamp burning atop a barrel. A man sat beside it, wearing a plain tunic and cloak. He could see a sword set beside him; a guard then.

"You don't want to speak, eh? Too embarrassed to say. Then let me guess. I should have a good chance to get it right. You are Curio."

He winced at the name. His thoughts turned to Falco and Curio descending a rope ladder. Both naked and seemingly on the verge of death, their escape seemed uncertain. He was alone in the cage, and straining to see either side, he did not spot anyone else.

"Varro."

He turned to his name and the guard chuckled again.

"Ah, you are the one called Varro."

"Why do you want to know? What does it matter who I am?"

"It doesn't." The shadowed figure leaned forward from resting against the wall. The lamp light spread across his right side, revealing the handsome guard who had spoken to them in the palace once before.

"Then why are you asking?"

"Because I want to know the name to write over the head we'll hang at the gate. The other two have escaped for now. But that the day is new. They will be run down like wild dogs. We'll hang their heads beside yours. I'm the only one who will care if the names are over the correct heads. It is my habit to be accurate in all I do."

A dozen questions backed up behind Varro's tightly drawn lips. He knew both Charax and Demas were dead. So the Spartans could learn nothing more from them. But Charax had mentioned family. By now King Nabis must have arrested all of them. He wondered if they were in this prison but in different rooms.

"You're looking around as if you have somewhere to go, Varro. Did you notice you are chained hand to foot and locked within a cage?"

"You fear me that much?"

The Spartan laughed, leaning back out of the lamplight.

"Yes, I do. And why shouldn't I? You have been brave and lucky. Those are fearsome traits to have in an enemy. Don't you agree? So not only have you been doubly bound, but I have been set to watch you right until the moment of your death."

Varro curled his lip and shoved back to rest against the hard bars. He recalled this man seemed to be some sort of palace guard captain.

"Why do you serve Nabis? He is clearly a tyrant and hated by many of your fellow citizens. If you are such a great man, then you shame yourself in service to scum like him."

The man shrugged. "I am Spartan. I serve who I wish, and I wish to serve Sparta. So, I must serve Sparta's king. It is not difficult to understand."

"You'll serve Sparta better by preventing the suffering that is coming."

The guard did not answer immediately. He shifted and seemed to look aside. But then he sighed and his shoulders slumped.

"That seems to be what many others say. But I can only answer that with my sword, Varro. We are not the soft people you Romans are. We are Spartans and we thrive under adversity. We live for the battle. I welcome the suffering that is coming. For I will return it tenfold upon those who deliver it."

Varro stirred, attempting to stand. His ribs ached and his legs trembled. He had to brace against the bars to slide upright. The cage pressed against the crown of his head, being barely large enough to hold him. But he shuffled to the front of it, his chains rattling as he did. He rapped the metal with his iron manacles.

"Then tell me your name, Spartan."

"Why do you want to know?" he asked, mimicking Varro's weak voice. "What does it matter who I am?"

"Because I want to write the correct name on your grave marker once I bury you. It is my habit to be accurate in all I do."

The Spartan's chuckle was cold and forced. He stood up and faced Varro, a shadow in the dark. Then he snatched something off the barrel and thrust it at Varro. Fluid struck him in the face, causing him to flinch back in shock. But the sour notes of wine leaked between his sealed lips. He blinked it out of his eyes while the Spartan laughed.

"Methodios. Take that name with you to Hades. I've sent better men than you there."

Then he vanished into the deeper darkness, leaving by an exit Varro could not see.

He was glad to see the Spartan leave. He had hoped that he was somehow connected with the spy that still must be hidden close to King Nabis. He spoke Latin, after all. Why should he know Latin if he was merely a simple soldier?

He had time to consider that question as no one returned for what seemed hours. The lamp had run dry of oil and snuffed him into near total darkness. A vague reflected light filtered in from somewhere beyond his sight. He heard nothing. No rattling bars, no wailing, no sign of life. Not even a rat visited him. He was in a special prison dedicated to him alone.

In the end, he realized Methodios never claimed to be a simple soldier. He could not be working for the spy, as despite having a perfect opportunity he had revealed nothing. For his part, Varro could not mention anything. Certainly in the coming days he would be tortured for information. But maybe in that time the consul would arrive and Varro would be forgotten.

The timeline for the arrival of the Roman and Achaean armies had never been revealed to him. Again, it was one more bit of intelligence that could not be tortured from him. If they did not arrive soon, then he realized he would die under torture before. The thought turned his hands to ice. It would have been better to perish on the board.

Yet why torture him now if not before? Perhaps the King would simply dispense with him a second time, demanding a more immediate end to his life. But being caught with Charax and Demas might indicate a wider conspiracy that the king would want to reveal.

Sitting against the cold bars, he groaned. Maybe if Falco and Curio reached the consul in time they could convince him to act sooner. But would the consul commit to a battle before he was ready just to save him? Of course he would not, and Varro's face heated at the thought of such vanity. He was a soldier, and as such his life was to be spent by his commanders. He swallowed hard, knowing his death had just become more painful than if he had simply hung from the walls.

In the fugue state of time brought on by silent darkness, he was shocked upright when the vague light brightened and he heard feet clapping against the stone floor.

Six men arrived in addition to Methodios. He gave curt orders to his men. One unlocked Varro's cage and two others dragged him out of it.

"What's happening?"

But Methodios ignored him. He once more wore his Corinthian-style helmet, as did those he commanded. They seemed like soulless monsters incapable of expression beneath their closed faceplates. They yanked him into place at their center, then shoved him forward with Methodios leading.

Being bound hand to foot, he could not move at better than a shuffle. The guards were uncharacteristically patient with this, neither rushing nor shoving him. In the end, it was a short walk up narrow stairs into the morning light. He stepped out of the stale air of the prison onto a street.

There he found a line of six carts with iron cages in the backs. In each cage were men and women dressed in fine tunics and cloaks of red and green usually reserved for the upper classes.

Spearmen lined these carts all around, carrying round shields and wearing their inscrutable helmets. A sullen and silent crowd of commoners watched from doors and alleys, not daring to enter the streets.

The captives in the iron cages behaved in various ways. Some were shouting protests with raised fists. Others shook the bars as if they intended to snap them. Some did nothing more than stare listlessly ahead. Varro noted that none of them cried.

Methodios turned to Varro and produced a key to the lock of his manacles. Within moments the chains were stripped away and the guards collected the iron cuffs. Methodios's helmet faced him.

"Who are all these people?"

"Your guides to Hades, Varro."

Now the guards shoved him ahead, no longer patient. They herded him at spearpoint toward the lead cage where one guard worked the lock and two others stuck their spears through the bars to keep the other captives at bay.

With a painful jab to his shoulder blade, Varro knew he was to enter the cage. The guard who opened the door grabbed him by the arm then forced him up into the cart. He stumbled through the cage door, which slammed shut to set all the bars rattling. The spear shafts hissed against the wood as the guards withdrew them then stepped back.

The lead driver gave a shout and the column of carts tugged forward. The jerk forward caused Varro to fall back against the cage door. When he turned around, he faced the crowded men and women imprisoned with him.

He counted thirteen people in the cage, men and women aged from their late thirties to what must at least be the sixties for others. They wore fine clothes and the women had expensive combs to hold elaborate hairstyles that had become disheveled from their protest. All of them were silent and thin-lipped, glaring at Varro and huddling away from him as if they might catch lice. The cage was not so large that they could get more than an arm's length back.

"What is happening? Who are you people?"

They looked to each other in confusion, some tentatively shaking their heads. One woman with a high nose and haughty brows stepped from clinging to her husband and slapped Varro's face. The bright crack of her palm on his flesh was echoed by a shout from the lead driver.

Varro recoiled both at the pain and the anger. She spouted curses in Greek that seemed to grow more impassioned as she shouted. Eventually her husband collected her and she at last stopped cursing. Instead, she buried her face against his chest and began to sob.

Many of the prisoners seemed to be on the verge of the same collapse. But they all turned their backs to Varro, leaving him alone in the rear of the cage.

The carts bumped and rattled through the streets. All along the roads the citizens of Sparta watched. Unlike his last trip through the town, he saw a tamer citizenry. Women looked in sympathy while children clinging to them stared in confused wonder at the procession. Men either remained expressionless or turned aside in disgust. Varro guessed it not disgust at the captives but at their fates. The folk lining their path were simple in dress and appearance. But the prisoners were clearly a cut above them, likely wealthy and influential families.

As they passed, Varro heard someone shout what sounded like defiance. The shouting seemed to come from nowhere specific. The guards following the carts turned to search, but only succeeded in cowing the people watching the procession. They faded away or ducked back into their homes. The single act of defiance was a seed blown onto fallow ground. Nothing more happened and the carts continued past.

Eventually they rolled beneath the city gates and onto the stone bridge. Varro could not help but look up to where he had been hung to die. He half feared Curio and Falco would be there still. But nothing remained to mark where they had been except for the crane that had been set atop the wall. But even now workers were disassembling it.

He smiled at this, knowing that at least his two friends had escaped. If Methodios was truthful, then they would be running like mad by now. Escape from this land would be harder than entering it. Without supplies or weapons, they would be in a hard place to reach the consul's camp. They would be on the march, but where? His smile faded. Maybe they were all going to Hades at different times. He would just arrive there sooner.

The carts and the guards marched along a well-trodden road. Varro wondered where they were headed. The prisoners in his cart began to murmur together, collapsing against each other desperate for comfort. He noticed they were all looking up at the same point. So he followed their gazes.

They all looked to that impossibly high peak Varro had faced yesterday. The carts were traveling parallel to it now, but it seemed everyone in his cart and the cart behind were staring at that peak. He could not figure the significance of it.

"What's happening?" he asked in desperation. "Why are you all looking at that mountain?"

His fellow prisoners looked at him with disdain. One of the youngest men spit on the plain tunic Charax and Demas has gifted him. He growled and balled his fists. As he was about to strike to release his anger and frustration, another voice called out.

"Stop, Roman! Do not make these final moments worse than they are."

He turned to his left. A man with mixed gray and black hair faced him. He had jowly cheeks that seemed to press against a pointed nose, giving him a pinched look. His eyes were small and sad and he shook his head at Varro's fists.

Instead of punching the offender, Varro glared at him then wiped the spit from his chest.

"Where are they taking us?" he asked. "Who are all you people?"

The Spartan gave a bitter smile.

"We go to the highest peak in the Parnon. At least the highest peak close to Sparta. As to why we go, you must know it already. We are to be thrown from it and broken in the chasm below."

Varro blinked, stepping back from the man whose bitter smile trembled.

"As for who we are. We are the rich and powerful. We are the best-known citizens of Sparta. And through our deaths, Nabis demonstrates his willingness to destroy even his finest subjects. How frightened will commoners be to see this done? What worse fate awaits them should they defy the mighty king?"

"That is madness. It will only enrage the people."

The man gave a dry chuckle.

"No common man will grieve us. The poor are always glad to see the destruction of the successful, as if it somehow enriches them. Fools."

"But anyone could be Nabis's next victim. How does that make a man obedient when his obedience might still be rewarded with death?"

"Well, the common man will not talk about siding with Rome to spare their livelihoods as some of the rich have done." The man raised his brow and looked Varro from head to foot. "Such talk is the privilege of the wealthy. And so is the penance."

They fell to silence and the man soon turned away from him to stare back at Sparta as it retreated into the haze. Varro looked down the column of carts, where everyone pressed to one side to stare at the peak where they were all going to die.

The ride up into the mountains was arduous. The paths were narrow and rough, and not built with carts in mind. But the determined leader of the column ensured every cart went as far as it could before they halted. It was midday and the air was thankfully cooler in the heights of the mountains. Yet Varro thirsted, as must all of his fellow prisoners. None of them showed any sign of weakness. Even as they were herded by the hundreds-strong group of spearmen up the final paths, where they stumbled and bruised their feet against stones, none gave any sign of suffering.

Varro had to credit these Spartans. He doubted the richest of Rome's citizens could endure such torment in the face of death without complaint.

They completed the climb to the peak by late afternoon. It seemed to have been built by the gods for the purpose of hurling men from its height.

The track emptied out to a wide ledge marked only by time-worn boulders on each side. The end of the ledge was like a road that led off into nothingness. It simply fell away as it hung out over a chasm below. Varro could not see it, of course. Such a dramatic height must simply be for terrorizing the victims. For as he knew from falling off Sparta's walls, a much shorter drop could easily kill a man. From this height, Varro expected his body to shatter like a barrel of wine and end up the same consistency.

In the end, he occupied his final moments counting the number of victims following him into death. The guards seemed to be confused about the next step in this procedure, for most stood with spears lowered while a large group huddled together in what seemed debate.

He counted twice, arriving at eighty Spartans plus himself. It seemed a round number to him, one King Nabis probably chose at random.

Unlike the others surrounding him, Varro had made peace with death yesterday. What more was to be cried for? What else was he to regret? The gods had granted him a few more hours of life, one last fight so that he could feel less a fool for being ambushed by an old man. That was generous and he was thankful.

The hardened facades of the others began to crack now. More women cried openly. Some men wiped tears. It was still a far better display than what he expected from people who had lived in ease and wealth. He watched with interest, anything not to think of what hitting the ground would be like. Would he feel pain? Probably not. But whatever he felt would be the most incredible pain any human could endure. His entire body was about to explode across jagged rocks at the base of a mountain. What could hurt more?

Finally the group of soldiers broke up, turning to shout orders at the others.

They lined up in ranks, shields up and spears lowered. They blocked any retreat down the path for the eighty-one victims. For Varro and all the others, the only way out was to go over the side.

An officer shouted an order, and the line of Spartans in their enigmatic helmets began to march forward with spears out.

All composure of the citizens broke. They began to scream and curse, throw rocks at the oncoming soldiers, and seek places to hide.

But there was nowhere to hide. Varro guessed being speared a dozen times and then being hurled over the edge would be the more painful way to die. So he backed up as the soldiers tramped forward. He clung to life, happy to at least be high above the world where the horizon was lost to clouds.

Some decided they could stand no more. They ran for the ledge then leaped off, screaming. Some couples jumped hand-in-hand, their horrified screams sharply dropping away.

Open ground had given out. The soldiers were now driving more over the edge.

Varro looked up and tears did blur his eyes. He saw an eagle soaring among the peaks.

It was a good sign to die upon.

He turned, then stepped off the ledge into oblivion.

12

Varro landed on his back with a heavy thud. He tucked his head to his chest out of instinct rather than any hope at surviving the plummet down the tallest peak in view of Sparta. But it saved him from being brained senseless. The impact of whatever he struck, however, still jarred his ribs and set him screaming in agony.

But rather than continue to fall, he looked up at the late afternoon sky. It was a deepening purple with new stars faintly visible through the haze. The ledge was high above, about as high as Sparta's walls had seemed. Bodies flew over as flailing black shapes, shrieking past him so fast the air current threatened to drag him along.

Yet drag him from where?

A spur of rock protruding from beneath the ledge held him in place, the very palm of Fortuna herself. When he had jumped, unlike the other terrified victims, he had not run over the edge. He had simply turned and stepped off to drop straight down.

This ledge was hardly wide enough to catch him, succeeding

only because he had hewed so close to the ledge when he jumped. If he shifted even a thumb's length he might continue his fall.

Two more bodies shot past him, their horrified screams rapidly fading to nothing and the air current clawing at him.

Yet he remained in place staring at the heavens and mumbling his thanks to the gods. The eagle he believed he saw now winged overhead. It was a black point, and he was not sure the bird was an eagle. No matter its form, he knew it as Fortuna herself watching him.

"My life is yours, my goddess."

To speak pained his chest, even as a whisper. So he remained waiting in silence for others to drop past him.

Yet no one else fell. A scattering of pebbles struck his face, stinging his flesh like miniature sling shot. The purple overhead deepened and no one peered over the edge. For why would they need to? Varro guessed he must be the only person to have ever survived such a fall. Even with the intense pain through his torso he surged with joy.

The gods had chosen him to live a while longer yet.

But as the sky darkened and the stars brightened, his elation dissolved.

He was injured, perhaps badly enough that he would not be able to move. Worse still, his position on this spur of rock was tenuous at best. It seemed rather than be shattered into bone fragments and shreds of flesh on the rocks below he would die of thirst while trapped here. One day someone might look over and find his bones here.

They would laugh at how the owner of those bones had probably thought he had been saved.

But he was not saved. Just not dead.

The saving part was for himself to figure out. Fortuna had only swept aside Nabis's decree to execute him. His next actions would determine what he made of the goddess's pardon.

He first gently flexed both hands and feet, relieved he had not broken bones in his arms or legs. Next he slid his left hand up to his head, seeking blood either in his hair or on the rocks. But he found nothing. In fact, as he oriented himself he realized the distance he had fallen was not even as far as he had from the walls of Sparta. Had his ribs not already been injured, the worst might have been a bruising. He would not question what had happened, but gladly accept that it had.

Of course, he realized the counterpoint to this was he could still plunge to his doom. He would not be blessed with surviving a second fall.

He now tested his body, raising his head to look down its length. Just this motion pained his ribs, but he saw nothing protruding from his tunic. But it still did not mean he was in the clear. As Curio had pointed out before, seriously injured men often did not realize their wounds and would suddenly fall dead even while laughing and drinking with their companions.

If he was to do anything, he would have to shift upright first. Lying prone and facing an ever-darkening sky was pointless.

The first move took a long time. Shadows had begun to crawl down the cliff face like black tar seeping over the rocks. At last he shifted and got one arm behind himself for support. Lifting upright hurt bad enough for his moans to echo off the walls of the neighboring mountains. But soon he was sitting on the ledge with his legs hanging over the sides. He barely had room to lean back against the cliff wall.

A handful of scree slid past him and vanished into the dark below as if showing him the way to death.

Just sitting upright had winded him and now his ribs throbbed and his chest hurt as he panted. He felt short of breath, something he had not experienced before this fall. He cradled his side and realized that what must have been a mild injury before was now a full-blown break. Despite the pain and the complications it would cause him in his effort to save himself, he could not be upset. He was alive.

Looking down, he felt dizzy, for the shadowed lines of the mountain face seemed to dive straight down into an abyss. He had to press back against the wall and close his eyes.

"Were I an eagle," he said. "No, even a sparrow would do. I cannot go down. There might not be a bottom to this chasm. But I cannot climb up."

When he opened his eyes, twilight had crept up on him. Shadows now oozed over his ledge. Across the chasm only the peaks of the mountains shined with rose-colored light. But within the hour even the peaks would vanish into indigo shadows.

Climbing up seemed impossible. He was barefoot and beaten, his strength sapped from all of his ordeals. But sitting here made death a certainty. Fortuna had not saved him just to cast him back into the abyss.

Drawing his feet to his chest, he suffered bright shocks of pain that radiated out from the point of his break. He was already gasping and sweating from the effort of getting his feet under him. But he shoved back against the wall and slid up it. Stones and dirt broke away, tumbling off into silent darkness below. He pressed so hard to the wall that the rough points of it scored his back.

Now he had to turn around on this tiny ledge. He had enough room, but did not trust the edge to hold his weight. Still he pushed against the wall and slipped around until his face hugged the cold stone.

Salty sweat rolled along the top of his lip and into his mouth. He struggled to breathe and looked up. It was a long climb that seemed impossible from this steep angle. Yet he had no choice.

His hands felt for grips as his feet sought support. Once he began, he would have to continue no matter what. He wavered, hoping the gods would send a rescuer. But a wind plucked at him as if this was the gods' answer, "Move or we will continue your fall."

There was no clear way up, but certainly a clear and swift path down. In fact, the mountain face seemed to become smoother as it stretched the peak.

Yet to his left a long span of rock almost like a pole protruding from the mountain face jutted out. It was rough and jagged and vanished straight down into the darkness. He stared at it while he hugged the rock facing.

It was a large protrusion, so large that it must be sitting upon something that could support it. Otherwise, he reasoned, it would have fallen away under its own weight by now. It led down into darkness, but how far down he couldn't tell. Looking up once more into the shadowed peak above, he saw nothing but the shallowest of handholds. If he got halfway up, he would never get back down again. With no way to mark his path, he could not retreat to the safety of the ledge.

But with this obvious spur of rock, he could always follow it back up.

Groaning with indecision, he leaned his head against the hard wall. Trapped either way, he chose the easier climb but the uncertain destination. He would follow that ridge down and see where it took him. Even if he did not reach the bottom, he might find shelter farther down the mountainside.

Yet that ridge was still a distance away. He would have to climb sideways along the wall to reach it. In this, he had more confidence, for he saw long, horizontal cracks and ledges that would be no use in climbing up but would serve to traverse this distance.

It took all his bravery to set his left foot into a crack then to force in his foot up on the ball of his big toe. He found a protruding rock for his hand and stepped from the safety of the ledge. The initial success at finding hand- and footholds emboldened him. But soon he had truly abandoned the ledge and was clinging to the wall. He imagined himself like a spider with arms and legs thrown at wide and awkward angles. But he was succeeding.

He had not realized the strength of the wind until his footing had become so precarious out on the wall face. Even the slightest gust seemed likely to plunge him to his death. But he continued along the crack in the wall. It helped to imagine it as a length of rope that he toed his way along. It was harder to find purchase for his fingers, and at points he was clinging by his nails.

All the while sweat dripped down his back, frigid in the cold air of the mountains. His chest ached and some movements sparked dazzling pain in his chest. But to yield to it would doom him. So he grunted and kept pushing sideways until he at last was able to grab onto the vertical stone ridge.

It was a perilous transition. Yet as he shifted his weight onto the ridge and enfolded it in his arm, he felt as safe as stepping onto solid ground. He had not gone far from his ledge, but to his bleeding toes and fingers it was as if he had traversed the world barefoot. He hugged the rock protrusion like a lover and caught his breath.

A deep breath hurt too much. But the strain had somehow numbed his body to the pain overall. Again the wind buffeted him, again is if warning him to continue while he still had strength. The simple act of holding onto this rocky protrusion consumed the scant stores of energy left to him.

The terror of descending into darkness threatened to overwhelm him. Lowering his foot to find a toehold stiffened him with fear, for each step down would have to bear his weight. He had no rope or piton to aid in his climb. He was one poor choice away from death.

Each step down took him deeper into darkness. Twilight had already filled the chasm below with inky darkness. The golden light bouncing off the mountain peaks no longer reached him.

The descent was painfully slow and soon Varro found his arms shaking from the effort of holding to the rock protrusion. He was engulfed in darkness, feeling his way by bumping his toes along the rough ridges. Every time he found a ledge wide enough to hold his feet, he paused and gave thanks to the gods. Though it was only a respite from the torment of his predicament, he savored them.

His patience was rewarded, however, for the lower he went the easier the descent became. The long spur of rock must eventually lead him to another ledge where he would rest and wait for daylight to reveal the remainder of his path down. This hope carried him ever deeper into the blackness.

Then came the moment his foot felt only air.

How long he had been crawling down this rock spur, he could only guess. His mind was numbed. Without light or sound beyond the gusting wind, he hovered in blank timelessness. Death swirled around him, ever ready to sweep him away into the cold forgetfulness of the grave. The slow, methodical search for an anchor point and the deliberate testing of each step down had become automatic.

Until his foot swished through air. At first, he thought he had come to a gap in the rock. But his foot sought all around and found nothing. His arms shook with the effort to cling to the column of rock. He shifted sideways, hoping to find a continuation on one side or the other. But he found nothing, and the slow process of crawling back and forth had further depleted his strength.

He was still trapped.

Hanging from the rock by willpower alone, he set his cheek against the cold stone and closed his eyes. It made no difference, other than to press out the tears that welled there. He had never known such frustration as this moment. To have expected life and found yet another path to death. The incredible struggle down so far had been a long joke told by those gods that wished to see him suffer before death. He had at last come to that moment when they would lean back in raucous laughter. For he had expended himself to go nowhere.

He looked up, seeing the dark sky above only as pool of dark blue spangled with stars. Even if he had strength to climb up, and had the skill to find his way back to the ledge, it availed nothing.

Below was yawning darkness.

Listening to the wind gust and flattening his body against the rock as it did, he wondered if he could hold on until morning. Light might reveal another path. But the wind seemed to turn to laughter. Where would the strength come to hold in place for an entire night? He was already beginning to lose grip. While descending, each limb enjoyed a break from exertion, however short. But now he burned all effort to hold in place. He might last half an hour, even with the most heroic effort. He'd not last the night.

Rock broke off from underfoot and clattered beneath him. He gnashed his teeth and moaned at his misfortune.

But then he realized he had heard the rock strike a surface.

And the report of the falling rock had come within moments of its drop.

Until now he had not understood how far he had descended. He still could not estimate the distance to the bottom, but could at least look up and see he had gone much farther than he expected.

With great care, he clawed off more rock from his handhold. It was a firm knob of stone that did not yield at first. But it broke away suddenly and he nearly pitched backward. Once stabilized, he dropped the rock.

Within a moment he heard it crack on something below.

He began to laugh. Whatever the distance, he could survive it. That rock sounded close.

So he began a careful descent so that he could dangle from the edge before dropping off.

Then the rock face collapsed where he had broken off the stone. It sloughed away under his hand as more stone gave way underfoot.

He dropped into darkness and crashed hard on his feet. He rolled backward, a pain entwining him like streaks of lightning.

He stopped. The rock continued to clatter from above, landing around him and sprinkling dust over his sweat-soaked body. But he was on a firm surface at last.

When he realized he was not dead he gave a shout of relief and celebration. Lying on his back, he thrust his fists into the air as he proclaimed victory. He had reached the bottom. He was safe again. Nothing could defeat him now.

Then the ground beneath him gave way.

It was like being in a river of stone that flushed down a mountainside. It also seemed as if every stone was aimed at his injured ribs. Yet for all the chaos and terror, he felt as if he rode atop this slide and therefore avoided being churned into bloody muck.

He slammed into something hard, then shot forward to roll head over foot. He bounced like the myriad of rocks and stones flowing around him until he flopped over on his face. Stones and dirt rushed up to him, washing over his body like surf.

His face was in something hard and wet. A foul stench filled the blackness.

Throbbing pain lit up his body bright enough that he thought he could see by its intensity. But of course he remained in horrific blindness. Worse still, he could not rise as something pinned his back.

He closed his eyes and struggled to breathe. With the dregs of strength left to him, he asked his question of the abyss.

"How long does a man need to beg for death?"

13

The spectral light of the otherworld shifted and swirled around him. It was a faint yellow glow that revealed a shadowy land of death. Bodies and parts of bodies were intermingled with old bones. Red-eyed rats stared at Varro and squeaked before darting into the remnants of rib cages and vanishing from sight.

He had expected to feel no pain in death. The length of his body burned with agony along with a heavy weight crushing him. The shifting light made him feel like vomiting. Could a shade vomit? he wondered. Despite the urge, he expelled nothing but dry air.

If he were to meet Charon at the River Styx, then he had best set off now. His current surroundings were a disgusting pit of festering flesh, and he wished to escape it even if he dreaded his judgement.

But he could not rise. Indeed, the pain was too much, but also something pressed him to the ground. It seemed a heavy, cold hand that shoved his face into the bloody dirt. He hadn't the strength or endurance to look over his shoulder at what force pinned him.

The light bobbed along, flickering wildly and scattering rats. He heard their panicked chittering, some close to his ear. Now he heard the scrape of stone and the occasional muffled curse.

As he lay flattened, struggling to breathe, he realized he was not dead. He was breathing and it hurt. It seemed like torchlight from someone seeking among the wreckage surrounding him. At first he could not figure where he was or why he hurt so badly. But as the scrape of sandal on stone drew nearer, he remembered his desperate circumstances.

"Help me."

But his voice was so weak he barely heard it himself. Further, the weight on his back drove out the scant air he pulled into his lungs. He felt as if he could not repeat the same plea.

The searching light continued along parallel to him, with more frustrated curses following.

Finally, Varro realized his arms were both free. He scooped up rocks near to hand, then hurled them toward the light. They rattled over the stony ground and he moaned. Even an enemy would be welcomed at this point.

"This way," he said, barely louder than a hoarse whisper. "Come kill me, please. I must die at last."

The swaying light stilled and the scuffling noises ceased. Varro scratched up more grit then flung it so feebly it hardly traveled any distance. But it made enough noise.

A Greek voice spoke tentatively. The tremble of fear was clear to Varro.

"I'm not a ghost, at least not yet. Over here."

"You are Roman?"

The voice was full and deep, like the voice of a king. Tones so smooth and automatically commanding could only be that of a god.

"Are you Mercury come to show me to the Styx? I am ready to go, my lord."

He heard feet on stone, the crunch of gravel, then a slip and curse. The light wobbled but brightened and widened until Varro felt welcomed warmth spill across the back of his neck and head.

"By all the gods!" The commanding voice was directly overhead, so Varro could not turn to see him. "You are the Roman called Varro? The very one thrown from this peak?"

"Never thrown, friend. I jumped to my own death, and failed to find it."

"How did you come to be pinned beneath a rock?"

"By the same magic that has brought you to save me."

The deep voice chuckled. "You speak clearly for a man who should be little more than a stain. I came here expecting to find your cloak and some tatters of flesh, not your body, and you still alive."

"There's a story, friend. Please, get this rock off of me. I may die yet, and I don't want it to be facedown in the blood of rich Spartans."

The man gave a sigh and Varro heard his feet shifting on the gravel. From the corner of his vision he could see the shape of his legs as he sought a good position. He set the torch between rocks, then began to push at the rock.

"Can you help?" he asked.

"I'll give you encouragement, friend. I've strength for nothing else."

The man groaned, but Varro felt the stone digging into his back as it shifted. Soon, it slipped to the side to thud into the mucky dirt beside him. The man clapped his hands together in satisfaction.

"That alone should have crushed you. But another stone kept its full weight off you. Fortuna has had a busy night."

"The goddess has been with me every day since I joined the army."

Though the weight lifted off Varro's back, he remained flattened and the pressure on him did not feel less. It was the result of his broken bones and his exhaustion. His eyes fluttered even though he wished to see his rescuer. He feared he might pass out.

"Clearly you did not fall, though you jumped. That was confirmed by Methodios himself."

Varro's eyes flicked open at mention of the Spartan's name. The connections all joined together now. If his rescuer had heard Methodios's report, then he must have been in the audience with King Nabis.

"You are the spy Consul Flamininus told us about."

The man knelt beside him but did not answer. His silence was confirmation, and Varro realized his rescuer had ingrained a habit of secrecy.

"You are too secretive, friend," Varro said. "Who will I tell? I'm hardly able to breathe as it is. But at least offer me a name so I know who to thank."

"I am afraid to move you. You are so cut up and bruised I cannot tell your flesh from shadow. You were already suffering a wound when they tried to crucify you."

"It's a lot worse now," Varro said. "Breathing and speaking are like inhaling and exhaling fire."

"Then rest. There is a cave nearby. I will relocate you there. You'll need someplace to heal in secrecy. It is truly a wonder that you are coherent enough to speak."

The process of turning him over felt as if his chest were being crushed. When he flopped on his back, his vision flashed white as if he were looking into a fierce lightning storm. But when the pain faded he realized from the roughness of his throat that he had been screaming. He looked up at the shadow of the man lit with a yellow stripe of torchlight to his left.

"I'm going ahead to clear the path to the cave, as I won't be able to carry you and the torch together. I'll be back."

"I'll try not to wander off."

Though once the man left, his eyes drooped and he found himself slipping into confused nightmares. When he returned, it was as if he were being jarred from sleep.

"Still alive, Varro?"

The words were distant and echoing. But he nodded and tried to smile.

Once he rose off the ground, pain lit up his world again. Only now he found something soft in his mouth. His rescuer had put a leather strap between his teeth for him to bite, and he hadn't even realized it.

The journey through the darkness was more pain than he could bear. He hung limp in the easy strength of his rescuer's arms. Each step ahead jarred his ribs and he wondered how he had found the strength to have descended the mountain as he had. But soon he realized they moved toward light which grew brighter.

"The cave mouth is narrow but enough for a man to fit."

Varro looked up now that the light had grown stronger. He still could not see his rescuer's face as it was all shadow.

"This will be tricky." His rescuer paused and angled himself, jumbling around Varro who bit down on the strap against the pain in his chest. "I'll do this fast."

Then they began to slip through the narrow entrance. Varro pressed against cold and rough stone but it surprisingly did not hurt as bad as the simple jostling he endured while being carried. They popped out into a brightly lit cave with a high ceiling that came to a shadowy peak. It was rough with many nooks filled with blackness. It spun around as his rescuer eased him onto a soft cloak spread into a cleared space among the uneven floor.

"This is going to be home for a while," he said. "Until you can move on your own power again."

The softness touching his back was what he imagined a cloud felt like. While it must be nothing better than a Spartan's cloak, the comfort was unparalleled compared to what he had endured since his capture.

"I've got something here for you to eat. It's not much."

His savior foiled any attempt to identify him again, as when Varro looked toward the man he was turned away and going through a small pack.

"This was to be my breakfast if I needed to stay out for the night. But if you can talk then you can chew, and I think you'll need sustenance after all your trials."

"If Falco were here, he'd say that's fancy talk for being fucking hungry."

The man laughed and set aside a bronze mess pan that a Roman soldier would carry, a patera.

"Here, you can enjoy salted fish and what wine I have. It is not much, but then you shouldn't eat much now."

At last the man turned with the patera filled with strips of dried fish. Varro saw him clearly at last, the torch light illuminating his face. He looked every bit as royal as his voice, with a broad forehead and piercing eyes. He had an easy, handsome smile that must have won him scores of women. His swarthy flesh shined with the sweat of his exertions, and his cheeks were smeared with dirt. But still, he seemed to radiate a healthy and confident glow. It made Varro feel safe, for he had the look of man who was competent in a great many things.

"I can't keep calling you friend," Varro said. "Especially when you seem to know more about me than I know of you. What is your name?"

The man shifted closer to Varro and offered to help him up. As he did, his ribs ached but he experienced no sharp pains. The man shoved a stone under him, softened with his emptied pack, for a pillow. Then he provided him a half-filled wineskin.

"You may call me Castor."

The wine was as sweet and refreshing as any Varro had tasted. Once again being swept to the edge of death made even an ordinary wine all the more vibrant. He gulped it down until Castor pulled the skin away.

"Castor? You speak perfect Latin for a Greek. Or is it that you speak perfect Greek for a Roman?"

"You mustn't gorge yourself," he said with a smile full of glaring white teeth. "I will be leaving you only this for a short time. You'll need to preserve it until I can arrange for better ways to deliver your meals."

He chewed the fish with more thoughtfulness now, despite his appetite. He would draw the full measure of flavor from it, and make it last even though he wished to cram all of it into his mouth.

"Castor, if that's your real name," Varro said as he chewed. "I owe you my life."

"You have saved it yourself. I came here simply to bury you, or what parts I hoped to find of you."

The spy nodded toward the cave entrance, where Varro could turn to view without pain. A worn shovel rested by the exit.

"I don't understand." He picked up another strip of fish, noticing his fingers were swollen and raw. The salt from the fish burned where it touched broken flesh. "Why risk your cover to throw dirt over my shattered bones? I'm just another dead soldier."

Castor's smile turned sly. Then he reached around his back to pull out something wrapped in gray rags. It was narrow and almost as long as his forearm.

"Another dead soldier, you say? And you accuse me of being too secretive." Castor held the wrapped object forward. "The man who carries this is no ordinary soldier, even if that is what he tells others."

He leaned forward and set the object by Varro's hand. He stared it, afraid to find what might be hidden within the rags. Castor smiled knowingly, raising his brows as if challenging Varro to deny what he seemed to know so well.

Forgetting his pain and hunger, he let his fingers run over the rags before collecting the object to his side. Even as he picked it off the rocky floor and set it on his lap, he realized what it was. After a moment's hesitation, he pulled away the rags.

His pugio sat on his lap in a nest of gray rags. It's leather-covered wood sheath still had a divot where it had stopped a killing blow from finding its mark. He tugged the blade half from the sheath. It revealed polished bronze with a white-razor edge.

"This is mine," he said. "Where did you get it?"

"I collected it from your confiscated belongings and determined it should be buried with you." Castor's handsome face brightened with satisfaction. "I had not thought to return it to you directly. When you have more strength, you must tell me how you came to be pinned under a rock in this chasm of death."

Varro stared at the pugio, his ravaged fingers resting on the leather sheath.

"I don't understand. How did you know the significance of this to me? It is just a common pugio."

"You are indeed fortunate that I noticed it. I went to investigate your confiscated gear; I was simply looking to remove anything that might betray my true purpose to Nabis. He rightly sees enemies everywhere, and his henchmen would bring him anything unusual. I saw you had wisely erased the contents on your wax tablet. There were still some impressions left, and I ensured they were completely filled."

A smile flicked on Varro's lips, but he did not correct Castor.

"I was satisfied you had left nothing else to incriminate me and was about to leave. That is when I saw the mark on your pugio. I learned it was yours from Methodios."

"What sign?"

Castor's brilliant smile faltered.

"It is just the two of us," he said. "I understand the need to maintain secrecy, but you needn't pretend with me."

Varro examined the sheath, but it was like any other soldier's weapon and distinguished only by the cut in the leather.

"There are no markings," Varro said. "Unless of course you mean this decoration."

On the pommel was a worn, decorative gold inlay. It was small enough that it did not invite theft or even comment from others. He had burnished it and kept it clean and never once considered that other soldier's pugiones lacked decorations on the handle. However, he had not cared to examine them beyond routine inspections of his own soldiers.

The mark itself was a stylized owl's head. Certainly it was an odd decoration for a soldier's weapon. But Varro had never questioned it and his mother never mentioned anything significant about the design. Now the owl's wide eyes seemed to stare into his.

"I do mean that," Castor said. He reached to his hip, then pulled his pugio from its sheath. Flipping it around in his palm, he showed a matching owl head to Varro's, only his was a silver inlay. "You outrank me, and at such a young age."

He met Castor's easy smile and made his own feeble one.

"I am centurion of the Tenth hastati, First Legion. You are a soldier, then?"

Castor's smile wavered and he retracted the pugio.

"You are feeling well enough to toy with me, Centurion Varro?"

The shift in Castor's tone was unmistakable. His eyes narrowed and his smile vanished.

"I don't know what you are talking about. That is a design I haven't given any consideration to beyond maintaining its polish."

Swift as a striking hawk, Castor drove the edge of his own pugio beneath Varro's neck and held it firm against his pulsing jugular. He gritted his teeth and hissed through them into Varro's face.

"Then who did you steal this from? Who owned it before you?"

The keen point of Castor's pugio pricked into his flesh. Even though he held a pugio of his own, he was too weak and hurt to present any threat. Castor could kill him with the flick of his wrist. So he pressed away to relieve the pressure of the blade from his throat.

"Easy, friend. My uncle carried this on campaign when he was a legionary. It came to me through my mother. She had it blessed at the Temple of Mars before sending me off to the legions with it as a gift. It has bought me nothing but good luck and saved my life a dozen times."

"Who was your uncle?" Castor's gritted teeth were framed in a leonine snarl.

"Tiberius Plautius Camillus." Varro studied Castor for any expression of recognition, but he did not shift from taut rage.

"And did you know your uncle? Did he have nothing to say to you about this pugio?"

"He died when I was a child. A fever took him in the night, at least that is what my mother told me."

"And she inherited his pugio, which she gifted to you? That is unlikely, but perhaps it is so."

Varro swallowed in answer, as Castor's eyes now seemed to be searching his own thoughts. At last he sat back and retracted his blade.

"I have wasted my time and risked much to honor a man long dead."

"Wait." Varro shifted upright. "What does that mean? You're not going to abandon me now? Not after all this?"

Castor stared at him, no longer the smiling and kingly man he had seemed. Instead, he looked more like a buyer at a slave market.

"I need to return to the palace before I am missed. I will send someone to mend your wounds, and then we'll see if you are a useful man or not."

"I'm sorry, Castor. I did not mean to offend you, and I am grateful to you for rescuing me. I would've died without your aid."

Castor stood and dusted down his tunic.

"There are worse fates than dying, as you might soon learn."

14

Light barely reached the interior of the cave, though it bounced into the recesses over Varro's head. It was a mere stain of brightness and he could not determine the hour. After Castor had left him with a cloak for a blanket and the remainder of dried fish and wine, he had collapsed from exhaustion. At some point he had awakened from the void he dwelled within, but was unsure when.

In fact, he realized his ribs were wrapped and his body cleaned. A linen blanket covered him and the rock under his head had replaced with a stuffed pillow. His hands and feet were bandaged as well, and a small clay pot with a wooden spoon sat on a flat rock where other, older dressings were laid out. A clay jug had been set beside it. Next to that, his pugio sat in its sheath.

He rubbed his eyes. "How long have I been asleep?"

"Two days before today."

The answer startled him, as it came from behind. It was a feminine voice, and he twisted to see her. Now that his ribs were tightly bound, the pain was bearable. Still, he could not get a full range of motion.

"Rest, I will come to you."

He settled back on the cloak as he heard the light movements of someone approaching from behind where the cave entrance was. Castor had set him facing the back wall of the uneven cave and he had not moved since.

The woman circled around him to where the clay jug sat. She produced a matching clay mug from behind it. The sound of the clear water pattering into it revived Varro's thirst.

She was a statuesque woman with presence, far too beautiful to be a common servant. Her skin was dark olive and her black hair caught the vestiges of light reaching into the cave. She had a smile that was a match to Castor's in its brilliance and easiness. Though she wore a plain gray stola in the Greek style, it formed to her body. Despite his weary state, Varro blushed at his reaction to her appearance.

She smiled as she knelt beside him, holding the mug to his lips.

"At last I no longer have to spoon water into your mouth. Can you take the cup?"

He blinked and felt his face warm as he realized she waited for him to drink. The water was cool and refreshing, and he gulped it down.

"You have been caring for me for two days?" The vague scent of rot reached him along with the feeble light from the chasm outside. "This is a place of death."

"So it is," she said, her smile never faltering. "Though not for you."

She leaned back and returned the cup to the makeshift stone table. The low light and intense beauty of this woman made Varro wonder if he was dreaming. Were it not for the dull ache in his side and the terrible throb in his head he would not be so certain.

"Castor sent you? I can only assume he has decided that I should live after all."

The woman hesitated at the mention of the name, but she glossed past it and stood to her full height. His perspective on the ground made her appear even more like a statue. Even her sandaled feet, peeking from beneath the hem of her stola, were unsullied by the filth she had to have crossed to reach him.

"I just changed your bandages," she said, sweeping the dirty rags off the rock into a small wicker basket. "I think that wakened you. You have murmured in your dreams. Who are Falco and Curio?"

He set his head down on the pillow and tried to recall his dreams, but found only blankness. In fact, he could not recall anything between jumping off the mountain peak and Castor's threatening him over his pugio. Those memories had crumbled into the emptiness that had engulfed him since his rescue. He realized the woman was staring at him.

"Ah, they are two of my companions who escaped the crucifixion with me. They got away, or at least that is my hope. Speaking of names, what is yours?"

"I am called Ione. Indeed, it was Castor who asked me to tend you for now. You have slept deeply." She looked back toward the cave mouth, exposing her graceful neck beneath her black hair. "It has been a lonely two days in this cave. My slave does not make for good company. She is drawing water from a nearby stream, and will return soon."

"You have sat with me for two days? How could I ever repay the debt I owe you?"

Ione lowered her flashing eyes at him with a crooked smile.

"Repayment will come in time. Nothing is free, especially goodwill. For now, you must recover and regain your strength. Then you can speak of repayment."

"You and Castor...you two are..."

Ione's laughter was deeper than he expected. She covered her mouth with her hand.

"Castor is my husband."

"Of course. Such a man could only be married to a woman of your beauty." His face felt fully enflamed now, and Ione's cheeks dimpled as she tried to restrain her laughter. He turned aside and looked back at the craggy ceiling.

"Well, have you any news of Falco or Curio? It was three days ago that they fled into the night. I hope they got away and back to camp."

He remembered their pale, naked bodies flitting away into darkness. Like himself, they carried nothing out of Sparta except their own will to survive. He hoped it was enough for them, and that Fortuna's blessings had found them as well.

"I would not be told if they were recaptured. I hope they escaped as well. You seemed so concerned for them."

He looked to his wrapped hands and then his torso. "You've done this sort of work before. I've had doctors who could not wrap as tightly as this. It's strange work for a woman, but I am grateful nonetheless. How long will I be on my back? Consul Flamininus's army could arrive any day, and I need to return to my century."

Ione tilted her head with a concerned frown. She gently touched his shoulder. "You need a good six weeks of rest. From all I've heard, the Roman and Achaean armies will be here long before then."

"Then let me ask a different question. How long before I can leave this cave and let the camp doctors decide on my recovery time?"

"You don't trust my judgement?" Ione gave a small pout, and Varro could not tell if she played with him.

"I don't mean any disrespect by it. Understand that I am a soldier and I have a duty to report as soon as I am able. Otherwise, I would not want to be judged a deserter."

"Your consul would be so cruel?" She arched her brows and again Varro wondered if she were mocking or sincere.

"That is the way of the army. If I decide that I should rest while everyone else is fighting, then what am I if not a deserter? I need to report back as soon as I can. If I am to be excused from duties, that order will come from my tribune."

"What were you doing here?" Ione now stepped behind him and he heard the scrape of something soft against the stone, probably a sack. "Why would you be in Sparta before your army arrived?"

"None of it matters anymore," Varro said, thinking back to Charax and Demas and their grisly deaths. "We failed, and now just hope to survive until Consul Flamininus brings his army to Sparta. I've no right to beg more favors from the gods, but I pray all three of us can return to him safely."

Ione did not speak, but soon reappeared to sit at his side. She had a small clay pot in her elegant hands, and carefully removed the lip.

"Here are pickled vegetables and goat meat. When the slave returns with water, I will make you porridge. You need to eat to regain strength.

The thought of food flooded his mouth with saliva. She propped him up and began to feed him. He tried to wave her off and feed himself, but realized with his wrapped fingers he could not get the food out of the pot. Ione smiled and continued to feed him.

Chewing made his head hurt, but he fought through it. The pickled vegetables and meat were more flavorful than anything he had eaten in days, so much so that the spicy taste was painful. He blushed at her care but realized he had no choice. He was lucky to be able to chew at all.

"Still won't you tell me of your adventures? I have sat in silence for days and I would hear stories of your bravery. I fear I must remain with you a good many days longer, and then I do not know what will happen if your consul arrives. Did he give you a time to return to him? Once the siege begins, there will be no way back into the city."

"I think we were to remain in the city until he arrived, and so he gave us no definite time. We were to incite dissatisfied citizens to an uprising against Nabis. That was a doomed effort from the start. It did not work in Argos, and it seems to be even less likely under Nabis himself. Still, I cannot question my orders."

He looked past Ione at his pugio resting on the flat stone. The owl symbol was hidden from this angle, and he wondered if Ione would know about it. She was Castor's wife and should have some idea of his dealings. But then, he thought of his own family. Certainly both his mother and father had kept secrets from each other, as might Castor and Ione.

"Did Castor mention anything about me? Other than that I needed help?"

She set aside the dish while Varro finished chewing the last of it. She cocked her head and frowned.

"Only that I should care for your injuries until he could join us in a few days' time."

He paused and considered whether he should share more. Yet the worst outcome could be that she sincerely knew nothing.

"You have seen my pugio. There is a mark on the handle, an owl's head. Castor has a mark just like that on his pugio. Have you seen it?"

Ione's brow creased in confusion, and she turned to reach for the pugio. She held it gingerly in her hands, her eyes glittering as she studied the weapon. She pointed to the owl.

"This? I have never seen such a mark. But then I do not study my husband's weapons. I would not even be allowed to touch them."

"But you are aware of your husband's true work, or else you would not be here." He paused to match Ione's sly smile. "So, that symbol is the entire reason he came to find me here. Did he not explain any of this?"

Ione shrugged. "I am his wife. I do as he commands me."

Something bothered Varro about this, but he could not put it together. He was still weak, and even chewing vegetables had worn out his strength. Ione was as beautiful as any woman he had ever seen. Castor had married an outstanding woman. Yet a question that would not form tugged from the garbled and black recesses of his mind.

"What did he say this owl meant?" Ione displayed it to him.

"Only that mine was gold and his silver, and that I outranked him. He found it among my belongings after I was thrown from the mountain. He was ensuring I had not left anything behind to expose him. So he came to bury me out of respect. But found me alive, and so you are here now."

"But you do not know what any of this means?" Ione returned the pugio to the flat stone. "How did you come to possess it?"

Varro explained the same story to Ione as he had to Castor. When he finished, the effort of so much speaking left him exhausted.

"Very well, you have talked enough. You should rest. Over the next few days, you can entertain me with your stories."

"I must return to the consul as soon as possible. I need to find out what happened to Curio and Falco."

"Curio and Falco," Ione repeated. "And you. Such brave men."

"More like simple fools. Everything we tried along the way failed. They may even be dead."

Ione patted his shoulder. "Do not fret over such things. Rest, now. When the time comes that you can move, I will help you reach your camp. If my husband cannot join us, then I will leave a message for him. Do you know Greek?"

"My family is not poor, but we are farmers. Our tutors did not teach us Greek, since we could not afford the extra lessons."

Ione nodded. "I will write the message in Greek then, in case he sends a servant."

He heard motion from the cave mouth, and Ione looked past Varro and her expression turned haughty.

"Set the water there, and tend the fire. We will be cooking for two tonight."

Varro heard the water sloshing as the slave set it down out of his vision. Ione then took another clay container and opened the lid. The stench of something like spoiled cabbage filled the air. She did not appear bothered at the odor, but Varro thought he would cough. She smirked at this.

"It does not taste as bad as it smells. Drink this and it will ease your pain and aid your sleep."

She placed it to his mouth and he sipped in the cold liquid. The bitter flavor was tolerable and the draught felt slimy on his tongue. But he dutifully swallowed it all. Ione smiled then replaced the cover with a soft clink.

Overwhelmed with weakness and exhaustion, he settled back into the pillow as Ione stepped from his side. The pugio remained on the rock, now shifted to present the owl face to him. What did it all mean?

And as he drifted into sleep, his strange foreboding lurked at the edge of his mind as if preparing to ambush him. Soon he collapsed into dreams full of shadowy threat and vague dread.

15

By the time Falco understood he had been rescued, he had run halfway across the open fields outside the walls of Sparta. Fear had propelled him naked to the night. That and the stomach full of wine Varro had given him. It burned going down and it threatened now to gurgle back up. A taste like vinegar bubbled at the back of his throat as he finally slowed his run.

His side cramped, and when he saw the line of trees ahead, he pushed harder to reach them. He at last crashed into the bushes, their sharp branches scraping his flesh. He crunched into the dead leaves and debris, then rolled onto his back. As he lay heaving, Curio's footsteps thumped along the ground and continued past him.

"Over here," Falco shouted.

Now that his terror ebbed away, every sort of agony seeped back in. His neck was raw and throbbed. All his joints ached from having been stretched on that accursed board. He realized blood had crusted at his wrists and ankles. He had been falling forward into the cold grip of death when suddenly Varro had appeared beside him. His old friend had seemed like a shade with bulging, blood-shot eyes and hollow cheeks. That had been the work of a single day hanging over the walls of Sparta.

Curio's naked body flashed white in the starlight before he thumped down into the grass behind the line of scrubby trees. With all the branches and stones poking his flesh, Falco could have laughed at his choice of landings. But he was too weak.

So they both lay there, panting and facing an indifferent sky. The wine in Falco's guts sloshed around and again he felt about to vomit. He wished he had not drunk anything, but his thirst had been fiery.

"Curio, are you alive?"

"I think so. Are we dead? I thought Varro saved us."

"He did." Now the thought of his old friend's whereabouts made him sit up again. "Where is he? Didn't he follow you?"

Curio was a gray streak in the grass. His chest rose and fell in the aftermath of his efforts. The question seemed to have silenced him, and Falco realized immediately something was wrong.

"He can't be far behind," Curio said. "He gave me this bread and wine and said he was following. But once I realized I was free and not dreaming, I started running. I never looked back."

Tired and pained as he was, he struggled to his hands and knees then peered into the darkness toward Sparta. He could see the well-lit main gate. Up where they had all been crucified, he saw nothing. In between there was only empty, night-shrouded fields.

"I don't think he escaped."

"What?" Curio rustled the grass behind as he crawled to Falco's side. "We were eye to eye just before I climbed down the ladder. He was going to follow me."

"So if he had, he'd have been here by now. Unless he ran in a different direction."

Falco scanned the wide fields, noting scattered copses framed against the dark. Varro could have run to any of them, but none of them were in direct line of sight from their starting position. Falco realized both he and Curio had come here without having to coordinate because it was the most obvious landmark.

Curio crawled forward as if to get a better look. Just like Varro, he appeared gaunt and haggard, his usually vigorous glow vanished. Falco wondered if he looked as bad as them. He certainly felt disjointed and broken.

"He didn't escape," Curio said flatly. "Listen."

Falco leaned forward with Curio. He heard the muffled notes of horns sounded across the distance. They were signals from beyond the walls of Sparta. The black spot where they had been crucified was torchlit, if he recalled correctly. The blackness told him no one stood there anymore, neither Varro nor the other Greeks who had freed him. They had all been captured or perhaps killed.

"This is not fair." Falco's fists tightened and his arms shook. "We were all supposed to escape. He could've gone without us, but instead he delayed to get us loose."

"Varro would've never left us." Curio sat back now, scratching his head. "His luck finally ran out on him."

"I'd sooner believe Jupiter is my father than believe Fortuna stopped looking after her favored son."

He leaned back, and as the flash of anger subsided, he melted back to lie in the grass. The contents of his stomach rolled with him.

"He gave you bread? I need a bit of it to settle my stomach. That wine made me sick."

The bread tore softly and Curio sat beside him, extending the small hunk to him. He stuffed it into his mouth and began to chew. His saliva had dried with his thirst and the bread went down in a hard clump. But as it splashed into his guts he already felt better.

"What are we going to do, sir?" Curio asked.

"Sir? Are you now happy to let me make the decisions?"

"Yes, sir. You're the senior officer now."

"Shit, Curio. Don't you have a heart? Varro is still in there and probably will be flayed alive for what he did for us. And you're talking about protocol?"

He did not answer, but flattened out in the grass.

Falco was not new to leadership. He had always been in charge of some gang since he could remember. He was always bigger and stronger than the other kids. And he had the face of a brute, as his father had so often told him when he was sober. He had said far harsher things on the more frequent occasions of his inebriation. That he had died early in the war was no great loss to Falco. But the thought of losing Varro was too much for him.

They had promised to get through their six years together and return to be neighbors again. With all the silver they now possessed, they'd make a great pair of businessmen. He hadn't floated his ideas to Varro yet. But it seemed they could move up in the world with that much silver. At the least, they'd both attract beautiful wives from good families. Things were going to be incredible for them in only a little more than two years' time.

But now Varro remained a prisoner. Of course, he might have also been killed in the escape. But he chose to discount that possibility. He had to, for the sake of his own willpower.

"I'm cold." Curio's voice broke into his thoughts.

"I asked him for a tunic."

Curio shifted in the grass, but Falco remained looking at the stars. "Asked Varro?"

"He told me to steal one along the way back to camp. I can't believe my last words to him were a demand for something as stupid as a tunic. I should've thanked him at least."

The grass again rustled softly as Curio reclined. He sat quietly a moment before breaking into the silence.

"I just asked him if he was coming. I didn't thank him either. I thought he was behind me." Curio's fist made a soft thump as he struck the ground. "If I had just turned around, I could've gone back up the ladder and helped him."

"Don't go hard on yourself," Falco said. "We just always assume Varro is going to be all right. Because he always is, no matter what shit he finds himself in. It's that magic pugio of his. Well, the Spartans took it from him, and so he was captured."

"You don't think he was killed?"

"Of course fucking not." His reply echoed over the fields and he tucked his head down in surprise at his own shout. "Don't say that again, or as senior officer I'll have you on latrine duty for the next ten years."

"Best you can do is two years."

Falco sat up and blinked at the vague gray shape of Curio lying next to him.

"And as senior officer, I'll make all the wise remarks from here on. You just keep your mind on the plan."

"So there's a plan?"

"Yeah, let's finish that bread and wine. I've a guess we couldn't eat it once we're anything short of desperate for our lives. Then we'll sleep. Tomorrow, we've got to get some kit again and return to Sparta."

Curio sat up and gathered the flaccid wineskin and hunk of hard bread. "I thought Varro wanted us to get word back to the consul."

"Well, we don't have anything to tell him that can't wait. As it is, I think that plan to start a rebellion must be squashed now anyway. If Varro was caught, then so were his rescuers. Nabis will have the plan out of them and uncover the other traitors. But Varro can't wait for the army to show up, unless they are showing up right now. So we're going to do what we can to save him."

They ate the rest of the stale bread and drank the sour wine. Even as hungry and weak as Falco felt, he nearly spit out the last mouthful of it. "You'd think they were working for Nabis from the quality of this piss. It could kill a man."

"It's bad, all right, but I think in the coming days we're going to miss it."

"Don't light up the night with your flame of hope, Curio. You'll give us away."

The two of them did not make any attempt at bedding, but curled up under the bushes and pulled the debris over themselves for a bit of warmth and camouflage. Falco dropped into a deep sleep, and if he dreamed he had no memories of them the next morning when his eyes fluttered open to sunlight.

The branches covering him were like an out-of-focus lattice. The sun was already high in a cloudy sky and wind gusted across the fields. He shot upright.

"Shit, it's midmorning. We've wasted time. Come on, Curio."

Curio was stretched out on his side beside him, face hidden. He gave a soft kick to the back of his legs.

"Wake up, man. We've got to find something to cover our naked asses."

Curio did not stir, and Falco ached all over. His joints cracked and protested, still inflamed from the torture of being stretched on the board. The cuts on his wrists and ankles burned. He realized he had only slept out of exhaustion.

Rolling out from beneath the bushes, he gave Curio another shove.

Then his stomach roiled and he retched on the grass. The wine and chunks of bread from the prior night ejected in a blast. His stomach clenched and he heaved. The foul odor reminded him of spilled intestines after a battle. That thought made him double over again and heave until clear, phlegmy spit was all that came up. His head and eyes throbbed from the effort.

When it was over, he did not feel any better. He stared dazedly at the puddle under his face, then pulled away to wipe his mouth with his wrist.

"Gods, that has to be the worst wine I ever drank. Feels like it rotted out my stomach." He looked to Curio again, who had still not moved. He stretched his arm to his extended leg and shook. "You slept through all that? I about coughed up my guts. You're not such a heavy sleeper. Stop being lazy."

When he still refused to respond, Falco felt his face grow hot. He slapped his hands to Curio's naked shoulders and hauled him over.

"Enough rest. Time to—"

Curio's face was pale and stiff. A spray of vomit had dried out in the grass and still clung to his cheek. His head flopped back as Curio cradled him off the ground.

"Curio! Wake up!"

He slapped his cheeks and his eyes fluttered open. Falco nearly cried with joy.

"I feel sick." Curio's feeble voice was barely audible. He lifted his hand as if to reach for Falco, but it collapsed to the grass. "I think I'm dying."

"As senior officer, I order you to not say that again. Listen, I had to throw up my guts. You probably need to do the same."

"It hurts." Curio again lifted his arms, to the same effect.

Falco sat back, looking around the wide plains. He saw nothing except for a long line of carts and soldiers leaving by the main gate. They seemed in no rush, and to have a purpose elsewhere. So no one had come to search for them. He turned back to Curio.

"If you mean your whole body, then I understand. Me too. But it's no excuse. On your knees at least, soldier. Get that poison out of you. Come on."

He wrestled with Curio, who either by design or just bad luck slipped all around Falco. He could not get him to grips. All the while he flopped and rubbed against his body while moaning with agony.

"Would you just fucking cooperate? Is it so hard, Curio?"

"I'm dying."

"You're not dying. But you're making me want to kill you. Work with me."

At last he clasped him in a full bear hug, the two face to face. Curio leaned his head back and groaned.

Then Falco heard the crack of a branch behind him.

He turned to the sound, and a young man with a thin, reddish beard stared at them. He had a walking staff and a small knife cinched by a cord at the waist of a dull green tunic. His eyes were wide and his olive-skinned face flushed.

With Curio clasped to his naked chest, he smiled at the sudden arrival.

"This is not what it looks like. My friend is ill and needs help. We both need help, actually." He smiled at the man, who stared confusedly between the two of them. "Say, you don't speak Latin? My Greek is limited to curses."

The man replied in Greek, as Falco had expected.

While still holding Curio upright, he smiled and extended a hand to the man.

"Give us a hand up and we'll sort this out."

But the man shook his head and backed away, putting out both palms in refusal.

"Wait, no, I'm not asking you to join us."

But the man turned and began to flee. Falco could not allow him to get away and warn others, not while he was unarmed and Curio incoherent.

He struggled to stand while Curio now remained entangled with him. With a grunt of frustration, he sloughed him off. Curio vomited a vile stream of acidic juice across Falco's legs and feet. He continued to retch, splashing Falco with more vomit until he could break away in pursuit.

"I feel better!"

Curio's exclamation faded behind him as he ran after the young man. He was naked, coated with dirt, dead leaves, and Curio's vomit. Despite all his suffering of the last days, he was still in the condition of a Roman soldier, and this shepherd or whatever he was could not compare.

Within a dozen strides he came within reach of the fleeing man.

He whirled around and slammed Falco in the side with his walking stick. The heavy sheet of muscle over his ribs absorbed the worst of the stinging blow. He slammed into his target, tackling the man to the ground and driving the wind from him.

The Greek shouted curses and reached for the knife in his belt. But Falco had expected as much and seized the Greek's arm then wrenched it around, causing him to shout with pain.

"You should've been more helpful, boy. Now it's dreamtime for you."

With the Greek pressed beneath him and one hand pinning the knife and the other pinning the man's shoulder, Falco angled his forehead and slammed it into the head of the enemy.

The head-butt opened a gash over the man's brow, sending dark blood flowing down the side of his head. Falco had been throwing head-butts since he was a boy, and knew how to do it without hurting himself. The man was dazed but not out. Falco sat up then pummeled his face and head until the Greek slumped unconscious and likely half-dead. He had broken the man's nose and probably his cheek.

He wrested the knife from the Greek's limp hold then began pulling the tunic over his head. Curio swished through the grass behind him.

"I think the wine was poisoned," he said. "I hardly drank any of it and it almost killed me."

"We'll have to thank Varro for it once we find him." He wrested the bloodied tunic over the Greek's head, then held it up for size. "You wear it. Take this knife and belt, too. I'll take his staff. It's no gladius but I can still knock some heads if I need to."

Curio slipped on the tunic and tied the cord to his waist while Falco surveyed the landscape. The long line of carts moved like a funeral procession and seemed to be headed toward the mountains. Sparta itself remained at rest, with the smoke of a thousand hearths rising from behind its walls.

"Falco, you look like shit."

"Thanks for vomiting on me. As if I wasn't suffering enough."

Curio belched in answer, then recoiled. "Ugh, that tasted awful. It's like I ate rotten fish or something."

"How do you feel? Good enough to march? Something about standing naked in an empty field before the fortress of my enemies is disconcerting. Call me a coward, but I'd like to get out of here."

Curio shrugged. "Everything hurts. I feel weak. My sight is blurry."

"Then you're doing great. It means you are alive, which is better than what we were expecting last night." He toed the unconscious Greek sprawled in the grass. "He's someone's son, and he'll be missed soon enough. But he must live someplace close. On one of the farms that supply Sparta, probably. Let's go steal me something to wear so you don't have to feel jealous of my naked glory."

"You look like a god, Falco."

"That's right. So follow me like one too."

He had learned from watching Varro and others he respected that a leader has to project confidence. He did it through the application of belligerence, which was his natural bent, and humor, which he had developed while enduring the absurdities of army life. Curio would whither under a bellicose command, but he took well enough to a softer touch. Falco needed him to believe they had a chance.

Because he doubted they actually had one.

They strode across the grassy plains which looked far wider and more exposed than they had during the night they arrived at Sparta. Mountains of impossible height loomed over the valley like stony gods sitting in judgement. No doubt part of the austere Spartan attitude must have leeched into them from the land itself. Falco felt like an insect crawling across the floor and hoping to remain unseen by giants that might crush him.

After he secured clothing and weapons, he had no idea what came next. It was a frightening prospect, and he wondered how Varro had always seemed to come up with a next step. He had been such a soft child, a real wilting lily. But over time he had hardened into a sharp leader with a quick mind and the love of the gods to support him.

Now it was Falco's turn to step up. Varro needed him. He couldn't have died. Not like this. Not in some summary sword strike to the liver. Varro was too dramatic for such a prosaic end. Besides, he had dreamed of Varro's death many times, probably for fear that it should come too soon. In those dreams it was always raining on that day. He turned his face toward the sun and felt its warmth.

Varro lived and he was going to find him.

"Up ahead." Curio grabbed Falco's wrist and pulled him to a stop.

On the other side of the short rise, they saw a farmhouse in the distance where smoke rose from the main home and a dog barked somewhere out of sight.

"Well, time to take what we need." Falco started off for the farm, slapping the heavy walking stick against his palm.

16

Falco lay in the grass with Curio beside him. Being flat on his naked stomach, the poisoned wine still made his stomach ache and gurgle. He had nothing left to vomit, and the scent of cooking wafting up the incline from the farmhouse made his mouth water. To his dismay, a dog barked wildly somewhere out of sight.

"I don't have the strength to fight," Curio whispered, lying beside him. "And I can't see straight."

"We're not going to fight, just get me something to keep the breeze off my bare ass. Maybe find a weapon or something useful."

"How about food? Sick as I am, whatever they're cooking smells great. It's meat, too." Curio inhaled deeply, then coughed.

Falco continued to study the house. Unlike Curio, his vision had not been affected by whatever they had drunk. The main house was stuccoed wood atop a stone foundation and a faded red tile roof. It was typical of most farmhouses he had seen throughout this accursed land. They burned easily enough, and he wondered if setting a fire might be the way to get them all out the house long enough to steal what they wanted. Unfortunately he had no way to start a fire, and sparking one from two dry sticks required too much time plus a touch from Vulcan's divine hands.

Curio's coughing turned violent and he rose to his knees as if to take pressure off his stomach. Falco watched him, hoping he did not rise high enough to be spotted from the farm. But Curio had to ride out the moment, and once he had he then flattened out.

"That dog is going to be our problem," Falco said. "He'll find us out even if we avoid whoever is inside."

"Depends on what you want to get," Curio said. "We might be able to snatch some clothes and run."

"We can't outrun a dog," he said flatly. "Feeling like I do now, I couldn't out run my lame grandmother. Shit, Curio, why do they have a dog?"

"Well what farm doesn't have a dog?"

"I never had a dog."

Curio twisted in the grass to frown at him. "I thought you grew up on a farm? You didn't have a dog to warn you of danger?"

"Well, we had one when I was younger. No one fed it and I think it ran away or maybe it died."

"That's horrible!"

"Don't shout, you idiot. Forget about my dog. It's this fucking animal we're facing."

He stabbed his finger at the farmhouse. Curio squinted after it then cocked his head.

"It's barking like it's mad, and we've not seen it. That means they have the dog chained up."

"Hey, you're probably right. What good luck, after all. But the little monster is going to bark when we get close."

"Falco, how's your hearing? The dog is barking now and no one seems to care."

"I meant to say that it might change the tone of its bark, like growl at us. That'll bring the master out for sure."

"Then why not just say the dog might growl?"

Falco watched for more activity at the farmhouse, but did not see anything. The farmers must have all gathered for their meal and chained the dog outside for some reason, hence its barking. Now was their chance.

"Curio, if you're done being a complete asshole, I'd like to share my plan."

"Some work is never done. But go ahead."

"We need what's inside the house, but that's where they all seem to be at the moment. We could wait until they come out, but then they might let that dog off the chain. We can't chance it. So I need to get them out of the house, but keep that dog chained."

"Are you just going to knock on the door and ask them to step outside?"

"Yes, and while I do that, you'll get in there and grab whatever looks good. Then we both run and meet back in the trees where we came from this morning."

Curio stared at him with his mouth open. "You're not serious? You're going to knock on the front door and I'm slipping in the back to steal what I can?"

"A simple plan works best. Fewer points where it can go wrong."

"But, I don't understand."

"As senior officer, I'm the only one who has to understand. You just do your part. Be fast, because I probably won't keep them busy for long. And try to hide your work so they don't come running after us."

"Well, yes, sir. This can't go wrong."

"Even if it does, what are they going to do? They'll be glad just to chase us off. It's not like we're raiding a guard post. We'll do that later on when we get into Sparta."

Curio moaned but made no other protest.

"You go wide and position yourself back from the farm but still in view of me. When you give the signal, that means you've found a door inside. Then I'll go distract them to the front. We'll be in and out before they know what happened."

"These easy plans always end up going to shit." But Curio backed up to his knees, paused to cradle his stomach, then rose to a crouch. Falco followed, and both swept down the incline to part ways before reaching the farmhouse.

Falco watched Curio go, then he ducked into the taller grasses as he sought his vantage point. The ability to vanish even in a sunlit field cleared specifically to avoid such things amazed Falco. He often wondered where Curio learned the trick, but he never said much about his past. As much as Falco wanted to learn more of it, he never asked. Somehow Curio made it feel disrespectful to pry into his background, even though he had never expressly forbidden it.

Nonetheless, he was glad for having such a sneak on his side. Between himself and Varro, neither of them could hope to sneak up on a sleeping drunk never mind an alert guard. Yet somehow they'd managed all they had been tasked with, despite the consul's strange confidence in their abilities.

At last he saw Curio sit up in the grass and point toward the farmhouse with a nod. He had parked behind the stump of a tree and hunkered behind it.

Now Falco leaned on his walking stick and bent over. Being naked, beaten, starved, poisoned, and desperate meant he did not need to act much to look his part. He used the rest of the approach to the farmhouse to perfect his charade. He let his head list to the side and quiver. He leaned on the stick, pressing hard on his strained knees to further complement the look of complete helplessness. His gait was unsure and he hoped others would see him on the verge of collapse.

Once he was near the door, he started to moan and make incoherent shouts and gasps like he had lost his tongue. He doubted the farmers would inspect his mouth to verify if his tongue was actually there.

He heard merry laughter from beyond the door as he approached. He glanced toward Curio and raised his hand to wave him forward. He glimpsed the top of his head as he dashed out of his hiding spot. The dog on the other side of the house continued to bark wildly.

Keeping a strong grip on his walking stick in case he needed to break heads instead of hearts, he rapped hard on the door.

The laughter beyond died. He started moaning and struggling to speak, calling out as if he were trying to form a greeting. He knocked again, more insistent this time, and continued his jumbled muttering.

An eye regarded him from the peephole and he tried to cavort like an overly excited fool when he saw it. Shortly after, he heard a bolt lifted then the door swung open.

Varro faced a potbellied man with skin so dark and shiny that it reminded him of Consul Flamininus's lacquered desk. He had curly gray hair in stark contrast to his skin, and wore a simple tunic and cloak of brown cloth. He glared at Falco and asked a clipped question, likely asking why he came to the door.

He held out two hands as if to beg, tilting his head and trying to act pleading.

The farmer backed up as if offered a cobra and snarled something in Greek. But then an older woman and a girl came to the door behind him. Both of them did not share the man's revulsion, and the woman spoke in chiding tones to her husband. He narrowed his eyes at Falco and seemed to repeat his question.

The dog continued barking like mad beyond, and as expected it started to growl. But now with Falco standing in their doorway, the farmers likely thought the dog growled at him.

When the farmer did not get an immediate answer, he raised his arm as if to strike Falco, who fought his instinct to punch first and instead recoiled in false terror. He tried to wail and snivel like the beggars in Rome did, throwing his arm across his face.

But the wife again intervened and stayed her husband's arm. She spoke softly to him. Falco had not expected this, and realized that while he had a good excuse for not speaking, he had no excuse for not understanding.

He pointed at his ears and shook his head, then shrugged all while offering up more mock speech. Now the daughter became animated, her big brown eyes flashing with a sudden realization. She seemed to explain Falco to both her parents. The father wrinkled his nose and shook his head, but the wife matched her daughter's enthusiasm.

Within the next moment, the wife stepped out and gently guided naked Falco into the house.

His heart leaped with terror. What were they doing? They were supposed to spit on him, curse him for a beggar and thief, and with luck throw rocks at him while he ran off. But these women seemed intent on aiding him.

Falco tried to act elated as they guided him into the house. The husband let out a long stream of frustrated breath and watched Falco pass. He ducked his head in a show of gratitude, all the while wishing he could escape.

Inside the scent of cooking was even stronger, and a black iron pot sat atop a low-burning fire. An old man with the same swarthy skin as the farmer slept with reed-thin arms folded over his stomach. He was bald but his beard was long, fuzzy, and stark white. He might have been by the fire to tend it or to warm his aged body. The interior was made up of a main room, but directly across an archway into the next area showed light from an opened back door.

Curio stood framed within it, his arms loaded with objects Falco could not see.

Terrified that they would be discovered, Falco twisted out of the woman's arms and feigned violent coughing. He spasmed and thrashed as if he might die. As expected, the woman and daughter focused on him and the husband likely cursed him for a diseased beggar that should be thrown out of their house.

The old man awakened with Falco's coughing, then stood up from his stool. Rather than ask any questions about what was happening, he simply walked into the same room where Curio had been.

While Falco pretended to recover as the woman patted his back, the old man went to the opened door and shouted at the barking dog outside before closing the door.

Whether Curio escaped in time, Falco could not be certain. But now he was surrounded by the farmers and the old man did not leave the other room.

A flurry of questions hit him and his actual confusion and fear must have leant him tremendous credibility. For the two women were now speaking with each other, the mother ordering the daughter to some task. That he was filthy and naked seemed unimportant to them, though the farmer sat back at his table with arms folded and a deep scowl.

The daughter returned with a gray tunic. This drew a protest from the father as the mother took it. He raised his fist as if threatening violence, which the woman ignored and sized the tunic to Falco's body. She then cheerfully offered it to him.

As he slipped it on, the farmer howled with rage. But then the old man in the other room shouted back, and the farmer fell into stony silence. His glare alone could kill Falco.

Satisfied that they had clothed their guest, the daughter then brought him a clay mug of wine. Falco grinned and babbled, but accepted it and drank deeply. The wife was already ladling some of their gruel into a bowl. The husband began to speak, then the wife sharply reminded him of something. Before Falco could finish his wine, he was already seated at the table with the bowl before him.

The husband shoved away and went toward another opened door that Falco had not seen. It was a small room where the daughter had gone to fetch the tunic. Even with his stomach still clenching, the wine had opened Falco's appetite. He gobbled down the gruel, not even sure what it was except for the barley. It was salty and hot and had bits of fatty meat. What more could he ask for?

The farmer started talking to his wife. No one sat with Falco as he ate, but the daughter watched. Her eyes were watery and full of compassion. What was wrong with these people, he wondered. If this had happened at his own farm back in Rome, both his parents would have cracked the skull of the fool who came begging to their door.

The father's measured speech grew more intense, and he kept pointing into the opened door of the room.

Falco finished the stew and remembered not to wipe his mouth so he might seem more simple and harmless to these people. He glanced to the other room where the old man had vanished, which was now dark and quiet but for the dog continuing to bark beyond the closed door.

He looked now to his benefactor, who argued quietly with her husband, her hands wringing together. Behind them he saw an armor rack in the small room, where a Spartan helmet and spear rested. Now Falco looked again to the farmer, potbellied and old. It could not be his.

Realization struck him. They probably had a son. But if his gear was set on rack while Nabis searched for every available warrior to fill his ranks, it meant that son must be dead.

Falco's arrival had somehow touched the mother's heart. The girl stared after him with a strange curiosity as her parents continued their low-volume argument. Did he remind them of the dead son, he wondered? In the end, it didn't matter. He had been fed and clothed, and now he wanted to leave. In fact, if he stood up and walked out now, he doubted anyone would stop him.

Then Curio vomited in the other room.

Falco heard the heavy shove of wood on the floor as he stood from hiding and retched with the intensity of a waterfall. The old man screamed in shock, and the two women jumped in surprise.

Only the potbellied farmer understood, seeing how he had suspected Falco all along. He grabbed his wife and pulled her into the room where the helmet and spear lay.

Realizing everything had gone to shit as Curio aptly predicted, Falco grabbed the daughter.

She screamed as he locked her head into the crook of his arm. He then smashed the clay mug on the table to put a shard to her neck.

"I've got what I want," he said. "Let's just part in peace."

But the father burst out of the door with the spear in both hands and leveled. He had enough room to thrust, but he was confused by Falco's transformation.

Curio moaned then something heavy smashed, like the hollow breaking of a pottery vase, and now he screamed. He thudded to the floor as the old grandfather shouted in triumph.

"Fuck! All of you listen!" He dragged the girl back and stuck the pottery shard harder against her thin neck. She couldn't be older than twelve. He felt like a monster as she cried and struggled. But the farmer was shouting and the wife screaming with hands atop her head. The farmer threatened him with the spear again, but seeing his daughter in danger he did nothing better than get between Falco and the other room.

The old man continued to shout in triumph and now fell upon Curio. He could see his thin arms and balled fists rising and falling as he pummeled him.

"Fight back, Curio! Let's get out of here."

But whatever Curio said was lost as the old man pounded on him. Being all in darkness, it sounded as if Curio was taking the beating of his life.

"Stop that old shit or I'll kill your daughter!"

He pressed the shard hard enough to the daughter's neck that she cried out. Falco doubted he could really break the skin with such a blunt piece. He'd be better off snapping her neck, which he could do but hoped he would not. But in any case, the farmer seemed to understand and shouted into the other room.

The old man cursed Curio, kicked him once more, then backed up.

"Are you alive?"

"Maybe."

"Then get out. I'll keep them busy with the daughter. Head for the trees and I'll meet you there."

He heard Curio slide heavily across the floor, then in the next moment the back door flashed open and the dog's barking echoed through the house.

"Good," Falco said with a smile. He nodded to the spear. "I'll trade you. Spear for your girl. Be sensible, you fat bastard. I just want to get away from here."

The wife understood it immediately but the husband refused. Falco let them argue until the wife snatched away the spear. She held it out to him. He dropped the clay shard then accepted the weapon. The look of hatred in her eyes, filled with kindness only a moment ago, cut him as well as any sword.

"I'm sorry it happened like this," he said, knowing she couldn't understand. "I just needed clothes."

She shouted what must be a curse and grabbed her daughter whom he released.

He then flipped the spear around at the farmers. The old man emerged from the other room, glaring in disgust and rage.

Falco backed out the door, then began to run. He left the

barking dog behind and headed for the trees where they had left that morning.

He found Curio there, panting in the shadow of a tree trunk. His face was covered in blood from a cut to his head.

"If I wasn't half-dead I'd have snapped that old man in half."

"Don't worry for it. You probably made him feel twenty years younger for beating you up. At least someone in that house will go to bed happy."

Curio's left eye now had a dark circle forming under it, adding to his already defeated appearance. He spread his arms wide.

"I had clothing, food, and even a knife. But I dropped it all when I had to run."

"It was a success as far as the plan went," Falco said. He stared back up the rise and shook his head. "But they're angry now and they know we're out here. That fat bastard is going to take his dog off the chain, get his friends together, and hunt us down. I've got his son's spear, and he didn't want to let it go. I'm sure he'll have it back."

"I guess we're not cleaning up in the river?"

"No, we're not," Falco agreed. "It's too dangerous to be out here now. Besides, Varro needs us and we're not doing him any good battling the local farmers. You and I are going back to the walls of Sparta, and we're getting inside."

17

Falco balled his fists as he stared at the impervious walls of Sparta. Had the gods constructed this place? The walls stretched up to the heavens and threatened the stars floating in the sky. It seemed they might collide with the parapets as they wheeled across the night. Worse still, it seemed King Nabis had increased his guards atop the walls. For now they no longer patrolled but were stationed to look out across the plains. Each one carried a torch, which he could drop to illuminate anything that stirred near the walls.

He sighed, then wondered if he could bait enough of them into dropping torches that the whole place might burn to the ground. Surely Varro could find his way out during the confusion.

"We can't sit here all night," Curio whispered, crouched next to him in the darkness. "We're not going to stare a hole through the walls, though that seems to be your plan."

They had circled the entire city during the day seeking a way inside. But traffic was all funneled through the main gate, and while Curio and he could have attempted to pass inside unseen, they had not found the chance. Only the column of soldiers and their carts returned from the mountains. Cages mounted on the beds were empty and rattled loud enough that he could hear them from his hiding spot in reeds below the bridge. Whatever they had set out to capture, they had returned empty-handed. Once the gates closed on that column, they did not open again.

"It all seemed possible in my head," Falco said. "But it's not working out."

Curio snorted. "You've got a good imagination, Centurion Falco. Were you hoping they left that rope ladder for us?"

"They might've forgotten it." He felt Curio's eyes on him as he stared at the walls and the points of yellow light lining it. "You know, someone always fucks up. Just not this time."

"No, we fucked up," Curio said. "We had one chance to get inside when those carriages returned from the mountains. Now we're stuck out here. It's nighttime, and we've no means of scaling the wall. Tomorrow, we have to sneak inside with whatever traffic they're allowing in. If the consul is near, no one will be allowed inside at all."

"Are you giving up?"

Curio did not answer. Falco knew he could not admit it. Neither could he. Varro would not have given up on them. But he was nowhere near as clever as Varro. When he saw a wall, he thought about smashing it down. If Varro were here, he'd have a plan to get over or around it or otherwise make the wall unimportant to their plan. But for Falco, all he saw was a wall that required siege engines to bring down.

"Well, we can't fly and it's not like someone left the back door open. We're not trying to break into someone's woodshed. We're trying to break into Sparta. It's different."

"Are you convincing yourself or me?" Curio shifted back to sitting in the tall grass. They were far enough to be out of sight from the wall sentries. But even having rounded to the southeast of the city, it seemed much like the opposite side they had first approached.

"Do you have to rub my face in it? All right, I didn't come up with a great plan."

"Or any plan, really."

"So you are going to push my nose in it, aren't you?"

"Why not, you let your dog starve to death. You deserve it."

"What?" Falco sat back with Curio and let his mouth hang open. But even in the dim starlight he could see the smile in his friend's swollen face. "Ah, well, if the old man hadn't worked you over so bad I'd give you a beating of my own."

"You at least found us another river far enough from the walls," Curio said. "And that's worth something. We can clean up there, make a camp, and try again tomorrow. Hopefully, Varro remains alive until then."

Falco groaned and imagined seeing Varro's head set over the gates to Sparta. It was a bleak thought, but highly likely that Nabis would take action by tomorrow. Time was not to be wasted, but they could achieve nothing more this night.

Gathering his captured spear from the grass, he stood to a low crouch and began to head for the river. Curio followed and the two kept bent at the waist until they reached the slow-flowing river that pulsed along Sparta's southern side. It was wide and seemingly deep. At points it ran close to the southern walls. It made a fine natural barrier to any enemy approaching from this angle. While siege engines could hit the walls from across the river, sending in any troops to exploit an opening would be a challenge. Of course, Falco knew Romans could do it. But these Spartans had just been fighting other Greeks in recent years, which did not count for much in his estimation.

Now they selected a clump of trees and brush that grew along the riverbank to be their hiding place for the night. It was fortunately balmy weather, but being just in tunics the nights were still cold enough that he would welcome a blanket. Besides, the earth near the river would be wetter and colder. Given the state of his body after recent days, he dreaded what the morning would bring him. He would be glad just to stand upright.

They cleaned off in a calm pool along the river's edge. The cold was soothing to his aching bones and battered body. He scrubbed the grime and blood from his skin and when done he let himself drip-dry higher up on the grass where he set his spear. Curio enjoyed a deeper soak and lingered in the water.

A tremendous wave of exhaustion flowed over him, and he felt like dropping to his back and just sleeping.

But then he saw movement from the clump of trees.

As fast as a frightened hare, he snatched the spear and rushed to the riverside. He flattened out, still naked and smearing himself once more with river mud. Curio popped out of the water, but followed Falco's gaze. He did not speak or move and water dripped off his body into the river with a bright plinking noise.

"You see him?" Falco gave the barest whisper he could.

A dark-cloaked figure had emerged from the clump of trees. He was bent over something, moving and arranging things all joined into shadow. He looked up occasionally, but always to look toward Sparta in the distance. After a few more arrangements, he seemed satisfied with his work. The man was nothing better than a living shadow carrying a heavy spear. Only as he rushed off to the northeast, away from the river, did Falco see that the man carried a shovel and not a spear.

Neither one of them spoke, but waited for the man to grow smaller and eventually melt into the night. They waited until sure no one else followed the man, then both gathered together on the grass up from the bank.

"What was that all about?" Curio whispered.

"You saw what I did. He just appeared out of nowhere. But he took pains to hide something. Let's get dressed and find out what he left us."

"I hope it was something to eat."

Falco smiled in the dark at the comment. At least he had the gruel from the morning to fill his stomach. After expelling whatever polluted his guts, Curio had not only felt better but had become hungry.

Falco first looked to where the man had gone, but he could see nothing. So he lowered his spear and led Curio in a cautious approach to the trees. While Curio had only a small knife, he held it ready in case something should burst out at them.

But they reached the trees and bushes and found nothing.

"It's like he grew out of the ground," Falco said. "What was he fooling with?"

"Something he didn't want found," Curio said. "Let's clear these bushes away. Whatever he didn't want to be discovered is here."

Falco prodded the bushes and ground with the butt of his spear, and within three attempts he produced a hollow thump against wood.

Digging into the spot, Curio cleared the bushes and dropped to his knees to clear away dirt.

"It's a trapdoor."

Falco straightened up and smiled, narrowing his eyes at Sparta.

"He's from the city. He kept looking at the walls. This is a secret way inside."

The trapdoor was set into the ground. The wood seemed in good condition, which suggested to Falco this passage was maintained. An iron ring was set into it, which meant the door was for entrance and exit.

"Well, we have a way inside," Curio said. "What's your plan now, sir?"

"Same as it ever was. We need to get Varro out of whatever trouble he is in, or else die in the attempt. Are you still with me?"

"Let's change the part of the plan where we die. But yes, I'm with you. Let me go first. I have the knife."

Falco would've questioned Curio, but he realized his spear was as good as a war elephant in the confines of what would probably be a crude underground tunnel. Besides, Curio already had the knife clenched in his teeth and squatted over the door.

"How do I work this thing?"

He tugged on the door by the iron ring, but it did not immediately release.

"They probably have another latch to keep it from accidentally opening," Falco said. He skirted around Curio and swished his palm around the frame until he found a release. It was made of bronze and kept the hinges pinned. Once he held it down, the door released and Curio stared into the opening. A faint orange light outlined his swollen cheeks.

"There's a light down there," he mouthed, barely speaking across the gap.

"Nothing for it," Falco whispered across the opening. "Still going first?"

Curio lowered himself into the trapdoor. Falco followed, placing his foot on the wooden rung of a ladder. He heard the splash of water as Curio reached the bottom.

"We're alone," he announced, his voice echoing off earthen walls.

Falco climbed down, keeping his spear to his side as he fit into the narrow hole. On the bottom side of the trapdoor was a rusted chain, which he pulled to shut the trapdoor over him. It made a soft puff as it blanked out the stars overhead.

He stepped off onto a pile of roughly shaped stones that were set under the wood ladder protecting it from water that seeped up from the ground. Curio held a large bronze oil lamp in one hand and a dagger in the other.

"It was set in that alcove." He nodded beside the ladder. "I guess that man is coming back tonight. This won't burn but for more than a few hours."

"No, it'll burn longer." Falco moved out of the puddle beneath the ladder and studied the lamp. "But still, he's going to know someone else took his path tonight. We need to see where we're going. So keep the lamp and lead the way. I've got you covered with my spear."

The passage was the rat hole Falco had expected. He struggled to bring the captured spear around and face it forward, but once properly gripped he could fight in the cramped tunnel. It was wide enough for a single man abreast. While he had to stoop, Curio could stand without trouble.

He held the lamp up and created a semicircle of light before him. The walls had been reinforced in places with stonework. But mostly it was all earthen. The floor was sodden and the air in the tunnel was thick with earthy scents. They proceeded slowly, uncertain of the direction they traveled. This tunnel might have been the work of miners from some long-ago siege and never plugged, for if it led under the walls and into the city as Falco knew it must, Consul Flamininus could exploit this.

While Varro was foremost on his mind, he could not forget the reason for their sacrifices. They had to prime Sparta for an easy victory. Even if the hope of an uprising had guttered out, providing the consul a secret path into the city might be even better. Teams of men could be rushed inside and capture the gates, depending on where this tunnel exited.

"Now I know what a rat feels like," Curio said, his voice strangely muffled in the tunnel.

"Rats and soldiers crawl through a lot of shit. I'm surprised you just noticed the similarities."

"I think this tunnel is going up. The ground is drier and I feel it in my legs."

"I'm trying not to think about how I feel." Yet Falco did notice the increased effort to progress through the tunnel. "No talking until we learn where this goes. Don't want to announce ourselves."

They bunched together, and Falco's spear reached past Curio as if pointing the way. They were not so far from the walls of the city that it should have taken this amount of time to cross beneath them. So Falco expected they would emerge in the middle of Sparta somewhere.

At last, the monotonous passage ended in a ladder much like the same they had used to descend into it. Curio's lamp shined on the sturdy ladder set atop rough-hewn rocks to protect the wood from rotting on the ground. Falco peered up into the weak illumination and saw another trapdoor.

"Does that look higher to you than the one we entered from?" he whispered into Curio's ear, unsure if his voice would carry.

"It is," he whispered back. "We better snuff the lamp. Don't want light leaking around the door to give us away."

Falco did not reply, and Curio snuffed the lamp as they stood at the bottom of the ladder. The instant darkness left him as good as blind. Touching his finger to his nose, he could not see it.

"Fuck, this is dark. Curio, are you on the ladder?"

He heard Curio's hand slapping around on the wooden rungs.

"I've got it. I guess I'm going first."

"Just open the door enough to see what's there."

"I wasn't planning on jumping out to join the guards' dice game if that's what you're thinking."

"I'm just making certain."

"Rest easy, sir. And don't stick that spear up my backside if things get hot. We'll just run back down the tunnel."

"Hurry up, Curio. This darkness terrifies me."

He shivered as a tingle ran along his neck and back. The darkness settled on him in thick silence.

"You're afraid of the dark?"

"Just get up the ladder or I'll stick this spear through your asshole and out your nose. Yes, I'm fucking terrified."

Ignoring Curio's childlike tittering, Falco wrung his hands around the spear shaft. It was a comfort to have a weapon in hand, however impractical. He heard the slap of Curio's feet on the rungs and the creaking of the wood as he ascended. The ladder went up beyond the reach of his spear, but he was not going to set foot on the ladder until Curio got a measure of where they had arrived.

Now he heard more wooden trembling and a metallic rattling. He heard a latch release, then a right angle of dim gray light appeared in the sea of blackness. Curio's body eclipsed it.

He resisted any urge to ask what Curio saw. Sweat beaded on his brow and he started to pump his leg in anxious anticipation. Curio remained still for a long while, until Falco thought he might scream. Yet then he pushed the door wider and spilled enough light to streak his body in gray shapes.

"See anything?" He squeezed the whisper out as if he expected to be beaten for the transgression. But Curio answered by pushing the door still wider.

"No one. But we're inside a building."

Falco rubbed his face, swiping away gritty sweat. A building? This was not a tunnel left behind by ancient sappers trying to defeat Sparta's walls. This tunnel served another purpose, but he could not imagine what it could be.

"Is there a place to hide?"

Curio made a gesture lost in the minimal light. Before Falco could complain about it, he opened the trapdoor and let a square of light strike Falco in the face. Even having only been in absolute darkness for a few minutes, the sudden brightness made him squint. Curio's shadow filled the square and then he exited the tunnel.

Heart thudding in his chest, Falco stared up and clutched the spear to his side. Sweat rolled back into his hairline as he stared up. Eventually, Curio leaned into the opening and spoke louder.

"What are you waiting for? I thought you were afraid of the dark?"

Eager to reach the top if only to give Curio the slap he richly deserved, Falco scrabbled up the ladder and accepted a hand from Curio to pull him out of the tunnel.

The terrible odor was the first thing to strike him. The tunnel air had not been fresh, but Falco considered the earthy scent tolerable. This dark space smelled of waste and death. He now crouched with Curio behind a shattered crate that sat against other equally shabby crates. Barrels had been set into a dark corner. Great black chains hung from a wall. Light spilled in from an open archway that led into a vague grayness.

"Where are we?" He gathered his spear closer and looked to Curio. He stared back, his swollen eyes wide in confusion.

Then someone in the distance screamed.

It was not a scream of rage or frustration, but a scream of acute, intense pain that pierced not just a man's flesh but his very soul. It was the mad wailing of man enduring unthinkable torment, and it continued until Falco felt sympathetic pains of his own.

"Gods, Curio, I know where we are. We're in a prison."

"Then that's got to be Varro screaming."

Falco sat back in shock.

Curio raised his knife. "He needs us. Let's go."

18

"Hold on." Falco grabbed Curio by his wrist, pulling the dagger down. His swollen eyes widened in surprise as Falco wrestled against him. But being stronger, he prevailed and kept Curio in place.

The screaming continued until it turned to sobbing. The pitiful echoes filled Falco's head, and it drove him mad as he knew it did Curio. But they had not come so far to throw their lives away yet.

"We don't know it's Varro who's screaming. Listen, it doesn't sound like him."

"What does anyone sound like when he's getting his eyeballs plucked out?" Curio made to stand again. "We've got to hurry."

But Falco's grip was iron. "I love the man, too. But let's be smart. It's what he would want us to do."

The screaming renewed, the voice ragged and hoarse but overflowing in expression of agony. Now a Greek shouted over the screams, and each of his shouts drew more agonized groans from the victim. It was obviously an interrogation, Falco realized.

"It's him," Curio repeated. "Who else could it be?"

"Anyone in the city." He tugged Curio back to emphasize his need for quiet.

The groaning continued and the Greek interrogator barked his questions.

"There's no way Varro could answer. He doesn't know Greek," Falco whispered. "No one is translating for him."

"Maybe they're just torturing him for the fun of it," Curio said, pulling his arm free. "I need to see it for myself."

Falco wanted to protest, but realized Curio would not be satisfied any other way. Nor could they hide in this room indefinitely. They would have to seek Varro out in any case. So he shook his head and sighed. Curio immediately crept to the archway and Falco followed. He kept a high grip on the spear, but regretted the impracticality of the weapon.

They leaned out into a long hallway. Down one end was a row of doors with small barred windows. Two heavy bolts, high and low, were set across each one, indicating these were prison cells. The bright light down the other end of the hall spilled in from a side room. The amber glare cast the rest of the hall into indistinct haze as columns of dust and particle swirled within it. But Falco thought he saw stairs beyond.

The screaming started again and blared out of the opened room.

"They certainly work late here," he muttered to Curio.

"I bet they don't let him sleep longer than a few hours," he said. "They're trying to break him."

It turned out the room they had emerged from was part of a row of cells, though not one itself. It might have been an old storage room or jailor quarters. Now it was for trash and junk.

Curio swept out of hiding and down the hall. He pressed against the doors on one side, careful to keep his head below the tiny windows. If anyone watched from the opposite side, they made no noise. Still, as Falco kept right up against Curio's back, he watched the black rectangles for signs of activity. It would only take one prisoner to call out to them and their cover would be ruined.

At last Curio stopped by the entrance. Falco came upon him and the two looked to each other. Beyond the opened door the screaming continued, ringing in Falco's ear. He now heard the man struggle against his chains and mumbling in a foreign language while another man gave a deep chuckle.

He shook his head at Curio. That was not Varro, which meant he could be inside any one of these cells. They would have to locate him without giving away themselves. Still, both he and Curio leaned into the doorway to see what lay beyond. Falco barely let one eye slip from behind the wall, but it was enough.

Heat brushed the sliver of his exposed face. The room beyond was nearly ablaze, or so it seemed. A black iron bucket roared with fire and long irons rested in it. A strong man, stripped to his waist and with black hair limp with sweat, stood with his back to them. He wore a heavy leather glove and selected another iron from the fire.

Chained to a table so that the top of his head faced the door was another man who appeared naked. His head rocked from side to side as he groaned. His large nose was like the rudder on a capsized ship. Falco was glad this was not Varro, for the torturer repeated something in his thick voice then held the glowing iron over the man's face.

Falco pulled back just as the victim screamed again. He grimaced, imagining where the hot iron had been stuck. Curio had gone pale as well and both now slinked back the way they had come and regrouped at the emptied room.

"I saw stairs," Falco said. "But Varro must be in one of the cells."

They both looked to the cell doors. Getting Varro out was as simple as removing the bars. They could then slip out of the secret entrance and be away before anyone realized what was happening.

"We'll have to look inside each door," Curio said. "What if whoever is inside see us and raises an alarm?"

"How would he know we're not guards? If he makes too much noise, open the door and I'll spear him."

Curio stared at him. "That's murder, isn't it?"

"Of course it is. It's also survival. If we're caught, then what happens to Varro and to us? These prisoners are as good as dead, anyway. I'd be doing them a favor."

Fortunately Curio's sense of self-preservation was stronger than his morals and he nodded. Falco smiled and patted his head.

"Are you tall enough to see inside?"

"If I stand on the ledge of your eyebrows I'll be fine."

They split up, each taking one side of the long hall. They timed their first look together, both pressed against the wall then shifting to look inside. Falco strained to see anything in the darkness beyond. But no one moved, and if Varro was present, he couldn't tell.

"Damn, it's dark."

"That seems to be the challenge," Curio said. "If only I had taken that lamp."

"We'd be caught with that. I don't think there's anyone in there."

Curio nodded in agreement.

"This isn't going to work," Falco said. "The gods would never set Varro right next to a secret escape route. In fact, he's probably not anywhere near us."

"It's a big city," Curio said. "We're not going to find him without help. And no one will help us."

Help. The world tumbled through the empty spaces of Falco's mind. He had never experienced what Varro had called inspiration. But he did now. It was like sudden inflation of an idea into those empty chambers in his usual thoughts. Inspiration was bright and warm, like sunlight. And he felt unable to contain it. He seized Curio by his arm and hauled him back to the trash-filled room.

"Of course, you're right," he said. "That is exactly what we need."

They ducked back into the room and Curio once more pulled his arm free then turned his shoulder aside.

"That's why I said it. What's with you, Falco? Do you have to relieve yourself?"

"Help is coming, and we're going to get it." He presented the spear, tapping the butt to the stone floor. "Help is coming right under our feet through that trapdoor."

Curio looked down behind the wall of discarded and shattered crates, the wood gray and brittle and coated with dust.

"You think the man with the shovel will return?"

"If he wasn't going to return, he'd have not left the lamp burning."

"Maybe he didn't care if it burned out."

"There was enough oil in that lamp to walk the length of that tunnel three times. Do you carry five torches on patrol when you need only one? No, he is coming back. I did not see him clearly, I'll admit. But he didn't seem to carry anything beyond his shovel. He'll show up here because he's the spy the consul told us about."

Curio cocked his head and frowned.

"I can't be completely sure," Falco admitted. "But it makes sense. A spy would have his secret ways in and out of a city like this. He left for some task, but he's coming back. When he does, he'll meet us."

"What if he's not that spy?"

Falco slapped his palm against the shaft of the spear and smirked.

So they settled into the darkness to wait. At first, the elation of having a good idea kept Falco unworried for how accurate his guess had been. But as time dragged and no one returned, he began to wonder if he had miscalculated. They'd have to retreat into the passage again, for they couldn't risk moving around in daylight wherever they were. A prison meant guards, and during the day there would be twice as many to deal with. He sat listening to the drawn-out screams echoing down the hall. The interrogator knew his work and kept his victim screaming for at least another hour.

But then the door rattled. Falco and Curio snapped up and Falco lowered his spear.

The trapdoor opened just enough for someone to peer through. But Falco and Curio had wisely positioned themselves behind the hinges, so that the door itself blocked them.

The door hung open like this for a long while. Falco had held his breath and was finding it increasingly harder to not let it explode from his lungs. But at last, the door opened wider and he let his breath leak out as the hinges and wood creaked.

Curio had crouched at the ready with his knife and Falco had the spear poised. They wanted the man committed to coming out of the trapdoor before acting. But he was too canny and remained in place with the trapdoor no wider than a thumb's width.

His body quaked with the effort of remaining so still. But at last the figure committed. He pushed the door open and Falco slid around it to stick the point of his spear at the figure's head.

"You better be a Roman spy returning to the job, or you're getting a new eye socket."

A black-hooded man shrank down from the shining bronze point aimed at his face. He seemed to realize the reach of the weapon ensured his only choice was to drop straight down or surrender. Falco know how long that ladder was and wouldn't drop of his own choice.

The man now turned his head up into the wan light. He had a

kingly look to him, with stunning eyes and heavy lines of someone who seemed accustomed to a much harder life than a king's. He smiled at Falco.

"You are the other two Romans who escaped? You are back here?"

The Latin was perfect and eased Falco's anxiety. But he kept the spear level.

"We are, except we don't know where here is. We slipped in your secret way after you popped up out of the ground. Now, I assume you're not eager to let anyone else know about this hole. So come up and play nice."

The man nodded and waited for Falco and Curio to back away. He scrabbled up out of the trapdoor with ease that made Falco feel shame for how he had rolled out of it like a landed fish. In fact, he recovered fast enough to have made a grab at either of them. Yet he held one hand up as he indicated he would set the old shovel against the wall. When Falco nodded him on, he then slowly unclasped his black cloak then folded it up before sticking it into one of the old crates.

Now he looked like a Greek aristocrat, though his tunic was a simple gray. His bold smile and bright eyes made him instantly likable. But Falco was not going to be swayed by someone who looked in command. He held the spear and so made the demands.

"You are beneath King Nabis's palace, in his dungeon no less. Your only way out of here will take you through a series of guard stations. You'd never pass through."

"But you did?"

The man gave a cool smile but said nothing. His likability slipped in Falco's estimation, since he seemed to hold a secret.

"So, you're just going to smile? Look, we're both working for the same side. So let's cooperate a bit better."

"I'd be inclined to cooperation if you lowered the spear and this one stopped trying to slide behind me."

Falco had not even noticed Curio slowly shifting, but when he was called out his face reddened.

"You just had the shovel?"

"And a dagger in my belt, which I still carry. Lower your weapons and let's talk. This is the best time we have to speak then you can both escape through the tunnel."

"We're not going without Varro."

The man's smile widened. "I've recently come from speaking with him. A remarkable man. Which of you is Falco and Curio?"

"I'm Falco. You mean, Varro got away?"

"No, he was executed along with eighty of Sparta's most prominent citizens. They were carted off into the mountains and hurled from the peaks into the abyss below. Death is assumed, but I found your companion alive but in rough condition."

"Varro was thrown off a mountain?" The spear lowered naturally in Falco's hand as he imagined the terror of being driven off a mountain peak.

"How bad was his condition?" Curio asked, plainly less astounded that Varro should have survived than Falco had been.

"His ribs were broken and his hands and feet horribly torn up. I actually found him under a rockslide. He had no memory after being driven from the peak. But it's my guess he did not fall the complete distance, then climbed down the rest of the way until the rocks collapsed and deposited him at the chasm floor. He is of no use to anyone now, and so I have done what I can and will send someone to aid his recovery."

Looking between the man and Curio, Falco could hardly believe what he had heard. Varro had survived certain death with no more than broken bones and cuts. His chest warmed with pride at his oldest friend's ruggedness. Those beatings had toughened up the boy, after all.

"And what's your name?" Curio asked, again being more practical in his response. "And why would you go out looking for him? How did you know he survived?"

"Call me Castor," he said. "I did not know he was alive, but went to bury what I could find of his remains. You can imagine my surprise at finding any part of him much less finding him alive."

"We've been trying to get back inside to help him escape," Falco said, shaking his head. "I can't believe it."

Castor moved past Falco, who collected his spear to his side. He stopped at the archway and nodded to the trapdoor.

"Well, he can use your aid and protection. I could try to tell you the path to him, but it would be better if you're guided. You should leave the city and return to where you planned to camp. Tomorrow I will send someone to aid him and guide you to the place where he is hidden. I moved him into a cave above the chasm floor. He should be safe enough for a while."

"You wouldn't have anything to eat?" Curio asked.

Castor shook his head. "I left some rations with Varro. I thought only to carry enough in case I had to remain out all night. Now, I dare not be gone for so long. You two get back beyond the walls. But before you go, I would send a message to the consul. King Nabis is planning a trap should the Romans breach the outer walls."

Then a heavy door thudded in the distance. Castor leaped at it, and Falco noted the look of terror in his formerly confident face. He also noticed that the screams of the tortured victim had ended. Now the hall echoed with loud voices of several men.

"Go," Castor shoved Falco at the trapdoor. "You'll be caught otherwise."

His panic spread to Falco, and he snatched at the trapdoor. But it did not come up. He tugged again yet it simply bucked against the frame. He set aside his spear to put both hands on the iron ring.

"There's that lock," Curio said. "Press the lever and pull."

"Shit," Falco ran his hand along the side of the doorframe, but Castor hauled him back.

"Too late, they're here." His whisper was rough with fear. "Cover the door. It cannot be found."

The voices from the hall were loud, boisterous, and proud, and just outside the archway. Falco and Curio both stumbled back as Castor shoved the crate atop the door. He looked to Falco's spear as he deftly removed the knife from Curio's grip.

Just as the voices came to the archway, Falco kicked the spear to roll behind the shattered crates.

Castor snatched both of them by their collars and dragged them forward.

"Methodios!" he exclaimed. Falco guessed it was a name, for the next words were all in Greek.

A strong and proud figure filled the door, and he led three other men. Falco noted that all but the lead figure, the one called Methodios, seemed shocked to find them.

Falco knew to follow Castor's lead. He held them both close by their collars, and shook them occasionally as he spoke. The fluid exchange of Greek was amazing. Castor had moved from one language to another with no effort. Moreover, he seemed back in command of his fears.

Even without knowing what was said, Falco realized the two men were locked in a verbal duel. Castor had to explain himself while this Methodios fellow seemed to have the upper hand. At last Methodios held up a hand and looked to Falco with narrow eyes. He spoke in accented Latin.

"Tell me what you are doing here, Roman?"

Falco blinked in astonishment. He looked to Castor for guidance, but he just stared back at him as if he were dog shit scraped from sole.

Figuring out things like this was way beyond Falco's comfort.

This was the kind of ruse Varro would pull off. In the time allowed to him, he had to think like Varro. What would he say?'

"We're being held prisoner, sir."

A slight smile flashed on his lips, then he backhanded Falco across his face. The pain exploded bright across his vision and his head flopped to the side.

"There's an opening on the interrogator's table. He does his best work once he's warmed up. Now, answer me."

Castor did not help him, or if he did Falco couldn't see it. He simply held him in place by his collar.

Then it struck him.

"We're deserters, sir."

Methodios bent his mouth and inclined his head to Castor. They exchanged snippets of Greek, and then focused on him again.

"What's your name?"

"Titus Calavius Pilus, sir." He gave the name of the old neighbor who used to terrorize the local children and who was ostensibly watching his and Varro's farms while they were enlisted. Methodios seemed to accept this then shifted his gaze to Curio.

"Canus Curius Crassus, sir."

Methodios frowned at this. Falco winced at the ridiculous name as well. Yet it passed, as the Greek now turned back to Castor.

"Deserters, then." He spoke in Latin, and Falco guessed he was looking for surprise at anything he said. Falco resolved to look the part of a crestfallen deserter.

"King Nabis is culling all able-bodied men to fill the ranks," Castor said. "Anyone will do, including prisoners."

"I had not heard this."

"That is not my concern," Castor said. "I knew we had Roman

deserters scheduled for interrogation. Rather than waste them, I am delivering these two to the auxiliary guards."

Falco did not flinch. But he was amazed that Castor had adopted a Greek-accented Latin. The man knew his business well, and Falco realized he could never play at games like this man.

Yet Methodios did not seem convinced. He stepped closer and removed Falco from Castor's grip. He studied him head to toe.

"Prisoners, then. Did you give them a bath? They are very clean."

"They have not been a day in the prison," Castor said. "They were by the river when caught."

Methodios rubbed the fabric of Falco's sleeve between thumb and forefinger. Water squeezed out and he looked knowingly at Falco. But he let the sleeve go then turned to Castor.

"Then, I am sorry to delay you. Take these captives away to their new duties. I will accompany you, I think."

Castor smiled and thanked Methodios, then he collared Falco and Curio once more.

"Come on, you two. Time to meet your new commander."

19

Falco swung the club he had been issued, a crude length of wood that was more likely to deliver a thorn to his palm than hurt anyone else. He arced it back and forth across his thigh, the head of it weighted with an iron band. In his other hand was a wood buckler that might have once been a barrel lid. Curio walked beside him with the same kit. They patrolled one long street near Sparta's main gate. There was no traffic outside beyond guard patrols and a handful of messengers trotting about on errands.

The city smelled of hearth fire and too many people. Pigeons stood sentry on rooftops and men stood sentry on the walls. The hush over Sparta was palpable. The grim-faced citizens stocked up for a siege and waited for the arrival of the Romans.

The soldier called Methodios had taken them from Castor, who acted as if he did not care for their fates. Perhaps he was not acting. The Latin-speaking Spartan explained their situation to the captain, who awarded them a sleeping area in a stable where other scabby and lice-ridden men huddled when off-duty. Auxiliary guard apparently meant former prisoners and masterless slaves. Falco had no doubt they would be forced into the Roman lines as body shields against the pila storm.

In any case, Methodios translated their orders, which were simple enough: patrol the assigned street until relieved. Never leave the street or else face execution. Never interact with a citizen except to order them back into their homes, forcibly if needed. Or face execution. Never take more rations than provided. Or face execution.

Death was the only punishment for an infraction of any degree, at least for an auxiliary whose only purpose was to die in some way useful to Sparta.

So they walked together, surprisingly not separated as Falco expected. The empty street in the late afternoon offered them no challenges. The stuccoed buildings were dark and shuttered, and people watched them pass with a mixture of fear and hatred. So they patrolled slowly, sticking to the shadowed side of the street to avoid the heat of the sun.

"Curius Caelius Carinus?" Curio stuck his club under his arm and scratched his head.

"Why by all the gods didn't you pick a name of someone you knew?"

"Caeso Coruncanius Castus?"

"No, it wasn't that. But it was a stupid name, like something a child would make up."

"I was terrified we'd be tortured," Curio said. "I didn't know what to say. It was the first name that came to my mind."

"Your children are going to hate you."

"Caeso Curius Crassus, that's it!" He swung his club in a wide arc as if celebrating. "I need to remember it."

"No one is going to call you anything other than whatever the Greek word is for dog shit. You will be dog shit and I will be the other dog shit. We're not even human to these Spartans. We're here to catch Roman pila with our faces. That's their plan for their so-called auxiliary guard."

Curio mumbled his name again, then tilted his head. "Actually, I don't think Caeso is right."

"Forget about that. We should be using this time to plan our way out of here."

He looked at Curio with his beaten, swollen face, bruised and cut flesh, bare feet covered in dirt, and he sniffed. "Dog shit is about right for us. I don't suppose I look much better than you."

"What? I think it was Canus. Canus Curius Crassus." He put his hand to his chest. "I feel better."

"All right Crassus, would you listen now? We're not going to patrol this street forever. We're getting out of here."

"I feel like I should call your plan a pile of horseshit before I even hear it. But so far your ideas have been working out. I haven't any idea how we'd get out of here alive."

"Wait, have you not had any thoughts of your own?"

"Did you order me to have thoughts, sir? Your last command was that I only need to understand my orders."

"Would you look around? This is not a joke. We're up to our Roman noses in Spartan shit here. If you have an idea, then I'd like to know."

"Well, I suppose you think we can go back the way we got inside. But getting to that tunnel feels impossible now. It might as well not even exist."

Falco paused before a short alley and stared at Curio. "As tempting as it is to sneak through the gates of the acropolis, into the palace, and down into Nabis's torture chambers, I think I'll come up with a better idea. One that doesn't lead us directly through every fighting man in Sparta."

"Good, I don't ever want to hear screams like that again." Curio resumed their patrol. Thus far the only living thing they had to chase off the street was a gray cat, and it obliged them by fleeing into the dark at their approach. He started swinging his club in a lazy arc. "So how are we getting out of here? Nothing goes out of these walls. The consul must be near and they're expecting the attack any day."

"That's right," Falco said, catching up to Curio and continuing back the way they had come. "The attack will begin any day, and when it does, what do you think happens to us?"

"We die by onager attack from our own side."

"Seriously, Curio. That's not going to happen. But you're not far off in thinking we'll be shoved in front of our own side. They'll use the auxiliaries as a screen if the Romans get over the wall. If they don't then that means they'll be busy defending the walls. In either case, we can use the confusion to escape."

"Did you think of that yourself?" Curio asked. "Or did one of the children at the stables give you that plan?"

"What? You have a better plan? How else are we getting out of here? We'll have to use the chaos of the attack to escape. I can't see any other way."

Curio looked around at the buildings along their path. "Are we watching them or are they watching us? People keep peeping out when we pass."

"Everyone is pissing themselves. Wouldn't you if you thought someone was coming to burn down your house, rape and enslave your women, and kill you?"

"Falco, you make it sound like we're the bad guys here. None of that would happen if this rotten Spartan king just did what he was told."

"Well, that's enough philosophy for the likes of us. Besides, you haven't heard my complete plan yet."

"I'm shivering with excitement. But I've got to tell you, Falco, I think we should just enjoy our last days as free men. We're either going to die fighting our own side or the Spartans are just going to kill us if it comes to a siege. They won't waste food on us.

Maybe they'll let us starve. Honestly, execution would be a mercy."

"Why so negative? We were hanging from those walls a few days ago, and now we're patrolling their streets with weapons they gave us. Even Varro is alive, and he got thrown off a mountain. We're doing great. We just need one final push, and we'll be free. Then we fetch Varro, return to camp, and all get drunk."

Curio shook his head throughout the speech. "Maybe Varro will get back. But we trapped ourselves."

Falco sighed and they continued the patrol. No matter what Curio felt, Falco was not ready to give up. Defeat started from within a man's heart. Over the recent days, he had no time to remember the ordeal of his crucifixion. Yet during the brief hours of sleep before his first patrol, he dreamed of it. He remembered how he had clung to life. How he refused to surrender to the pain and the crushing iron around his neck. If he had surrendered when the sun set and his physical strength shattered, then Varro would have found a corpse. But his will endured even when his body could not. And that force of will had ensured his survival. This time was no different.

Their patrol came to the main road that led to the gates. They were not supposed to pass this point, but turn and continue patrolling until someone told them to stop. But they paused to look down its length into the bright haze.

Bales of hay were being carted along the walls while teams of soldiers hauled them off then sent them down short lines of workers. These workers seemed to be lined in front of homes.

"What are they doing?" Curio asked.

"It looks like they're storing the bales in houses. What would that be for?"

Falco shielded his eyes from the sun for a better look. But as he did, the first person he had seen all morning stepped into the street. A broad-shouldered man stood in the purple shadows cast from a nearby building. Falco was about to wave him aside when he realized the man was armed with a bow and had an arrow on the string. He leveled it with Falco's head.

"We're surrounded," Curio said, bumping up against Falco's back.

Looking about the crossroad, bow-armed men had them covered from every angle. They wore dull red tunics and had thick and curly beards. Falco counted six of them, and they all could have been brothers.

"I don't think these barrel lids are much hope against arrows," he said, pressing against Curio.

"It was an ambush," Curio said mildly. "Even if we had our own shields, we're done for."

"Come on," Falco shouted at the man before him. "At least let me die fighting. I earned it."

The men said nothing but remained poised to draw and release faster than Falco could hope to reach the closest archer. They either did not understand or ignored him. But another voice spoke from the left.

"Who is Falco and who is Curio?"

Both he and Curio whirled to the familiar, jaunty voice. To their left three men in chain armor and fearsome Corinthian helmets with black horsehair plumes approached. Two carried spears and one set his muscled arms akimbo over a sheathed sword. He repeated his question.

"I don't know what you're talking about," Falco said, shifting his flimsy shield to face the three men. He held his club against it like a gladius, a habit formed of long training and utterly incorrect for the use of a cudgel.

The man laughed and raised a hand to stop his followers. He removed his helmet, revealing the charming and handsome face of the soldier who had captured them last night, Methodios.

"It's not so important that I correctly identify your heads," he said. "But it is my habit to be accurate in all I do. My king wishes to carry them to his negotiations with your consul, to show him what he thinks of Roman tricks. It would be a nice touch if he were to name you correctly when he produces the last of your remains."

"What game is this?" Falco said. "If you know who we are, then why did you arm us and set us here?"

Methodios shrugged. "I thought I might learn more of what you planned if I just watched you in action. But to my delight, Castor has told us all I need to know. I expected him to take days of effort to break. Still, I will credit the man. He had his skin flayed off from his toes to the middle of his thighs before he spoke."

Curio hissed. "This is bad."

"Fuck, we can't even fall on our swords. If we rush him, maybe the archers will kill us."

"I'm not letting them torture me, Falco. We die here."

"Agreed."

But Methodios either guessed the plan from their stances or else had excellent hearing. With a swift bark in Greek, the spearmen behind him lowered their weapons and the archers drew their strings back. He stood smiling.

"These are Cretan archers, the best in these lands. If you think to die here, they will not allow it. Each of you will take an arrow through both your knees and arms. And since we must conserve our supplies for the coming battle, for every arrow wasted on you I will double your suffering. If you surrender and answer some questions for me, then I will make a soldier's promise of a swift death. No more crucifixions or lingering punishments. I will have your heads struck off in one go."

"Can we trust him?" Curio asked.

"Do you want arrows in your knees?"

Falco set the cudgel and shield on the road. Curio did as well, and both raised their hands in surrender.

Methodios closed his eyes and nodded with an expression of deep satisfaction.

"A wise choice. The war is over for you now. I know you are just two simple soldiers, but there are some things I would know. Then I will send your souls to be judged."

"No tortures?" Curio asked.

Methodios nodded in agreement.

The spearmen drove them down the road at the points of their weapons. Falco hung his head, his mind spinning with confusion. He was aware of the faces peering from the doorways and windows of the buildings lining the road. A few dared to shout curses as they passed. Methodios herded them toward the acropolis.

As they climbed the steep road leading to the highest point of Sparta, Falco gave a bitter smile. They were going to pass through the soldiers massed here and reach Nabis's palace after all.

"You're taking us back to the torture chambers," Falco said. "You lied to us."

"Did I?" Methodios followed behind. Though Falco did not turn or else risk a jab from the spear at his back, he could easily imagine the Greek feigning hurt feelings.

"You can ask questions anywhere, and I'm sure the people would enjoy the execution of enemy soldiers. So there's no need to take us back to the palace except to torture us."

"Depending on how you answer me, you might be better kept alive," Methodios said. "But whatever you say will need to be verified. I promise, the interrogator will only just poke you a bit to check the truth of your words."

"He's going to cut my balls off," Curio mumbled beside him. "We should've been shot through with arrows."

The Greeks herding them up the long road did not appreciate Curio's muttering. One jabbed his shoulder with the spear, causing him to leap and shout with the pain.

"That's it," Curio said. "I'm running. Let them kill me."

"No!" Falco grabbed him as he started to run.

Methodios shouted at his guards, and they reversed their spears to batter the shafts across Falco's back. He fell atop Curio, protecting him from the blows that slammed over his body. He gritted his teeth and endured it long enough to whisper into Curio's ear.

"If Castor didn't reveal the tunnel, we can escape that way. When I act, run to the spear we hid there and save me. If I'm doomed, save yourself."

Then the guards ripped him away and began to beat Curio, who now held his forearms over his face as the two spear shafts slammed into him. Falco sat heaving on the road, aware of onlookers gathering to the spectacle. His back and shoulders throbbed from the beating. Methodios drew his sword and stood over him.

"Going to take my head now?"

His easy smile now vanished, Methodios ignored him. The guards recovered Curio, who bled from his shoulder and nose, then forced him into a line with Falco at the lead. One spearman went ahead, and Methodios and the others followed behind.

Falco hoped Curio remembered the spear that he had taken from the Greek farmer. Just before being caught, he had kicked it behind the crates hiding the secret tunnel. If Methodios had learned of it from Castor, then he would have bragged about it. In fact, Falco guessed that they were going to be tortured into revealing how they had entered the city. What else could Methodios want to know from them?

They reached the top of the acropolis and Falco's heart beat both from the effort of his exhausted body and the excitement of his plan. His stomach burned with fear that escape was just within his grasp. The lead guard signaled to the men stationed all along the streets leading to Nabis's palace. Falco realized he was actually beginning to learn the way around this area, something he had never hoped to achieve. As expected, they passed through checkpoints and Methodios was well known to everyone they encountered.

Soon they entered the cool shadows of the stone palace. Falco had glimpsed the entry areas busy with servants and guards. It was full of indistinct tension. While he did not understand their language, he understood their postures and the timber of their voices well enough. He held back a smile at the fear shown by the so-called fearless Spartans. They might be inheritors of a brave warrior culture, but here he saw soldiers barely better than thugs who were worried for their futures against the Roman legions.

The scene was cut short as they took the familiar turns into the darkness of the dungeon entrance. Methodios's spearmen transferred Falco and Curio to other guards who wore only short swords at their hips. The guard room was smoky and lamplit and filled with a half-dozen men. But only two accompanied them into the darkness, with Methodios following behind.

Both he and Curio held their heads in defeated silence. At least for Falco this was an act, for his heart raged with anticipation for both revenge and escape. With one guard to lead the way with a lit lamp and the other chatting softly with Methodios, Falco believed his enemies were confident in their capture. They had not secured their hands, likely believing that even an attempt to grab weapons would be unthinkable.

Descending the stairs into the long hall filled with emptied cells, Falco located the torture room by the orange light spilling from it.

"I've prepared a bit of encouragement for you." Methodios's voice was once more alive with good humor. "Take a look inside."

The lead guard stopped beside the entrance. The bright illumination spilling out colored half his body in golden light. The sweaty, lanky torturer stepped out while tugging off his heavy leather gloves. He wore a blood-splattered apron and smiled to reveal missing teeth.

The guard behind shoved Falco at the entrance. Within he saw a dark shape strapped to a chair, which he shortly realized was the ruin of Castor. His kingly countenance had been brutalized into the warped shapes of a man who died in agony.

His skin was expertly flensed from his feet up to his mid-thigh, the exposed muscles glistening red. A bucket of blood and gray flesh strips sat beside his chair. He hung with his head to the side, both eyes opened wide enough that they bulged. His excruciation had been complete and Falco could only guess that the shock of his torments had killed him.

"Castor has long been on my list of potential spies. It took too long to catch him." Methodios stood beside Falco and Curio, arms folded and smiling in admiration of the corpse slumped against the leather straps of the chair. "But your arrival here brought him out and confirmed my suspicions."

He turned to Falco and narrowed his eyes.

"And I lied about the torments. The two of you will suffer as Castor did, as all Roman dogs should, and you will die begging for its release. Your flesh will be flayed back to your necks, and then your heads will be sent to the king. Let's see how long you can endure. Trained soldiers ought to last longer than Castor did."

"I thought you wanted to question us?" Falco fought to keep his voice from quaking and never looked from the ruined corpse before him.

"You don't know anything useful now that Castor has told me everything." Methodios grabbed him by the shoulder and spun him around so that he had to look into his smirking face. "I know about that secret passage. I sent my agent to explore it right after I caught Castor with the two of you."

Falco's eyes widened and his stomach filled with cold fear. Methodios's smirk widened.

"That's right. I even know where Varro is hiding and sent my agent to watch over him. If I originally had my way with all of you, I'd not have ordered your executions but questioned you before having your skins for a new cloak. It seems the gods have granted me my wish. Varro's survival is especially fortunate. Who knows where that will go? My agent might even be able to infiltrate the Roman camp with your friend's aid."

A numb wave of fear crawled over Falco's flesh. Methodios and his two guards smirked at him while the torturer turned back to his tools by the flaming iron basket as if to prepare for his work.

They never had any hope. Methodios was just enacting his sick pleasure at their torment.

He felt the strength in his limbs ebb away.

One of the guards screamed and then collapsed out of sight.

Curio had snatched the short sword from one of their guards and cut out his legs.

"Come on, Falco! Strike!"

20

Falco struck forward, throwing himself at Methodios. He was larger and stronger than the Greek, but the extraordinary trials of recent days had dulled his power. His shoulder rammed into Methodios's chin, driving him back into the room. He slapped his powerful hands to Falco's shoulders to stop his backward skid, but both men stumbled into the hot, bright torture room.

The fallen guard was screaming and holding his cut legs. Falco could not hear any more of that struggle, as he was now locked with Methodios.

Both collided with the torturer, who cried out in shock at the sudden violence. All three slid along the table, sending iron tools to crash on the stone floor.

Methodios grunted then shifted his hand to Falco's face, where he pressed his thumb into his eye socket. The pain and blinding pressure shot instant panic directly into Falco's brain. As the Greek drove his thumb deeper, Falco had to relent or else risk losing his eye.

A knee rose up and slammed into his gut, doubling him over

and sending him back from both Methodios and the torturer who now had shuffled aside to Castor's body.

"You're trapped here," Methodios said. "Your fight is pointless."

In the doorway, figures whirled in combat and Falco could not dare more than a glance. But Curio was not out of the fight yet.

Neither was he.

Methodios rested opposite him against a table where various bars, tongs, and blades were set out beside a bucket of fire that both lit the room and heated iron pokers in it. The lanky torturer stood to his left beside Castor's corpse. He spread his arms wide as if preparing a tackle.

Falco himself backed up to the heavy bench where the torturer conducted most of his work. It pressed against his hamstrings and prevented retreat. It was too heavy to shift with his body weight.

His eyes swept all of this information into his mind, and even as cold sweat rolled down his face, his plan of attack formed in an instant.

Methodios reached for his own sword, and seemingly confident in Falco's capture, he glanced out the door where Curio's fight had spilled into the hall.

That was Falco's moment.

He pivoted to the torturer, who lurched back from Falco's attention. Yet he rushed the unarmed man and threw his arms around him in a bear hug. He smelled of blood, sweat, and sour wine. He was tall and thin, but not particularly strong. Falco slammed his body back against the wall beside Castor's corpse. The force of the blow struck the torturer's head against the rock wall.

Falco pressed him back, seizing the torturer by a lock of greasy black hair, then slammed his skull against the wall three times in succession, dazing the man.

Without delay, he spun the torturer around as a shield against the attack he knew Methodios planned.

The lanky torturer flopped about in his arms, but with raw fear powering him, Falco whisked him around like a child's doll. Methodios indeed had stepped forward with his drawn sword. But he had enough discipline to pull his strike before skewering his own man.

A scream echoed in the hallway. Falco could not determine if it was Curio or his enemy. But Methodios blocked the exit, and his self-satisfied grin had turned to one of rage. The veins of his neck stood out and his face had shaded to red.

The torturer mumbled and began to struggle.

Falco charged forward with him held as a body shield. Methodios backed up, cursing and skipping over the tools that had fallen to the floor in the scuffle.

The man in his arms now suddenly roared to life and tried to spin around to face him. Yet Falco had wrestled him over to the iron bucket.

"Time for payback, you fucking maggot."

He shoved the torturer's head at the flames. Out of terror and instinct, the torturer screamed and tried to protect himself by bracing both hands against the iron bucket.

His flesh seared and hissed, then Falco twisted him aside toward Methodios with a triumphant grunt. With his hands melted to the iron, the twist unseated the bucket and spilled the burning coals and hot irons over his workbench. The torturer himself fell into the flaming coals, setting his arms, face, and hair aflame.

Screams echoed in the room, no worse than those of his former victims, and the torturer began to flail wildly as the room filled with the sweet stench of his burning flesh. He staggered in the direction Falco had shoved him, and now was a flaming bulwark against Methodios who had already backed out of the room.

"Burn like Sparta!" Falco surged with newfound strength. Even though he was still boxed into this room of gory horrors, he smiled at his small victory.

The flaming man bounced around the opened doorway, pawing at his head with arms of fire. His screaming echoed through the hallway beyond.

Falco searched for a weapon, finding many hooks, chains, pliers, and other tools that made no sense to him. The best weapons were now covered in flaming cinders. But a series of red-hot iron bars had rolled out before him, and the heavy leather gloves of the torturer rested on the nearby workbench.

He had just put on the gloves and picked up a bar when Methodios reentered the room. The torturer had collapsed and the flames from the spread-out coals were now easily sidestepped.

Methodios cut down in an overhead chop, relying on his own strength and the weight of the heavy blade to cut Falco's head off in a single strike.

But he held up the bar in both hands overhead. The bronze blade clanged against the iron bar. The heat of it reached through the gloves and still threatened to burn Falco's hands. But the iron had saved his life. Methodios and he both looked up in surprise at it, as if neither of them could guess where it had come from.

But now it was Falco's turn to smile. It takes no skill to wield a searing-hot iron bar.

He let it fall from his hands, and it struck Methodios first on the face and then rolled down his proud nose onto his chest.

Falco dodged back from the iron as it bounced on the stone floor, but Methodios shrieked and dropped his own sword as he grabbed at his face. Blood surged out of the burns as he accidentally pulled the flesh open while trying to protect himself. Falco grabbed him by the tunic then thrust him aside. He had hoped to knock him into the coals, but instead he tumbled to land at Castor's feet. The bucket of blood and flesh spilled out over him.

Not wasting any more time with Methodios, he raced into the

hallway. He looked first to the left, toward the room where the secret tunnel was hidden. It was dark and silent that way. There were no bodies in the hall besides the smoldering corpse of the torturer and the first guard Curio had disarmed. Blood pooled beneath his legs, but it seemed Curio had stuck him in the neck as well, creating a brilliant red spray across the hall onto the opposite wall.

Down the hall toward the stairs, he saw shadows moving in the guttering light there. Screams from this place would not draw their attention, but by now they must have counted too many screams.

Methodios wept from within the torture room. Falco considered killing him with his own sword as a final act of humiliation, but he heard voices calling tentatively from the stairway.

"Enjoy your new face," he said. "I'll be looking for it in the rubble of this fucking city."

Methodios groaned in answer, and the voices grew sterner from the stairway.

He swept out of the room, and he heard someone call out to him.

The chase was on now.

His legs filled with desperate strength. Curio might be dead. Varro was in danger that he wouldn't recognize. Everything rested with him now.

The men down the hall began to give chase, but they would doubtless pause at the carnage left behind. They might also seek to aid Methodios. Falco hoped it would be enough time. For if they had blocked the trapdoor, then he was running to his death.

Skidding around the corner, he stared into the gloom.

The body of the second Spartan guard lay across the entrance as if he were napping. His arms rested at his sides and his eyes were closed. However, a sword protruded from his stomach just below the rib cage on the left side where a bloom of red showed on his gray tunic. Also, a swathe of blood showed where the body had been dragged across the floor. This was set here to trip anyone racing into the room from around the corner.

"Curio?"

No answer came from the room, but shouts of surprise and anger echoed down the hall. Falco set his naked foot to the dead man's chest then yanked out the sword. It was longer than a gladius but much shorter than the typical Greek sword. It was the right size for fights in close spaces like this room. Not that he planned to make a stand here.

He jumped the corpse and found the empty crates had been cleared aside and the trapdoor sat open as a flat-black space in the gray gloom. To his surprise, the spear he had taken from the farmhouse had been rolled to the wall and forgotten.

He dropped it butt-first into the hole, then sat at the edge and lowered his legs into the darkness. His feet felt around for the rungs, which were hard and smooth against his soles. Tucking the sword underarm, he started down. He tried to pull the door shut by a short chain that had been set for this purpose, yet in his rush to escape, he could not grasp it and so left the door open.

The faint light hardly illuminated the ladder into the darkness. His feet slapped on the rungs as he scrabbled down until he at last touched cold, wet stone.

He leaped off the ladder, then felt around the darkness for the spear he had dropped. The narrow shaft did not leave room for it to vanish into the darkness, and he soon wrapped his trembling palm around it.

"Curio," he called down the tunnel, but dared not repeat himself. For now he heard the surprised voices of the men in the room above.

While Methodios might have known about the trapdoor, he might not have shared the knowledge with others. By now, Falco imagined they were wondering where he had vanished. They would soon discover the truth, in any case. But he had a spear and sword, and now felt the chance of survival was much higher. He had no idea how many had pursued him. If he recalled correctly, there had been six total guards in the room and two were already dead. He would have to even up this fight.

As the voices mumbled in confusion above, and already one shouted in what sounded like surprise, Falco set his trap.

He drove the butt of the spear into the softer earth of the tunnel floor, angling it so that the blade faced the ladder. Whoever climbed down would have his back to it, then when he turned and walked forward he would impale himself on the sharp bronze blade. He smeared dirt on it to hide the metal from any flame they might bring into the tunnel. Even if they discovered it, they would still have to pause to remove it. Every moment aided Falco, and hopefully Curio as well.

Now he took the short sword in hand and began to rush down the narrow tunnel. While he had not memorized the details of it, he knew enough that the floor was fairly even and from this point would slope down in a nearly straight line to the boggy ground of the river behind Sparta. Unlike his pursuers, he could just put one hand to the wall and race forward knowing what to expect. Anyone else would need a light source and would advance without knowing where they were going.

His fingers flapped against the rough-hewn wall. Sections had been built up with stone walls, feeling hard and cold under his fingers. Most areas were naked earth still holding the ruts and divots of the tools used to create this tunnel.

As he expected, he heard voices echoing behind. Shortly after, he heard a shocked, painful howl and he smiled. His spear trap had succeeded.

"I hope it pierced your black heart," he muttered as he continued following the tunnel, increasing his pace as he heard other voices join with the screaming man.

He raced ahead and heard them calling into the darkness as if he might answer them. Certainly, they were not the smartest enemies he would ever face. Yet he knew they were fearful. Like him, they might fear the darkness. But worse, they would fear the unknown and fear being below the earth. They would pray for any reason to turn back. All he had to do was keep his lead and their own doubts would cost them the chase.

His own fears of the dark did not outweigh the fear of being caught once more. These men would just hack him to pieces, and with his luck they might not even do a proper job of it. The gory thought kept him running, until his feet struck something.

It was fresh dirt mingled with hard stone. He knew this both from its scent and from the hard smash of rock against his toes. He cried out as he felt atop the pile, and his sword slipped from his grip.

He lay flat, surprised at what he had found, which was not there just a day ago. As if to insult him further, dirt drizzled over the back of his head as he lay prone. He listened for his pursuers. The screams of the injured man had faded away to nothing. Either he had died or they had carried him out of the tunnel and left. As he lay atop the cold earth, he heard nothing, but soon he heard a man crash and curse. They were still following him into the dark.

Padding around for the sword, he snatched it up and resumed fleeing down the tunnel. His heart raced now that he realized the tunnel might not be entirely safe. While his toes hurt, if he was careless he could twist his ankle or break his leg.

Yet despite the fears he reached the end of the tunnel. He felt the ground growing wetter and soon he was at the ladder. Yet the trapdoor remained shut.

"Curio?" he dared to call out again, hoping he was just holding the door closed against enemies. But when he did not answer, he once more tucked the sword underarm then clambered up the ladder. He shoved the door open to spill in both bright light and fresh air. It was as forceful as a slap, and he paused before leaping out in case Curio might strike him out of fear.

"It's me," he said, then pulled up into the bushes.

Branches and leaves pressed against him like old friends welcoming him home from the war. The sun was bright in a sky filled with puffy white clouds. A fair breeze blew across his face, clearing the earthy smells from his nose and bringing him the watery scent of the nearby river.

He looked around, but found himself alone and no sign that Curio had gone ahead of him.

But it made no sense. Curio had killed his enemy then set him in place to trip up pursuers. He had even left Falco a sword.

He collapsed among the rough branches enfolding him. No matter what it seemed like, Curio had not fled down the tunnel. For whatever reason, he still hid inside Sparta.

"What are you doing, you fool?"

He wiped his face and stared up at the sky. His pursuers were still below, and Falco couldn't just close the door then shove rocks atop it as he would have done were Curio here.

So he waited.

He left the door open, hoping to coax the pursuers out of the hole. Then he could spring on them. There might be as many as three, but likely two at best. With surprise on his side, he considered himself in the better position even if outnumbered.

It took a long time for the voices to begin echoing in the darkness below. Falco crouched opposite the ladder, so that he could skewer the first man out before he could turn. Yet he noted the cautious tones of the voices. He counted two, but as they spoke together he was not certain of the numbers.

Yet soon curiosity won out and the ladder began to shake and creak as someone began climbing. Falco grabbed the sword in both hands, raising it to his shoulder for a powerful thrust at the first enemy to come through.

The head and shoulders of an enemy popped up from the hole. But rather than leap up, he stood there trying to ascertain his surroundings. Falco held his breath. Being directly behind, the enemy did not spot him. So when he spoke again, then set both hands to either side to push up, Falco struck his blow.

The enemy rolled to his side, then saw Falco. He let out a warning cry, but it was cut short as Falco rammed his sword into his neck, nearly decapitating the man. He screeched as blood sprayed onto the bushes and he crashed among them. Falco now sprung to his feet to face the next man through, but instead he heard him fleeing away into the darkness.

"Shit!" Falco stared at the black hole in the ground. "Shit! Curio, where are you?"

The question hung in the air unanswered. The splashing of the other man's feet in the muddy tunnel quickly vanished. He was going back to report what he had found.

Falco glanced at the dead man, whose blood flow had slowed to a trickle that dribbled over the bushes where he hung.

"What am I supposed to do now?"

He turned to look at the mountain peak that stood so prominently over Sparta. Varro had been thrown from it and survived, but was being tended by Castor's spy as a way to gain his trust and thereby use him to access the Roman camp. He looked back at the darkness. Curio was down there still, inexplicably hiding within Sparta doubtless now a captive of whatever foolish plan he had made. Methodios was injured but not dead. If he found Curio, his torments would be legendary.

Then he looked to Sparta.

Every large city has a plume of smoke over it from the hearth fires of its citizens. But this was more smoke than he expected, especially given the breezes.

And as he listened, even from this distance, he heard the faint clangor of battle on the opposite side of Sparta.

At last, Consul Flamininus had arrived with his army, and to the trap that Castor warned of but never explained before his death.

Falco looked to the sky, raised his sword, and screamed.

"Are you entertained? What am I supposed to do?"

21

Falco knelt by the river, scooping cool water with both hands. He had scrubbed his face in a calm in the swift current. The blue sky and clouds reflected behind his head. The rippling of the drops splashing from his face to the water distorted the image. But he had glimpsed himself and did not care to remember what he had seen. Even his mother would not recognize him, given he did not recognize himself. The beard growth and dirt smears alone made him look wild. But he had met his own eyes, the hollow, staring eyes of a madman.

He had tried to scrub that face off. But it was not something to wash away. He thought back to his childhood and of Old Man Pilus's son, a young man just discharged from his service in the war against Hannibal. What was his name? Lucius, maybe? It was too long ago. But even with a name faded from memory, Falco had never forgotten his face.

He had been mucking about behind the Pilus farmhouse and decided to piss on their barn wall. It was the sort of foolish, malicious activities he loved as a boy. He was trying to write something in the stucco with his urine. Then Lucius found him out. His sudden appearance behind the barn scared him enough that he ended up pissing his own tunic.

But it was not from the fear of being caught. It was that horrid, dead look in Lucius's eyes. He had been a survivor of Cannae, a battle his father said was butchery and that only a handful had survived. Lucius stared at him while he tried to come up with an excuse. But soon he marched forward, and now the older Falco realized Lucius had moved like a man formed up in a battle line. Those empty eyes were not looking at him, but something else, and it seemed he would tear young Falco into strips of bloody meat.

He ran home, tears in his eyes. Of course, by the time he arrived at his own house those tears had dried. But his heart remained beating long after that encounter. Old Man Pilus's son never did return from Cannae, and his eyes beheld only battle and carnage forevermore.

The face Falco saw reflected on this cheery day, where the clank and crash of distant battle carried on the breeze, was the face of Lucius. His face had covered Falco's own. And scrub as viciously as he could, that face remained reflected in the river.

He rested with hands on knees, letting the water drizzle back into the river and turning his reflection into a spinning zigzag of tiny waves.

Old Man Pilus's son hanged himself later that summer. Everyone for miles around came out to comfort the old man. Lucius had done it in the same barn that young Falco had tried to deface.

"Jupiter save me. What am I thinking?" Falco set both hands to his head and turned aside from the river. "I just need a mug of wine and a bit of food. That couldn't go wrong."

He climbed back to the grass embankment where his captured sword lay flat with a dim tidal mark of blood on its blade. With war now come to Sparta, he had less to fear from men watching on the walls. Even if they saw him, they would not come out to do anything about it. Still, he wanted to remain unseen as long as he could.

The presence of the hidden tunnel weighed on his thoughts. He once more sat where he and Curio had originally discovered Castor sneaking away to find Varro in the mountains. Now that its existence was revealed, he wondered how long before it was sealed up. What resources could King Nabis devote to closing it off while he had a battle to fight? He certainly could not guard it, not with Rome now assaulting his front gates. With Methodios seriously injured, would Nabis even learn about the passage in time to do anything?

Falco sighed at the unhappy prospect of having to yet again find a way into Sparta. He snickered at this, laughing alongside whatever gods were laughing at him now. At least this time he was certain someone worth saving was on the inside.

He stared back at the mountain towering over Sparta in the distance. Throwing anyone off that must surely leave only bone fragments and bloodstains behind. That Castor sought Varro's corpse in these circumstances dug at his sense of logic. If Varro had been thrown off with a bunch of nobles, there would be no way to determine one body from another. Yet he had acted that very night, and at such risk that he paid for it with his life.

Why? Falco had no answer, and he wondered if Varro would know.

But for now, he had to make a choice. He was needed in three places and did not wish to be at any of them. Curio had stayed behind in Sparta for some reason. Varro was a broken man lost in the mountains and at the mercy of a hidden enemy. Then there was the entire army that was going to face a trap that Castor had felt dangerous enough to mention within moments of their meeting.

He rapped his knuckles against his skull as he struggled with the decision.

"Why are you making me choose?" he questioned the gods, but knew they would remain silent. So he rocked back and forth as he tried to pry out the right choice from his conflicting possibilities.

Methodios had been down the hall from Curio. By now, he might have caught him. But Curio could disappear when he wanted. Falco had seen him do it often enough. So maybe he was not in as much danger as imagined.

Varro was being deceived into believing an enemy was a friend. As long as he did not discover this fact, he was likely safe. Methodios's so-called agent wanted to use him to infiltrate the Roman camp. But he had to get Varro healthy again so that he could at least move him. Now that the consul had brought the attack to Sparta, would the agent change plans? Would he just kill Varro after learning all he could? It was possible, but this seemed like a patient game that was planned before anyone knew he and Curio had survived to potentially ruin it. So Varro might be the safest of all.

Then there was Consul Flamininus. By strict procedure, he should report back to him with all he had learned. He was duty-bound to at least warn of potential traps set within Sparta in case of a breakthrough by their side. But he did not know the specifics of the trap. His report would be as useful as reporting that the Spartans were planning bad things for Rome. Wouldn't Consul Flamininus know to be aware of traps when penetrating into an enemy city? How valuable was his report to the consul? But then he thought of Lucius and Old Man Pilus. If he did not do what he could to help his fellows, would he be creating more scenarios like theirs? Would he kill himself one day like Lucius had? Perhaps, especially if the trap killed thousands of his own side and he could have warned them to greater caution.

That seemed to make his choice. By force of logic, something he always struggled with but admired in others, he decided the greatest harm to the greatest number of people must be prevented.

"But without more to report, I'm not doing anything better than telling them to be careful." He groaned and fell flat in the grass, still rapping his knuckles against his head. "This is killing me!"

Worse than the struggle to make the correct decision was his realizing his own indecisiveness. He was a centurion, after all. In battle he had to make snap decisions and the lives of his soldiers hung on them. Yet somehow those decisions were easier than this one.

"Well that's it, isn't it."

He sat upright, a sudden sense of clarity infusing him with energy again. He just had to make a decision. All of his choices had good and bad sides. He could never know which would be better than the other until he saw the outcomes of all three. So he could stop feeling sorry for himself and crying over circumstances beyond his power to dictate. He was a centurion. He read the enemy battle lines, read his own men, then made a decision and fought at the front of the battle line.

So that's what he did now.

While saving the army was important, he only knew they faced a trap. But it would only manifest if they breached the walls, which wasn't going to happen overnight. Falco had seen enough of the walls of Sparta to know. Therefore, he would go after Curio. Not only would he be able to save Curio but he might also learn the details of the trap set for the consul. He had more to gain by going back into Sparta than going after Varro.

He sprang to his feet and felt ready to jump back into the tunnel. But then he paused.

"Falco, you handsome bastard, you're assuming you'll just walk in and out of Sparta like a trip to the market."

His life meant nothing without friendship. He never had a true friend when growing up, nor a brother or sister to call family. Now he had friends worth dying for. He didn't need to worry for himself. If he did not give his all to save them, then his own death would be a mercy. There is no life ahead of the man who abandons those he loves for safety and comfort.

He snatched up the sword, then stalked back to the slain guard. He lay tangled in the bushes, suspended over a congealing puddle of his own blood. He wrested the body to the ground, then flipped him over. The Spartan's face was frozen in a bizarre expression, as if he were just getting to the punchline of a bawdy joke. Falco frisked his tunic for anything of use, pulling away a ring with three ponderous iron keys. Judging from the wear marks and smoothed edges, these saw frequent use. He decided to take the entire belt as it had a sheath for his sword, a dagger, and a loop for the keys. When finished, he rolled the body into the bushes. Crows and other animals would eventually find the corpse and call attention to this spot. For a short time, at least, the scavengers would be busy with a feast north of here. Still, Falco could not help but feel the battle was a distraction and all of Sparta truly wanted to hunt him. It was a foolish thought, but having twice been sentenced to death he could not help but feel the Spartans wanted him personally.

"Varro," he said, looking toward the towering peak against the deep blue sky. "I will come for you. I know you would come for me were our positions reversed. I swear it on my life. I'd cut my palm and swear a blood oath to you right now. But it'd probably kill me, I'm so weak. Anyway, hang on. Curio's just right here."

Whether or not he had made the correct choice no longer mattered. He had decided his path and would not wonder if he had chosen well. All his life, he had never doubted a single step until today. Maybe until this moment, he had not made a meaningful choice. That thought alone was sobering, and he resolved to live a better life when this was all done. Maybe he would make a vow like Varro had, except one that would at least be possible to keep in a world mad with violence and warfare.

Yet even that thought faded as he once more descended into the tunnel. He made no effort to close the trapdoor. No one would find it now that the battle had started. Besides, he would be looking for the column of sunlight when he doubtlessly came feeling back this way with Curio. He slipped down the passage, following the same wall back in the darkness as he had before. He still did not correctly estimate the point of the cave-in and tripped once more, though not onto his face. His hand had braced against the wall. He considered the pile of fresh earth. That this tunnel suffered collapses must mean that it was maintained. Otherwise, over time it would have become blocked by a major collapse. Perhaps that's why sections of the wall had been built up with stone.

But who maintained the tunnel and why? Certainly it could not have been Castor alone.

It was something to think about other than his own impending death from returning to the carnage he had wrought and within hours of it happening. Had they even time to clear the bodies? Would he run into a crew at work or would everyone be called to defend the walls?

The answer would be learned soon enough, for the beam of wan light of the opened trapdoor was as bright as a beacon in the utter blackness. As he closed in on it, he smiled to himself.

"I'm not so afraid of the dark anymore. There's one good thing from all of this."

Evil spirits dwelling beneath the earth or in the darkest places of the world were not more fearful than what Methodios would do to him if caught. He had never seen a man with his skin flayed off before Castor, and that image would haunt his dreams forever. That was the work of human hands and human evil. In fact, given his choice, he'd rather just hide in this tunnel until the battle was settled. So much for the darkness being a source of terror.

He paused at the bottom of the ladder. The spear he had set as a trap was gone. If there was blood on the floor he could not distinguish it in the dimness. But his devious trap had likely saved him. Now as he set his feet and hands to the ladder rungs once more, he was undoing all the good work his trap had done. He drew his captured dagger and set it between his teeth as he climbed.

There was no point in caution. Either men were waiting for him or not, and he had no patience to discover which. He scurried up the ladder to pop up like a weasel from its den, head jerking side to side to take in everything in a glance.

Relief and a hint of disappointment suffused him as he realized the room was empty. Even the corpse Curio had set across the entrance was gone. A lamp sat in the corner, guttering away and likely forgotten atop the old crates and junk stacked here. He pulled up and was tempted to take the light after suffering so much darkness. It seemed brighter than it actually was. But he left it in place and crawled forward to peer out the archway.

The iron keys on the ring slid and clinked as he leaned forward, and he hurriedly set his palm over them. The cool iron pressed into his thigh as he peered down the hallway. The torture room was dark. The hallway was lit by lamps at wide intervals, leaving pockets of darkness.

Thus far he had no choices to make, but now he had to decide where to go. In fact, dressed as he was, he could pass himself off as one of King Nabis's thugs that he called auxiliary soldiers. He carried their weapons and even had a ring of keys. If no one spoke to him, he might actually walk out of this prison.

He turned to the row of cells and found one door hanging open. Now that was different from before and his heart leaped with excitement. Crouching down, he sped across the hall to back up against the door. Closing his eyes, he dared a whisper.

"Curio, are you in there? It's me."

When no answer came, he felt burning embarrassment. Of course if he hid inside, by now he would have escaped down the secret tunnel. Shaking his head, he stepped into the cell doorway. Again the darkness defeated him, but he opened the door wider. The bolts had been thrown into the room, which seemed odd. The guards would want to set the bolts beside the door to be used again. Inside smelled of rotten hay and feces. But he found nothing even with the additional light. He was about to leave when he noticed blood stains on the floor. These were fresh and sticky to his touch. They clustered by the door, as if someone had hidden right behind it.

Curio had been here, he was sure. He followed the blood out into the hallway, but the trail was only viable until reaching the room he had just come from. Then there was too much blood spread on the hallway floor to continue the trail. But Curio did not go to the tunnel. So he had gone back up this passage.

Then he was caught, Falco decided. Curio's only logical choice was to flee down that tunnel at the first possible moment. That he did not, meant he had been discovered and taken elsewhere.

Falco scratched his head, wondering why they wouldn't just bar him into one of these cells. If Methodios had anything to say about it, he would have taken Curio to the torture room. Realizing this, he rushed back to it. The dead were gone but the scent of blood and seared flesh still hung in the unmoving air. The room was empty and torture implements were splayed out everywhere and black scorch marks covered the wooden tables and bench. Castor still hung limp in death, his blood and flesh dashed at his feet where Methodious had fallen. Even the hot bar used to burn him had not been moved from where it had landed.

He crawled back toward the stairs and waited in the darkness.

But he heard no voices or sounds of activity. Drawing his sword, he climbed one step at a time until he reached the top doorway which also hung open. The guard room beyond where Methodios had traded them to the jailers was empty. The door leading into it was closed. On a nearby table was a jug of wine, cheese, and some bread. Without hesitation, Falco sheathed his sword and stuffed the food into his mouth. Forgetting everything else, he savored what he would have otherwise called stale bread and moldy cheese. He washed it down with wine little better than vinegar but relished it with a smack of his lips.

Wiping his mouth with the back of his arm, he felt sudden shame. Curio was likely getting a mouthful of hot coals while he ate and drank. But gods, he needed the food and it helped him concentrate on what he needed to do next.

The path they had followed into this room remained unclear in his memory. If Curio had not been put to torture, then he must be in the other prison where they had been held prior to crucifixion. That was not within the palace, but in a separate building on the acropolis. He knew Greeks did not believe in prisons, and instead exiled or executed their criminals. But they maintained holding cells for those awaiting sentencing. Curio must be held as a prisoner of war now that the consul had arrived. Maybe the Spartans held him to be included in any future exchange of prisoners. In any case, those cells were likely where he was, as the cells he had just quit seemed reserved for victims of torture. He patted the keys at his thigh and hoped they worked on all the locks in both prisons.

He listened at the door, both eyes pressed shut with intense concentration, and heard nothing. Stepping beyond it, he entered into a short corridor that gave way to a much wider hall. He followed it because its brightness seemed to indicate sunlight. Also, the area seemed completely abandoned.

But when he slid around another doorway into the wider hall, he found himself in a long gallery that was opened to a courtyard on his right, blocked only by a waist-high decorative fence. Directly ahead, a procession of armed men surrounding people in the center marched directly for him.

At first he wanted to sprint away, but realized no one had yet seen him as the door was recessed from the gallery and in shadow. He had nowhere to flee but back into the dungeon.

Yet as the group proceeded ahead, he glimpsed the man at the center. He had only seen him this close once before, but he could not forget that haughty, lined face.

It was King Nabis and his royal guards. And they headed directly for him.

22

With only a moment to act, Falco seized up in terror. The king and what might be his family charged down the open-air gallery ensconced in a ring of guards wearing shining mail and carrying glittering bronze shields. He would have no chance against them and their trajectory would push him right back down into the dungeon. For the moment, he stood unseen in the shadows.

What was Nabis doing here? He should be leading his men in battle against Consul Flamininus. Yet the king and all his men seemed set with grim determination and were marching directly at Falco. If he moved, he would be seen. His best chance now was to retreat and hide until the king finished whatever he planned to do in his dungeon.

Then it struck him.

Nabis and his family were escaping Sparta. It all made sense. The secret passage had been maintained by someone, and of course that could not be done without the king's knowledge. It was his own escape tunnel, leading to a river where no doubt a ship could be prepared to lead the king away to safety before any enemy could reach his palace.

Falco's eyes flicked wide at the realization. The Romans must have breached the gates and entered the city. Why else would Nabis flee? But this did not change the fact he was about to be discovered. He had to escape back into the dungeon and await the king's exit.

But in the next moment, a group of soldiers rushed out of the courtyard toward Nabis. Among them was another royal-seeming man dressed for battle. He called out to the king, halting their party in its headlong drive. There was no immediate threat from these soldiers to their king, but neither was their exchange marked with joy. The king and his guard seemed to recoil from the new arrivals who cut across the open courtyard to block Nabis's way ahead.

With the fortuitous distraction, Falco's options multiplied. Nabis shouted at the man who had cut off his progress, and his soldiers formed a wall across the gallery. If he kept his head down, he might remain unseen behind them.

He crouched low then slipped out of the shadow. The sun struck his skin, warming him instantly and eliciting fear of exposure. But he leaped the short, decorative fence, then raced along the shadows of the courtyard. The king and his troubles faded behind him, as he hewed as close to the walls of this courtyard as he could. Even though he still feared discovery, his heart lifted with excitement at having pulled out of a trap.

Various barrels, crates, and filled sacks lined the courtyard walls. These were not trash items, but things that seem staged for delivery or else immediate use elsewhere. They afforded him cover from the others in the palace grounds. He could not see them, but heard them well enough. The bass notes of speaking men penetrated the wall directly behind him. He heard shouts in the distance. But as he crouched and studied his surroundings, he did not hear the crash of battle any longer. If Rome had entered Sparta, then screams of terror from the population would shatter the sky, never mind the clamor of destruction Rome would create on its path to the acropolis.

This was too silent. Whatever engagement they had fought had ended swiftly and without Roman victory. Certainly, the Spartan king was not with his soldiers but trying to escape. To Falco, it meant Sparta was dealt a hard blow but not a final one. Nabis was a coward, as all power-mad dictators are eventually revealed to be. He feared the retribution of Rome, which might be simply to turn him over to his own people to be thrown from the same peak as his best citizens.

As satisfying as it was to think on Nabis's disgrace, it did not serve Falco's immediate needs. He realized that a Spartan soldier was far braver than his king, and more capable of driving a spear through his guts. The matter of rescuing Curio remained, and then getting themselves out of Sparta to find Varro as well. He wiped the cold sweat from his brow and focused.

The scuffle across the courtyard with the king grew louder. No one had come to blows yet, but shouts and curses were being traded. This would draw attention, and Falco could use it to escape the courtyard. Farther down the wall, a light-filled archway showed the way out. It also seemed the only way inside, and anyone coming to aid Nabis or the other faction would likely pass through it. So, he could not risk that way. However, there were points where shuttered windows broke the monotony of the courtyard walls. Yet he might be trading for greater danger if he rolled into a guard room.

In the end, he slid along the walls toward the open archway. He drew his dagger rather than his sword, and his sweaty hand clamped down on the leather-wrapped handle as he hid it behind his leg. Shadows appeared in the archway as he stepped out from a stack of barrels beside it. Fortunately, it was still dark along the wall leading to the archway, and as three men entered at a jog, Falco jumped back against the wall to slam flat against it.

The three men would have passed him, their eyes intent on the squabble ahead, but as Falco hit the wall, three pigeons perched overhead burst into flight at his sudden motion. They swooped low, aiming from the opposite wall. But this flurry of action drew the attention of the three men.

Suddenly, Falco stood in beside of them with dagger in hand. They slowed and frowned, but did not immediately attack. They were not dressed in the same armor as some of the better soldiers, like Methodios and his men. They were dirty with unkempt beards and short swords strapped to their sides.

"Nabis!" Falco said, pointing toward the king excitedly. The three then turned back toward the scene, and their attention was recaptured. They resumed stalking off toward him.

His knees buckling from the sudden release of fear, Falco watched them go. Whatever argument Nabis had with his detractors seemed to be heating up, and these three seemed like his typical thugs or freed slaves. But one of the three might have been smarter than the others, as he slowed down and turned to face Falco.

He spoke something in Greek, a command or a question. Falco was already sliding for the courtyard exit. But the thug now broke from his companions. He was muttering angrily at him, and Falco did not know what to do. He couldn't speak a word of Greek. So he held up his key ring and shook it so that the iron keys rattled. He then pointed out the archway as if he were too busy to answer.

This actually caused the thug to stop short in surprise. Falco narrowed his eyes at him, then proceeded to walk out of the archway as if this had been his plan all along. He felt a tingle at the base of spine, expecting the thug to drive his sword into his back. Yet the man only called after him, and Falco just raised a hand to wave him off as if he could not be bothered for a response.

He stepped out of the courtyard that led to a wider parade ground that was mostly empty but for pockets of men flitting about at its edges. The way out to the acropolis remained open, and while guards were posted there, they allowed people to pass without question.

So he set the keys back on his hip and continued forward.

But the thug had followed him out now, calling in a more demanding tone.

Realizing he would not be able to shake him, he looked around for a place to rid himself of the man. Beside the archway was a large cart with more of the hay bales he had seen being delivered to the front gates. Clay pots were stacked beside it. As it created an obscured pocket against the wall, Falco decided he could use it to rid himself of the thug.

He wheeled on the man, putting hands on his hips as if he had had enough of his questioning. Again the thug caught up short and changed his demeanor. He spoke more quietly, and gestured back toward the courtyard as he did. Falco shook his head violently, then pointed at the cart as if ordering him to it.

The thug followed the pointing finger in confusion. He had a heavy brow, not unlike his own, Falco mused, and it gave him an ignorant but threatening cast. A deep scar filled with shadow on his cheek and he wore the white scars of a brand on his exposed shoulder. Definitely one of Nabis's hired thugs.

He questioned Falco, who ignored him as he stalked over to the cart. He glanced at the clay pots, noticing they overflowed with pitch from beneath their lids. His act was so forcefully confident, that the thug followed him even as he questioned in Greek. Falco noted the almost pleading tone in his voice.

Once they both stepped behind the cart, Falco snatched the keys off his belt, then held them in the air. He gave them a hard shake.

"Look up here, you ignorant bastard."

The thug first looked at the keys, then glared at Falco's foreign speech.

He struck up with his dagger, plunging it into the thug's throat to the cross guard. He staggered back, both hands reflexively grabbing for the bronze blade in his neck. Falco guided him by the dagger so that he wouldn't collapse in view of others, then shoved him against the wall and yanked the dagger out with a twist.

It was his training to stab and twist on withdrawal, so that the wound would be widened and bleed more swiftly. In a battle, this was key to getting an enemy to collapse, where he was no longer a factor in the battle. But now, the hole torn in the thug's neck sprayed Falco's face and chest with gore as if he had cracked a pressured cask of wine. He recoiled from the thug, who gasped and squirmed as he slipped down the wall to die behind the wagon. But the geyser of blood had marked him, ruining any chance that he could walk out to the acropolis past the posted guards.

Stifling a curse, he stepped back from the decaying flow of blood. The puddle beneath the dead thug began to widen and would soon flow out the bottom of the cart. Thinking to sop up the spreading pool, he snatched hay from the wagon. But it came away in oily clumps and was too thick and matted to do much good.

Dripping blood from his face and wiping pitch-soaked hay from his hands, he felt as if he might as well start a bonfire and announce himself to the enemy.

He stared again at the bales of hay. These were being loaded into the buildings by the walls. It all made sense to him now.

This was the trap. The Spartans would lead the Romans into the city and then create a massive conflagration around them. The panic would disrupt the unsuspecting Romans, causing frantic retreats that would likely generate more casualties. The consul would lose half his army in a blaze of fire, and possibly his own life as well.

"They can't be serious," he whispered to himself, touching the hay bale again as if to confirm its reality. Even if concentrated along breached areas, a fire on such a scale would be hard to contain. Sparta would be consigning a huge portion of its area to ashes and likely at terrible cost to themselves. Without prepared fire breaks, all of Sparta might eventually burn.

"These damned Spartans would kill themselves before defeat. No wonder Nabis wants to flee."

Then he realized he would be trapped in the inferno along with his enemy.

Bloodied or not, only a single path led to where he wanted to go. He tore his tunic so that the worst of the blood stains hid under the ruined flap. Wiping what blood he could from his face with the backs of his arms, he stepped out confidently and made for the gate. Varro always said acting like you belonged someplace made you belong to that place. He hoped he sold the illusion of a Spartan thug as he walked toward the gates.

His pulse soared as he closed in on the two guards leaning on spears and staring out through the shadow of the archway to the brightness beyond. The gods had laid a clear path ahead, with the only other Spartans leaving the wide parade ground. He held his dagger tight to this thigh, ready to strike if he was grabbed or attacked.

Walking with swift purpose, he strode between the guards and realized why they stared ahead rather than look to him.

From high on this hill, the road spilled down into a wide area where masses of troops assembled in the shadow of the acropolis. Falco's experienced eye took in the defeat at a glance. The injured were being separated from the others. Officers did not enforce order, and formations of pikemen, their weapons set aside, milled in confusion. They had just quit the battlefield, and the gates, out of sight from here, must have closed on the Romans and condemned this war to a siege.

Yet he did not delay. Instead, he looked to the stern, low building to his left and was certain there was Curio's cell. Men stood guard there, also looking down the wide road at the sad confusion below. He shot across the two guards, confidently walking past them. Neither challenged him until he was beyond their reach. He did not understand the command, but knew they were asking him to stop.

He turned to see both of them staring after him. He also saw the bloody footprints he made through the gate.

Without another thought, he raced down the road toward the soldiers. The two guards shouted and started after him. Yet halfway down the road, they dropped back. Falco slowed as he ran, realizing they couldn't abandon their posts and he was not likely worth their time.

"Thank the gods for standing orders," he said.

But now he was nearly upon the throng of recovering Spartans. Their muttered curses, groans, coughing, and occasional maniacal screaming all brewed up into a wavering cacophony that thrummed against his eardrums. He could turn back up the hill now, but would just be handing himself over to his pursuers. Going forward seemed impossible.

Yet he seemed more like these men than the cleaner, rested men of the palace. In fact, that horrid, empty face he had seen reflected in the river might serve him well here.

So he wandered down among the enemy. In his mind he cursed himself for an utter fool. He suspected that some part of his darkest soul was hoping he would be captured and put to death. It would be easier than what lay ahead. Men stared into his eyes, not looking for him but looking for someone else. For a friend who did not return from the battle. But when he did not fulfill their hopes, the soldiers ignored him.

In fact, bloodied as he was and being slovenly dressed, many of the Spartans disdained him for a skirmisher or maybe even an auxiliary. He found himself somehow being channeled through the crowd to the edges, where the rougher and poorer men huddled together.

He was grateful to slide out of this mix of defeated and angry men into the alleys of Sparta. Yet now he was hopelessly cut off from the acropolis and the building where Curio must be held. The officers pushing through the ranks of pikemen were at last generating a semblance of order. He would not be able to pass through them again without someone trying to fit him into a unit. This was their likely rally point, right before the main road leading to Nabis's palace and the other important buildings of the acropolis. Also, it would be a highly defensible position against attack and maybe even the fires they planned to set.

So he crawled away into an alley, away from the sun and his own foolishness. He had passed among the Spartans unsuspected by anyone. It was a feat he could never imagine achieving, but ultimately it served no purpose. He hung his head, shamed at the thought of being lost and alone in this city, unable to help Curio, himself, or even the consul at this point. He wasn't even certain what he could do now.

"You blew it, Falco. Let's face it. You're not good at this sort of thing. If only it had been a stand-up fight. Or even just a cheap shot. I like cheap shots. But this sneaking around." As he crouched against a wall, he stared at his pitch- and blood-stained hands. "I'm only good for cracking skulls."

He rested in the shadow and listened to the commands of Spartan officers and the groans from their subordinates. If he remained here longer, he might be discovered, and so he slowly rose to his feet, using the rough stucco wall to brace himself.

Not knowing where to go now, he proceeded down the narrow alley. He ducked under a window, even though it was shuttered. He would have to return in darkness to reattempt Curio's rescue. He only hoped he would still be alive by then.

Varro had insisted they meet on the southern end of the acropolis in case they ever separated. Well, if this wasn't separation, then he didn't know what was. Besides, he must have had a reason for it. So he followed the abandoned streets around the base until he reached the southern side. Nabis's palace towered high overhead, casting the whole area into deep shadow.

The area was abandoned, or more likely residents were cowering in fear at what might come next. A dog barked in the distance and he did smell a cooking fire. He could not see what was special about this part of Sparta, other than it was easiest to see from nearly every location within the city.

He wanted to find a place to sleep the day through, and the houses built up against the base of the acropolis seemed to offer the best hiding places. So he studied the crossing for anyone watching before he dashed into the light to eventually reach the shadows on the other side. He did not have to act so guilty, he realized. Nothing overtly marked him as Roman. In fact, given his state others might mistake him for a deserting soldier, which could have repercussions of its own.

Yet he settled into a narrow alley behind a tall building that seemed boarded up, though he was not entirely certain if that was just precaution against invaders. He hoped no one would hear him. Once he lay down in a sandy patch and found a comfortable position, he closed his eyes which throbbed behind his lids.

Then someone spoke in Latin.

"Time to get up."

23

His eyes flicked open and a smile formed on his face before his sight could focus on the man speaking to him.

"Curio, you little shit," he said. "Don't you know you're supposed to be locked in a prison atop this rock and I'll break you out during the night?"

"It's a great plan," Curio said, his feet sliding across the gritty sand as he drew to Falco's side. "You'll have to tell me if I escape."

Falco sat up as Curio crossed out of shadow into the light. He looked no worse than when he had last seen him, except his tunic was torn and stained with dried blood splatter. His boyish face had vanished, and though he smiled with warmth he had the same hollow-eyed stare as Falco had seen in his own reflection. The felt of a beard now fringed that smile.

"I told you he would come to the south of the acropolis," Curio said.

Falco accepted his extended hand and eased onto his feet. But he looked past Curio to the shadow, where another dim shape resolved into a man who stepped forward. When he spoke, his voice was sonorous and arresting, like that of a great orator.

"So you were right. We have not wasted time after all."

He was taller than Curio, which was true for almost any man, but he stood nearly even with Falco. That was unusual. He had long, muscled limbs and pronounced features such that his face seemed carved from marble. His left brow raised over eyes so dark as to be black.

"You made a friend?" He spoke to Curio but continued to study the new man. Despite his regal cast, his Greek-style tunic was dirty, torn, and bloodied. He also had a thick crust of blood at the edge of his hairline.

"Maximus Surius," the man said, inclining his head. "I am glad you returned, Falco. Though you will soon regret that you did."

"I regret nothing," he said, looking to Curio and slapping his shoulder. "Do you have a rank, Surius? Am I to call you sir or am I to remind you that I am a centurion?"

"A soldier of a different sort," Surius said, his sheepish smile making him less commanding. "We work for a common purpose of survival. So let's forget formalities for now."

"I'll agree to that." Falco looked between Curio and Surius. "So, you two have a story? Last I saw Curio, he was fighting for his life down a hallway."

Surius turned to the building that hid them from the main streets. He looked up the two floors, where only a single window on the second floor was shuttered. Seemingly satisfied that they would not be heard, he drew both Curio and Falco closer.

"I was Castor's partner," he said.

"Ah, sorry about what happened to him," Falco said. "He was still tied to that chair when I came back."

Surius lowered his head and bit his lip. "It was hard to see, and it pains me to leave him in such a state. But there is nothing to be done for him now, other than to be sure he receives a burial that will allow his soul to rest."

"I was pushed back to the tunnel," Curio said, taking over where Surius seemed caught up in mourning. "The fight wasn't going my way, but I thought if I could get to that spear I might gain some advantage. But he was too good and had a better reach. Then as we fought, the trapdoor opened and Surius stepped out of the tunnel. He joined me against the Spartan and we killed him."

Surius roused from his thoughts. "Enemy of my enemy. I wasn't sure who Curio was, but after all I had guessed correctly. Still, when the fighting was done, your fight was still continuing down the hall. You had set a man on fire and he blocked the hallway. I took Curio here as a hostage, and dragged him into one of the cells until I could confirm his identity. I needed to get through to Castor, but didn't realize at the time he was already dead. In any case, I watched you being chased into the tunnel."

"And you didn't think to help me?"

"You're not my mission," Surius said with a shrug, "and you were a good distraction. You emptied the hall. Methodios eventually staggered out of that torture room and I was free to get Curio away with me."

"I knew you'd come back," Curio said. "Didn't have much choice about leaving you anyway. He had a dagger at my neck. Once we escaped, I told Surius to wait for you here. And look!"

"And look," Falco repeated with a grin. "What a great stroke of luck for you. But most of the men following me went back out of the tunnel. You didn't run into them, eh? And you just walked out of the palace? That's too fucking easy."

"The battle outside the wall was just finishing," Surius said. "All attention was focused there, and not on someone leaving the palace. No one cared about us, and it seems the same for you."

Falco looked at the fresh blood stains on his tunic.

"I'm a lot taller, not to mention better looking, than you two. I get more attention. I had to mix in with the regular soldiers to lose some pursuers. Turns out it was a good thing. But, Surius, were you inspecting the tunnel or something? What were you doing there?"

"He's been to see Varro!"

Curio's smile widened and he slapped Falco's shoulder.

"Was he all right?" Falco asked. "Methodios said he sent his man to look after him, but as a way to get into his favor and infiltrate the Roman camp."

"Well," Surius said, rubbing his head. "Curio is exaggerating the story somewhat. Castor contacted me and said I was to see about relocating one of the Roman operatives that had survived execution. All three of you are Fortuna's chosen, you must know."

"I know it all too well," Falco said. "And I'm afraid to have used up a lifetime of favor so early. But, what were you going to do for Varro alone?"

"I am a capable man," Surius said, a frown crossing his handsome features. "But I never got to ascertain Varro's condition. Methodios had sent his agent. He must have been watching Castor's activities to have gotten his agent in place before me. When I came to the cave entrance, I decided to watch it from across the chasm. Something seemed off, and I was not wrong. Methodios's agent emerged from the cave shortly after I got there. I knew her on sight."

"Her?" Falco folded his arms. "Methodios sent a woman?"

Surius gave a sly smile. "Who better to gain a man's trust? She is a crafty woman, capable of playing any part."

"Well, hopefully you saved Varro from her?" Falco asked, but from Curio's sad look it seemed he had not.

"I cannot just attack Methodios's agents. That's not how this game is played. But in the end, it didn't matter. The precipice where I had hidden gave way, and I fell backward into a pit. I struck my head and was unconscious for at least a day, and dazed after that. When I finally had my wits, I hurried back to report to Castor. The rest you know."

Falco narrowed his eyes at this Surius fellow. He did have a head injury, but it might not have happened as he described. Falco was tempted to comment on how well he was doing for a man who had been barely alive for several days in the wild. But rather than challenge the story, he decided to be careful around him for now.

"Enough of the introductions," Falco said. "We've got to get out of here and warn the consul of the trap set for him, then get over to relieve Varro of the enemy he doesn't realize is hovering over him. In fact, I suggest we split this duty so we don't waste time. Surius, do you think Methodios's agent will try to kill Varro?"

"She should follow whatever orders she was issued. But she'll be smart enough to adjust plans to any changes. Namely, if we charge in on her then your man is going to become a hostage rather quickly. But in any case, as much as I'm sorry to say it, one man is not as important as the entire Roman army. There lies our duty."

While Falco did not disagree, it stung him to be corrected on understanding his duty. But once more, in an effort to cooperate, he bit down on his words.

"We know our duty," Curio said. "But you can't fault us. If that was Castor instead of Varro, what would you do?"

Surius raised both hands. "Peace, brothers. I'm just focusing us on what you've made all the sacrifices for. You were supposed to start an uprising against Nabis, and get the gates opened for an easy victory."

"Even if we open the gates," Falco said, "Nabis has set a suicide trap. I assume you've figured it out as well. All those pitch-soaked bales?"

Curio clapped his hands together. "They're stuffing the buildings around the walls with it. They'll burn the city down that way."

"Along with our army," Falco said. "Even if that's madness."

"Fire is a dangerous weapon," Surius said. "But an effective one. They only need to start enough fires to make the Romans believe they are trapped in the flames. Once the infantry penetrates into the streets, they'll never be able to see the extent of the fire. The bales are set to throw more smoke than fire. The buildings might burn and the fire might spread. But not all of Sparta will be consumed. Yet, if the Romans try to retreat out of fear, think of the losses they would sustain. Their power would be broken, and Nabis could settle in for a long siege while Rome has to send for replacements."

Falco thought back to his own century. He had not been in command for long, but he had pride in his men. They were young hastati, mostly green and trusting their lives to him. He shoved away thoughts of those men being trampled in a mad rush down a crowded Spartan street filled with black smoke. He did not need to imagine it for long to understand how Sparta could exploit that chaos.

"King Nabis is trying to escape through the tunnel," Falco said. "If he does, then the Spartans will crumble. Some men were trying to stop him, and when I left it seemed more of his thugs were joining him. Maybe we just need to wait for his authority to fall apart."

Yet Surius was already shaking his head.

"Nabis has ever been eager to use his tunnel, but now is not the time. That group you saw must have been led by Pythagoras, the overall commander of his army. As long as he lives, he will fight if there is any chance. So we must ensure Sparta breaks as fast as possible."

"Then we open the gates," Falco said. "And let our boys inside. Once they reach the heart of the city, it will be all over."

Surius nodded. "That is my thought as well. Except, we are but three men and the gate is guarded more heavily than ever."

Curio and Surius both looked at Falco as if he should have an answer to this question.

"Well, then we'll have to call for help." As his idea formed, he paused to increase the drama of it. Curio's eyes widened and he leaned forward. Surius just frowned at him as if impatient to hear more.

"It's obvious what to do. Tonight, we start the fires for the Spartans. Our side will see the flames and the consul will know he must attack into that confusion. That's when we enter the gatehouse and capture it."

"A night attack?" Surius asked, tilting his head to the side. "That is risky."

"Not when the city is well lit," Falco said with a smirk. "Besides, are you a soldier? I'm telling you, the consul wants this city to fall fast. If his enemy is distracted, then he'll take the initiative. All we have to do is keep the fires burning until the consul arrives. Then we capture the gates and warn him of the remaining trap. It will be a complete success."

While Surius raised his brow at the claim, Curio again clapped Falco's shoulder.

"Good idea, sir. We're going to finally give this city what it deserves."

"The both of you are talking as if we won't have opposition. The firetraps will certainly be watched so they aren't accidentally ignited. The gatehouse will be packed with men even if there are fires."

"You're a good fighter," Falco said. "You got that man off Curio. What are you afraid of? Trust your sword and the man at your side. We're trained for battle, and killing is the one thing we excel at."

"I don't doubt it," Surius said, tightening his folded arms. "But I'm not trained. I am an opportunist and not a soldier."

"There will be room for both styles," Falco said. "Now, we better rest while we can. It's going to be a long night."

"We stole some onions and wine," Curio said brightly. "We'll have a good meal and a quick nap."

"Raw onions," Falco said with a grimace. "Never thought the day would come when my mouth watered at the thought. Bring me to your hiding place and let's eat."

Their spot was not materially different from Falco's other than they had a clutch of onions and a skin of wine secreted in the shell of an old crate. All three of them ate like the starving men they were and left nothing at the end of their simple meal. Falco and the others tried to sleep in the shadows of the quiet buildings under the acropolis. Surius estimated they were directly below the temple to Minerva, or Athena as the Spartans called her. Falco whispered a prayer to her, both for protection while they slept and for wisdom.

After hours of fitful sleep, he found himself staring into the darkness of night. Perhaps he had slept more than he thought, but he did not feel rested. The onions shifted like a lead weight in his stomach as he sat up then belched the sharp taste of them. Curio was already leaning against the building wall opposite and Surius was gone.

"I figured you could sleep some more," Curio said. "You were kicking and crying and moaning. Once that stopped, it looked like you finally got real rest."

"There's not going to be real rest for a while yet," Falco said. "We're not done when Sparta falls. We've got to reach Varro. When Methodios's agent sees Sparta has collapsed, maybe she'll just kill him and escape."

"To where?" Curio asked. "She's just a woman, even if she's Methodios's agent. She'll have a rough life on her own. No, she'll want to take Varro back to the camp. She doesn't know about us yet or that Surius can identify her. Varro is safe."

Falco nodded, but he did not agree. No one was safe in an enemy's hands. Varro's life was only useful to a point, and if the agent decided his use was through then he'd die easily. She could feed him poison but call it medicine, and Varro would believe it.

"Where is Surius?"

"He went to scout the best locations, and to find a source of fire. We've got no way to make one on our own. Say, have you thought about how we'll move around with an open flame from place to place? That's even beyond my talents."

"I'm not like Varro," Falco said, violently scratching his head. "I don't have an answer for everything."

"He doesn't, either." Curio groaned as he stood. "Well, we better keep the fire small and just move fast. That's the best we can do."

They stretched and strapped on their swords. Falco checked that his was loose in the sheath. Surius returned out of the darkness, his face grim.

"There are five main points where the bales have been set, including by the front gate. All the lamps have been extinguished so that the areas are in total darkness. Three or four auxiliaries guard each point, probably just a precaution against an accidental fire. They should be easy to overcome."

"Sounds like a lazy swim in the Tiber," Falco said.

"Well, don't count on anything beyond the first blaze," Surius said. "There are plenty of soldiers encamped by the walls."

"That's just what we want. Make them choose between defending their walls or stopping a fire." Falco patted his sword. "Let's cut our way into history."

"We'll not be remembered for this," Curio said.

"Only good-looking heroes like me are remembered," Falco said. "Poor bastards like you just get to follow along."

Surius frowned but said nothing as he led them through dark streets and back ways. It was a long path to the northern walls.

Along the way he had procured an unlit streetlamp, one of the many bronze lamps that lit the nighttime streets in happier days. Such a lamp would not light without another flame to feed it.

"You've not said where the fire will come from," Falco said.

As they reached the first building, Surius paused in an alleyway. He drew them close to speak low.

"The lamp will help us carry a flame from location to location. But lighting it will be difficult. We'll have to capture a burning torch or other open flame." He glanced out the alley toward the walls. "In that tower, there should be a lamp or brazier. You two will have to get inside then bring the fire out. Once it is started, we can move on to the next point."

Falco stared out of the alley, and Curio laughed.

"No wonder this feels so familiar, this is where we first climbed the walls. We've fought these men before."

"There's five of them in there," Falco said. "Maybe more now that they'll be watching the Roman camp. There's two of us."

"Feels like good odds to me," Curio said.

"Right, then let's not wait to get this siege underway. We wouldn't want the consul to get over these walls without our help. Surius, you'll watch our backs and be ready to take whatever we come running with."

The three men nodded to each other. Falco and Curio drew their swords with a slow hiss of the blade against the sheaths.

"Gods go with you both," Surius said.

Then they swooped out of hiding for the tower door.

24

Falco felt as if he were flying. He bent at the waist, sword readied, following Curio through the thin darkness. Only a half-moon lit the sky, hardly enough for clear sight, and the sea of stars sparkled over the city. The gods would have a show tonight, he guessed, and they would see it clearly through the cloudless sky. His bare feet, cut and bruised from so much rough ground, slid easily across the gritty, packed dirt of the alleyways by the wall. Houses had not been built right up to them as in some cities, but kept enough distance that Falco feared discovery while making the short run.

But Curio dashed to the side of the door and flattened himself against it. His eyes were still puffy and swollen from his numerous beatings. Nevertheless, they were wide now and sparkling with excitement. He held his sword back and prepared to follow Falco into the tower.

This was not a moment for stealth. What he needed was swift and stark terror, to burst among his enemies and slaughter them before they could cry out. So rather than test the door or try to slip inside through some subterfuge, he charged at it.

He made the final strides as long as his legs could stretch, then leaped into the air to plant his heel into the wooden slats. The force shook up his legs, but the door was not bolted, and so smashed inward. Falco crashed through into the darkened room.

Three men slept there, off-duty guards who only now shook awake at Falco's explosive entry. It was little better than murder, but Falco stuck the first man he found through his neck. He crashed past a table to another who was fumbling for his sword leaning against the tiny wooden bed frame. Again, Falco stabbed true and ran the enemy through his ribs.

The final man could barely stand before Curio had slipped inside and finished him. When Falco looked to his short companion, the body of his enemy curled at his feet.

There was no light here, but a square yellow outline glowed from the next floor up. Falco roughly wiped his sword on a bedsheet, sheathed it, then drew his dagger. With his larger size, he was the better candidate to climb up the ladder first. Curio would follow on and pick up anyone at his back.

Brows furrowed in concentration, he jumped onto the ladder and sped up to the trapdoor. Again, lacking all subtlety he bashed it open with his palm then shoved into the bright opening.

Two more men were on this middle floor. They were bent over their own chores, each seated on opposite sides. They might have been chatting about the noise from below when Falco burst among them.

He leaped for the first man he saw. Unfortunately, he was polishing his sword and brought it up to block Falco's initial thrust. The dagger turned aside against the larger blade. But Falco roared and used his size to crash into the man's reach, denying him any use for his longer weapon. They fell against the wall, as Falco's dagger stitched into the enemy's side. He felt the hot blood welling up over his hands as he clutched the enemy to him. The Spartan groaned and went limp. Falco shoved back to find Curio wrestling with the other man. Somehow he had been disarmed and now held against the Spartan's attack by jumping behind a table.

A large clay lamp sat on it, and as Curio dodged out of the way he struck the table and nearly tipped it over. Falco let out a scream, more for fear of losing the lamp than danger to Curio.

The confused Spartan shouted for help, and Falco heard feet thumping overhead. They had to get out now.

"Get the lamp," he shouted at Curio. "I'll hold them off."

Curio dodged another strike with the table between him and the Spartan. But now that Falco had recovered, the man realized he was outmatched.

He flipped the table in the same moment Curio snatched the lamp away. Mugs, wooden plates, and a scattering of coins shot at them, achieving nothing.

But the Spartan used the table like a ram, battering Curio backwards into the opened trapdoor. He plunged through, dropping the lamp and vanishing from Falco's sight.

Cursing, Falco slid forward with dagger in hand. While the ploy had relieved the Spartan of Curio's threat, it had yielded space for Falco to get into his reach with his bloodied dagger.

"Here's a message from Rome!"

Falco rammed the dagger into the Spartan's ribs as he twisted to face him. The flesh sucked at the blade, and Falco let him fall back with it still quivering in his side. He collapsed against the wall, streaking red blood down its length as he slumped to the floor.

The trapdoor above opened and men shouted down.

He looked to the trapdoor below and found Curio hanging on with both hands while he tried to get his legs onto the ladder. Below him, brilliant yellow light spread into the darkness.

"Shit, that's not how I imagined us getting a flame."

"My feet are going to burn!" Curio shouted, though to Falco the flames seemed too low to harm him.

"Stop the acrobatics. We need to get out."

Falco grabbed Curio's wrists and let him dangle before safely dropping below. But as soon as he hit the bottom, he howled with the terror of the flames.

"It's burning up down here."

"Get back to Surius. Start the fires!"

Then Falco spun around to the sounds of men thumping to the floor behind him. The first man was strong and dark haired and his wild eyes gleamed with the light now shooting up from the floor below. As smoke began to filter up through the floorboards, those eyes grew wider.

"Sorry about the mess," Falco said. "Now out of my way."

The horrified Spartan held a short sword at his side. But his surprise cost him the fraction of time Falco needed to hurl into him. The Spartan had a moment to shout to his companions on the third floor before he stumbled backward.

They collapsed atop one of the dead Spartans, and both slammed to the wood floor. Smoke now chugged through the gaps and Falco could feel the heat. He slammed his fist into the Spartan's nose, flattening it against his face. The spurt of blood and snot covered his knuckles as he struck again, harder still. His superior size nullified the Spartan's better weapon. In two more punches, Falco beat him into unconsciousness.

Leaping to his feet, the floorboards felt hot on his bare soles. Smoke clogged the tower and blinded him. He heard heavy thuds on the wood ceiling. The men above were abandoning the tower. He could not go down, and this room was soon to be consumed with fire.

Burning alive was no choice. He stole the dagger from his most recent victim, then padded up the ladder. Each step up brought cool relief from the crackling flames growing below.

"I wanted a fire," he muttered. "So I got a fire."

Even though the top floor was not yet aflame, the guard station was thick with black smoke. Falco's eyes burned and tears flowed. His lungs drew heat but no air, and he doubled over choking. Within moments, his head began to swim and he felt as if he might faint. The air was clearer on the floor and he sucked at it with all the desperation of a suffocating man. A door hung open and smoke rushed out. He crawled for the exit.

When he rolled out of the door, coughing and blind with tears, he braced for the inevitable stab from his enemy's sword.

But he found that no one was on this side of the tower. With the blessing of the gods, he had gone out the opposite door from the Spartans. He scrabbled to his feet, staggering away from the smoke-spewing tower. He heard alarm horns and men shouting.

Down the end of the tower men rushed toward him.

There was no escape now. Already the light of uncontrolled fire shined from the doorway he had just exited. A rectangle of dancing yellow light reached to his feet. He leaned against the walls, feeling as if he might fall over the sides. He glanced out into the darkness.

Far across the field the ordered fires of the Roman and Aetolian camps glittered in the darkness. The sight of so many of his own kind, even if only unnamed points of light in the black, lifted his heart. Never had he seen his own side from the viewpoint of an enemy. How did anyone have the arrogance to stand against Rome in her full might?

But the glory of the moment curled away on the streamers of smoke flowing from the tower. The heat again licked at his side and he realized he stood too close. He would rather give himself to the enemy than burn.

As he pushed away from the wall to raise his hands in surrender, he collapsed. He fell into the corner of the parapet, all the energy of the moment burned off just as the flames consumed the wood of the tower.

But the Spartans rushed past him. As they did, their panicked voices shouting to each other, he felt the cool splash of water on his shoulder.

He looked up and found more men arriving with buckets. They came from the tower to make a vain attempt to douse the fire. Perhaps a dozen men had mobilized to the call, and they were more concerned with the fire than Falco lying at their feet.

In fact, Falco was now covered in sooty residue. The blood on his tunic and flesh vanished into the gray of its coating. He looked up at Spartans running past him. Some shouted disdainfully at him. At first he did not understand. But then one hauled him up and shoved him at the other tower.

They wanted him to join the brigade line forming to bring water to the fire. To them, he might have looked like one of their own to have survived the fire. On this side of the burning tower, the other Spartans could not correct their companions' error.

So he nodded and ran past the men charging at him with pale faces and buckets of water. He did not dare meet their eyes. But once more his poor condition made him seem like one of the rabble so common to Nabis's army.

As he jogged along the parapet, he glanced toward the Roman camp. It seemed placid amid so much chaos. But Falco understood what he was looking at and knew where to look.

He saw one fast-moving point of orange light, a messenger running with a torch. That light moved in a straight line down the center road of the camp, and was headed to headquarters. No doubt, he was bringing a message of the fire spotted on the Spartan walls.

When the consul received this news, his interest would be piqued. He would instruct his men to watch for developments. Then, as other locations went up in flames, he would order his men assembled. He would assume the rebellion he wanted had begun and that Sparta was ripe to be plucked.

Before he reached the door, he glanced into the city to see if Curio and Surius had started the fire in the houses. From this vantage he could not tell and he could not delay for a better view. If anyone questioned him then his ruse was over.

Instead, he vanished into the cool guard room of the next closest tower. Spartans were struggling up the ladders. But they were not bringing water, and instead carried empty buckets and coils of ropes. Falco realized they were going to deploy these from the walls to haul water to the tower, as getting it up ladders was impossible. The first men must have been using their own personal stores.

A small man grabbed him by the arm and spoke hurriedly to him, then slapped his back in the universal signal for a soldier to move out. Falco gave a sharp nod and started down the ladder. The man shouted after him, but he crashed down against the other climbing up.

The confusion aggravated them, and curses were shared. But they stopped when they saw him covered in smoke and let him pass down the two floors to the base of the tower. He assumed they considered him a casualty, and so he just staggered out as if barely alive. It was not far from an act.

The bright lights to his right caught his eye. The tower was truly ablaze, with flames shooting out of every opening and the wooden roof now surrounded in a haze of orange light. Men swarmed to the tower, soldiers and citizens both, and seemed to make no progress against the tower base.

Yet the actual fire he had nearly died for was not lit.

He searched for either Curio or Surius, but found no one near the houses. In fact, even the guards there had left their posts to help with the tower fire. He ran across the stream of men headed to the blaze from other encampments. With so much focus, the

Spartans would extinguish it, and if they did, then the consul might not be encouraged to attack. Fires were a constant threat in large cities like Sparta, and each one had its own means of firefighting. The Spartan system seemed effective, to Falco's dismay.

When he arrived to the darkened houses, he could smell the pitch over the bitter scent of the larger fire just behind him.

He heard Curio call out to him, and he followed the sound of his name to meet with both him and Surius behind the house. They huddled over a small, burning lamp.

"You're alive," Curio said without surprise. "You look like an old campfire."

"Glad you made it out, too," Falco said. Then he pointed to the lamp. "Why isn't this place burning?"

Surius shook his head. "This is not enough to get a fire going. We've tried and tried, but the fires burn out. We need a larger flame."

"New plan," Falco said, drawing them closer. "We can't start a fire here anyway. The consul saw the burning tower. I saw a messenger's torch headed for headquarters. We need to get another fire underway before this one is extinguished. If we start it here, all the firefighters are just two streets over. So let's get to the one by the main gates, as far from here as we can go. We'll first get our own brands lit, then we'll get the bigger fire going."

No one spoke as they threaded the dark streets. They kept the lamp flame between them and contained its light with their bodies. Were it not for the urgency of the tower fire they had inadvertently set, they might have been caught. At last, they came to the row of buildings that faced the wide-open space behind the main gates. No lamps or torches lit this area as they normally would. With the potential for a major fire so near to the gate, they had sensibly kept open flames away.

They crouched in the darkness, waiting for the motions of the guards to reveal their positions. While he waited, Falco imagined all the ways the Spartan plan could go wrong. Still, it was a devious trap and Nabis did not care for his people. He would be a king of ashes rather than a surrender to Rome. Fortunately for him, as far as Falco understood, Rome wanted Sparta mostly intact. If the consul shot flaming ammunition from his onagers into the city, Sparta would defeat itself.

At last the few guards surrounding this location were all accounted for. They mostly wandered around and craned to see the bright light of the tower fire. Falco thought he recognized some of their profiles from his few hours serving in the auxiliary guard.

Without words, the three of them elected to fan out and each eliminate guards as they could. Falco was soon alone, sliding along the wall and advancing on a reed-thin man who held his hand to the back of his neck as he stared at the orange glow over the rooftops. He collapsed with a dagger in his back and Falco's hand clamped over his mouth.

Within minutes, he was again advancing on Curio, who was moving toward him. They had taken out the guards, and Surius carried the lantern into one of the houses. Falco and Curio followed.

Inside had been stuffed with pitch-soaked hay bales. With a strong heat source, such as from several torches, this place would burn up in moments. He imagined columns of Romans streaming ahead, eyes fixed on their destination, then flames exploding all around. Even though it was not a large area the terror would be consuming. Black smoke and yellow flames would drive men to panic while centurions and optiones tried to maintain order, if they could marshal their own primal fears.

They gathered hay into clumps to form makeshift brands. These were easier to catch flame and soon they each held brands that shed twisting flame and oily black smoke. Yet it burned swiftly and they rushed to touch multiple points around the interior of the single-room house. Falco had to throw his brand aside when it threatened to scorch his hands.

But the fire had caught and was already racing along in a bright curtain through the room.

"To the next house," Curio shouted. "Once both sides are aflame, our work is done."

They raced across the street, where Falco saw the lump of a corpse of one guard lying in the middle. By the time the next fire started, the other house was engulfed. A hot wind formed between the two sides of the street, and flaming ash swirled all around them.

"We did it!" Falco shouted. "Onto the next trap."

As they fled the blazing street, they shot around a corner to escape the racing flames and ran headlong into a column of soldiers. Both sides stopped short in surprise, yards away from each other.

Sparta was no longer asleep to the danger within it.

What seemed an officer from his long black helmet crest pointed at them and shouted. The front rank of soldiers raised javelins and threw.

25

The javelins were pale gold in the combined light of the half-moon and the raging fires behind them. They whistled in an overhead arc. Falco raised his shield arm out of instinct and Curio did as well. While he lacked the comforting weight of his scutum, that he and Curio both crouched had saved their lives. Falco felt the clip of a javelin speed over his head and Curio yelped as one grazed his shoulder.

Surius, however, was not a soldier. He tried to run backward from the Spartans, and a javelin pierced his thigh. He screamed then collapsed onto Falco.

"Fuck!"

This was Falco's most concise order. It meant run for your life, and Curio did not hesitate to obey. He shot ahead and to the right, ducking into an alley.

Falco swept Surius off his feet and ran back the way he had come, toward the fire.

Surius screamed and his blood pattered down Falco's legs as he ran with him. Were it not for abject terror, he could not have found the strength to carry the Roman spy. He had no good reason to save him, other than Falco needed as many friends as he could make in enemy territory. So while he wailed and squirmed to grab his leg, Falco clasped him tight and sprinted away into the burning streets.

"Where are you going?" Surius's screaming stopped as he looked around.

Heat licked at Falco as he ran down the street narrowed by flames on either side.

"Somewhere they won't follow."

"We're going to burn to death!"

He wanted to shout him to silence, but the intense heat stole the breath from his lungs. Indeed, the Spartans had chosen to let him run to his doom and did not follow. They were far smarter than he was. But he could think of no other way to carry Surius and lose a column of pursuing Spartans.

Tears sprang from his eyes and his skin felt as if it were peeling back from his face. The flames were not close, but as buildings collapsed they shot bright sparks into the air that settled on him. Even as he was coming to the other side where the flames wreathed the exit to the cooler darkness beyond, he felt the burn at his shoulder.

"You're on fire!"

Surius, despite bleeding terribly from his thigh, tried to kick himself free.

The flames bit into his right shoulder and he now felt it on his ear as well.

Yet he cleared the end, sprinting across the way. He dropped Surius, likely killing him after all he had endured to save him, then began batting at the flames on his shoulder.

Curio leaped out of nowhere, slapping at the fire and finally tearing away the tunic. Falco ripped the rest of it away, screaming in agony as he did. The burn felt unlike any pain he had ever endured. Yet the flames were out by the time the section of tunic hit the street.

"They've turned back to the fire," Curio said, his shoulder bleeding from where the javelin had scored it. "They're not really after us. You ran into the fire? What were you thinking?"

"Fuck, Curio, I was thinking of escape. I couldn't outrun them while carrying another man."

"But running into a fire?"

Both turned to Surius, who lay quiet now with both hands clamped to his thigh. The javelin had pierced the meat of his leg and protruded from the hamstring. Judging from the flow of blood, his artery had not been cut. Yet, they could not risk removing the javelin.

"Surius, we're going to have to hide you around here. We'll come for you when we're done."

His eyes flicked open. "You're abandoning me?"

"Do you remember saying one man was not as important as the whole Roman army? It's true for you as well. We're opening the gates next. Sparta must fall tonight. The consul will come."

The burn on his shoulder felt as if the skin would tear when he and Curio lifted Surius. He noticed Curio staring at the burn as they hefted the spy off the ground. But he did not want to look at it yet. Seeing a wound only made if feel more painful, and he had more work ahead if he wanted to survive the night.

Surius screamed again, and Falco winced at it. Yet the roar of the fire and the shouting of the responding Spartans masked it, or so he hoped. They hauled him into an alley across the street, down to the next street, and then into another building. The area had been abandoned by the original owners. Nothing of value was left inside, including any furniture. Only a few dirty rags and assorted junk were scattered on the floor. A rat darted away at their sudden entrance. They set Surius on the floor at the center of the single-room dwelling.

"I'll wrap his leg," Curio said as Surius draped his arm across his eyes and moaned. "But I don't know what to do about your shoulder. It looks cooked."

"I can still hold a sword," Falco said. "And I can bear the pain. I'm not like those rich calvary men. I'll make it."

Falco enjoyed deriding the cavalry as spoiled children of the wealthy, even when he knew they were as brave as any infantryman and suffered the same hardships.

Curio nodded, then used strips cut from the discarded cloth to bind the area around the wound. Surius hissed and gritted his teeth until it was over.

"That will slow the bleeding," Curio said, leaning back and wiping his brow.

"This is too close to the fire," Surius said. "You're leaving me to burn."

"We'll come back for you," Falco said. "The wind is not blowing this way. Besides, what good is it carrying you around to other dangers? Listen, I don't forget my friends. I will come back as soon as we've opened the gates and the consul arrives."

Surius lifted his forearm from his eyes and fixed them on Falco. "I've no choice except to take your word. But I don't have faith in it."

"Then you'll be doubly happy to see me again," Falco said. "Now, we've got more chaos to create."

He and Curio left Surius in the abandoned house, stepping back into the chaos of Sparta. Horns blasted from all around and shouts reached into the sky. Now two orange blooms reached into the night sky above Sparta. If he could start another, the consul would not fail to take advantage.

They raced across the length of walls to where they expected to find another of the trapped buildings set by areas where the Romans might breach the walls.

But now the Spartan army had mobilized to the danger. A fire in a tower might have been an unfortunate accident, but a second fire in one of their trap zones ruled out chance.

Their advantage lay in the congested and winding streets in these poorer sections of Sparta, where they could easily duck into shadows thickened by the night. For the moment, they remained hidden, and as Falco had shown, they might not know him for an enemy even if spotted.

Soldiers now encircled the trapped zone, and more marched down the streets. The tower fire was easier to see from this vantage and bright flames still licked up into the sky over the walls. He could not see any of the fire brigades at work, but he was masked from their sight.

"We can't get past them here," Curio said. "I'm sure any other trap is guarded just as heavily. What do we do now?"

Falco shrugged. "I'm not sure if the consul will come just for a few fires that might go out any time."

"But you just told Surius that the consul would definitely come?"

"How long have we known each other, Curio? I was just telling him that to keep his spirits up. How do I know if the consul will come? He should, but then maybe he's made a deal with the Spartans already. I've been a little busy to keep up on the latest news."

They stared longer at the Spartans rushing around the streets. One file of soldiers stomped toward them, forcing a retreat out of sight. The Spartans made cursory glances into the alleyways as they passed.

"We should get the gate open," Falco said. "Even if we can't keep it open, the advance scouts will see someone is working for them on the inside. The consul will know it is us, and he'll be encouraged to attack. That's the best I can think of. If setting a tower and a city block on fire is not enough to get his attention, I'm out of ideas."

Both of them swept back down the darkness of the alleyways

and emerged onto a street empty of patrols. They worked back along the path they had come, their steps ever more confident for both their growing knowledge of the streets and their successes in remaining unseen.

But as they ducked into an alley, they heard a voice shout after them and a shrill blast of a horn.

"How did they know it was us?" Falco asked as he and Curio began to run.

Yet the answer was simple enough. By now, they were searching for men who looked as if they had been in a fire. Falco was blackened with soot and Curio had been coated as well. They might have crossed into a patch of moonlight, or else someone had followed them a distance to confirm their identity. No matter the reason, they were found out.

They burst onto the next street, both pausing to locate the next alley to lead them back toward Surius and the gate area.

A column of a dozen Spartans with round shields and spears lowered rushed to cut them off, forcing them to retreat up the street and toward the wall.

Their feet slapped hard against the streets. Falco felt every strike of his heel against the dirt as he fled, the shock riding up his torso and jolting the burn at his shoulder. The weight of the sword at his side felt as if it dragged against him. The Spartans gave chase, calling out for blood.

They emptied into another crossroads, and found two more columns converging on their position. The column at their left sounded a horn again, and the lead soldiers pointed at them. The blue moonlight and dull glow of orange fire painted them for their enemies. Falco cursed and jumbled up against Curio as both turned to escape down the only street remaining open.

And they ran into yet another column.

They were boxed into a T-shaped intersection, with high buildings to their left whose windows and doors were boarded up.

On all other sides, columns of Spartans raced down the streets. Both of them jogged to a halt and drew their swords. The only chance Falco could think of was to escape through the buildings. But they would have no time to pry away the boards. They were trapped.

"Curio, we really did well for a while, didn't we?"

"We did," he said. "But I guess it couldn't go our way forever."

"It never does. We got a few more days of life. We really should've died on those boards."

"Really? Feels like a hundred years."

"Well, maybe like a week. I don't know anymore. But I think here's where we end up staring at our guts in our hands just before we die."

"Don't paint me such a clear picture, Falco."

The Spartans on all three sides fell into crouches with shields forming a wall and spear points gleaming from between them.

To Falco, it seemed an extravagant gesture for the capture of two men. Yet, the Spartans could not be sure who else was near or what tricks they had prepared. He smiled grimly, tightening his grip on the short sword. He would be lucky to get under all those spears and nick one of them in the shins before he was brought down. But he was prepared to try.

"I'll take the east column," Falco said. "And you take the west column. Then we'll take down the center column together. That's about twenty men each. Seems fair."

"Don't make me laugh before I die. I don't want someone to find my corpse with a smile on my face. That'd be awkward."

"Definitely poor manners."

The Spartans saw that both intended to fight. One of the officers shouted at his soldiers, and all three columns resumed their jog forward with their spears extended.

Without a shield on his arm, Falco felt as if he were naked. The burn on his shoulder vanished into the overwhelming fear of death. Getting speared all over his body would hurt more than that shoulder. But he still refused to look at it. Instead, sweat rolled into his eyes and his heart thundered as the Spartans' sandals clomped down the streets.

Random memories flooded his mind. He thought of his drunk father throwing plates at his mother. He remembered hating Varro for his perfect family and tormenting him. He regretted that. He recalled watching tadpoles in the brook near his home. All manner of mundane memories sped past in a blur.

This was it, he decided. The spears gleamed. Curio butted up behind him.

"At least we won't be stabbed in the back," he said, and Curio chuckled.

Then a deafening crash exploded overhead.

The force of it blew him sideways, as timbers, splinters, and sharp debris showered over him. The Spartans screamed as well and vanished into a wave of dust.

The building on the left burst into a cloud and a massive stone careened out of it to plow down the street into the center column. The crash of the boulder into their bronze shields and their horrified screams mingled with the snap of bone and spear. Falco landed on hands and knees, his palm over the handle of his sword. He spit dust and squinted at the column.

It had vanished into the swirling brown crowd, but voices moaned and cried. The Spartans he could see lay still, crushed or bashed into silence.

Before he could say more, another two-floor home next to the destroyed building groaned and collapsed into itself, dumping its roof tiles in a shrill hiss and then folding into a jumble of timbers. He and Curio both scurried away from the structure, which now seemed like a skeletal hand reaching up behind the wall of dust left from its destruction.

Then another crash came from the wall. Falco and Curio both looked up to find the source.

The flaming tower top shattered into a spray of burning wreckage, sending trails of glowing and smoking embers streaking into the night. The fresh infusion of air into the tower caused the flames to roar higher even as men fell screaming from the walls.

"Onagers!" Falco shouted. "The consul is coming!"

All along the wall he heard the volleys of onager shot crashing into the parapets. Pulverized stone bloomed into clouds to shroud the wall and men plummeted out of sight. Horns sounded and shouts went up in every direction.

The remaining two columns of Spartans had both flattened out across the street from the stray onager hit. The center column had taken the unlucky strike and were either dead or fleeing. The other two columns looked to where the horns blared.

One officer stood then dispatched six men to handle Curio and Falco while the rest rushed away to answer the calls of their commanders.

Amid the settling dust, Falco and Curio stood. They were still outnumbered three to one, yet the men assigned to bring them down did not seem pleased with their orders.

"Looks like our boys opened the way," Falco said.

Without another word, they both ran down the now opened street. They leaped dead bodies as they darted away from the Spartans' lackadaisical pursuit. Falco hurdled a decapitated soldier and dodged another who gritted his teeth against a crushed leg. Others seemed to have done nothing more than lie down in the street. The huge stone had rolled to a halt halfway down the street, and Falco slapped it with a smile as he raced beyond it.

They cut into alleyways and the Spartans followed. But once he and Curio were lost to the darkness, blindly charging ahead with one hand on the alley walls for guidance, they surrendered the chase.

"Not a dedicated bunch," Falco said as he jogged to a stop, hands on his knees. He gulped his breath, feeling his legs trembling from the exertion and fear.

As they caught their breath, the deep thud of onager fire against the wall shook the night. Falco knew they would target the towers where Spartans maintained their own war machines. The bombardment was also likely covering the army's advance to walls.

"That rock could've taken our heads off," Curio said once he recovered his breath.

"No chance," he said. "We're Romans. The rocks will just bounce off us."

Curio laughed as another boulder slammed down among the houses where they sheltered. Falco heard it tearing through the night sky as a faint whine and had enough time to yank Curio out into the street with him to avoid disaster.

When the boulder struck the ground, the jolt sent both of them off their feet into the middle of the road. The impacted buildings exploded into splinters as if Jupiter himself was dragging his finger in a line through them. Falco heard the boulder slam against something then saw it spin into the air to once more crash down amid the buildings.

Curio picked splinters out of his tunic and stared wide-eyed at Falco.

"To the gates," he said. "We'll be safer there."

They made a headlong rush through the empty streets. Falco realized the Romans were also directing the onagers at the fire, probably in hopes of spreading it.

Their path took them close to the second fire they had set. More onager shots howled out of the night and crashed down into streets and buildings, the stones bouncing like children's toys and leaving destruction in their wake. The fire to their right blazed out of control, with massive clouds of black smoke smothering the area.

This forced them to go wider than they had hoped, but to do otherwise would either subject them to fire or the Spartans swarming the areas, for streams of citizens were now rushing toward the blaze to either relieve or aid the soldiers already fighting the fires.

At last, they arrived at the gates.

The Spartans had not yet come to reinforce it. Instead, they were swarming up the walls on ladders to lend their defenses against an attempt by the Romans to scale them. The gate seemed as if it had been forgotten.

"Well," Falco said to Curio as the two hugged the last shadow between them and the open area before the gate. "This is it. Our last duty. We act now, and end this tonight. Are you ready?"

He looked to Curio, who now was nearly as black as the shadow that contained him. His eyes seemed unnaturally bright as he stared back.

"For the glory of Rome," he whispered.

"Right then." Falco stood from his crouch and faced the gate. "For the glory of Rome."

26

Falco led a mad dash across the open space between the well-lit gates and the comforting shadow of the last row of buildings to provide cover. But at this point, being covered in soot no longer marked them as infiltrators. If anyone saw them running, they would likely be judged messengers dispatched to the gatehouse.

When he and Curio crashed against the gatehouse walls, he felt the rough coolness of the stone bricks as a welcomed relief. His shoulder burned as if his flesh still touched flame and he felt blood leaking from it. If he lived through the night, he figured he would shortly die from the unattended wound in any event. So he resolved to risk it all tonight and die fighting rather than sweating in delirium before finally being released from the world.

"The door's barred," Curio whispered. "We don't have to check it. They'll have locked themselves in when the attack started."

Falco realized this, and this door was not the flimsy wood of the tower entrances. Everything about the gatehouse was built to withstand an enemy attack from any side. The wood was thick and reinforced. Heavy iron nails reflected a dull orange sheen of the lit areas by the guardhouse. He would not dramatically smash open the door like he had for the tower.

"Well, we got this far," Falco said, looking around for inspiration. "I'm not giving up. Once we're inside, we've got to raise the gate then jam the winch. If we're still alive by that point, one of us will have to hold off the Spartans while the other lifts the bolts off the doors."

"Falco, you're starting to talk like Varro now. We can't even open the door, never mind hold off waves of Spartans while we unbolt the gate. There's got to be another way."

He gritted his teeth, understanding he had asked for the impossible. Even a strong man would labor to remove the bolts alone. He needed leverage and a dozen more men to keep the gatehouse guards occupied.

The heat on his cheeks was a match for the burn on his shoulder. He had been winging the plan until this moment. Maybe that was how Varro and others felt when they were leading their missions, but they never showed it. He pressed against the wall by the door, out of sight from anyone but guards who might look down from the top of the gatehouse or those approaching from the streets. They couldn't hang here indefinitely. But no plan came to mind. The guards within would not open their doors now that the Romans had started their attack. He would need a ram just to get this door down, and while there was plenty of wreckage to serve such a purpose, he and Curio would die before it could be opened.

He felt Curio's eyes on him, teasing out his desperation. To have come so far and then to be stopped by a locked door seemed impossible to him. A quarter of Sparta was in flames by his own actions, yet he could not figure out how to open a door.

"Looks like we're caught." Curio's words drew him out of his self-pity.

Marching out of the smoke and fiery haze were hundreds of

men huddled together. They marched with resolute purpose toward the gates. Spread among them, he saw the points of spears held high.

"Curio, I can't do the death speech again. I am so fucking sick of it."

"Honestly, I'm tired of hearing it. Look at all of them. This is why we shouldn't be sent to infiltrate an enemy city. We've alerted all of Sparta."

Falco heard the angry shouts and saw the raised fists as the mob closed in.

"We're not getting a second chance to infiltrate another city. We are literally pressed against the wall with nowhere to run."

The enemies marched closer, and Falco soon realized it was a mob. Perhaps they had lost their officers, or else with the smoke and burning ash swirling like orange stars through Sparta they had forsaken order. But it was a jumble of men with a miscellany of weapons. Perhaps the auxiliary guards were dispatched to bring them to justice. But as they drew closer, he identified them.

"Oh shit," he said to Curio. "They aren't soldiers. They're citizens."

As they emerged from the shadowed streets into the plaza before the gates, the light from the massive braziers over the gatehouse shined on the angered faces of common Spartan citizens. Some carried their old kit, with aged bronze shields and helmets and time-worn spears. Others brought what they could, from knives to clubs. Nor were there only men in the mob, but stern-faced women with swords and young boys with daggers. They were a motley group unified in their red-faced anger.

"This is the uprising," Curio said breathlessly. "This is what we failed to start, but it's happening anyway."

The approach of a mob of armed citizens did not go unnoticed by those in the gatehouse. From directly above, Falco heard someone calling down to the mob.

The crowd did not slow but shouted back at the soldiers out of sight above Falco. Dirt drizzled down on his head as whoever stood to the edge turned back with a curse.

"He's going to fetch archers or call the alarm," Falco said. "We've got to organize these people. Then we have a real chance to open the gates. But we've got to do that before they're cut down."

Falco emerged from the wall, hands in the air as if to call them to attention.

"We are Romans," he shouted. "You have tired of King Nabis and you wish him deposed. We can help you."

The crowd showed no sign of slowing or of acknowledging him. He knew these were the kin of the senselessly murdered, the oppressed and dispossessed inhabitants who still eked a living in the shadow of Nabis's terror. But now they had a chance to overthrow him and would not be halted in their purpose—for neither fear nor reason.

"We are Romans," he repeated. "Let us help you."

As the crowd arrived before the gatehouse, a group of young men who seemed as normal Spartan soldiers led from the front. One narrowed his eyes at Falco.

"How have you come to our city? Are you with the Roman army?"

"We are," Falco said. "We never left Sparta. We were to be crucified on your walls until two of your bravest men spared our lives. We would now repay them for their sacrifices. We will open the gates and guide our army to Nabis's throne."

The young soldier snarled. "Then let us honor my father. I am Arion, son of Charax, and I disown Nabis as a false king!"

As if to underscore his determination, the stark notes of an alarm horn blared from the gatehouse.

"They're calling reinforcement, Arion. We've no time to lose. If you lead these people, set some to lift the bars and give me your best fighting men. We will batter the door to the gatehouse and claim it for ourselves."

Arion and his rebels directed the mob, shouting over the blaring horns. The boulders from Roman onagers still whined overhead, crashing among the city and raising a cloud of destruction in their wake. One struck the nearby wall, and a section of the parapet slewed off to crumble outside the wall. Yet the frequency of the volleys seemed to be slowing.

The moments of organization seemed like hours to Falco. But Arion's rebels were less a mob than they had seemed. They had prepared a heavy beam which would never prevail against the main gate, but would be fine to batter the tower door.

"We'll draw whatever missiles the gate guards have," Falco said as he and Arion lifted opposite sides of the heavy beam. Curio had taken hold of it next to him. "If anyone has shields, they must cover us."

Arion nodded and shouted to his brethren. Now they marched along to the tower door with the ram held between eight men while others followed with their shields held overhead. The rest of the mob attacked the double-barred gate rather than lift the beams away as they should have.

Looking up, he glimpsed motion from the top of the gatehouse. He increased his pace and soon they were battering the heavy door. The beam was prepared with wooden handholds, indicating the depth of Arion's planning. It made it easy to swing back and slam into the heavy wood.

The throng at the gate screamed and cursed, and at last seemed to be lifting the gate bar aside.

Each crash on the gatehouse door weakened the planks. Falco saw bright yellow cracks of interior wood spreading from the nailheads.

"Just a few more hits and we'll be through."

Arion nodded with grim determination, and all of the men on the ram roared as they slammed it home another time.

The wood staved in and created a hole into the bright area beyond. Falco heard orders shouted inside. The team wound up for another strike.

The ram burst through the planks, collapsing them into long splinters. Arion and others dug at these, knocking them away to expose the bolt holding the remnants of the door shut. He flipped the bar away with a triumphant shout.

In the same instant, Falco heard a whooshing noise followed by a great wail of fear and pain.

The guards had dumped burning oil onto the mob at the gate. They scattered away from the splashing flames, many of them completely immolated. Many spun and staggered a few steps before collapsing into a burning pile.

But they had removed one of the two bars, and the second was half out of its braces.

With the gatehouse door destroyed, Falco and Arion threw the ram into the gap. It crashed into the first defender into the breach, who fell back with a breathless gasp. Inside, men with long spears and small shields had come to defend the winch. But Arion and his men had spears of their own.

The Spartan defenders surged forward to plug the gap with a wall of razor-edged blades. But brave Arion had grabbed a shield from his follower and was first to push into the thicket of bronze spearheads.

He shouted to his followers as Falco and Curio pressed in behind him. With the addition of Falco's size and furious strength, they cleared the space of the Spartan defenders enough that more of Arion's men could enter.

The winch dominated the room beyond, which was brightly lit with hanging clay lamps. Heavy chains flowed out of the ceiling and wrapped around the winch, which had two spoked wheels to turn it.

"Someone raise the gates!" Falco shouted, uncertain who could hear him. He pushed Arion deeper into the enemies, using him and his bronze shield for cover. He wished for his own scutum, which was built for an action like this.

Yet Arion screamed and staggered, held up only by the continued pressing from Falco and the others. The Spartans were sensibly aiming their strikes beneath his shield, which could not cover his legs. At least six men clogged the room, and others lined a narrow set of stairs leading up to the gatehouse roof.

"Curio, make sure the gate is raised and jam that fucking winch. I'm going to clear the room."

"Clear the—"

But Falco turned his mind over to blind rage. Training and discipline were fine and had their place. But now was a time for unrestrained blood-letting. It had been a secret longing since his first battle, to forego the line and crash around the enemy bringing them fear and death. Since he was a dead man no matter what the outcome of the night's violence, he was happy to die here in one final service to Rome, even for something as small as the winch room of Sparta's gatehouse.

He did not stray far from his discipline, though. He plunged past Arion, who slipped to the floor once the pressure at his back relented. He grabbed the shield and swept it across the stunned faces of the enemies staring at him. The bronze rim slammed through their teeth, spun their helmets over their faces, and sent the rest ducking back.

The longer sword of the Spartan guards felt familiar enough in his hands. He cut away half of an exposed arm, unsure which among the press of startled and snarling faces owned it. Blood sprayed from every stab and his feet danced away from every return thrust.

The men behind cheered and joined him, and soon he sailed a wave of gore to the stairs at the back of the hall. He did not hear anything but the thunder of his own heart. He did not see anything but for the red-rimmed images of his dying foes. He did not feel anything, no pain and no joy. Instead, it was an effortless lightness as if he might fly away up to join the stars in the heavens. Knowing that death must follow him, he had no cares for his safety.

And so he carried the rebels in the current of his own violence. He stepped over corpses and men gasping through bloody mouths. His feet found purchase in the gore-soaked wood and soon he emerged into the outside world, where smoke had tainted the night air with a sickening bitterness.

The roof of the guardhouse held six more men, all of whom were leaning over the wall to observe the effects of their horrific attack on their own citizens. It seemed more oil was prepared, reserved for the imminent Roman attack.

Falco shouted his challenge as he raced from the stairs toward the men. They held their spears ready, but he had Arion's mob behind him. The first Spartan held up his shield. Falco punched with his own. The collision of bronze on bronze was a bright echo over the surrounding clash of battle. This stunned the Spartan, pushing him backward and letting Falco's sword slip into the gap that opened. The blade shuddered home, slicing into muscle and across bone to puncture his guts. He collapsed with a groan and rolled onto his side to spill his dark blood onto the roof.

Whatever madness had gripped him now ebbed away. He stood on the roof with eight other rebels who raised their assorted weapons in triumph. Bodies littered the roof and blood puddles reflected the stars above. With his head clearing, Falco looked along the wall to the west and saw that reinforcements could not reach them here as the parapet had been destroyed. They would have to set a bridge across the wide gap. To the east, reinforcements were following the wall to reach the gatehouse and recapture it.

To his delight, he heard the gate beneath him clang into its housing. Curio has opened the way. At the same time, Arion limped up the stairs supported by one of his followers. A thick flap of skin had been cut from the inside of his left calf. Blood slicked his leg and foot, but he smiled at the carnage.

"We've done it," he said. "The gate is opened and unbarred."

"Wrap that or you'll bleed out," Falco said. "Order your men to move that pot of boiling oil to intercept the reinforcements. I'm going to get us help."

Arion called to his men, who did not seem to notice the column of Spartans approaching from the eastern wall. Falco now leaned over the front of the gatehouse and drew a deep breath, summoning his best centurion voice.

"This is Centurion Caius Falco, Tenth Maniple of hastati, Ninth Century. Can anyone hear me?"

He stared across at the gleam of the Roman battle line. They came with shields up, carrying long siege ladders behind them. In the brightness surrounding the bridge and main gate, he saw nothing. Apparently the consul had judged it better to scale the walls than try to besiege the gates.

He repeated his name and rank again, hoping some scout had seen him. At last, when no one answered, he tore a white tunic from one of the dead Spartans and waved it overhead and repeated his calls.

The Spartans from the east had now arrived, and Arion understood what to do. When they reached the roof, he had his men pour the flaming oil into their path. The reinforcements had not foreseen this, and the initial group fell back in terror, many plunging off the wall either aflame or knocked off by retreating men.

It was a good opening attack, but Falco had a dozen men on

the roof to twice that number. Yet Arion was shrewd and he piled flammable wood and even the corpses of their enemies to create a wall of flame.

"Who is up there?"

Falco turned from the blinding fire to answer the call from below. He leaned over and found what seemed like velite scouts from their wolf pelts. He repeated his credentials.

"We've captured the gatehouse and opened the way. You must get to the first tribune on your left flank and tell him to bring men to hold the gatehouse open. The way over the walls will be trapped. We've got this opened for the time. But it cannot stand. Be fast!"

The velites ran off into the darkness and Falco returned to Arion, who sat against a wall and still neglected his leg. He shouted for his men to build the fire to keep the Spartans at bay.

"Easy on the fire," Falco said. "If the gatehouse burns down too fast, our men cannot pass this way. We should prepare to hold the winch room. It can't be long before the king's men try to retake it."

Arion nodded, called his men to retreat, and Falco used the tunic he had stolen from a dead Spartan to tie his leg.

"If you live, I'll be surprised if you keep this."

Arion's eyes fluttered and he seemed on the verge of passing out. But he focused on Falco's shoulder like a drunk man trying to fix his gaze.

"You've been burned."

"Thanks for reminding me. It wasn't hurting until now."

He lifted Arion along with aid from the last of the rebels. They took him into the winch room, where Curio and a handful of other men had finished jamming spear shafts into the winch mechanism. Someone had also removed both spoke wheels, preventing any easy way to lower the gate short of cutting the chains.

"The gate won't be coming down easily," he said. "What is happening outside?"

"Velites are going to fetch us help." He let Arion slide to the floor beside the stairs and out of the way. "Now we just need to hold this gatehouse until they arrive."

In the short time they had, they moved whatever they could into the remains of the shattered doors. They created a wall from their shields facing the breached entrance. Another man was set at the top of the stairs to watch for Spartans arriving from the roof.

No sooner did they finish their preparations did the first column of Spartans arrive. The mob of rebels outside, temporarily scattered by the flaming oil, now emerged from hiding to swarm them on both sides. But this was not a small column but a main line of the army. There was no chance to hold the gatehouse against so many.

"Death speech?" Curio asked, nudging Falco with his elbow.

"Like I said, I'm sick of it." Falco had retrieved a spear from a fallen defender and now wrapped both hands around it. "Let them come."

27

The first wave of attackers attempted to breach the barriers around the doorway. Falco, Curio, and as many more as could fit into the fortified space stabbed their spears at the enemy. But they were in turn covered by the long spears of their fellows. It was a horrible stalemate, as they slew every man that did not benefit from a shield. Yet the sheer number of Spartans attacking back ensured more of Falco's men fell out of line, either dead or crippled from the enemy strikes.

As men fell to either side, those in the rear pulled them out of the way to step into their places. He marveled at his own luck in avoiding the worst of the Spartan attack. He stared over the top of the shields erected as a barrier along with barrels, crates, and furniture. The Spartans in their Corinthian helmets seemed faceless and implacable. They did not protest the deaths they suffered. They did not yield, confident in their eventual victory.

"Where is the consul?" Curio shouted.

Falco had the same question, and knew there could be no answer. It might even be that the velites failed to deliver the message, or were ignored due to their insignificance. He hoped that at least one of them remembered his name and rank, and that it might mean something to the tribune who received his message.

But he could not worry for such matters when spears sliced over his head and shoulders. Whenever the Spartans drew back for a strike, he would pop up and deliver his own. Their workers had dismantled enough of the barrier that soon they would just wade through it like rough surf.

"We can't keep this up," Curio shouted.

The grunting, sweating, and cursing press of men shoving against the barrier and the groans and shrieks of the wounded nearly drowned out his voice. But Falco understood how desperate their moment had become. He counted six men remaining. Arion no longer answered to his name, and had either died or fainted from blood loss.

"What's going on upstairs?" Falco asked, knowing no one could tell him. "We better not be in a firetrap."

The shields were at last worked out of place and a tight group of spears drove forward to keep the breach open.

Falco and the others naturally fell back, taking up their own shields. Thanks to his long training with a far larger and heavier shield, the bronze Spartan shield felt light on his arm. He did not know the art of fighting with a spear and shield as well as he did a sword. So as he stepped back, he was heartened to have both ready to face the enemy.

"We die here," he said.

The remaining men might not have understood the exact words, but they knew their deaths were at hand.

Falco stepped back and nearly fell over a body. Ahead, Spartans carefully entered behind the safety of their own spears, stepping across the corpses in the entranceway. One of them looked to the winch and let out a curse seeing that it had been jammed and dismantled.

Above him, Falco heard footfalls on the wooden roof. He

closed his eyes and shook his head. Without turning to face them, he heard the Spartans' triumphant calls as they descended the stairs. Whoever had guarded that way had either been killed or else was among the final men standing at his side. It did not matter now.

"Surrounded," he muttered. "At least we won't lack for an enemy to take with us."

Curio nodded.

Then the Spartans at the door erupted into confused shouts.

Falco heard the thundering of hoofbeats and the snorts of horses outside. Against the brilliant orange of the fires raging in Sparta he saw bodies flying. The men in the gatehouse now turned to back out, and the Spartans on the stairs looked back up as if seeking new orders.

In the next moment, the entire room had cleared of enemies. They all retreated to face new threats.

"The cavalry," Falco said. "Saved by the fucking horse-lovers."

"You're going to owe them an apology for all you've blamed them for." Curio's voice was again bright and relaxed, as if he had not just locked arms with death.

The surviving rebels cheered and embraced each other. They even swept Falco and Curio into their celebrations. They were crying, and if Falco hadn't been so thirsty he guessed he might have produced a bit of water as well.

"We'll wait here a bit," he said to Curio. "Let the cavalry clear the gate area. Besides, we look little better than an enemy levy right now."

"I don't want to have survived all this to get my head plucked off by one of our own."

Curio set both hands on his head as if to ensure it remained in place.

Falco knelt beside Arion, and this silenced the celebrations of the surviving rebels. He touched his neck and pressed hard until he detected a feeble pulse. He nodded to the others that Arion lived, but so tenuous was his hold on life Falco did not expect to be able to thank him for his timely aid.

They listened to the shudder and crash of battle outside the gatehouse. It went on for a long time and he could not be certain who had prevailed. It depended on how many cavalry had arrived to exploit the opened gate, since the Spartans had sent a large force to plug this gap.

Yet their rest did not last. A rider pulled up to the shattered doorway and dismounted. Falco heard others outside of the rectangle of the door clomp to a halt and leap off their horses.

A Roman cavalryman entered, flat shield and sword ready for any attack. He wore heavy chain and a shining bronze helmet. Falco was immediately jealous of his clean, good looks. The cavalryman looked first to the bodies strewn everywhere, then finally settled on Falco and the others huddled against the stairs.

Falco gave his name and rank, standing before the others. "I have never been so happy to see a fellow Roman as I am now."

The man's square jaw was heavily shaded with stubble. His deep black eyes sparkled and he nodded in acknowledgement.

"Good work with this gate. The tribune wants to see you. Who are these others?"

Curio introduced himself, and Falco swept his arm across Arion and the remnants of his followers.

"These are the men who helped us gain the gatehouse. They're Spartans, but do not accept Nabis as king."

The cavalryman frowned. "A Spartan is a Spartan for now. They'll be held as prisoners until we get other instructions."

Falco was too tired to threaten the man. Instead he tapped Curio and made for the exit he had so desperately defended moments ago. He paused beside the Roman and leaned in to him.

"The injured one is nearly dead. He saved our lives. Do me the favor of making sure he's seen to."

Now he had both Arion and Surius as well as Varro on his mental list of men needing his help. He would do what he could for all of them, but not until Sparta had fallen.

Outside, the cavalry had driven back the Spartan defenders and scattered them back into the streets. The infantry now followed them into the city via the opened gate. They seemed to be waiting their turn to enter, such was the crowd that now streamed over the bridge.

But victory was far from certain, and if they pursued Spartans into the firetraps they were sure to fall back to, then all progress might be reversed.

Two of the cavalrymen provided him and Falco an escort to the rear where their tribune monitored progress from atop his white horse. He frowned at the two cavalrymen when he saw Falco and Curio's condition.

"This is the centurion who captured the gate? Not Spartan prisoners?"

"Centurion Caius Falco, sir. Tenth Maniple hastati. I was sent into Sparta on a special assignment by Consul Flamininus."

The tribune nodded. The infantry swept past them in fast-moving columns, their officers shouting for them to keep pace and encouraging them for the fight to come.

"Sir, the city is trapped," Falco said. "At least these forward approaches. You see the fire we set. That is just one of at least four more we've found. They're willing to burn themselves down rather than let us take them. There is a way around these traps, sir. But if the men get too far ahead then they'll be led into the heart of them. It will be bad, sir."

The tribune frowned, his dark eyes glowing with the reflected light of the flames.

"You can guide us through the traps, then?"

"We can, sir." Falco looked to Curio. "He'll lead the men to the acropolis and avoid the worst traps. But I'm afraid you won't find King Nabis there, sir. He is escaping by a secret tunnel by now."

It was a guess, but Falco believed the king might have been persuaded earlier to remain in Sparta. But now that the fires had begun and the gate captured, he would certainly collect his wealth, his followers, and use his secret tunnel.

"How do you know this?" The tribune leaned forward in his saddle.

"I've learned it the hard way, sir. Not only have we used this tunnel ourselves, but I've recently seen Nabis trying to escape that way. His subjects prevented him then, but by now I am certain he is headed out the tunnel. It leads to a river on the opposite side of this city. A ship will be waiting for him."

The news set the tribune to thinking, and he cupped his chin in his hand. Falco watched more infantry tramping by and knew they were headed to danger.

"Sir, we cannot delay. If Nabis escapes Sparta he will flee to Argos, which will just dump us all in the shit."

"You have a way with words," the tribune said, raising his head again. He looked to the two cavalrymen. "Take him to Praefectus Paullus. Order this turma to follow Centurion Falco's directions to this hidden exit. Then they are to prevent the Spartan king's escape. The king is to be taken alive at all costs."

A turma was thirty horsemen, divided ten to a decurion, the equivalent of Falco's rank.

"Sir, the king's guard will number at least as much. We have to ensure he is captured."

"That's all I can afford to send now, Centurion. Curio, I will take you to the infantry commanders and we'll organize the attack on the acropolis."

Knowing he had no chance to change the tribune's mind, Falco accepted his orders. The cavalrymen guided him through the infantry to reach the reformed cavalry units now standing aside to await further orders. The infantry had sent the hastati ahead to form a wall around the area before the gate, expecting a counterattack which must come before the main Roman force could arrive.

He jogged between two horses, and when the cavalrymen introduced him to Praefectus Paullus, his eyes widened in surprise.

"Marcellus Paullus? You are Praefectus now?"

The haughty man peered down on him from his strong black horse whose coat shined with yellow firelight. He, Varro, and Curio had to drag Paullus back from his defection to the Macedonians nearly three years ago. At the time, he was besotted with King Philip's sister, Alamene. His short time as a traitor seemed to have been no hindrance to his career. After all, he thought, Paullus was the scion of a powerful and wealthy family.

"What is this? One of the Spartan slaves speaks Latin?"

"We've no time to fuck around, Paullus. King Nabis is set to escape and your turma has got to cut him off before he does."

The boot struck him in the face, and he reeled back more from surprise than the impact. He stared up at Paullus who sneered at him.

"You'll address me as sir. I've no idea who you think you are, but you do not speak to me like one of your piss-stinking gambling friends."

"Centurion Caius Falco, Tenth Maniple hastati, sir. You'll remember me from our first meeting a few years ago, when I—"

"Ah, Falco, my old friend! Now I recognize you. Yes, it has been a while since I rescued you from the Macedonians. Well, what is this about the king?"

Falco was silenced better by Paullus's claim than the boot to his face. Yet the cavalrymen explained their tribune's orders, and Paullus immediately began to organize his men. Before Falco could say more, Paullus had already left to address his men.

"Well, am I going to fucking run with you?" Falco looked up to his escorts, who looked between each other as if to see who would take him on his horse. The man on the left seemed to have lost some sort of silent contest.

"Get up with me, sir."

Falco struggled to mount into the four-horned saddle, but after a short struggle he managed to sit behind the rider. He slung the bronze shield over his back and adjusted the Spartan sword before clapping the rider's shoulder to indicate he was ready.

They rode out of Sparta with Paullus leading them. Falco was no great lover of horses, and the jolting gallop they rode around the walls of Sparta reinforced his distaste. Every time the beast's hooves struck the ground his burned shoulder lit up with fiery pain. He still had not chanced to look at it, other than to note reddened skin from the corner of his vision. As long as he did not see the burn, he would not feel the pain any worse than he had to. Or so he convinced himself as thirty cavalrymen thundered around the walls.

"Time to lead the way," Paullus shouted back to him. "Where is this tunnel exit?"

Falco looked to the mountain peak, a dark shape that blotted out the stars and the place where Varro was hopefully safely hidden. From there, he looked across to the clumps of trees. There were not many, but he found the right one. It seemed nearly a half mile away, and he was not certain how fast a horse could cross the distance.

He pointed to the location and Paullus led them in perfect formation, racing away from the glowing flames of Sparta. As they crossed the plain, he saw the sparkle of stars on the river beyond and the unmistakable silhouette of a ship. He called out in victory, and Paullus only nodded in affirmation.

They had not yet reached the secret tunnel exit when men emerged from it. Falco knew only a single man at a time could escape, and if the king took his honor guard, then he would never get them all out of the tunnel in time. Instead, he would be forced back inside and to his palace, which would soon be under attack.

"There they are," Paullus shouted as he sighted the first Spartans standing up against the horizon.

"Men are coming from the ship, sir!"

Falco's rider had sharper eyes than he did, for he noted how a dark line of men streamed up the shallow banks to meet their royal passenger.

"We'll to cut them in two," Paullus shouted.

Through signals and shouts and the motions of their leaders, the turma reformed into two halves. Paullus took one half and rode for the ship. Falco's half rode for the tunnel.

Their beating hooves announced their arrival and Falco saw both the men at the tunnel and those coming from the ship turn in surprise at their charge.

The men from the ship had bows, which Falco knew by the postures their shadows assumed and not by seeing the weapons through the darkness. But Paullus and his men held up their shields and continued their charge. Falco did not see the result of the first volley, as his fifteen horsemen cut severely to the right and now faced the men exiting the tunnel.

"Hold on, sir," his rider called. "I can't slow to let you off here. Try to protect yourself."

Before he could protest, the line of horsemen raked into the shadowy figures surrounding the tunnel. They surrounded smaller figures, which might be Nabis and his family. Falco clung to his rider in fear the horse would throw him. Their wild charge had nearly sent him flying a dozen times since leaving Sparta.

The initial pass did not thin out the enemy ranks as well as Falco had thought it might. Bodies showing gray in the starlight lay in the grass. However, the survivors formed a wall of shields around their wards, bracing spears against another charge. Across the field, Paullus had run his cavalry along the archers and scattered them.

The decurion called for another charge, and Falco's rider wheeled them around. He had renewed respect for the ease with which they guided their mounts. The horse and rider seemed bonded, as if the riders' thoughts passed directly to the horses' minds.

The next charge met more determined and organized resistance. Falco struggled not to scream in terror, for it seemed they were charging into a wall of spears.

He hid as best as he could behind the wicker shield of his rider, but it did not cover much of him. Fifteen horses thundered the short distance to the desperate cluster of spearmen and their round bronze shields. Falco closed his eyes at the last moment, helpless as he was.

Then something caught him on his shield. The bronze gave a hollow thump and slammed against his back.

He slid sideways and lost his grip. As he fell, he snatched at the saddle blanket, pulling away a yellow tassel as he plummeted to the ground. He slammed onto his back, and stared dazedly at the stars blinking at him in a deep purple sea.

His shoulder hurt and he struggled to breathe. But he lay in the bowl of his shield and his sword was still at his side.

A shadow loomed over him, and a faceless Spartan in a Corinthian helmet raised his spear.

28

Falco rolled onto his stomach as the spear struck down. The blade screeched on the bronze shield still hanging there then slid into the grass. He hooked his leg around the feet of his enemy, who had recklessly thrown his weight into the thrust, and used his momentum to splay him on the ground.

He grabbed the moment to scurry to his feet, step on the enemy spear, then draw his own sword.

The cavalry swirled around in zigzagging chaos. Yet the shell of bronze shields held its basic formation and tracked back toward the tunnel.

The man underfoot tugged at his spear, reminding Falco to finish his work. He rammed the short sword through the kidney of the Spartan. His back arched and he screamed when Falco twisted and withdrew his blade. He paid the fallen enemy no further attention.

Spartans had broken from the defensive shell to keep the cavalry from getting too near. It was a brave sacrifice, as these men were alone and easily cut down. But it succeeded in giving what must be Nabis and his family a chance to retreat into the tunnels.

Paullus and his men were equally engaged with the crew of the dark ship that waited on the banks to sweep Nabis to safety.

"I owe you a good beating," Falco said to the cluster of men sheltering the king and his family as they escaped back to Sparta. "Let's see if I can stick you once before you slip away."

He jogged for the spearmen, the lone foot soldier among the thundering madness of the cavalry. They were terrifying to behold and even unsettled him as they danced their horses around the enemy, never remaining in place long enough to suffer a return blow. He had to admire their dexterity and bravery.

Methodios stood at the front of the spearmen sheltering the king, his bronze shield reflecting what light shined on this frenzied hit and run battle. There was no mistaking the man. His stature and bearing, and the wrap around his head covering one eye beneath his helmet, all combined to create an unmistakable impression.

"Methodios, you prick! It's me, Falco! Let me finish what I started."

The Greek captain startled at his name, and he looked about before his shadowed eye settled on Falco.

He jumped out of the line, spear gripped for a charge in both hands, and his teeth bared in rage.

Falco presented his shield and sword, bracing for the impact and searching for the chance to get under his spear.

"I'll carve your heart out, Roman!"

"Not before I eat your liver!"

Methodios bolted halfway across the gap between them, then the black streak of a horse passed behind him and the blur of a rider's sword slashed across the back of his neck.

The Spartan's helmet flew from his head, which pitched forward along with Methodios. He crumpled into a heap at Falco's feet.

"Fuck! That was my kill! You stole my fucking glory moment, gods curse you!"

He bent to Methodios who had flopped the grass. The back of his neck was carved to the bone, nearly decapitating him. Surprisingly little blood flowed from the horrific wound. He flipped the Spartan over. His eye seemed to fix on Falco and his sneer resurfaced. But in the next heartbeat, the unbandaged eye turned upward and his body slackened.

"Dead is dead," Falco said. "Not a bad outcome, I suppose."

He stood then kicked Methodios's corpse. The men surrounding the tunnel were now vanishing down it after their wards had escaped. Falco knew they could only return to the palace and meet Consul Flamininus there. He smiled at the thought of Nabis fleeing back and forth. But now that the secret exit from his palace was exposed, he could no longer chance this route.

Paullus signaled for his men to reform. For all the fighting, only one rider had taken an arrow to his leg. Though he tried to laugh it off, the bleeding seemed lethal to Falco's experienced eye. One other had been unhorsed, but was not seriously hurt. Falco marveled at how his horse stood over him as he recovered from what must have been a nasty fall.

"The ship is routed," Paullus proclaimed, indicating the ship that was already under oar and angling into the river's current. "I left them half a crew. I'm sure they will not trouble us again. What of King Nabis?"

Looking up at Paullus on horseback rocked his neck and burned shoulder with pain. But he simply nodded to the stand of trees and the hidden exit.

"Like a scared rat, he retreated into his tunnel. It leads to the prisons beneath his palace. I expect he'll be running right into the consul, sir."

"Then we should pursue him. A king's ransom, imagine that!"

"Sir, there is no light in the tunnel and it is collapsing in places. I would not be surprised if they collapse a section of it as they retreat, or leave someone to collapse it on you if you pursue. I would not advise going down there without sappers and a good light."

Paullus seemed about to chastise Falco, but then he paused.

"Buried alive, eh? Not a fate for handsome men like us. Still, we must guard this tunnel until relieved. Centurion Falco, you are hurt and I have an injured man. Return to the tribune with my report. We will remain on guard here until otherwise instructed. Tell him the king is contained in his palace, then see to the medical aid of my men and yourself."

Falco remounted with his rider, who apologized for letting him fall.

"I ducked the spear but forgot you were there, sir. Glad you survived."

"Believe me, it's not the worst I've had these days. Now, I know you've got an injured man, but I want you to ride like you're racing for all the silver in the world." Falco looked to the mountain peak. "I've got a friend who needs my help before this night is done."

Two calvary men held up their wounded companion in his saddle, but Falco and his rider sped ahead of them. As they neared Sparta, the wail and thunder of destruction shuddered the ancient stone walls. Fires blazed everywhere, and it seemed as if this grand city must all crumble to ash and collapse into a pit of despair.

The gatehouse, a scene of a desperate battle an hour before, was now completely in Roman control. The cavalry was kept in reserve here, prepared to move where needed within the city. But a quick glance showed Falco the main column of infantry had reached the acropolis. The smoke and fire in their wake marked their progress.

Once the report was made to the cavalry tribune, Falco was on his feet again and glad for it. It seemed the ground was no longer so solid as he wobbled about on it. Men experienced this after long sea voyages, but was it possible after riding on a horse? He did not know.

"You need to get to the medical aid station," the tribune said. "You have done more than your duty, Centurion. The battle is over for you tonight."

"There is one more thing to do, sir. I need a man to help me. Would you loan your soldier for one last task? There is a Roman spy here, and I promised to rescue him as soon as I could. He's in hiding."

"The city is not conquered and dangerous for two men," the tribune said. "Take ten men."

So it was that Falco led ten cavalrymen back to the burned out remains of where he had left Surius. He could no longer tell one building from the next, and resorted to shouting out his name. The cavalrymen joined him, though they did not hide their irritation at the task.

Yet at length he did hear Surius shouting is response. One of the cavalrymen picked his way among ash-strewn ruins and opened the door to Sirius's untouched hiding spot. Falco was there when the solders carried him out. His fine features were slicked with sweat and the javelin wound in his leg was black with caked blood. But he smiled at seeing Falco.

"You kept your promise."

"I always do. You're one promise fulfilled, another to go."

The cavalry escorted them outside the walls to where a medical station had been established. They delivered Surius and Falco to the doctors then returned to their unit. The doctors wanted to review Falco's wounds, and were prepared to have him restrained when he tried to escape. But in the end, he relented. They cleaned his shoulder and doused it with what only seemed like more fire to him. After applying something they promised would numb the pain, they wrapped his shoulder before instructing an orderly to take him to the evacuation queue.

"I can't fucking lie on the grass," he shouted at the orderly guiding him away. The fresh wrapping on his shoulder hurt worse than when he had been running around exposed. "There's a man who needs me. My best friend, for fuck's sake!"

"Would your friend want you to lose your arm?" the orderly asked, leading him to a line of other wounded. Some seemed uninjured to his eye, but others were so hacked up they might as well be dead.

"His life is in danger. If I don't get to him, he'll be killed."

"All our lives are in danger," the orderly said, leading him to the end of the line of injured. "Now, we'll be evacuating you back to camp shortly. You've done enough to get yourself killed already. So just sit here and wait."

The orderly helped him to sit, then stared hard at him, pursing his lips.

"But you're going to run off the moment I leave you."

"You should tell fortunes in the Forum," Falco said.

The orderly sighed. "Look, scores of men have come through here all night. Many have already been evacuated. I'm handling the casualty reports. What is your friend's name? Maybe he has already been here."

"Impossible. He's trapped in a cave under that mountain." Falco nodded toward the black peak in the distance. "And his body has been shattered. He can't take care of himself."

"Centurion Marcus Varro, Tenth hastati," the orderly said flatly. "If you had arrived just a few minutes ago you'd have met him. He showed up under his own power. Amazing tale, if you can believe it. Seems like cover for something else, but I can't deny he had the wounds to back up the story. His ribs were shattered and his hands and feet cut to ribbons. He'll live, but recovery will take a good long while."

Falco blinked. "Centurion Marcus Varro was here? He walked in?"

"He had a woman helping him, and she was quite a beauty. Even the wounded stopped screaming to stare at her. But he made the journey on foot with a crutch and her aid. We just evacuated them back to the camp."

"Evacuated to the camp," Falco repeated. He looked toward the walls of Sparta. Curio was still in there. But that little bastard could dodge a tidal wave if he had a mind to. He would be fine as long as he was in line with other infantrymen.

"Did you receive a Greek by the name of Arion?"

The orderly thought on this but shook his head. "Not sure about that one. A few Spartans were delivered here by the cavalry shortly after we established this post. Maybe he was one of them."

"Probably was," Falco said.

That wavering, unstable feeling he experienced a short time ago returned. Only now it seemed to engulf his vision as the world blurred.

"So everyone is all right. I can relax now. I've done my duty."

The orderly squatted down then grabbed Falco's head by the chin.

"Look at my eyes, Centurion Falco. How do you feel?"

"Feel? I feel fucking great."

Then he rocked back and knew nothing more.

29

Varro awakened into a world of pain. The trek out of the mountains and across the open fields back to the Roman lines had undone all the healing he had enjoyed since Ione and her traitorous slave had joined him. He was under an awning where rows of men lay on the grass atop their cloaks. He remembered collapsing once he and Ione had been delivered to the safety of the camp. The cart ride had jostled his broken ribs, but the doctors had complemented Ione on her careful work.

He shifted his hand across the new dressings wrapping his torso. His hands and feet were also wrapped in clean linen. It was dawn after the battle, far from the walls of Sparta. Yet the scent of ash still carried on the breeze, only defeated by the smell of blood hanging over this field hospital. Shadowy forms moved around the edges of his vision, orderlies leaning over their patients as they made the morning rounds.

"This one is dead."

He heard the voice clearly just overhead, then shuffling as someone removed the body.

That was not his fate, he mused, staring at the yellow light shining through the covering overhead. He had been crucified over the walls of Sparta, then cast from a mountain peak. He still could not recall the details of it and believed his mind would hide that terror from him for the rest of his life.

There were so many questions built up in his mind. What had been Falco's and Curio's fates? Did they escape? Did they fight in the siege of Sparta? What happened to Castor, Ione's husband? For that matter, where was Ione now? Why did Ione's slave attempt to kill him?

That attack confounded him. But once Ione reported the fires burning in Sparta, her slave had acted with unexpected violence. Ione had only acquired her in recent weeks. Had she not reacted with unexpected calm and speed, her slave might have ended Varro's life with his own pugio.

Yet Ione had wrested it from her slave's grip and killed her instead. They left her corpse in the cave and began the torturous journey to meet the Roman lines. They were out of food, and the sudden violence of the slave had galvanized both of them to action. Ione had looked longingly toward Sparta the entire time. Yet she never complained, and her strong arms supported him when he stumbled.

Had she not been married to Castor, Varro would have pledged his life to her. Such extraordinary beauty and strength was rare in anyone. He only hoped Castor had survived the siege to reunite with his wife.

The dizziness that had plagued him the night before had abated with a night of rest. The grass under him was a welcomed change from the uneven stone floor of the cave, and the fresh air was far better than the rancid stench of decay that pervaded that chasm. So he lifted his head to take in his surroundings.

Falco lay beside him on the right. He was unrecognizable to anyone except the boy who had grown up fearing him every day of his youth. But he was covered in black ash and blood. His bulky muscle had shrunk and his heavy brow was even more pronounced over sunken eyes, which were tightly shut as if he were enduring loud screaming.

But worse still was the wrapping on his shoulder and part of his ear. Varro saw the red flesh peeking beyond some of the wraps and noted that his hair had been singed. Falco had been burned, it seemed.

Yet the joy of seeing his friend lying beside him filled him with strength. He wanted to leap up and embrace him but knew he needed as much rest as he could get.

Looking for an orderly, he intended to ask for Falco's condition. Sitting upright brought him fresh pain, however, and he had to lie flat. When he did, he looked to his left and found Curio lying there.

Now he gasped in shock, for what were the chances that the three of them would be set together? Then he realized the consul might have had a hand in it. Curio's wounds were not apparent. His shoulder had been stitched, but it was hardly something to put him in the hospital. However, he shared Falco's emaciated visage. The glow that usually suffused him had vanished, and he too seemed to cling to life.

He lay back in the grass, staring upright with a grin. They were all wounded, but they had all lived. From those first ill-fated moments on Sparta's walls right up to this moment, they had survived what no man could ever expect to survive.

The orderlies eventually arrived at Varro's row and found him awake and smiling.

"That's not something we see often here," said the orderly examining him. He pressed some words into a wax tablet as he stood by Varro's feet.

"What are Curio's and Falco's injuries?" He sat up again, eager to hear news of his friends.

The orderly glanced up from his tablet to look at Falco. "Both suffer from malnutrition and dehydration. Falco has burned his shoulder and neck. Provided we keep it clean, he'll have a nasty scar and he'll live. As long as the flesh does not die. Curio had cuts and bruises. He's in a rough state. All three of you have bad bruises and cuts around your necks and wrists. There's got to be quite a story there."

Varro shuddered to think back on the crucifixion and pushed aside the memory. "Why are we together?"

The orderly paused and raised his brow. "I wasn't on duty here when you were sent in. It's possible an officer might have asked for it. They like to keep their men in one place. Makes it easier for them to get their visits completed."

Varro nodded. "What of Sparta? Did it fall?"

The orderly shook his head. "We fought through to the acropolis, but the fires forced us to retreat. It's still burning. Can't you smell it? Anyway, surrender is expected this morning. The consul is already set up to receive an emissary from Nabis. Not a bad night's work. Whoever opened the gates from the inside is going to have the gratitude of the legions, that's for sure."

Varro's smile grew. "So they did it after all. And I missed out."

"You need to lie on your back, sir."

He obeyed his instructions and the orderly now stooped to inspect Falco's wounds. As much as he wanted to ask for the details, he let the man work and shuffle down the line. He could hear it from Falco's mouth once he awakened.

"You're awake."

He turned to face Curio's weak voice. He smiled as if he had just roused from a beautiful dream.

"I'm so glad to see you alive."

"Can't tell you how many times I nearly died."

Varro nodded. "There are going to be plenty of stories for us to share over a good mug of wine. Are you all right?"

"I didn't fall off a mountain, at least. I'm probably the best of the three of us. Falco burned his shoulder like a complete fool. He ran into a fire to escape the Spartans. Can you imagine?"

"Nothing about Falco surprises me, other than he survives his own ideas."

They both chuckled. Varro knew it was an unfair statement, but couldn't help a good-natured jab at him while he slept.

"The orderly said he'll live if the wound doesn't go bad. What happened in Sparta, Curio? Last I saw, you were both running away from it."

"Well, last I saw you had just fed us poisoned wine before sending us down the walls."

"Ah, I thought I might've mixed up the wines. Charax and Demas had poisoned the men in the tower to get to us. I think you got the dregs of that wine. But I see you lived."

Curio turned his head to stare up once more. "It doesn't matter. If you hadn't sickened me, I'd not have vomited when I did. Then Falco wouldn't have got that spear, which basically saved our lives. So it's all for the better. The gods were watching over us."

"Nothing you said made any sense," Varro said. "But I suppose it will after you explain everything. How did you get back into Sparta?"

"We found a secret tunnel. We caught Castor using it, though we didn't know him at the time. He was going to bury your body while we were resting by the river and figuring how to get back inside."

"That must be the way Ione used to get out of the city."

"Ione? Is that the name of Methodios's agent? Did you kill her?"

"No, she is Castor's wife. Methodios was involved? Now I will have to hear this story, though it might explain the slave who tried to kill me."

Curio shifted his head back to face him.

"Castor had a wife? Well, here's sad news. Castor is dead. Methodios flayed him alive."

"Oh gods!" Varro turned aside at the thought of it. "Gods, Curio. He saved my life."

"It cost him his own. I don't understand why he would've done so. But his partner still lives, or at least he did when Falco and I left him in that house."

"He's alive."

Falco's voice was weak but clear. Varro turned to him, a thin smile stretched on a wasted face with taut, red skin. His own mother wouldn't know him, but Varro did, and he felt tears stinging his eyes.

"Thank all the gods you are alive, Falco. I prayed every night that you and Curio escaped."

"Well, we went back to get you, since you were too busy poisoning us to follow."

"Sorry about that."

"It worked out," Falco said, shifting so that he looked up at the awning. Varro saw damp streaks running from the corner of his eye. "I'm glad you're back from that little vacation under the mountain. Just in time to try to claim credit for sacking Sparta. But Curio and I handled it, with a little help of course. I'd have gone to fetch you last night, but I heard you had Venus for an escort. So I thought I'd get some sleep first."

"That burn looks serious."

"You should know, I'm serious about all that I do."

Varro started to laugh, then Curio, and finally Falco. He laughed until his broken ribs ached then he laughed some more. All of them rolled in the grass, laughing like children playing on a summer's day. The men around them cursed and shouted for them to stop. But nothing could stop it. Tears followed until they gasped for breath and settled into quiet.

Over the next days, they recounted their tales in between their treatments. The consul apparently refused the first surrender terms, but on the second day won all his demands. The army had basically stood ready for battle over this period and celebrated victory the evening of the second day.

The stories they shared were unbelievable from either side. Varro could not believe all that Falco and Curio had suffered and achieved. They could not believe he had been shoved from a mountain peak along with eighty other people and survived. They both were interested in hearing about Ione's great beauty. They both hoped to meet her soon, and Varro expected her skills were currently put to use tending the other wounded.

The only thing he withheld from his friends was the owl marking on his pugio. Instead, he told them Castor had come to bury him out of respect for his sacrifice, which was not entirely a lie. But he did not share that his pugio seemed to indicate he had rank in some sort of secret society. Given Castor's initial violent reaction to his ignorance of the owl's meaning, he thought it best to shield his friends from any potential threats.

On the third day, the injured were to be relocated to the main camp at Elateia while the army accepted Nabis's surrender and the restoration of Argos, which Varro had nearly forgotten was the cause of all this suffering. Before they departed, however, the consul visited them in the hospital. It was not a surprise visit, since they were relocated to a section of the hospital tent that was screened off from others so the consul could debrief with them in private. The doctors still determined it better not to move either Varro or Falco unnecessarily. So the consul would visit them instead.

They waited on him in the screened section of grass for over an hour. None of them spoke during the time, but each stared pensively. In the end, they had not done what the consul had asked specifically, yet at least Falco and Curio had achieved the spirit of his command. They all wondered what his thoughts were, and dreaded they might not be favorable.

Flamininus entered the screened area, speaking to attendants out of sight. He entered alone, wearing his bronze breastplate and greaves, but eschewing his helmet. His soulful eyes seemed to light up at seeing them. And Varro at least felt immediate relief.

They tried to stand for a proper salute but Flamininus raised his hand.

"Do not stand or worry for any formality now," he said. "I arranged these screens so we could dispense with all of that. I am sorry to have kept you waiting, but I have been busy, as you must know."

Varro looked to Falco and Curio, and all of them seemed stunned.

"Sir, please, you mustn't apologize to us," Varro said.

"Ah, well, I suppose not. But I did, and I did it with cause. Thanks to the three of you, the dealing with Sparta has gone far better than expected. After our first battle outside the walls, I expected we would have to settle into a long siege. I had despaired of news from you. I knew I set you a hard task, and regretted that you might have perished in its attempt. But once more, you have demonstrated astounding resilience. My proconsulship has been all the smoother because of your service. So, you cannot imagine my relief to have found you not only alive but to have been the architects of Sparta's surrender."

"What of Sparta's surrender, sir?" Falco shook his head. "There was no science at all to my blundering. I just fell on lucky days and thanks to Varro I did not die on the walls of Sparta."

"That's true, sir," Curio said. "But Centurion Falco is not telling you all the truth of his efforts. He is a hero, sir. He never faltered in carrying out your orders, and was ready to give his life to open the gates."

"Which brings me to some important matters." Flamininus

lowered his gaze but smiled. "You three have of course all earned citations for bravery. I will be certain to make much about it once we are all settled back in Elateia. However, you must be patient as there is much to sort out before then. You've also earned leave time, the duration of which I will determine in due course. But you need to heal both your bodies and your hearts. I have debriefed with Surius, and understand you were all crucified in the Greek manner."

The matter-of-fact way the consul described it made Varro shiver at the reality. Yet he simply nodded in answer.

"Yes, well, that must be an ordeal to test any man's mind. And I need your minds sharp. The Argives are still not settled and I wonder for their reaction once news of Sparta's surrender and release of its rule reaches them. Nabis remains pacified for now, and still in command of his city. It is a shame that the rebels who enabled our success must now face his wrath."

"No," Falco said. "I mean, sir, those men gave you the gatehouse. You aren't turning them over, sir?"

Flamininus smiled. "I am not that heartless. I have named them prisoners for now. If they are smart, they will escape and never be seen again. But they are a proud lot, and consider themselves Spartans before all else. I think they will try to return home."

Falco sank back and lowered his head.

"There is only so much to be done for them," the consul said softly. "But there is brighter news for you, Centurion Falco. Surius wishes to nominate you for a grass crown. You saved his life, first by carrying him to safety and enduring that terrible wound to your shoulder, and then by returning for him before he was found by the enemy. I have agreed with his nomination."

Falco swallowed hard, and his voice was hoarse upon answering.

"Thank you, sir."

"Congratulations, Falco." Varro nearly patted him on the shoulder, but caught himself. He stroked his hair in embarrassment. Curio offered his congratulation as well.

"Well, I cannot stay longer. You have served me well, and I will see you all mended so that you may serve me again. Rome is lucky to have you. You are men who build empires."

Varro lowered his head in appreciation, but the idea of building an empire seemed a strange comment. But the consul was given to grand statements and was likely puffing them up after so much despair.

"There is a final visitor for you, as well," the consul said.

"Is it Ione?" Varro's heart suddenly jumped and both Falco and Curio sat up straighter at the name. Yet Flamininus frowned.

"No, not a woman, but Surius. He wishes to speak with you before he goes his way."

"He's not coming to Elateia?" Falco rubbed his leg as if feeling the spy's wound. "He took a javelin through the leg and nearly bled out."

"He'll recover elsewhere," Flamininus said. "See you back in the main camp."

Once the consul stepped out of the screened area, an orderly helped Surius hobble into the consul's place. Varro had only heard the man described as Castor's partner. Even tired and injured as he was, he seemed every bit as regal as the man. The orderly set him a stool and helped him sit with a short groan. He stretched his injured leg, wrapped in fresh gray bandages that showed spots of deep red where blood still seeped.

They made short introductions to Varro and spoke at length about their wounds and recovery. Surius thanked Falco profusely.

"You've earned the crown," he said. "I heard the fiery winds blowing and so many times the Spartans passed near my hiding spot. But in the end you came for me, or else I'd be back there and facing the fate of my brother."

"Castor is your brother?" Curio asked, leaning forward for a better look.

"I see the family resemblance now," Falco said.

Varro tried to remember Castor's face, but he could not. He just remembered the knife at his throat.

"Not of the same father," he said. "And we were not so close as you might think. But I still mourn his loss. Now, Varro, you survived the attack from Methodios's agent. Had I not knocked myself out, I'd have exposed her from the start. Thank the gods you were still able to defend yourself in this condition. She is quite skilled with a knife, if I remember."

"It was not me who disarmed her," Varro said. "But Ione, Castor's wife. If she had not been there with me, then I'd have been stuck through the neck. But she turned the pugio on her, in fact so easily I couldn't see that this agent had much talent with knives."

Surius's smile vanished into a frown and he stared in hard silence at Varro until it grew to an awkward length. At last Varro cleared his throat.

"Like I said, Ione killed her then the both of us decided that was the best moment to head for our lines. But I have not seen her since. I assume you have, though?"

Surius slowly shook his head.

"Castor didn't have a wife."

Varro coughed lightly. "Of course he did. She even wept at mention of his name. Maybe you were not close at all and did not realize this."

"I was close enough to know Castor did not favor women."

Falco sucked his breath and looked to Varro.

"Were you just imaging her?"

"Don't be stupid. The orderly told you about the beautiful woman that helped me here. Half the men in the hospital were slobbering over her, even if they had their hands cut off."

"A woman of such great beauty," Surius said wistfully. "I've not heard of one in Sparta's court nor have I seen mention of one in this camp since I arrived. You can be sure if such a beauty were among us, she'd be the talk of the camp. Every man would want to be with her."

"Especially the consul," Curio said. "But he didn't know what you were saying."

Varro stared down at his hands. "She wrapped these, fed me, talked with me. Her name was Ione and she claimed to be Castor's wife."

"She lied to you. Ione is not likely her real name, either," Surius said. "And how she knew to find you, and why she helped you, are for reasons of her own and nothing to do with Castor. If anything, she was in Methodios's employ and decided to betray him. That's the best I can think of."

"Well, I'm going to change your nickname from Lily to Mystery Man," Falco said. "You fall off a mountain and half of Sparta goes running to find you. What do you make of that?"

Varro thought of his pugio with the gold owl's head on the pommel. A gift from his mother, carried on campaign by her brother, and blessed at the Temple of Mars, his lucky charm. But he no longer had it and Ione was the last to possess it.

The pugio had vanished along with her.

30

Three months after Sparta's surrender, Varro was still not fully recovered. While his ribs had mended, his neck and joints still ached from having hung off a board over Sparta's wall. His dreams were only ever nightmares of plummeting into a yawning blackness. The poor sleep made the time since Sparta feel even longer.

Yet he had resumed command of his century a month ago, and on this summer morning, he had just completed a painful march with his men in full kit. His tunic clung to his back from sweat as he stripped off his mail armor inside his tent. One of the century's slaves helped him with this, carefully setting the heavy mail onto a rack while he stretched and tried to hide his pain.

He missed having Falco as a tent mate. He wished more than ever that Curio would learn to read so he could name him as his optio. Of course, he had a fine optio who had led the century during his absence and earned honors for the men and himself. But still, he was no friend and never could be while Varro was in command.

Now he hurriedly cleaned his face in the bronze basin set out for him. He had been summoned to a private meeting with an unnamed but exceptionally important man.

The camp was rife with important men with the preparations for the Nemean Games and Consul Flamininus's plans to at last proclaim freedom for the Argives after the senatorial ratification of his treaty with Nabis. Yet the order to present himself with all haste and in a formal toga to this mysterious man had come from the consul himself, delivered by his messenger.

So he changed into his toga, feeling awkward in it when he had just been slogging around the hills outside camp in full mail. He had considered wearing his grass crown but thought better of it. Falco would soon have one as well, and they were all to be publicly decorated at the summer Nemean Games during Flamininus's great moment—which was the consul's own description of the plan.

The slave straightened the folds of Varro's toga and then stood aside as he rushed outside. His command group was haggard and sweating, squatting around an unlit cooking pit. They smiled admiringly at him, and his optio teased him about looking like a senator. He rushed off across the camp to the billowing white tents of the important men who had recently arrived for the games.

He was met by guards who knew where to direct him.

With a glance over his shoulder, he caught Falco and Curio watching in the distance. They were no doubt dumbfounded to see him running off to headquarters in a toga rather than joining them for wine and gambling.

The large tent denoted a man of stature, for it was an even larger and grander tent than Flamininus's, and he was not a man to come up short in any comparison. Two triarii stood guard at the entrance and challenged Varro's presence. He gave his name, and one nodded while the other entered the tent to announce him.

Slipping through the flap into the shade of the tent, he was immediately relieved of the hot sun which bathed the huge space with diffuse light. Screens had been placed strategically to create private sections, florid with decorative patterns and pastoral landscapes. A small table had been set up with two couches. A gray-haired man in a white toga reclined on one, a plate of fruits and a silver goblet of wine set out before him. He was older now, but Varro recognized him immediately.

He snapped straight and at attention.

"Consul Galba! Centurion Marcus Varro present, sir."

His former consul smiled indulgently. "Ah, thank you for the reminder of old times. But please, I am only a senator now. Let us forget military rank for the moment. Be at ease."

"Thank you, sir." But Varro hardly relaxed.

Galba chuckled and waved him toward the vacant couch.

"Centurion? You have had quite a rapid rise. But of course, I always expected you would."

"Thank you, sir." Varro stepped toward the couch but stopped when he saw what rested on the table before it.

It was a pugio in a plain leather case, a deep divot on the sheath, and a stylized owl's head in gold inlay on its pommel.

He froze, staring at it. Then he looked to Senator Galba, who chewed on a handful of grapes while smiling.

"Please, Varro, be seated. We have important matters to discuss."

HISTORICAL NOTES

The Laconian War was fought between Rome and her allies against Sparta, Argos, and Cretan mercenaries in 195 BC. The genesis of the war was the Achaean League's dissatisfaction at Sparta maintaining control of Argos when they had only recently switched sides from Macedonia to Rome during the Second Macedonian War. Argos had been awarded to Sparta by Philip V as the price for his alliance. Rome agreed with the League, since they did not appreciate the threat of a reorganized and ascendant Sparta with free rein to cause trouble after they withdrew from Greece.

Of all the Roman allies, only the Aetolian League did not favor war with Sparta, as they hated the Roman presence in Greece and had made it clear they wanted to see an immediate exit of Roman power in the region. They wanted to deal directly with Sparta, but in the end the Roman alliance silenced them and aligned against Sparta with Rome at the forefront.

Flamininus sent an envoy to Sparta with demands to surrender Argos to the Achaean League. This of course failed and so Rome and her allies mustered their armies and marched on

Argos. They were promised that the Argives would revolt upon seeing Rome and her allies so close. Nabis had earlier terrorized the Argives by seizing the wealth of powerful families and inflicting tortures on those who resisted. So it seemed plausible that this uprising would happen, and they even had received direct word from the organizer of the proposed rebellion.

The Romans set up their camp in sight of the walls. They were attacked and the proposed rebellion never started, as the organizer and his followers were hacked down within Argos itself. Rome beat back the Spartan garrison and settled in to besiege Argos.

The Roman alliance waited for battle, but when none came Flamininus called a council, the outcome of which was Rome and the Achaeans would directly attack Sparta. They reasoned since Sparta was the instigator of all the problems, bringing Nabis to heel was the true work of the alliance. The other members remained in place before Argos, claiming their only goal was to retake that city.

Flamininus gathered allies along the route to Sparta and capitalized on the arrival of a Roman fleet along with Rhodian and Pergamene fleets at the Spartan-controlled port of Gythium. Cretan piracy, if not outright sponsored by Sparta then at least sheltered by them, had driven this fleet action. Gythium faced an intense siege and the Cretan fleet was destroyed. Along with the capture of the port, Sparta's only access to the sea, a large amount of siege weaponry was destroyed. Sparta had been dealt a serious blow and cut off from any potential aid by the Seleucid Kingdom across the Aegean Sea.

The Romans plundered the surrounding countryside and lands around Sparta before bringing their siege to her walls. Along the way, Cretan mercenaries attacked the rear of the marching column, but were turned away and suffered terrible losses. They were forced to retreat into Sparta. When Rome arrived, the Spartans gave battle outside of their walls, but it ended in a stalemate. Flamininus decided that a prolonged siege was undesirable, and so decided to take the walls by storm.

The Romans overwhelmed the wall defenses and were soon inside Sparta. They suffered rooftop attacks as they pushed through narrow streets. But once they reached the wider streets toward the center of Sparta, they had easier going. During this push, Nabis attempted to flee, but his general, Pythagoras, rallied Sparta. He ordered the buildings by the walls set aflame. The resultant fires and black smoke caused panic in the Roman ranks. Also, the fire itself claimed a large share of casualties from Romans still entering the city. Seeing this, Flamininus called for a withdrawal.

The Romans continued assaults for three more days, and Sparta successfully withstood the attacks. However, Nabis concluded he could not last much longer and sent Pythagoras with an offer of surrender, which Flamininus reused to entertain. The Spartan general had to return a second time to offer surrender, which Flamininus did accept. The terms were the same demands that he had set to Nabis before the war began.

Nabis was not beloved, but feared by most of his subjects. He had freed the helot slaves and incorporated them into his standing army, which he used as often on his own people as his enemies, and perhaps more. In fact, the Greek historian Polybius describes Nabis's army as a crowd of murderers. He was given to exiling his opponents and marrying their wives to his freed helots. Before the Romans besieged Sparta, in order to ensure his people feared him more than the Romans, he had eighty of his most prominent citizens executed by throwing them from a mountain peak. It was a shame that in the end he was allowed to keep control of Sparta for surrendering his claims to Argos and Gythium. However, as bloody-handed tyrants often end up, he was killed years later in a stunning betrayal by his erstwhile Aetolian allies, murdered in front of his own troops.

While this war is not as famous as other Roman wars around the same period, it presaged new wars that would eventually lead to Greece's ultimate fall to Roman domination. This will take many years yet, but the messy alliances and unanswered grievances Rome left behind would guarantee future interventions until at last Rome had cause to conquer all of Greece in the name of enforcing peace. Some scholars debate if this was part of a master plan for Rome to expand influence or just an unhappy outcome. Suffice it to say, after this war with Nabis, nothing was truly settled other than Rome had an excuse to garrison troops throughout the region to ensure Sparta honored the treaty.

The siege of Sparta as depicted in this book has been compacted into one night of battle whereas the actual siege lasted several days. Also of note, at the time Sparta was not entirely encircled by walls. Hence, King Nabis's intention to flee was as easy as leaving by the open areas. However, enough of Sparta was walled off that the Romans could not loop around them. I decided to fully encase Sparta in walls since it had better dramatic potential. Also there is no historical evidence of a secret escape tunnel, as it would not be necessary given the incomplete walls. The fires were also not a prepared trap, as far as my research shows. It seemed Pythagoras intuited that starting fires by the walls would both panic the Romans and inflict casualties. His actions spared Sparta immediate defeat, but ultimately only delayed the outcome.

The ancient Greeks did not imprison their criminals. More often than not, being exiled was worse than death. When they had to execute someone, there were two primary methods used. One was a so-called bloodless crucifixion where the victim was secured to a board and left to die. The other, more dramatic method, was to cast the victim off a precipice into a deep chasm, into the sea, or else onto rocks. While more gruesome, the physical suffering was nowhere near as prolonged as crucifixion.

Varro, Falco, and Curio still have almost two more years of continuous enlistment to complete out of a total potential of sixteen years over their lives. But Roman action in Greece is winding down for the time being. Perhaps they will be onto new frontiers or different battles altogether. No matter what, they will face their future together.

NEWSLETTER

If you would like to know when my next book is released, please sign up for my new release newsletter. You can do this at my website:
http://jerryautieri.wordpress.com/

If you have enjoyed this book and would like to show your support for my writing, consider leaving a review where you purchased this book or on Goodreads, LibraryThing, and other reader sites. I need help from readers like you to get the word out about my books. If you have a moment, please share your thoughts with other readers. I appreciate it!

ALSO BY JERRY AUTIERI

Ulfrik Ormsson's Saga

Historical adventure stories set in 9th Century Europe and brimming with heroic combat. Witness the birth of a unified Norway, travel to the remote Faeroe Islands, then follow the Vikings on a siege of Paris and beyond. Walk in the footsteps of the Vikings and witness history through the eyes of Ulfrik Ormsson.

Fate's Needle

Islands in the Fog

Banners of the Northmen

Shield of Lies

The Storm God's Gift

Return of the Ravens

Sword Brothers

Descendants Saga

The grandchildren of Ulfrik Ormsson continue tales of Norse battle and glory. They may have come from greatness, but they must make their own way in the brutal world of the 10th Century.

Descendants of the Wolf

Odin's Ravens

Revenge of the Wolves

Blood Price

Viking Bones

Valor of the Norsemen

Norse Vengeance

Bear and Raven

Red Oath

Fate's End

Grimwold and Lethos Trilogy

A sword and sorcery fantasy trilogy with a decidedly Norse flavor.

Deadman's Tide

Children of Urdis

Age of Blood

Copyright © 2022 by Jerry Autieri

All rights reserved.

No part of this book may be reproduced in any form or by any electronic or mechanical means, including information storage and retrieval systems, without written permission from the author, except for the use of brief quotations in a book review.

Printed in Great Britain
by Amazon